Praise for

TEEN TITANS
Raven

"Riveting from start to finish. Full of mystery, fierce friendship, and romance that might not be quite what it seems. Kami Garcia shows off her stellar storytelling skills in this fantastic first installment of *Teen Titans*. Once you start reading *Teen Titans: Raven,* you won't want to stop."

—**Stephanie Garber**, #1 *New York Times* bestselling author of the **Caraval** series

"As someone who spends half her life inside Rachel's head...it was impressive to see her so effortlessly come to life on the page! If you love Raven, this is a must-read!"

—**Teagan Croft**, actress portraying Raven in the **DC Universe** series **Titans**

"Kami Garcia's *Raven* shows us that family bonds are made by more than blood, and that the ties of sisterhood are more powerful than the scariest demon. It's the heart of this kickass "girl power" superhero book that keeps you reading and rereading and desperate for the next installment."

—**Ellen Oh**, author of **The Prophecy** series, and Cofounder and President of **We Need Diverse Books**

"I continue to be inspired by Kami Garcia's authenticity and keen ability to create raw and empowering stories full of strength, truth, and love."

—**Jennifer Niven**, *New York Times* bestselling author of *All the Bright Places* and *Holding Up the Universe*

"With *Teen Titans: Raven,* writer Kami Garcia and artist Gabriel Picolo have created a new and different look for Raven, yet she still shares the DNA of the mystical heroine created in 1980 by me and artist co-creator, George Pérez. Explore and enjoy!"

—**Marv Wolfman**, co-creator of Raven

"Raven might have a...questionable background, but this colorful twist on her story made ME want to fly!"

—**Nic Stone**, *New York Times* bestselling author of *Dear Martin*

TEEN TITANS
Raven

WRITTEN BY
kami garcia

ILLUSTRATED BY
gabriel picolo

WITH
jon sommariva
AND
emma kubert

COLORIST
david calderon

LETTERER
tom napolitano

Raven created by Marv Wolfman and George Pérez

MICHELE R. WELLS VP & Executive Editor, Young Reader
JUSTINE FUENTES Assistant Editor
STEVE COOK Design Director - Books
AMIE BROCKWAY-METCALF Publication Design

MARIE JAVINS Editor-in-Chief, DC Comics

DANIEL CHERRY III Senior VP - General Manager
JIM LEE Publisher & Chief Creative Officer
DON FALLETTI VP - Manufacturing Operations & Workflow Management
LAWRENCE GANEM VP - Talent Services
ALISON GILL Senior VP - Manufacturing & Operations
NICK J. NAPOLITANO VP - Manufacturing Administration & Design
NANCY SPEARS VP - Revenue

DC Comics
2900 West Alameda Ave.
Burbank, CA 91505

Printed by Worzalla,
Stevens Point, WI, USA. 2/25/21.
Second Printing.
ISBN: 978-1-77950-727-3

MIX
Paper from
responsible sources
FSC® C002589
www.fsc.org

Library of Congress Cataloging-in-Publication Data

Names: Garcia, Kami, writer. | Picolo, Gabriel, illustrator.
Title: Teen Titans : Raven / written by Kami Garcia ; illustrated by Gabriel
    Picolo.
Description: Burbank, CA : DC Ink, [2019] | Summary: "When a tragic accident
    takes the life of the only family she's ever known, 16-year-old Raven is
    sent to New Orleans to start over. She soon discovers that she can hear
    the thoughts of others around her...and another, more disturbing, voice in
    her head."-- Provided by publisher.
Identifiers: LCCN 2018043961 | ISBN 9781401286231
Subjects: LCSH: Graphic novels. | CYAC: Graphic novels. | Orphans--Fiction. |
    Psychic ability--Fiction.
Classification: LCC PZ7.7.G366 Te 2019 | DDC 741.5/973--dc23

dedications

For Nick, who encouraged me to write a graphic novel.
And for Stella, who loved Raven first,
and told me to choose Teen Titans.
—Kami Garcia

For Andrea, who gave me the determination
to keep working on my comics.
—Gabriel Picolo

dear reader,

As someone whose mother hand-made her a Wonder Woman Halloween costume—which I insisted on wearing for an embarrassing number of Halloweens—I can honestly say I've been a DC Comics fan for a long time. The idea that anyone could be a hero regardless of race, religion, gender, or sexual orientation (or, in the case of some of the Teen Titans, species) has always resonated with me. I'm the kind of person who roots for the underdog and who believes in magic, miracles, and the impossible.

I remember how hard it was to be a teen, and, figure out who I wanted to be and how to stand up for what I believed. I struggled to define myself in a world that was determined to define me—a world that didn't think I was old enough to make a difference or effect real change. So when DC Comics approached me about writing for them, the Teen Titans came to mind. Why write just one book when I could write a series about a group of badass teens—beginning with my favorite member, Raven? In the DC Universe, Raven has to fight to define herself and overcome the hand life dealt her. I wanted more readers to meet her, because the odds are usually stacked against her, but she never gives up. She's a fighter, like so many of you.

I had the honor of meeting Marv Wolfman, the co-creator of Raven, Cyborg, and Starfire from the Teen Titans. I wasn't sure how a legend like Marv would feel about me creating a new story for Raven, one of his most beloved characters. I asked for advice. Was there anything specific I should or shouldn't do? Marv's advice was to do what I wanted and make the character my own. He also said he was excited to see what I would do with her and he loved the idea of introducing her to new readers. Marv seemed to understand that the world needs Raven and the other Teen Titans more than ever—that with all the injustices in the world, there are plenty of battles left to fight. The world needs heroes like the version of Raven you'll meet in this book and her feisty foster sister, Max, a new character I created and artist Gabriel Picolo brought to life. But more than anything, the world needs everyday people like you.

Keep fighting and reading.

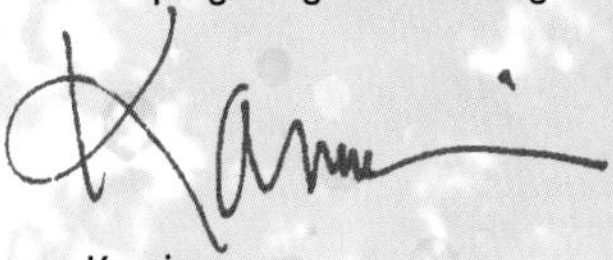

Kami

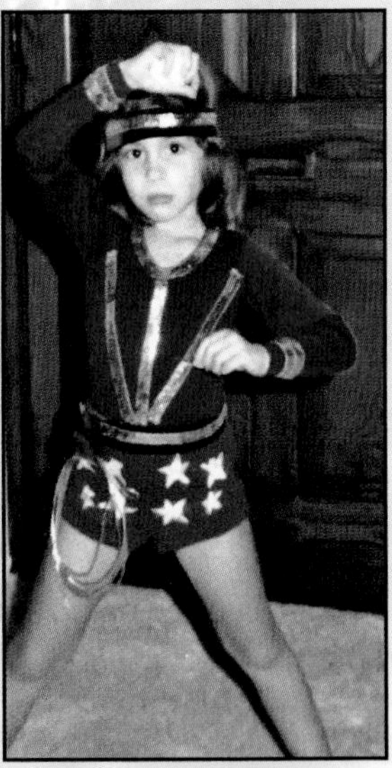

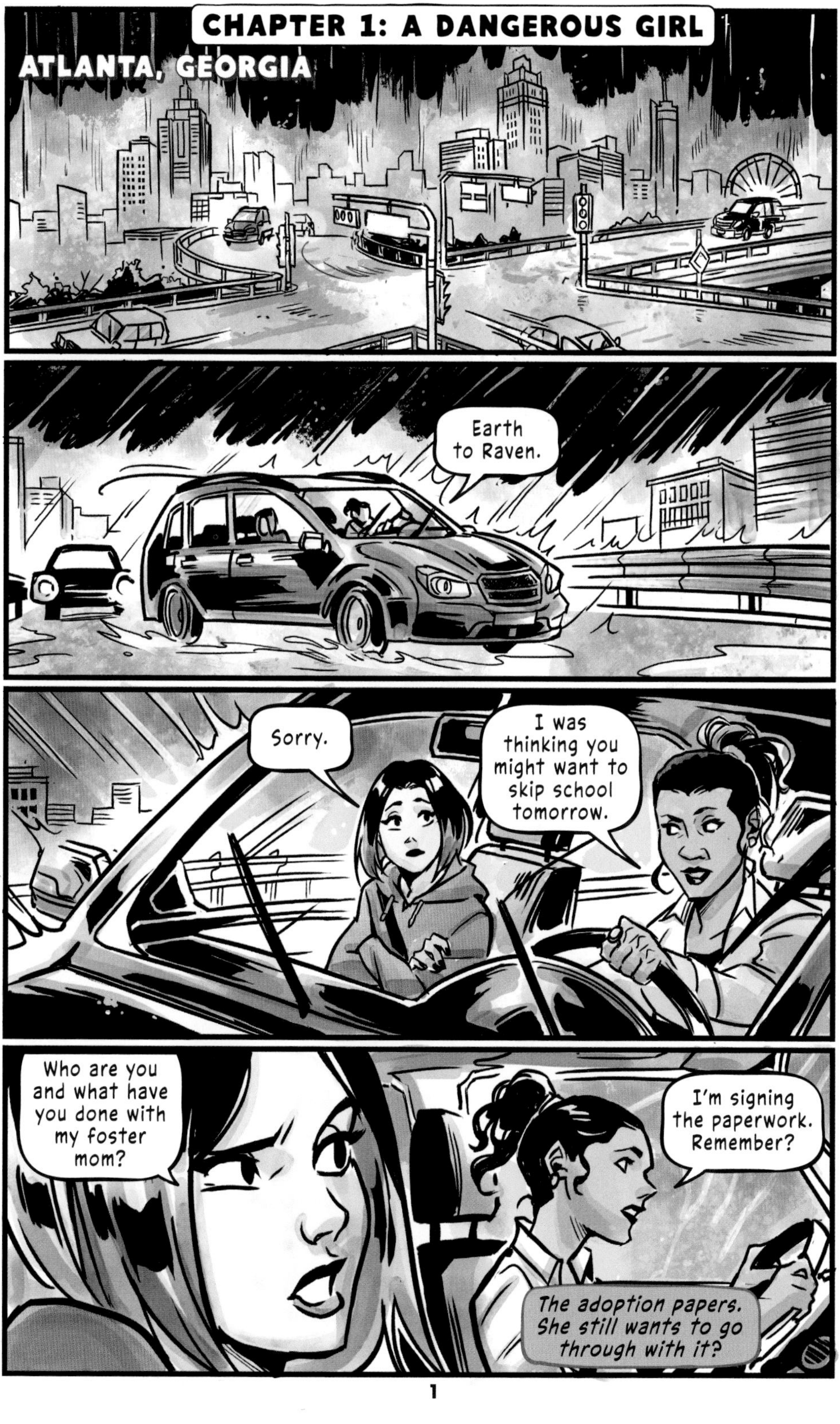
CHAPTER 1: A DANGEROUS GIRL
ATLANTA, GEORGIA
Earth to Raven.
Sorry.
I was thinking you might want to skip school tomorrow.
Who are you and what have you done with my foster mom?
I'm signing the paperwork. Remember?
The adoption papers. She still wants to go through with it?

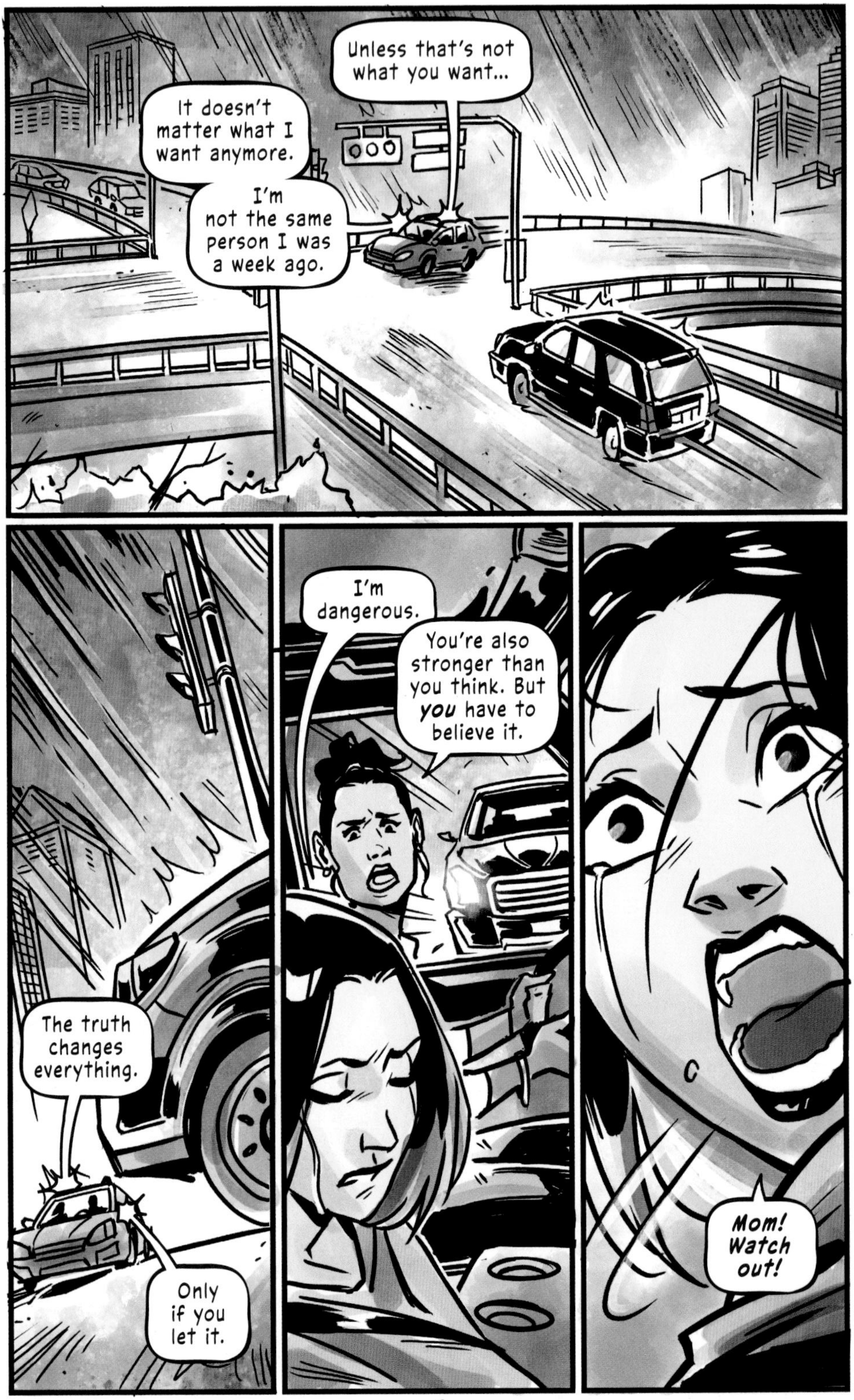
It doesn't matter what I want anymore.
I'm not the same person I was a week ago.
Unless that's not what you want...
The truth changes everything.
Only if you let it.
I'm dangerous.
You're also stronger than you think. But *you* have to believe it.
Mom! Watch out!

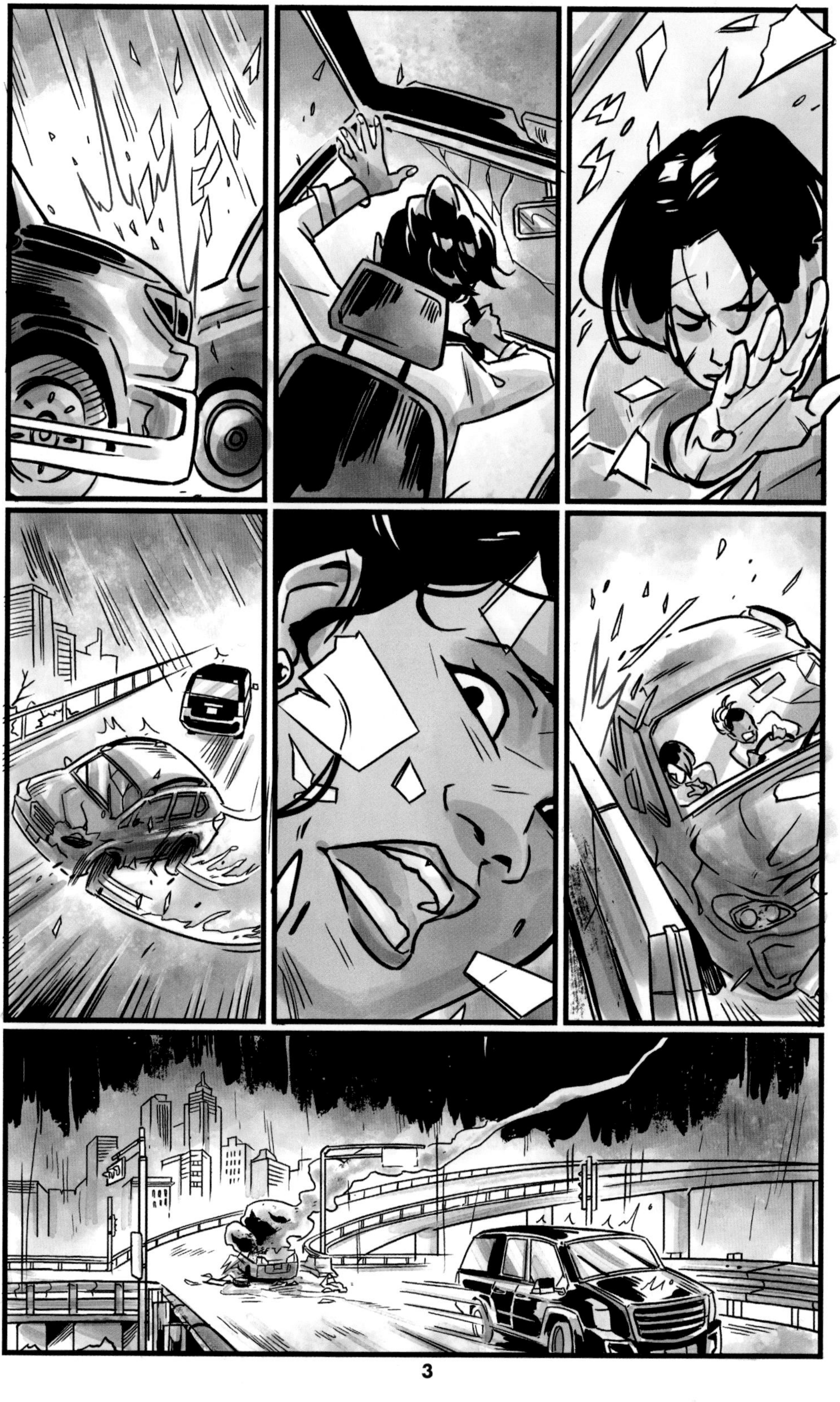

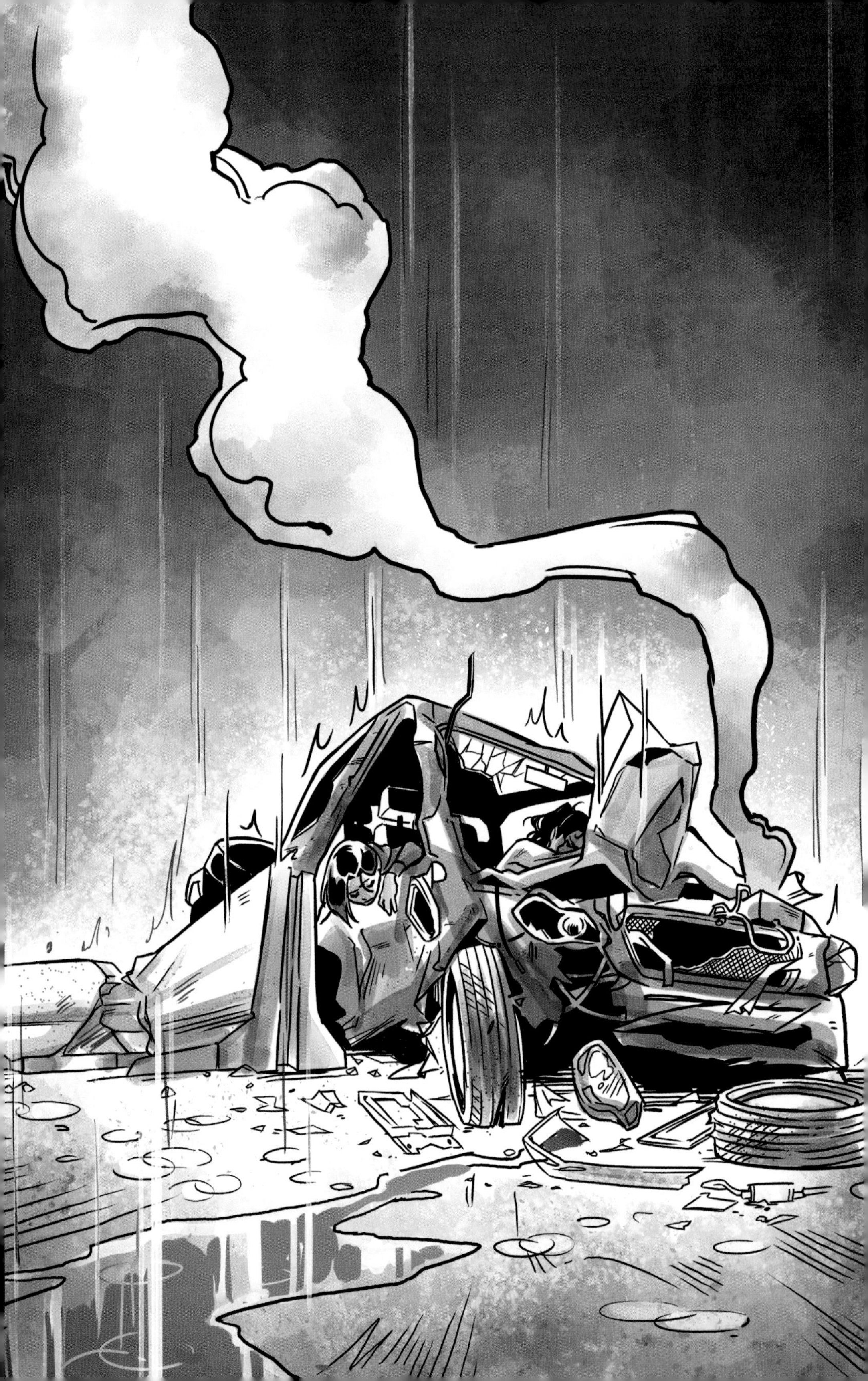

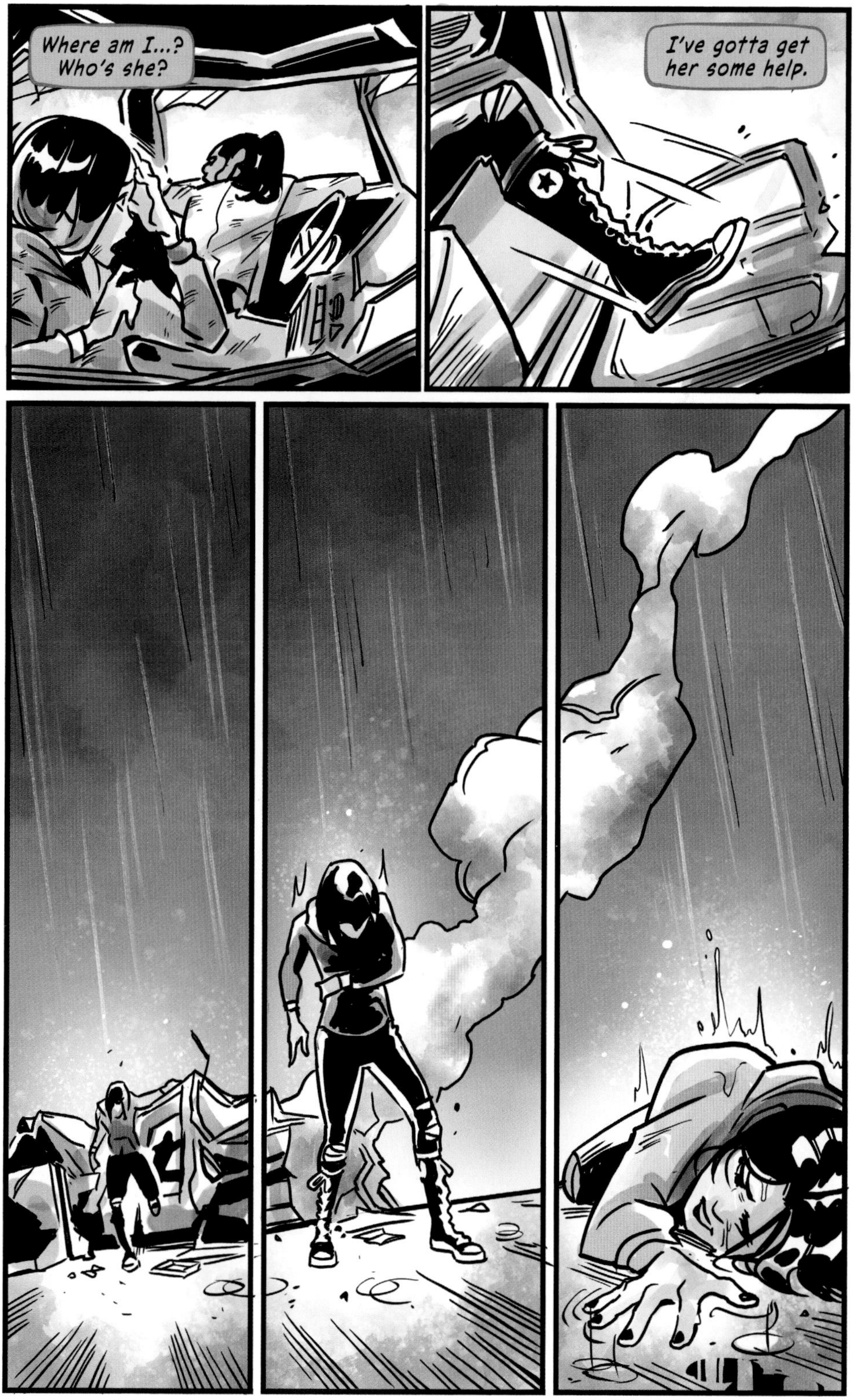
Where am I...? Who's she?
I've gotta get her some help.

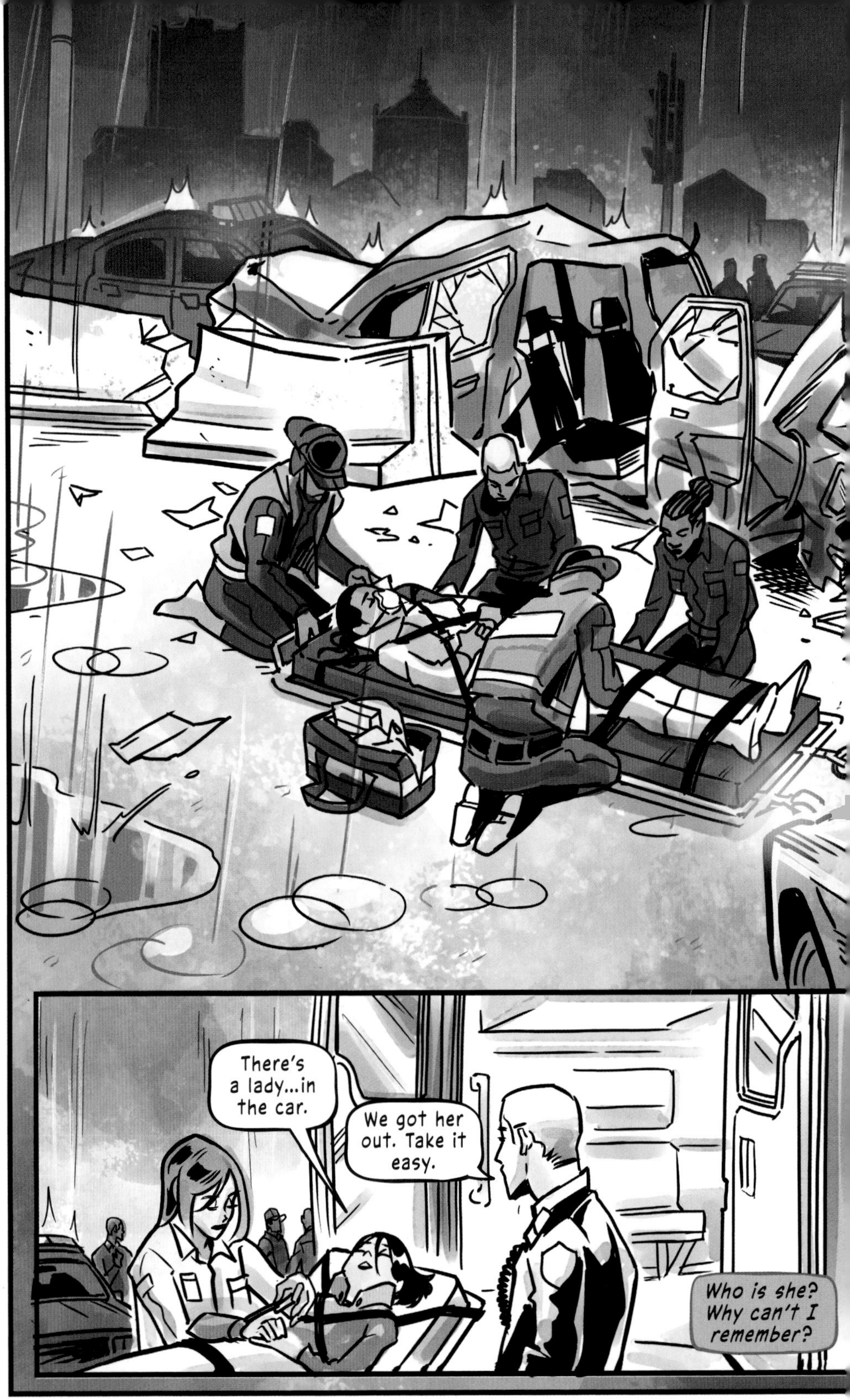
There's a lady...in the car.
We got her out. Take it easy.
Who is she? Why can't I remember?

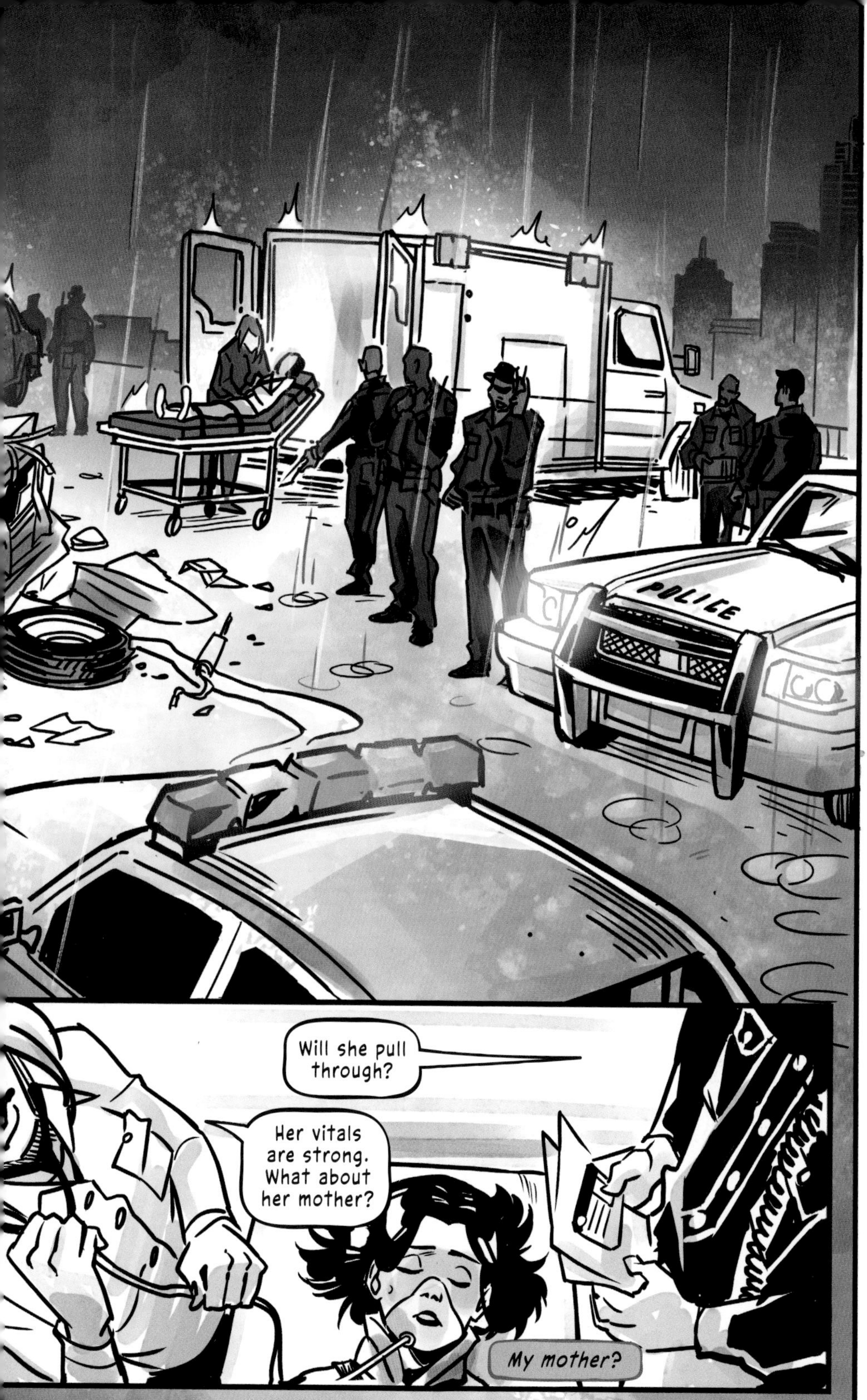
POLICE
Will she pull through?
Her vitals are strong. What about her mother?
My mother?

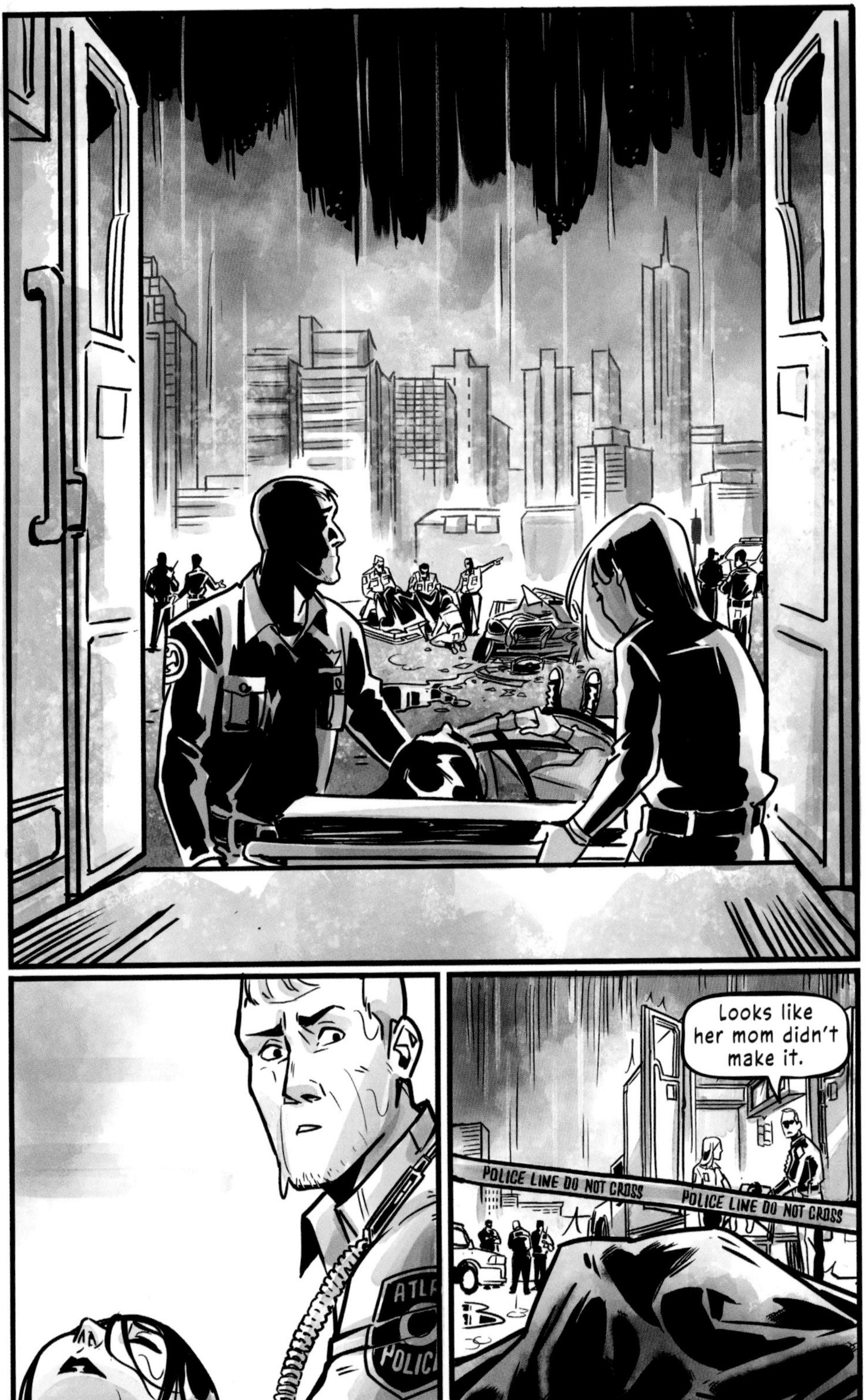
Looks like her mom didn't make it.
POLICE LINE DO NOT CROSS
POLICE LINE DO NOT CROSS

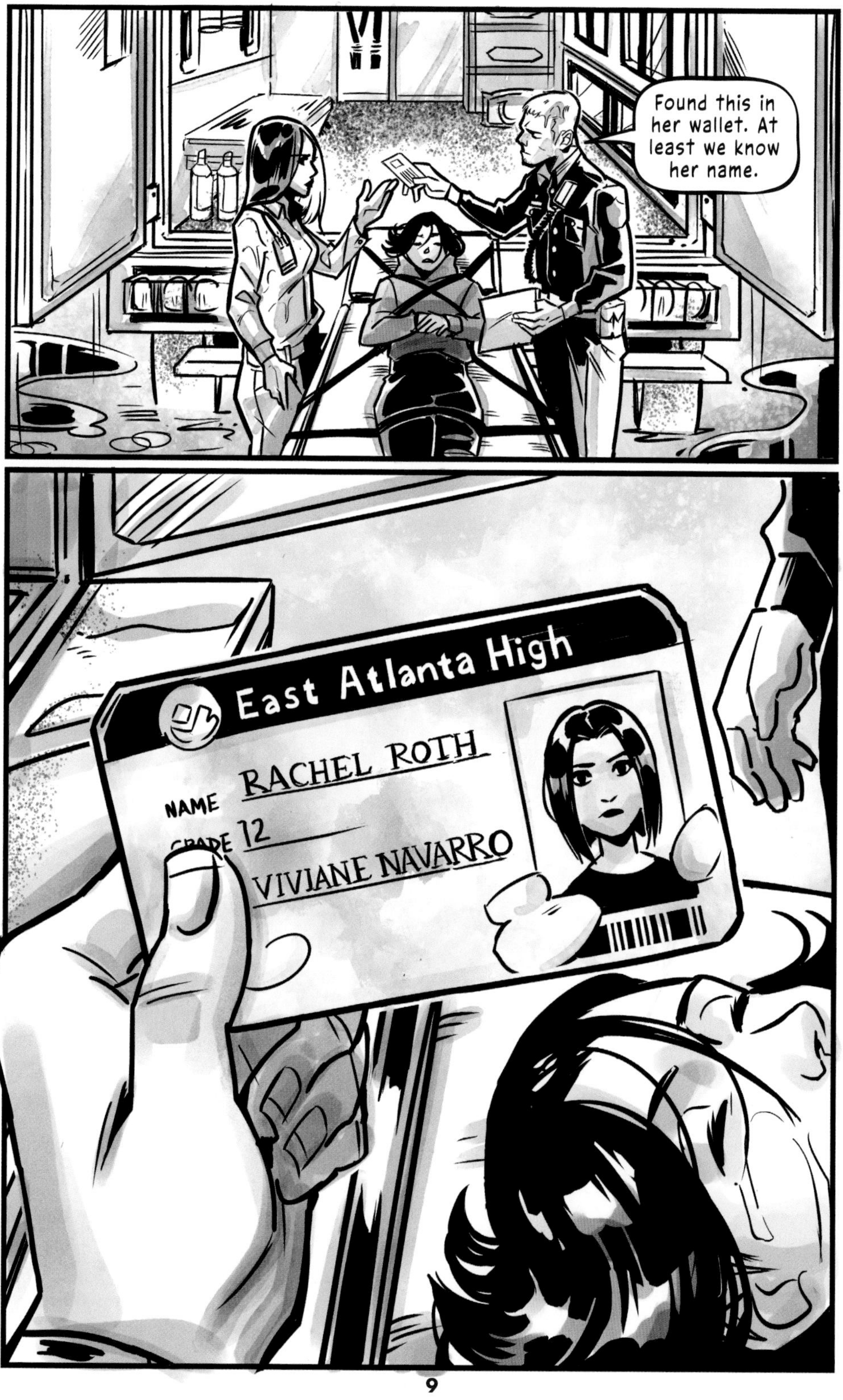
Found this in her wallet. At least we know her name.
East Atlanta High
NAME RACHEL ROTH
12
VIVIANE NAVARRO

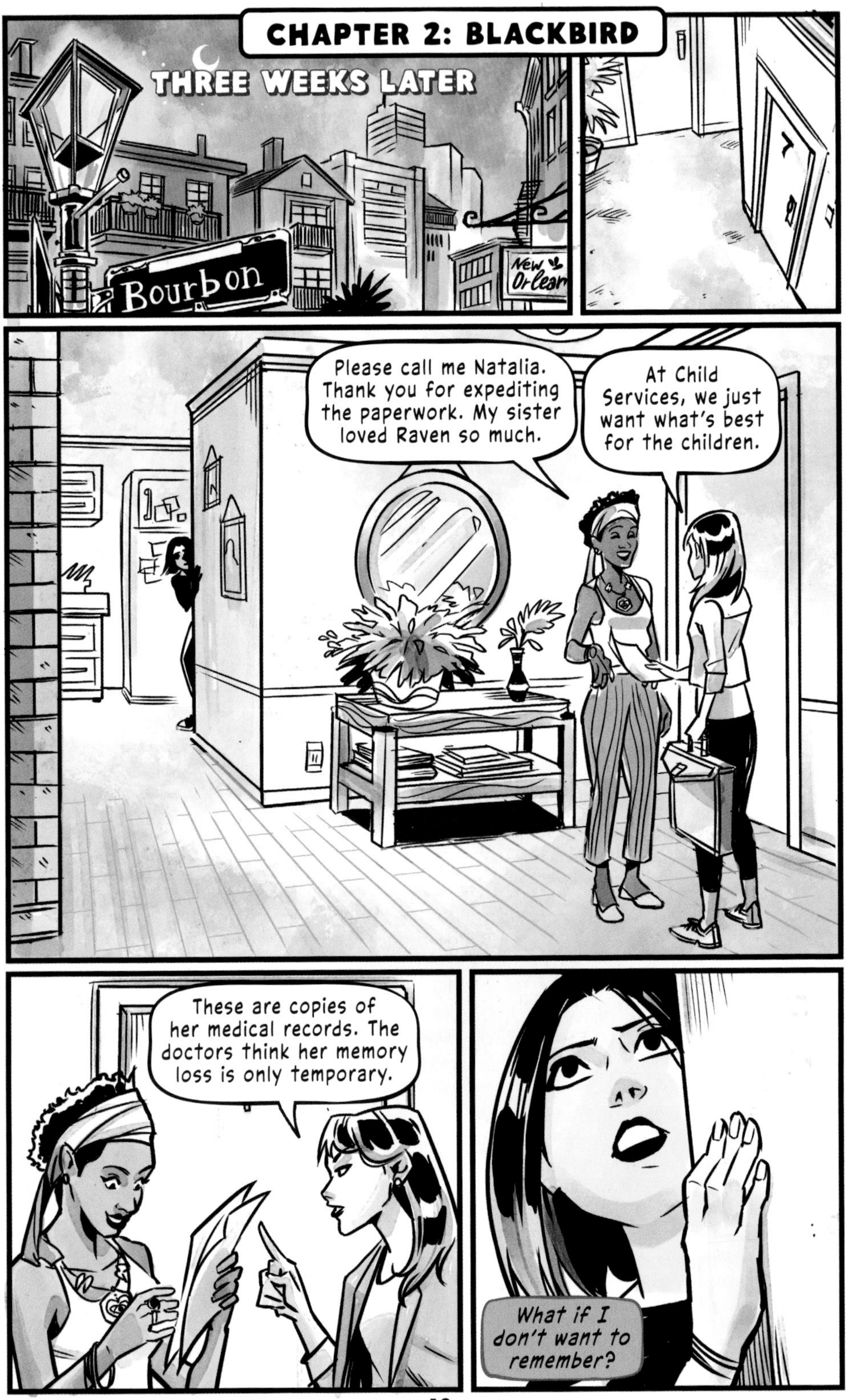
CHAPTER 2: BLACKBIRD
THREE WEEKS LATER
Bourbon
New Orlean
Please call me Natalia. Thank you for expediting the paperwork. My sister loved Raven so much.
At Child Services, we just want what's best for the children.
These are copies of her medical records. The doctors think her memory loss is only temporary.
What if I don't want to remember?

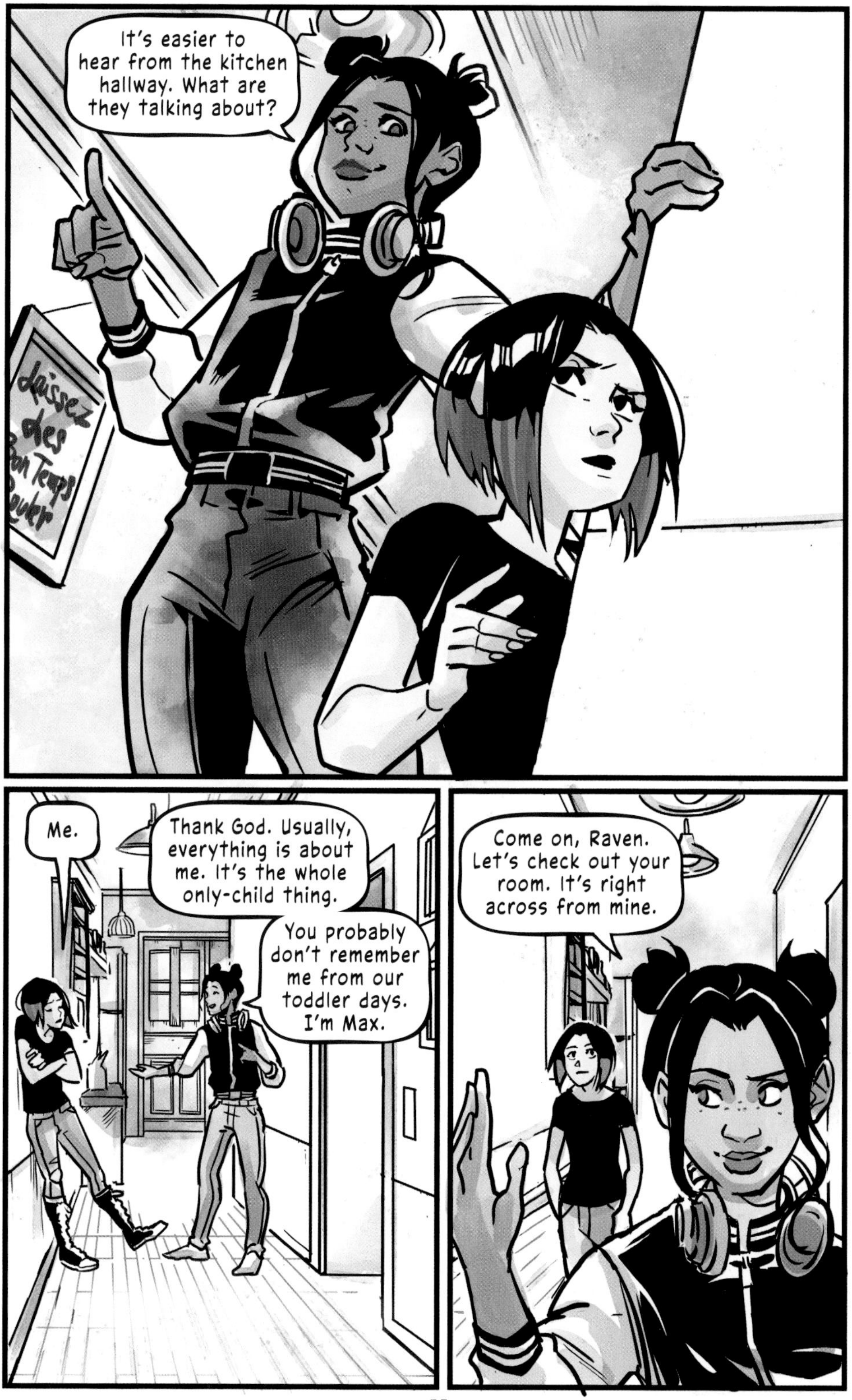
It's easier to hear from the kitchen hallway. What are they talking about?
Laissez des Bon Temps Rouler
Me.
Thank God. Usually, everything is about me. It's the whole only-child thing.
You probably don't remember me from our toddler days. I'm Max.
Come on, Raven. Let's check out your room. It's right across from mine.

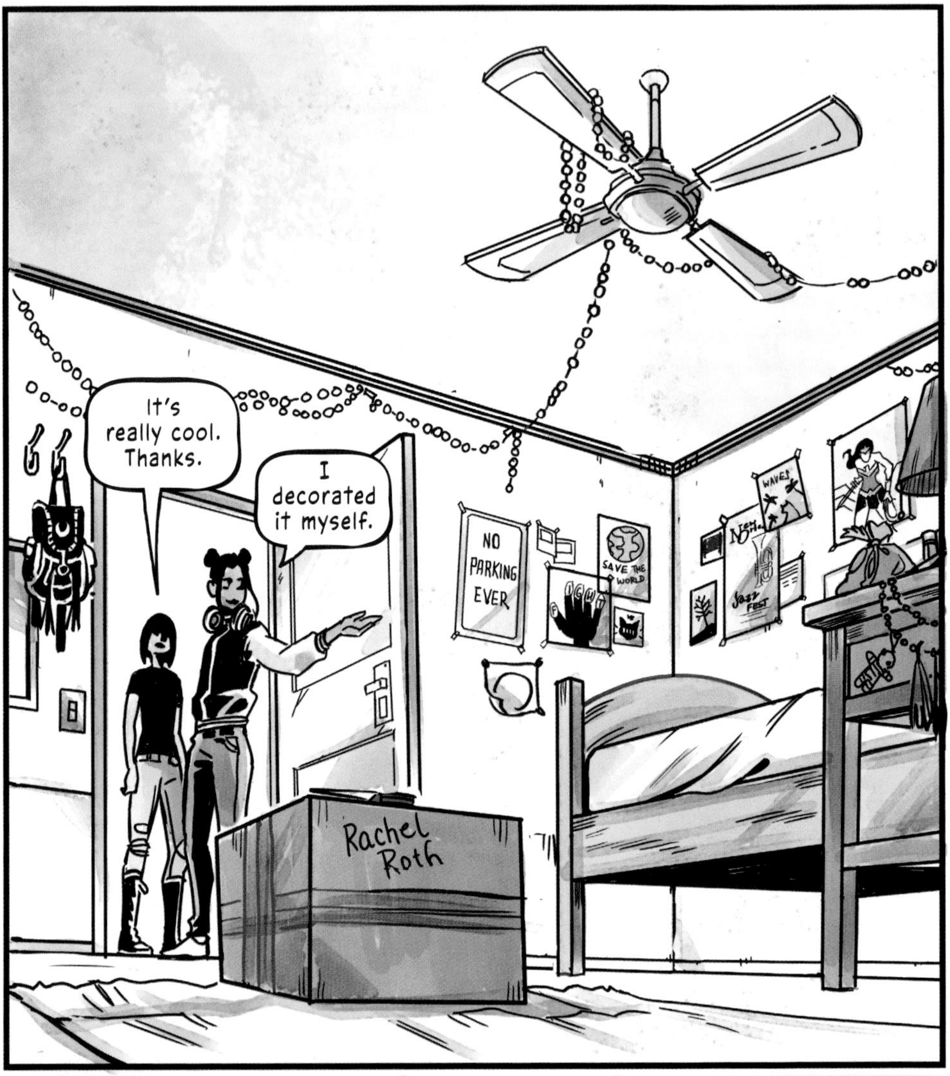
It's really cool. Thanks.
I decorated it myself.
NO PARKING EVER
SAVE THE WORLD
Rachel Roth

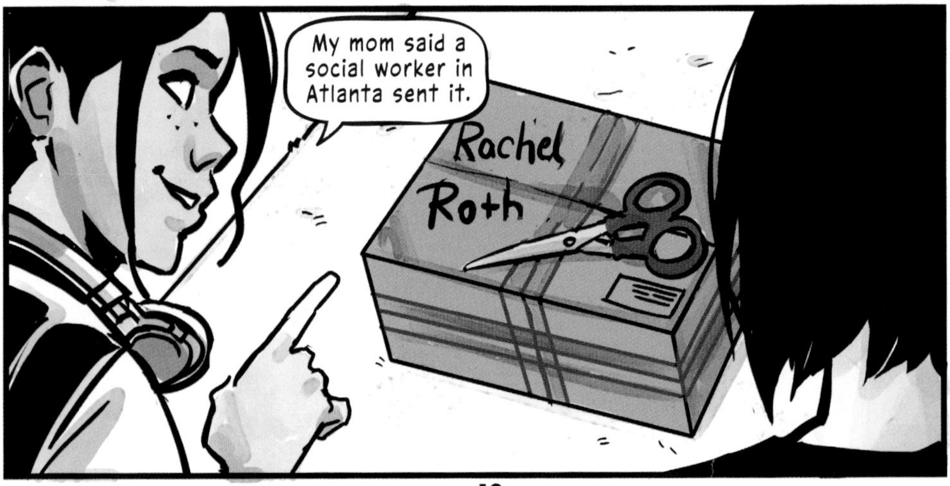
My mom said a social worker in Atlanta sent it.
Rachel Roth

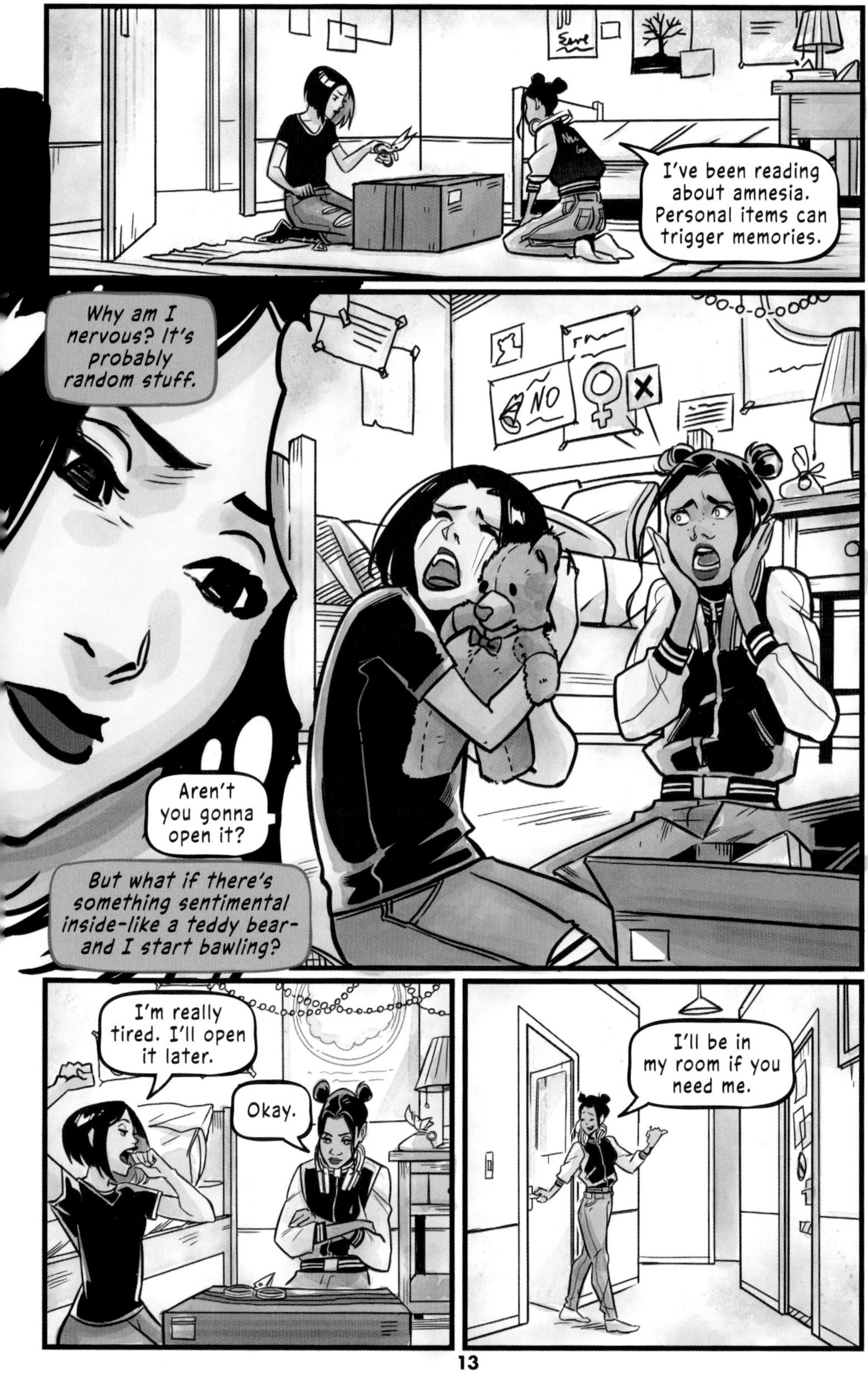
I've been reading about amnesia. Personal items can trigger memories.
Why am I nervous? It's probably random stuff.
Aren't you gonna open it?
But what if there's something sentimental inside–like a teddy bear–and I start bawling?
I'm really tired. I'll open it later.
Okay.
I'll be in my room if you need me.

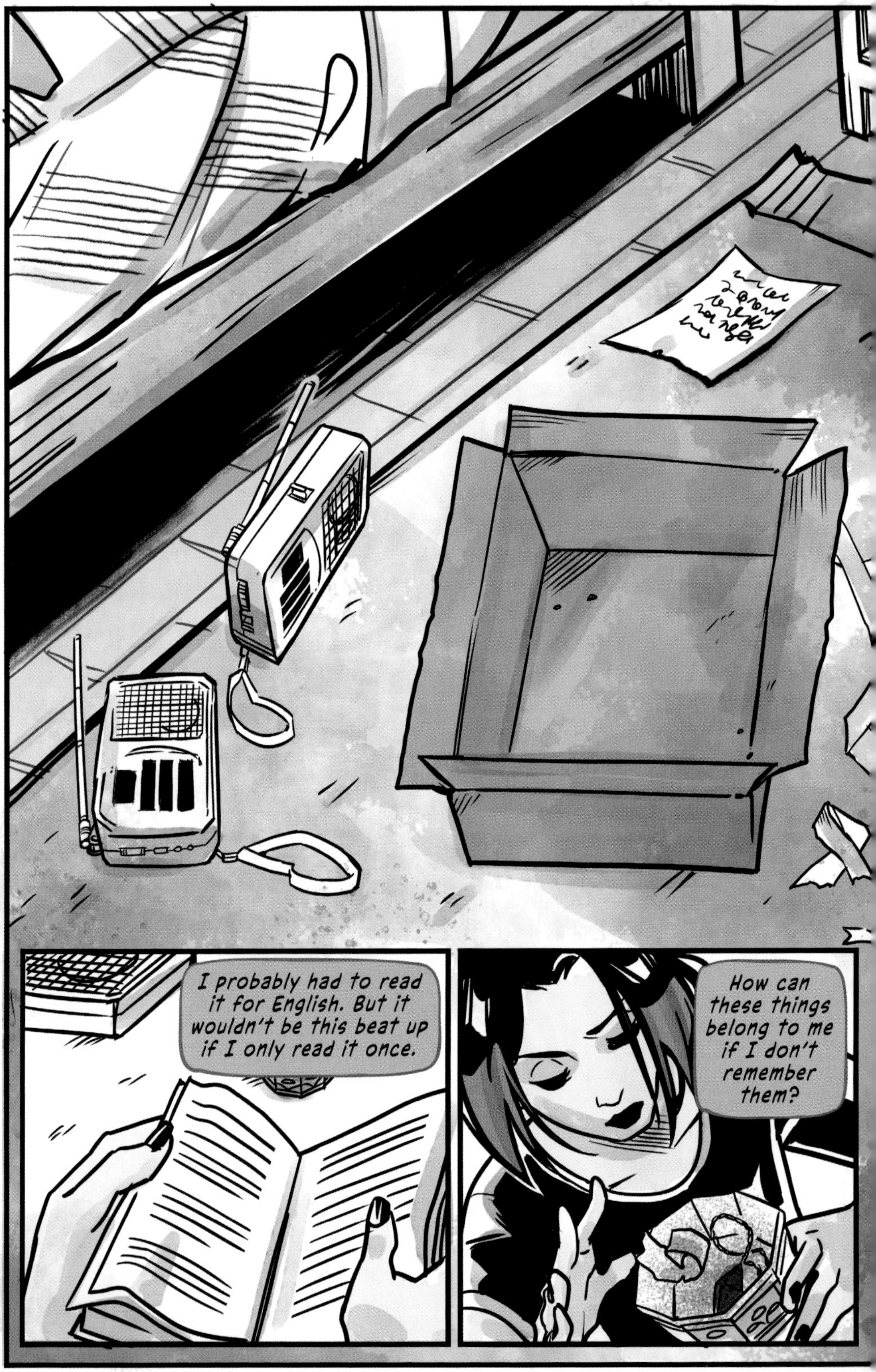

I probably had to read it for English. But it wouldn't be this beat up if I only read it once.
How can these things belong to me if I don't remember them?

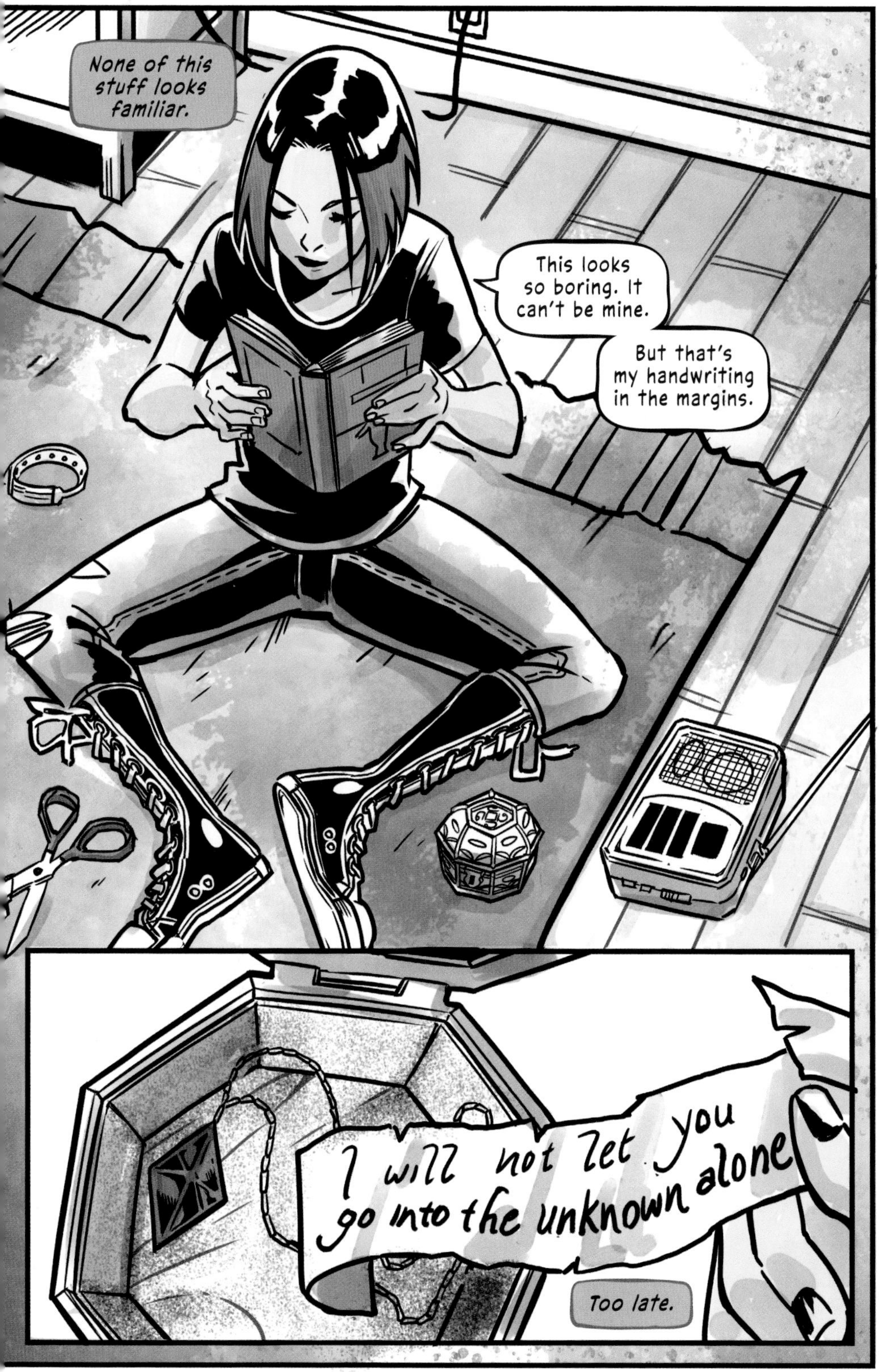
None of this stuff looks familiar.
This looks so boring. It can't be mine.
But that's my handwriting in the margins.
I will not let you go into the unknown alone
Too late.

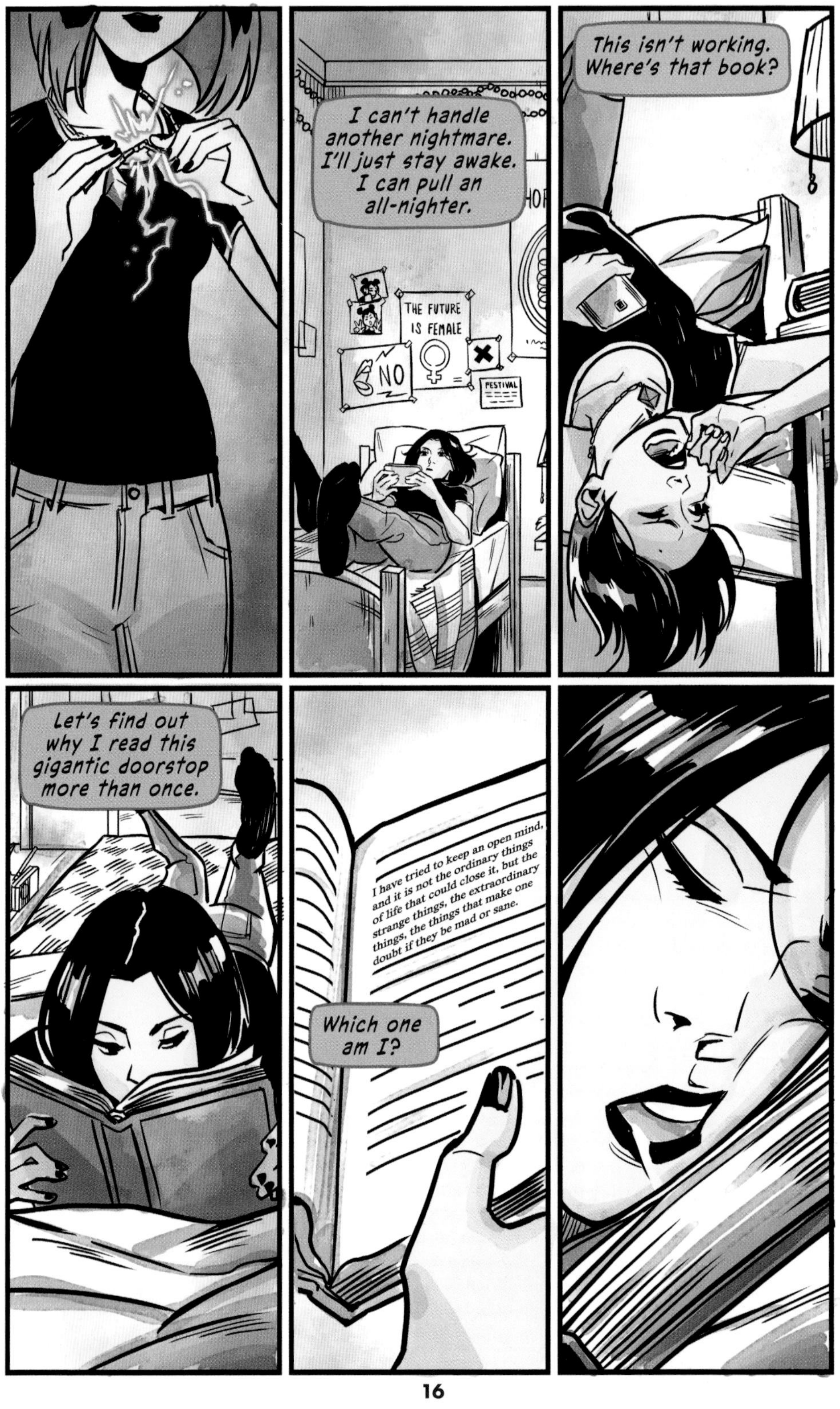
I can't handle another nightmare. I'll just stay awake. I can pull an all-nighter.
THE FUTURE IS FEMALE
NO
FESTIVAL
This isn't working. Where's that book?
Let's find out why I read this gigantic doorstop more than once.
I have tried to keep an open mind, and it is not the ordinary things of life that could close it, but the strange things, the extraordinary things, the things that make one doubt if they be mad or sane.
Which one am I?

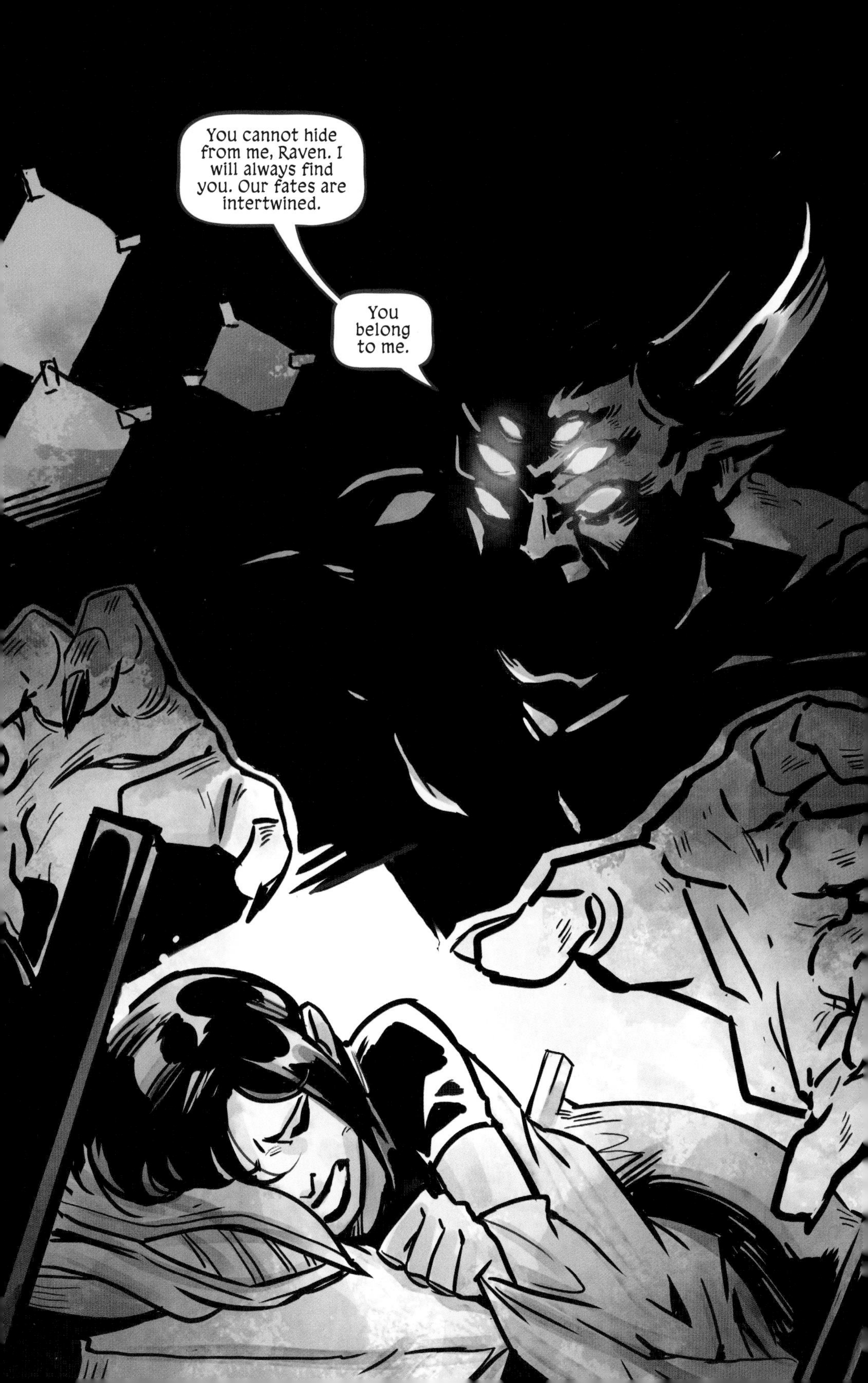
You cannot hide from me, Raven. I will always find you. Our fates are intertwined.
You belong to me.

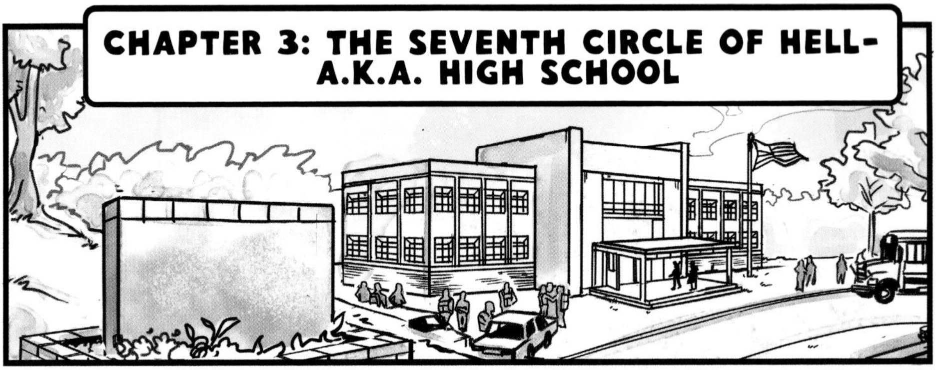
CHAPTER 3: THE SEVENTH CIRCLE OF HELL-
A.K.A. HIGH SCHOOL

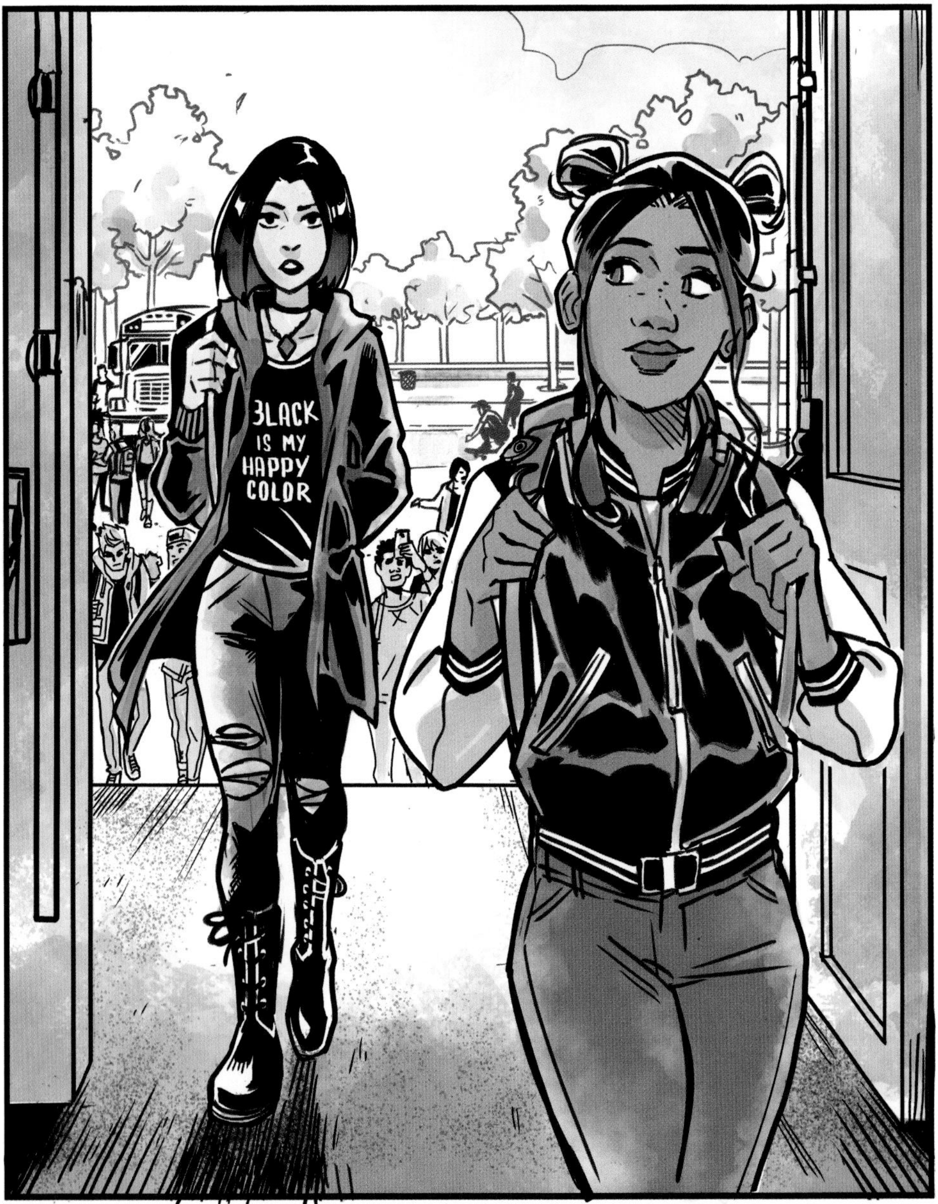
BLACK IS MY HAPPY COLOR

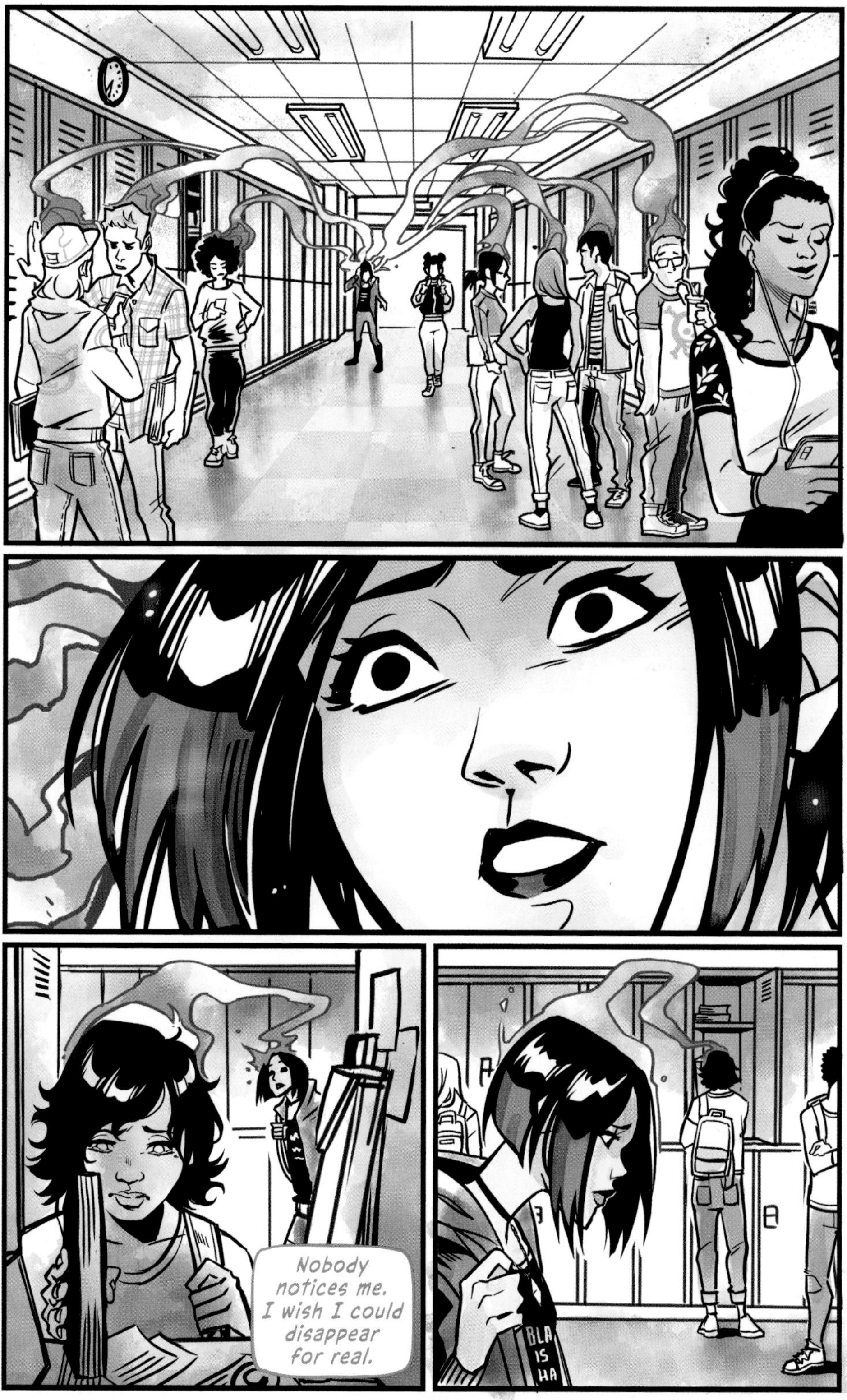
Nobody notices me. I wish I could disappear for real.
BLA
IS
HA

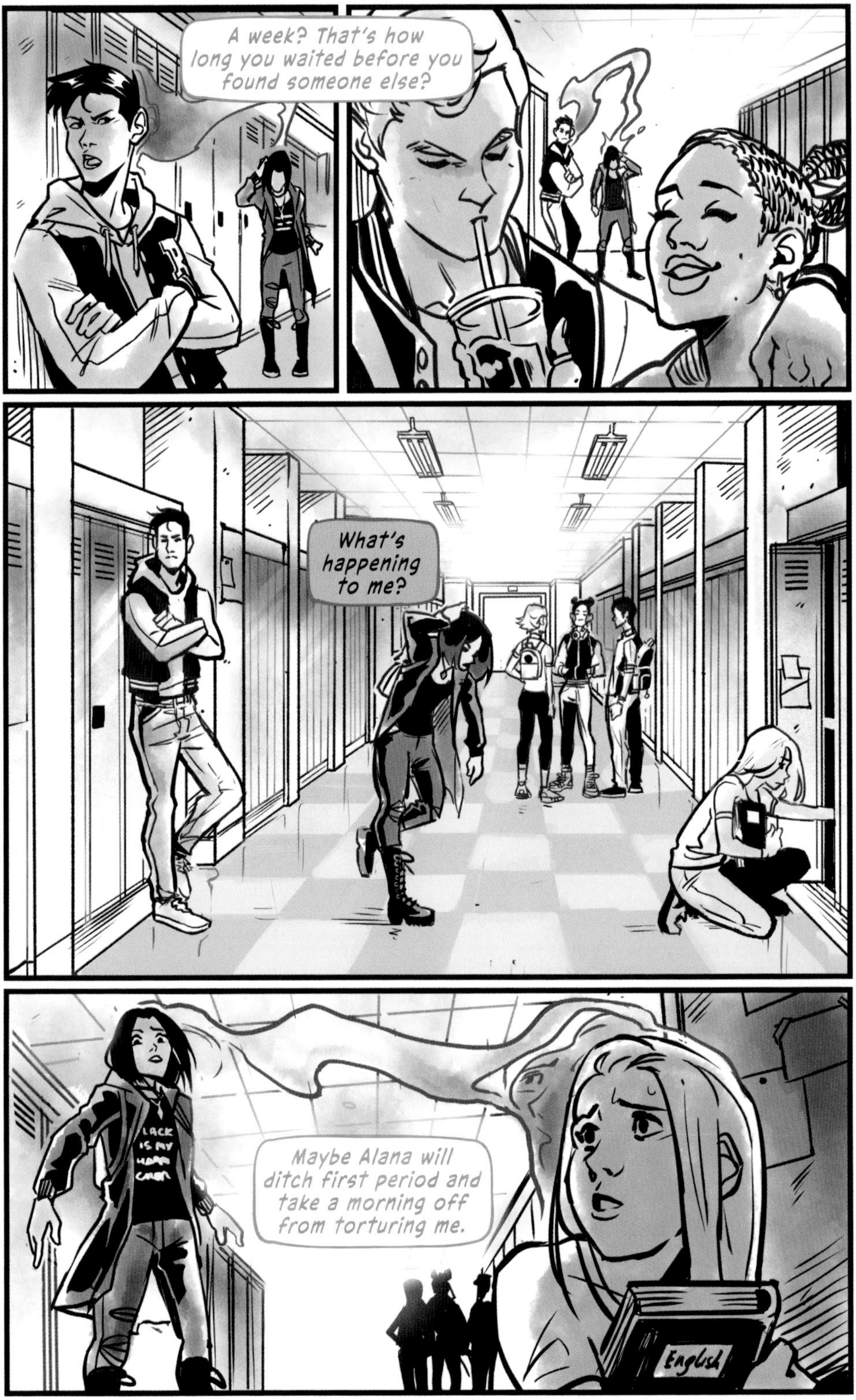
A week? That's how long you waited before you found someone else?
What's happening to me?
Maybe Alana will ditch first period and take a morning off from torturing me.
English

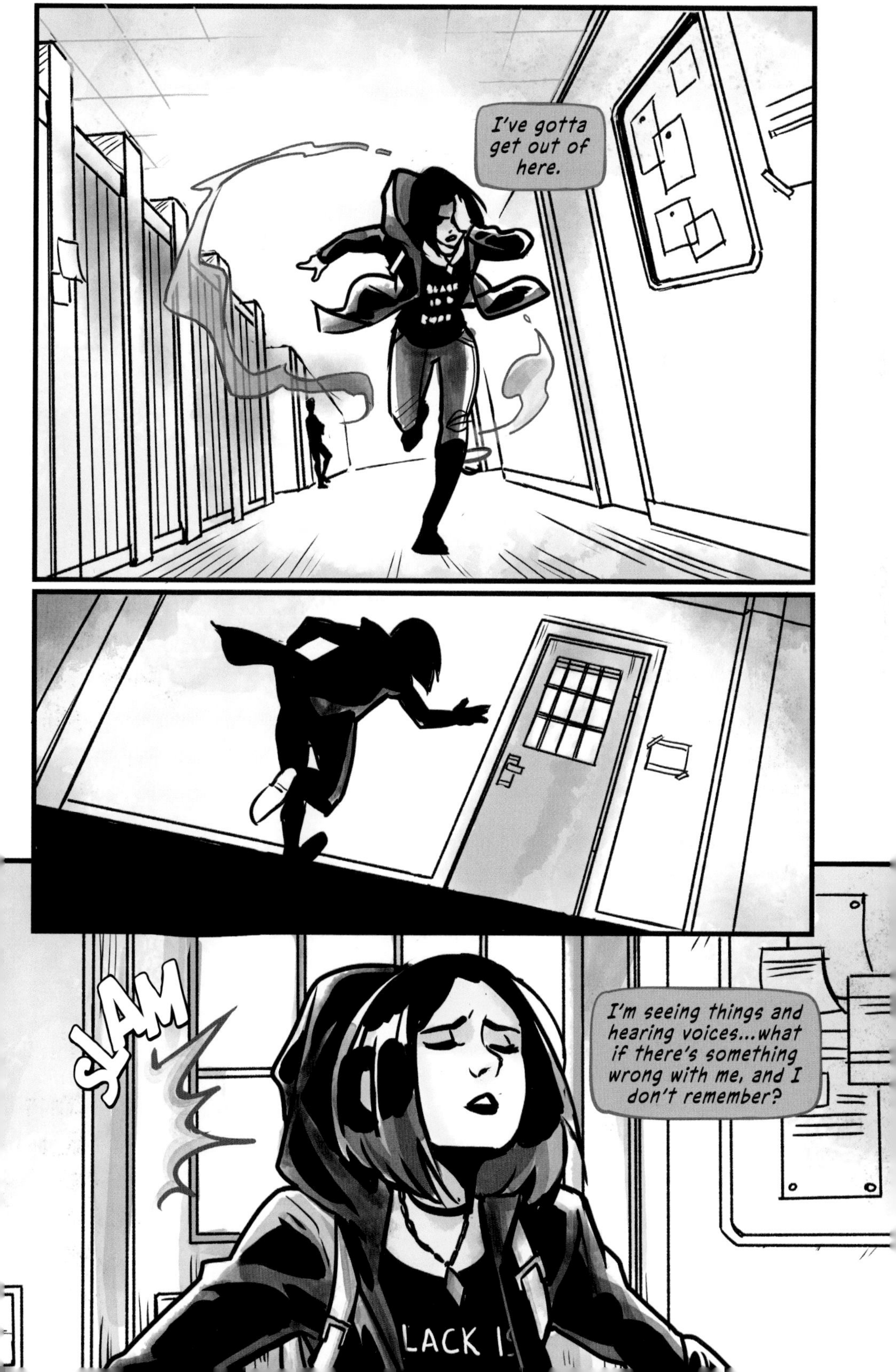
I've gotta get out of here.
SLAM
I'm seeing things and hearing voices...what if there's something wrong with me, and I don't remember?

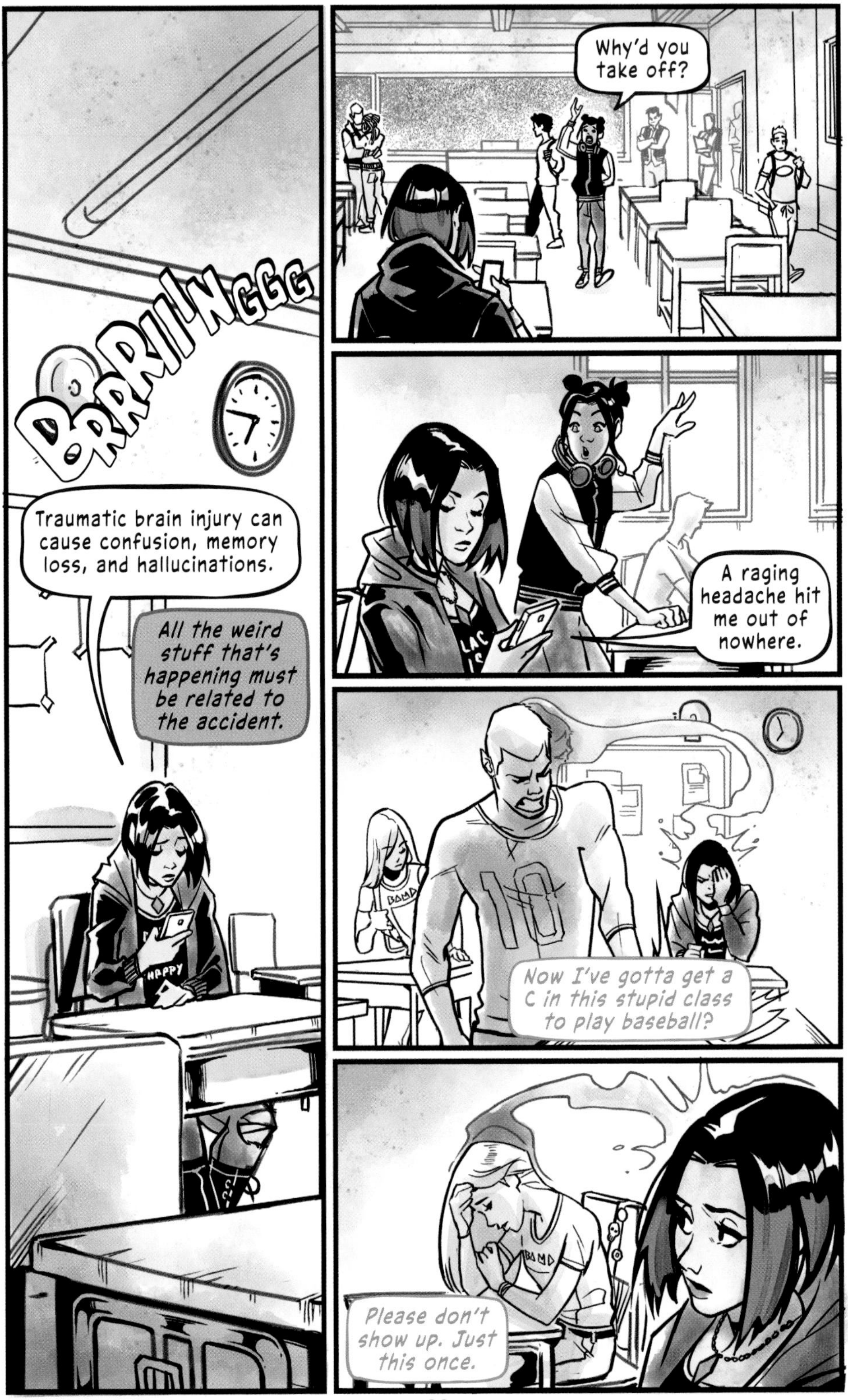
BRRRIIINGGG
Traumatic brain injury can cause confusion, memory loss, and hallucinations.
All the weird stuff that's happening must be related to the accident.
Why'd you take off?
A raging headache hit me out of nowhere.
Now I've gotta get a C in this stupid class to play baseball?
Please don't show up. Just this once.

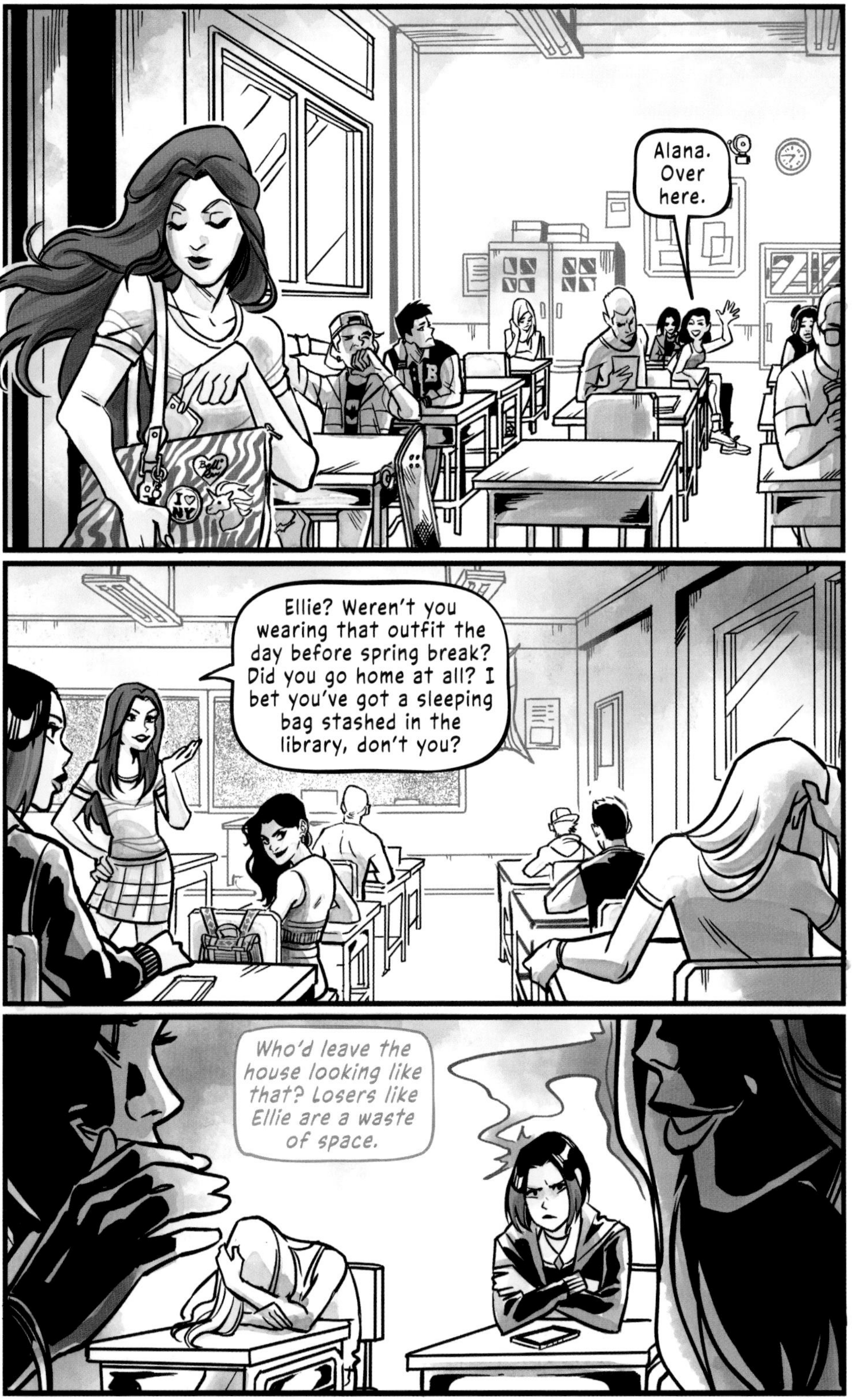
Alana. Over here.
Ellie? Weren't you wearing that outfit the day before spring break? Did you go home at all? I bet you've got a sleeping bag stashed in the library, don't you?
Who'd leave the house looking like that? Losers like Ellie are a waste of space.

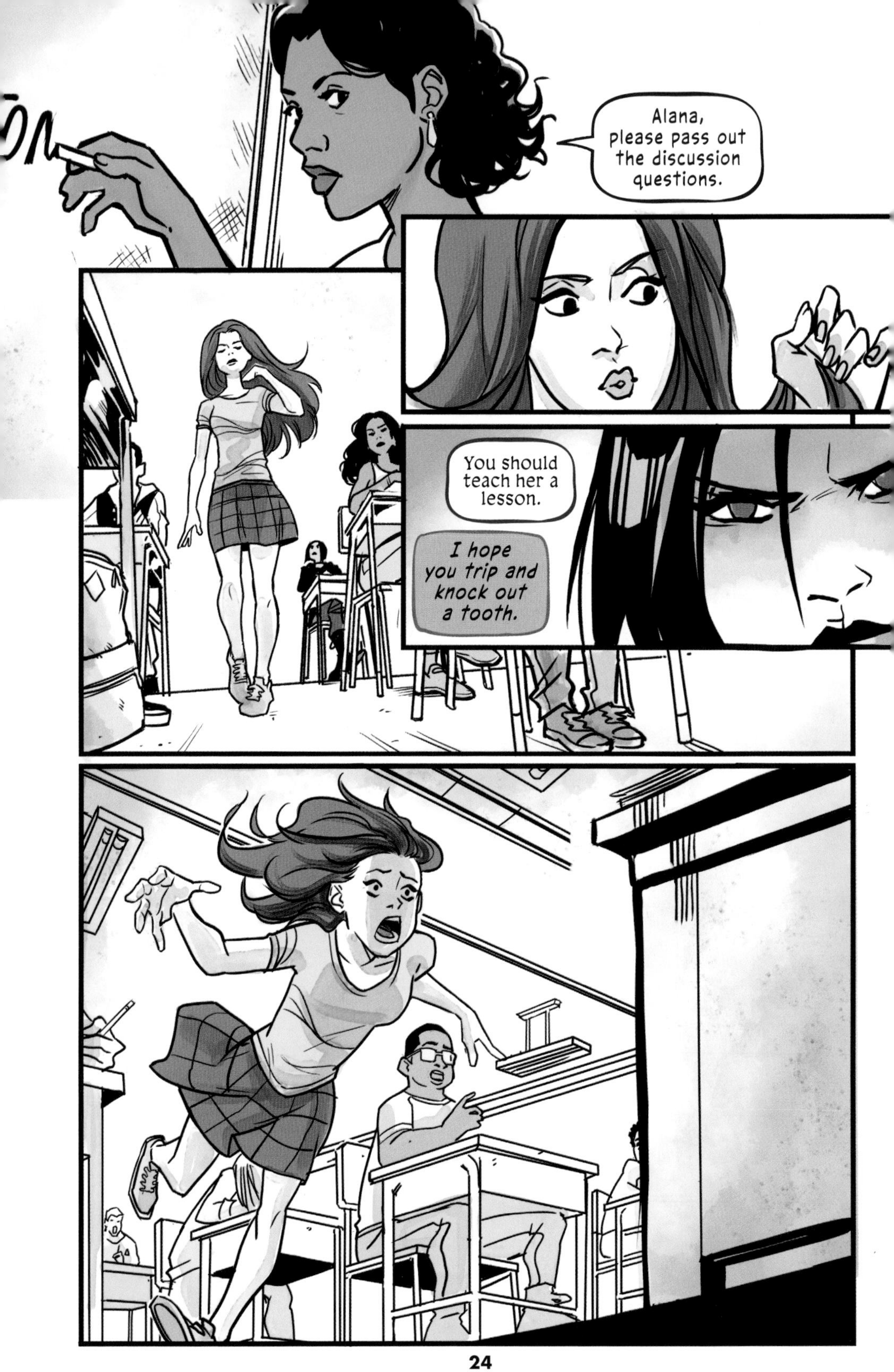
Alana, please pass out the discussion questions.
You should teach her a lesson.
I hope you trip and knock out a tooth.

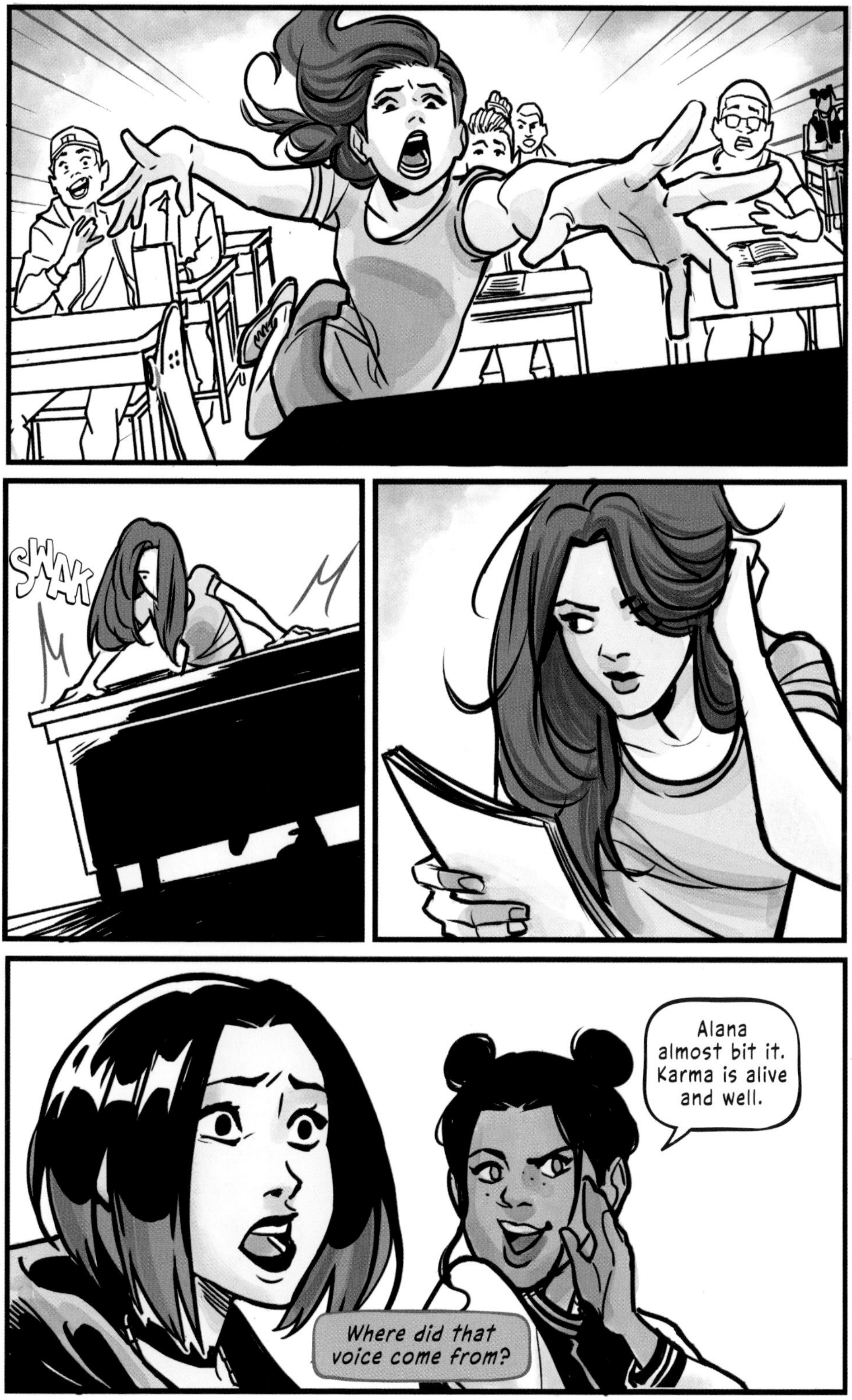
SWAK
Alana almost bit it. Karma is alive and well.
Where did that voice come from?

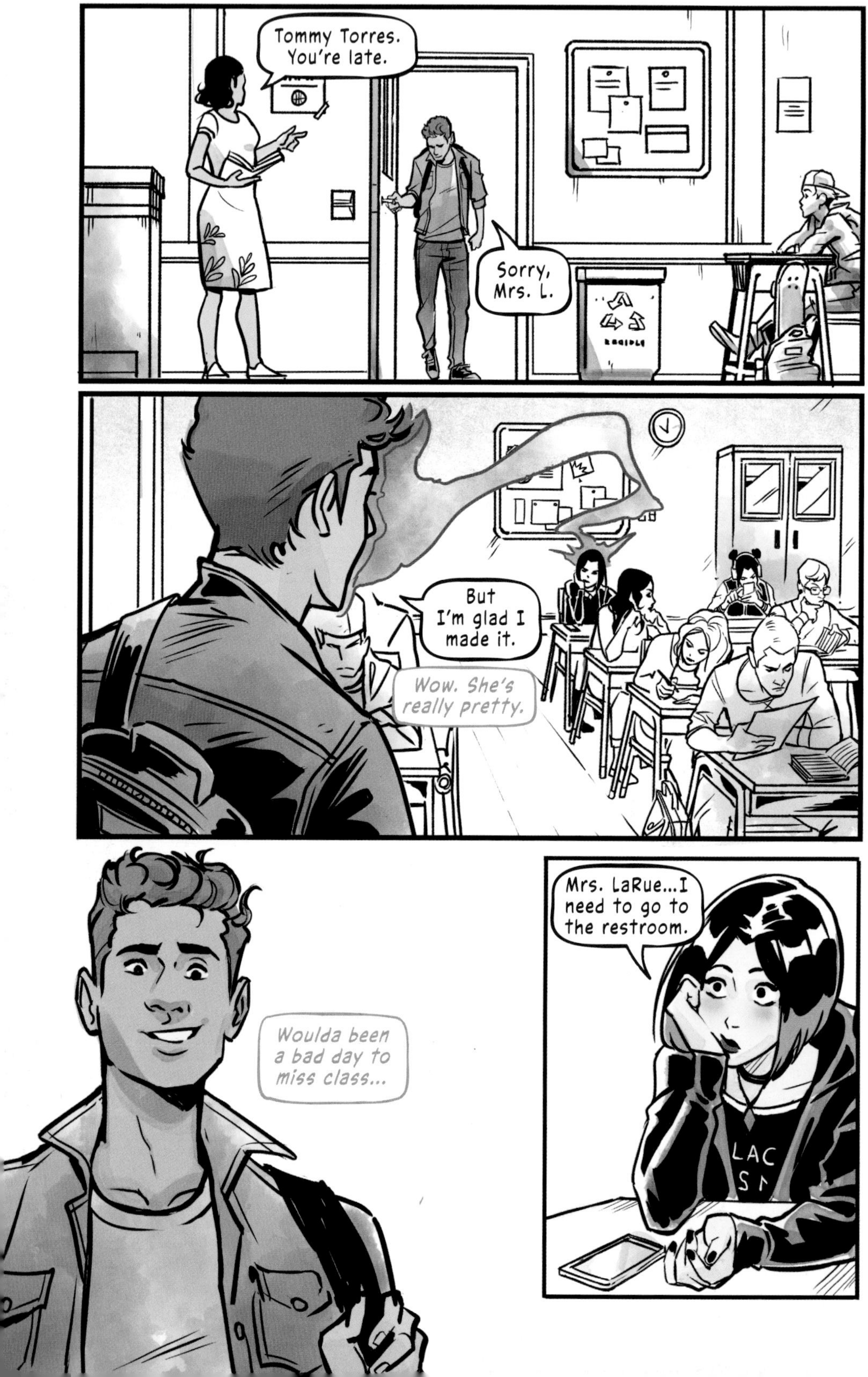
Tommy Torres. You're late.
Sorry, Mrs. L.
RECYCLE
But I'm glad I made it.
Wow. She's really pretty.
Woulda been a bad day to miss class...
Mrs. LaRue...I need to go to the restroom.

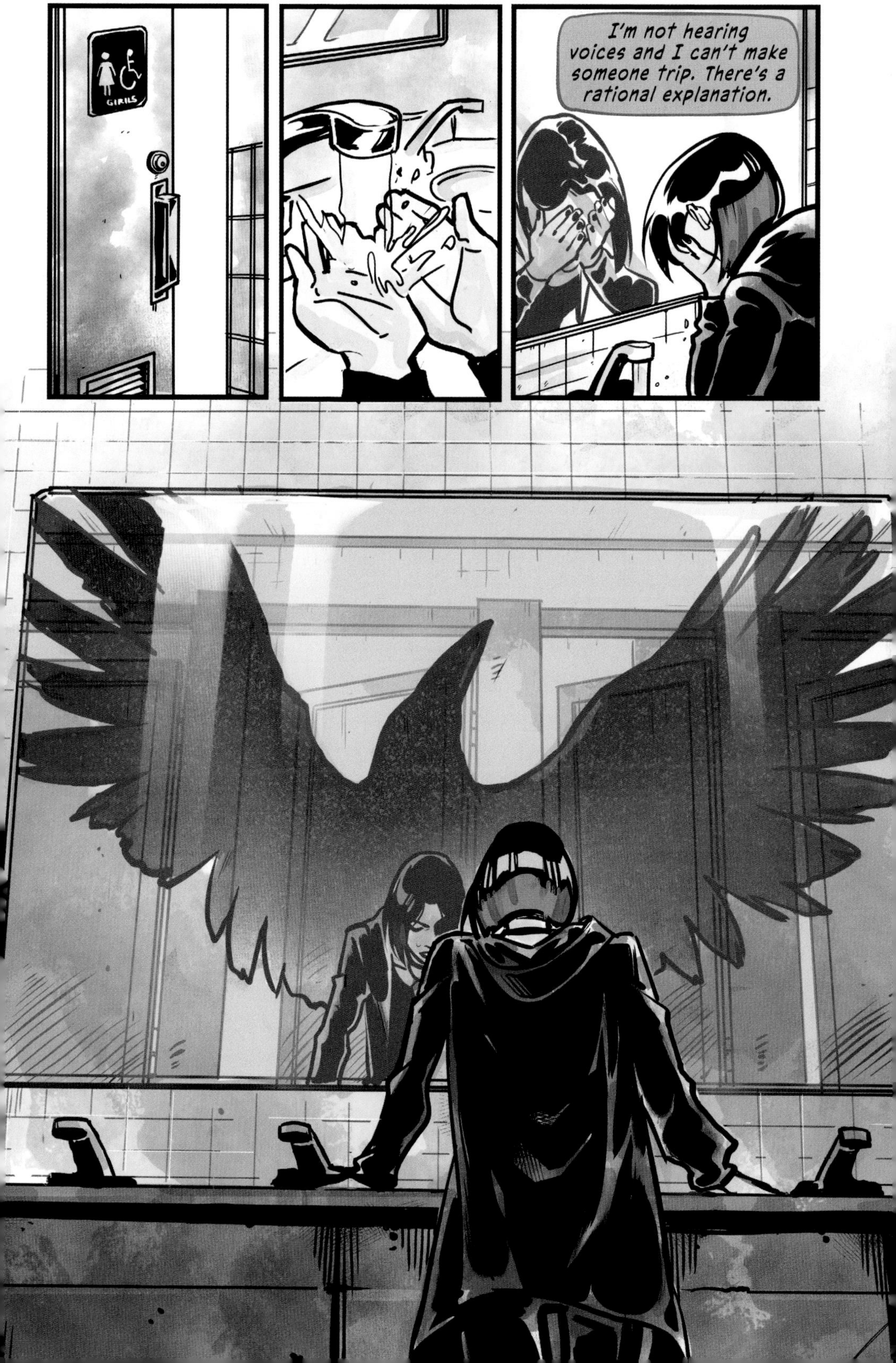
GIRLS
I'm not hearing voices and I can't make someone trip. There's a rational explanation.

CHAPTER 4: TEENAGE WASTELAND

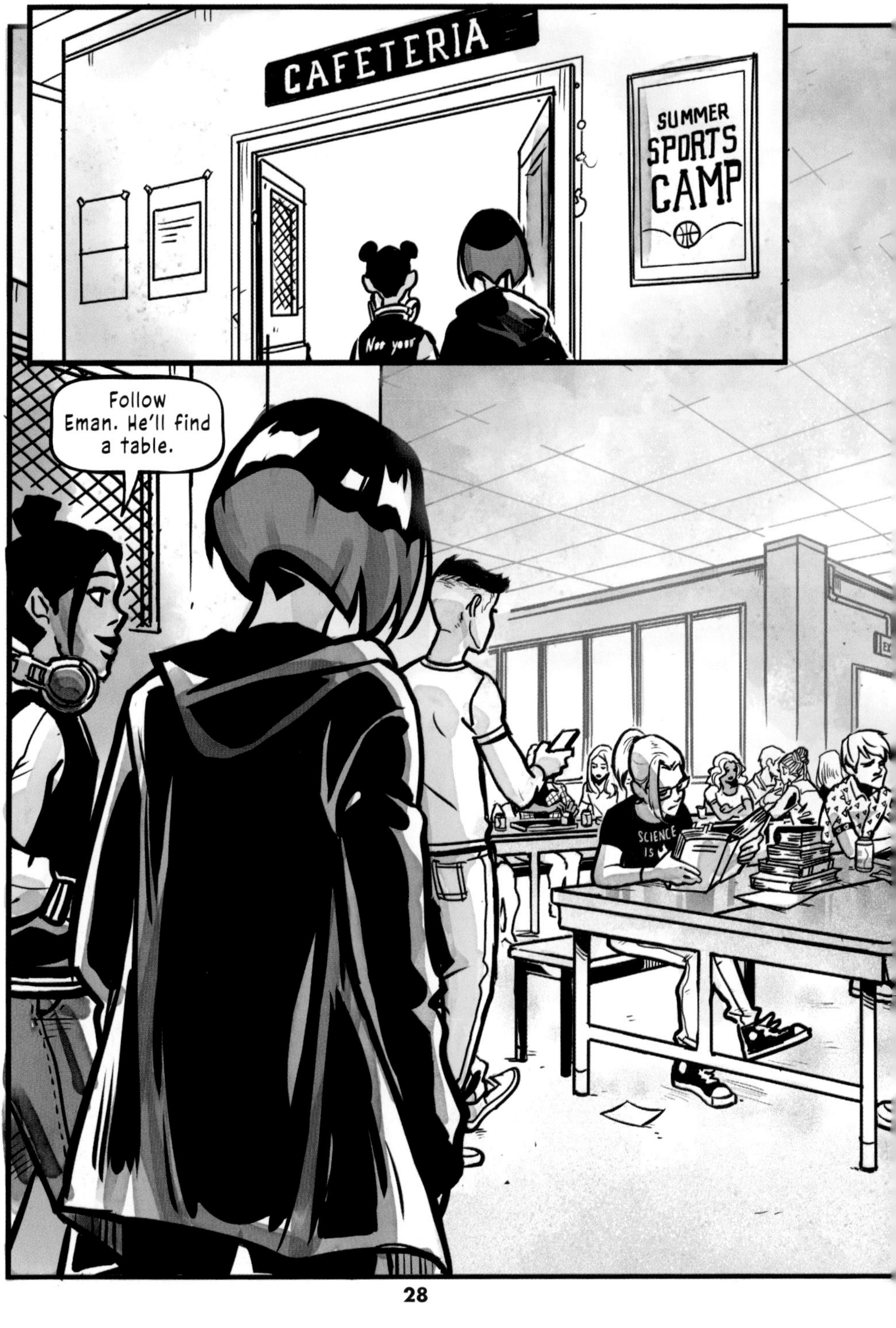
CAFETERIA
SUMMER SPORTS CAMP
Not your
Follow Eman. He'll find a table.
SCIENCE IS

BLACK

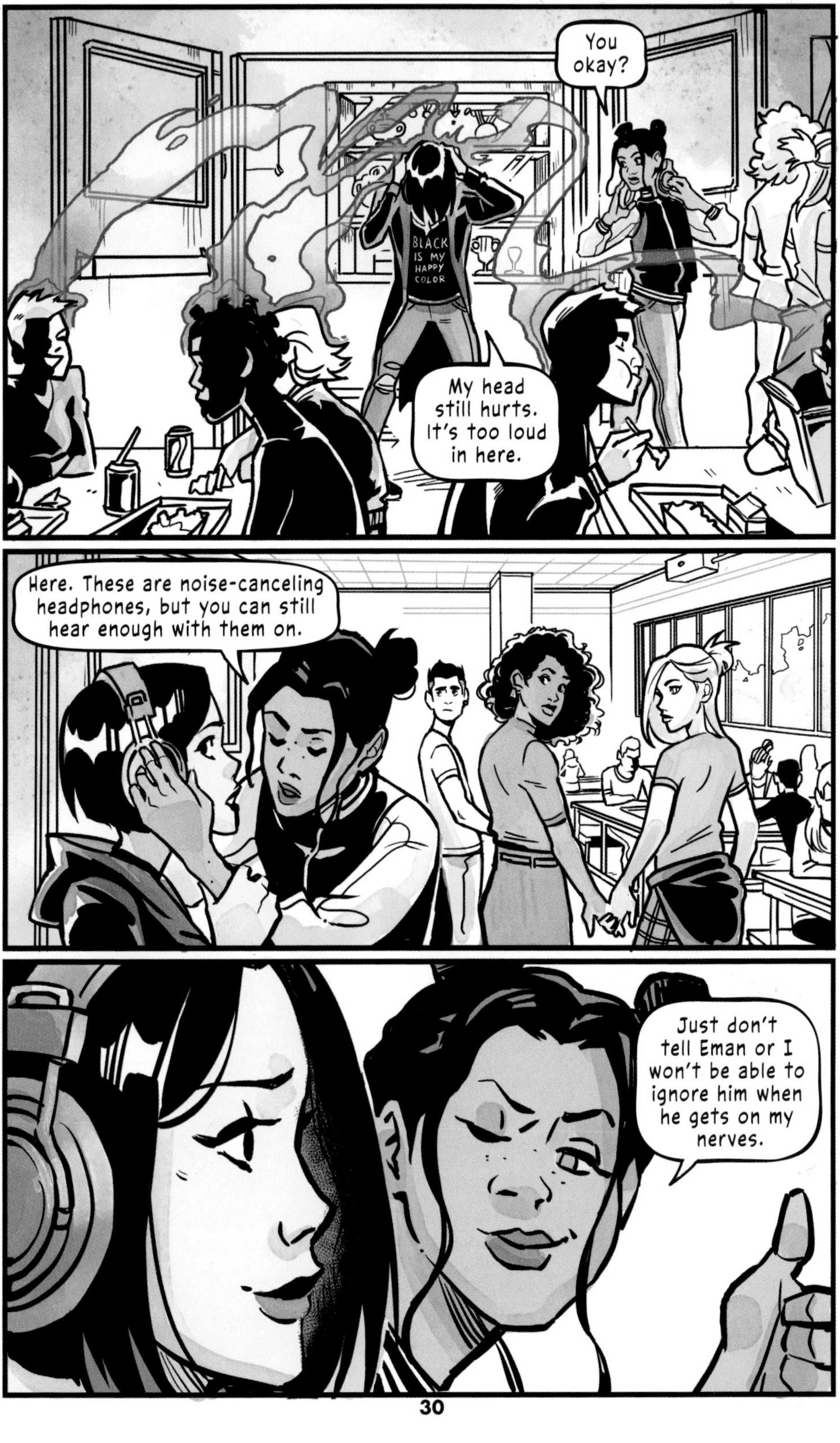
You okay?
BLACK IS MY HAPPY COLOR
My head still hurts. It's too loud in here.
Here. These are noise-canceling headphones, but you can still hear enough with them on.
Just don't tell Eman or I won't be able to ignore him when he gets on my nerves.

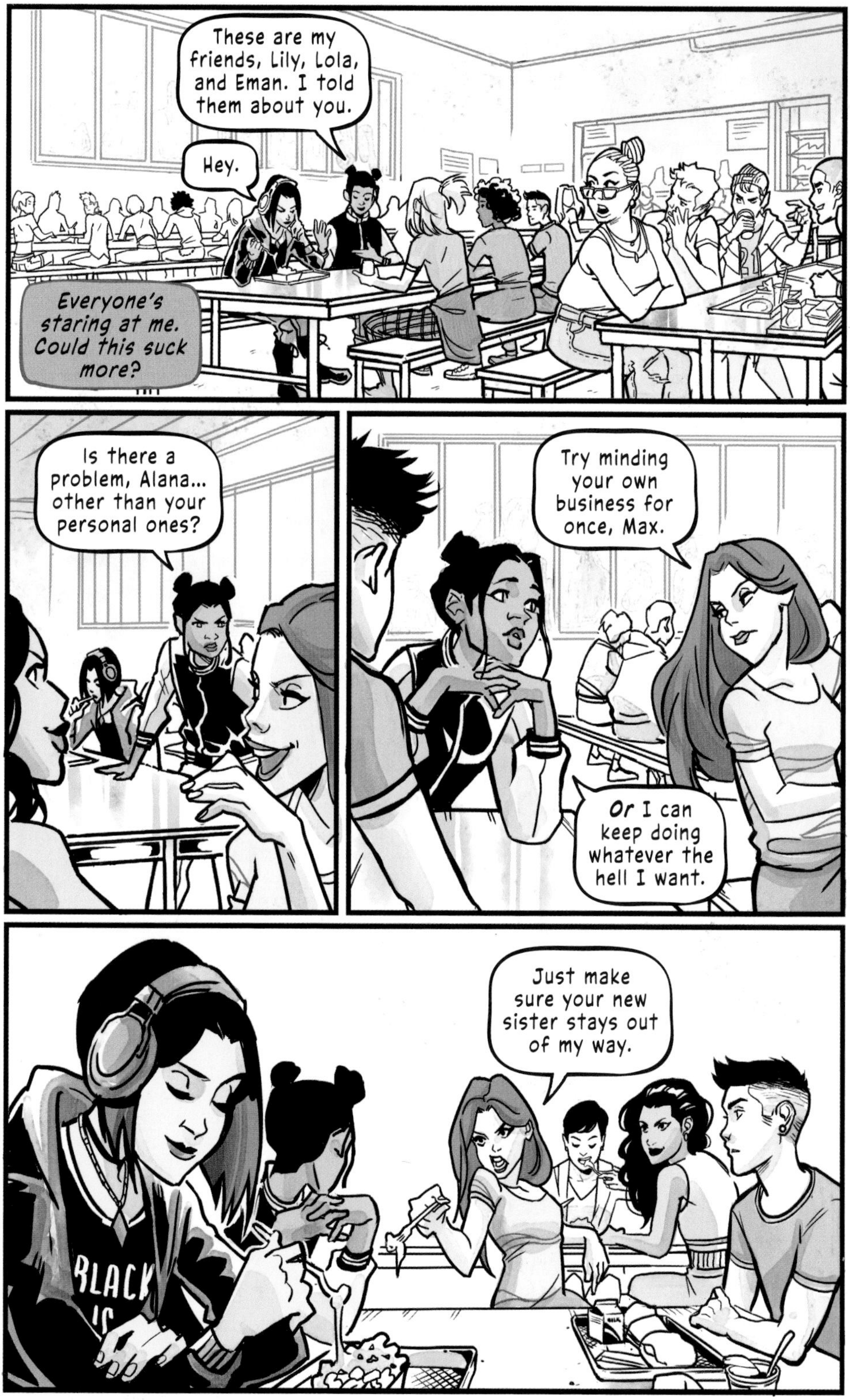
These are my friends, Lily, Lola, and Eman. I told them about you.
Hey.
Everyone's staring at me. Could this suck more?
Is there a problem, Alana... other than your personal ones?
Try minding your own business for once, Max.
Or I can keep doing whatever the hell I want.
Just make sure your new sister stays out of my way.

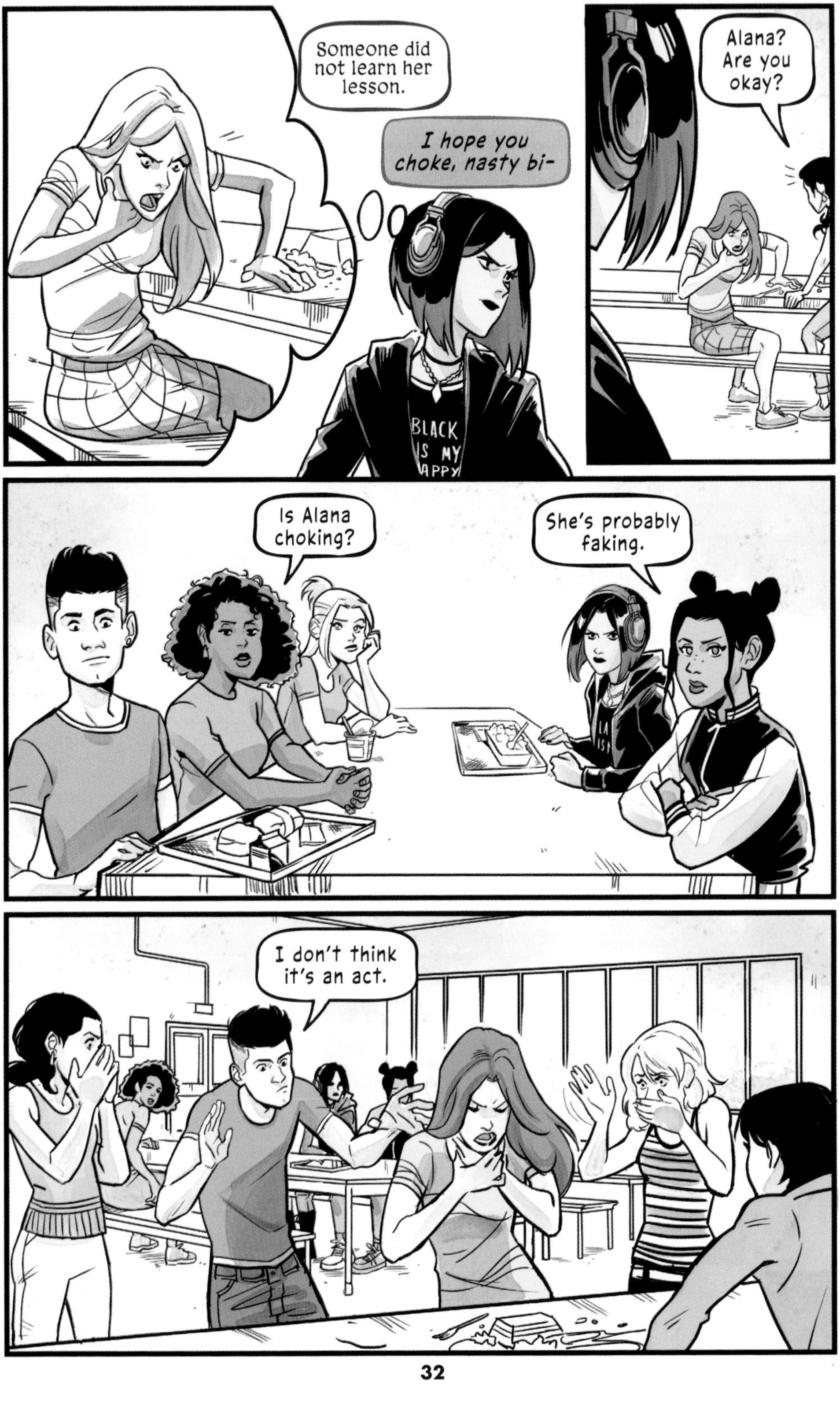
Someone did not learn her lesson.
I hope you choke, nasty bi-
BLACK IS MY HAPPY
Alana? Are you okay?
Is Alana choking?
She's probably faking.
I don't think it's an act.

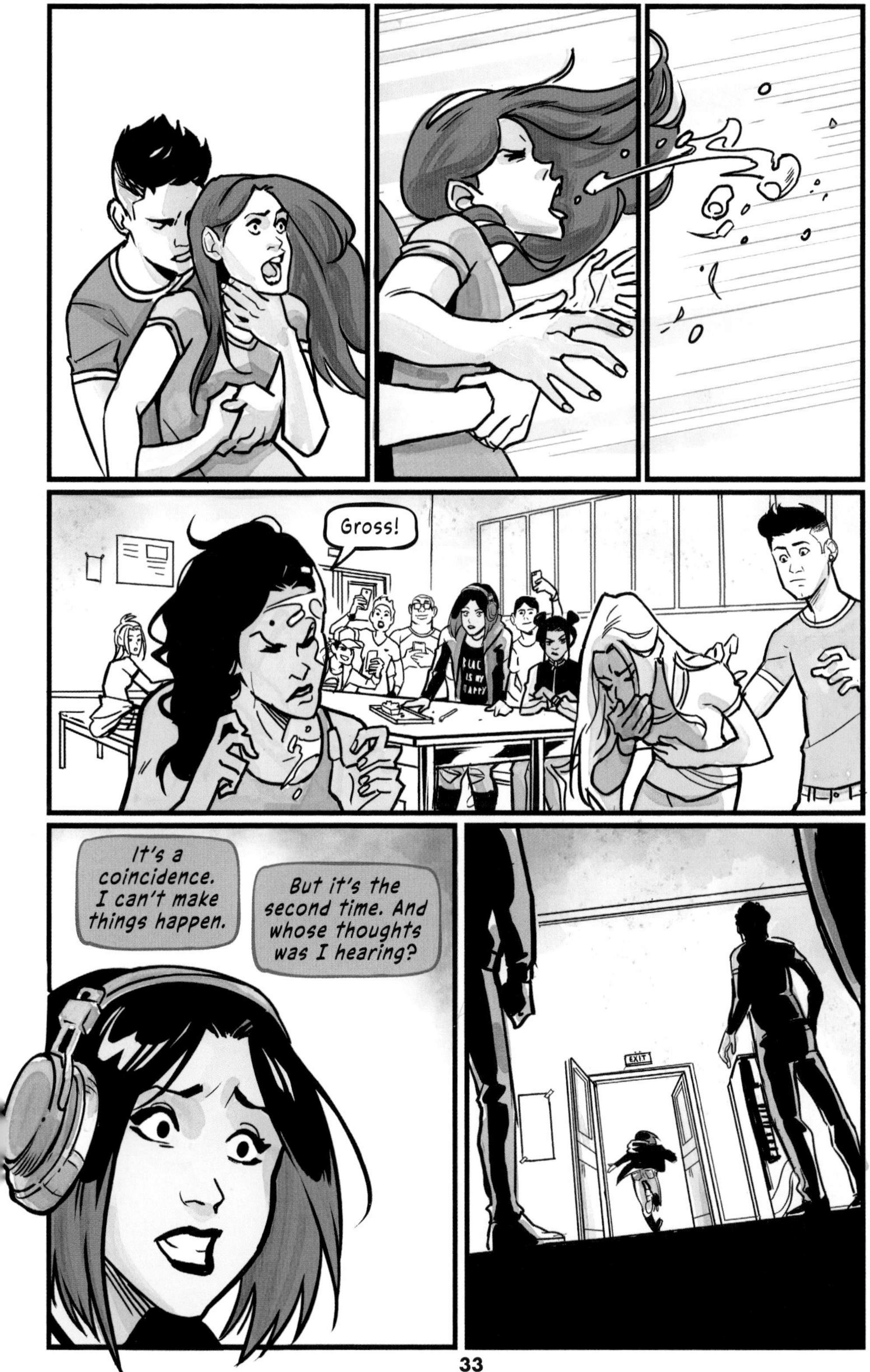
Gross!
It's a coincidence. I can't make things happen.
But it's the second time. And whose thoughts was I hearing?

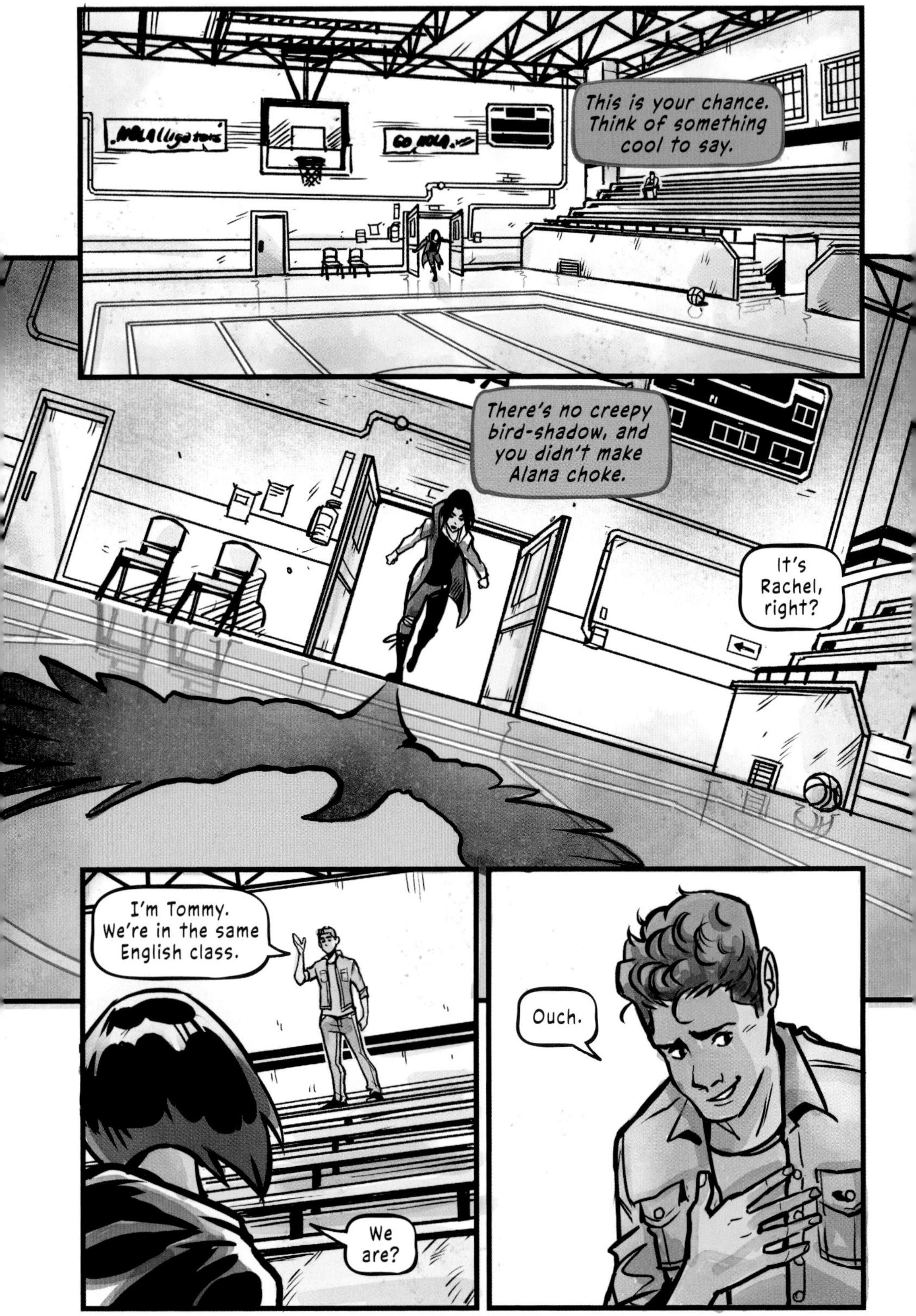
This is your chance. Think of something cool to say.
There's no creepy bird-shadow, and you didn't make Alana choke.
It's Rachel, right?
I'm Tommy. We're in the same English class.
We are?
Ouch.

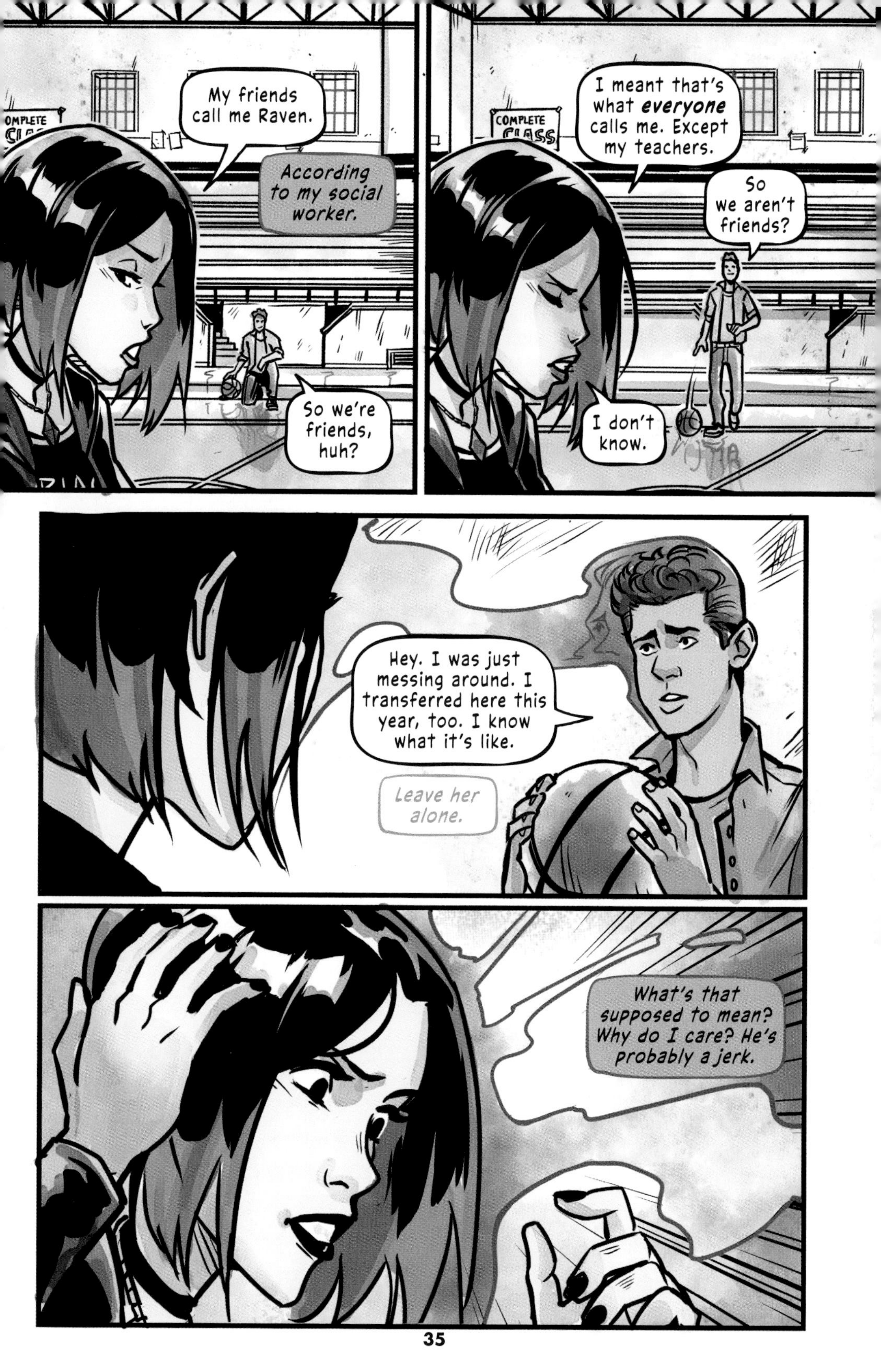

My friends call me Raven.
According to my social worker.
So we're friends, huh?
I meant that's what *everyone* calls me. Except my teachers.
So we aren't friends?
I don't know.
Hey. I was just messing around. I transferred here this year, too. I know what it's like.
Leave her alone.
What's that supposed to mean? Why do I care? He's probably a jerk.

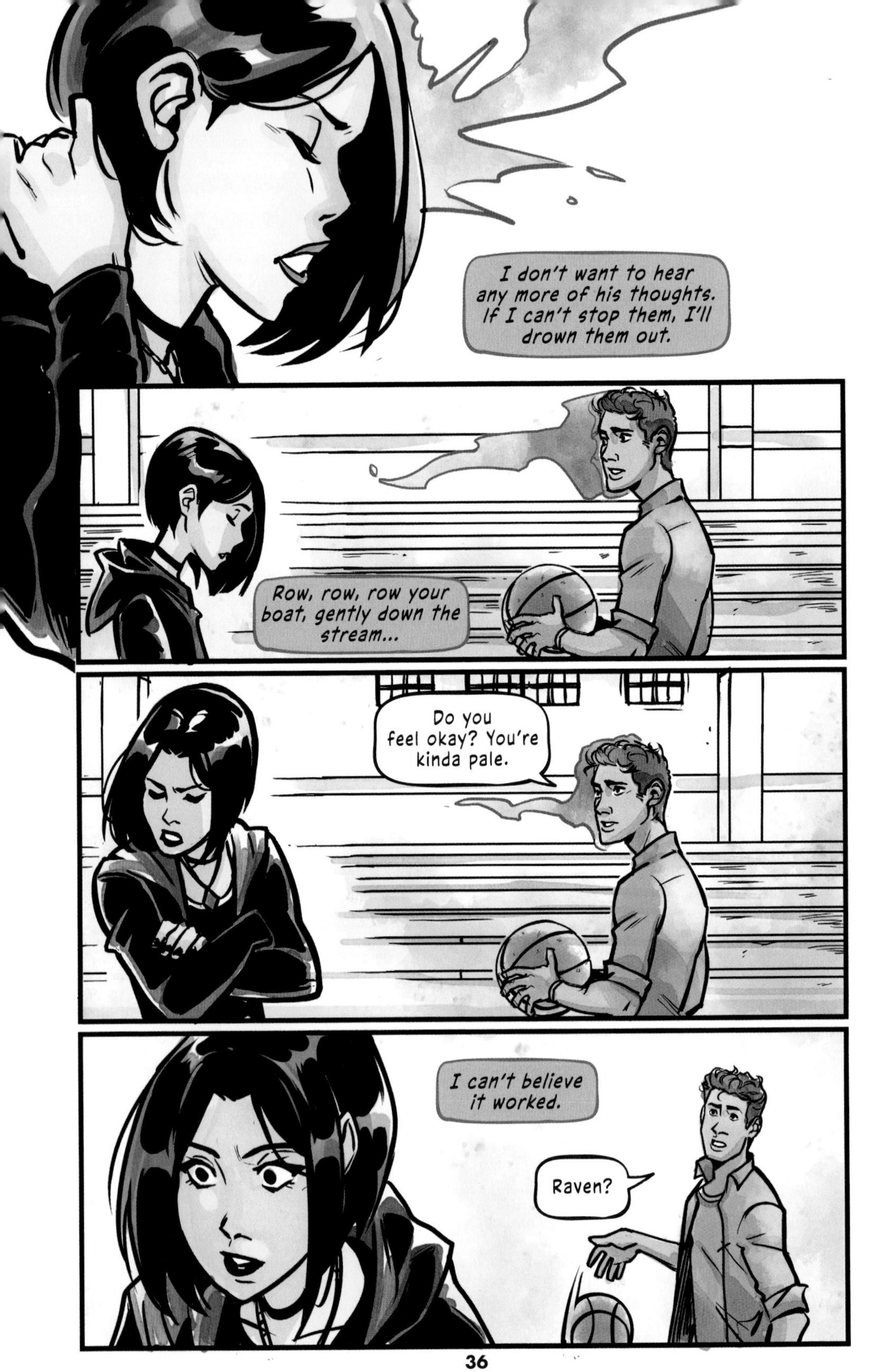
I don't want to hear any more of his thoughts. If I can't stop them, I'll drown them out.
Row, row, row your boat, gently down the stream...
Do you feel okay? You're kinda pale.
I can't believe it worked.
Raven?

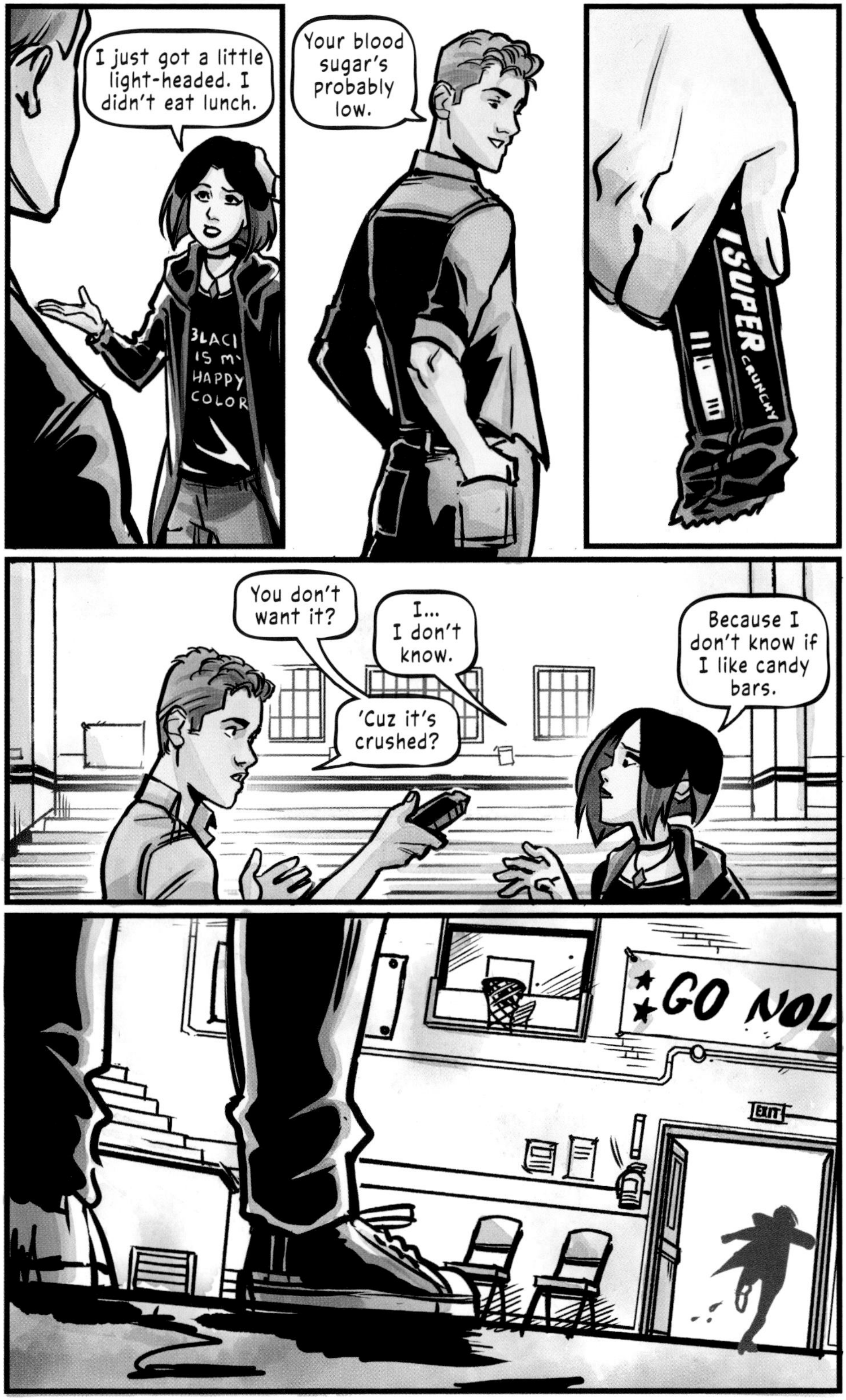
I just got a little light-headed. I didn't eat lunch.
Your blood sugar's probably low.
BLACK IS MY HAPPY COLOR
SUPER CRUNCHY
You don't want it?
'Cuz it's crushed?
I... I don't know.
Because I don't know if I like candy bars.
GO NOL
EXIT

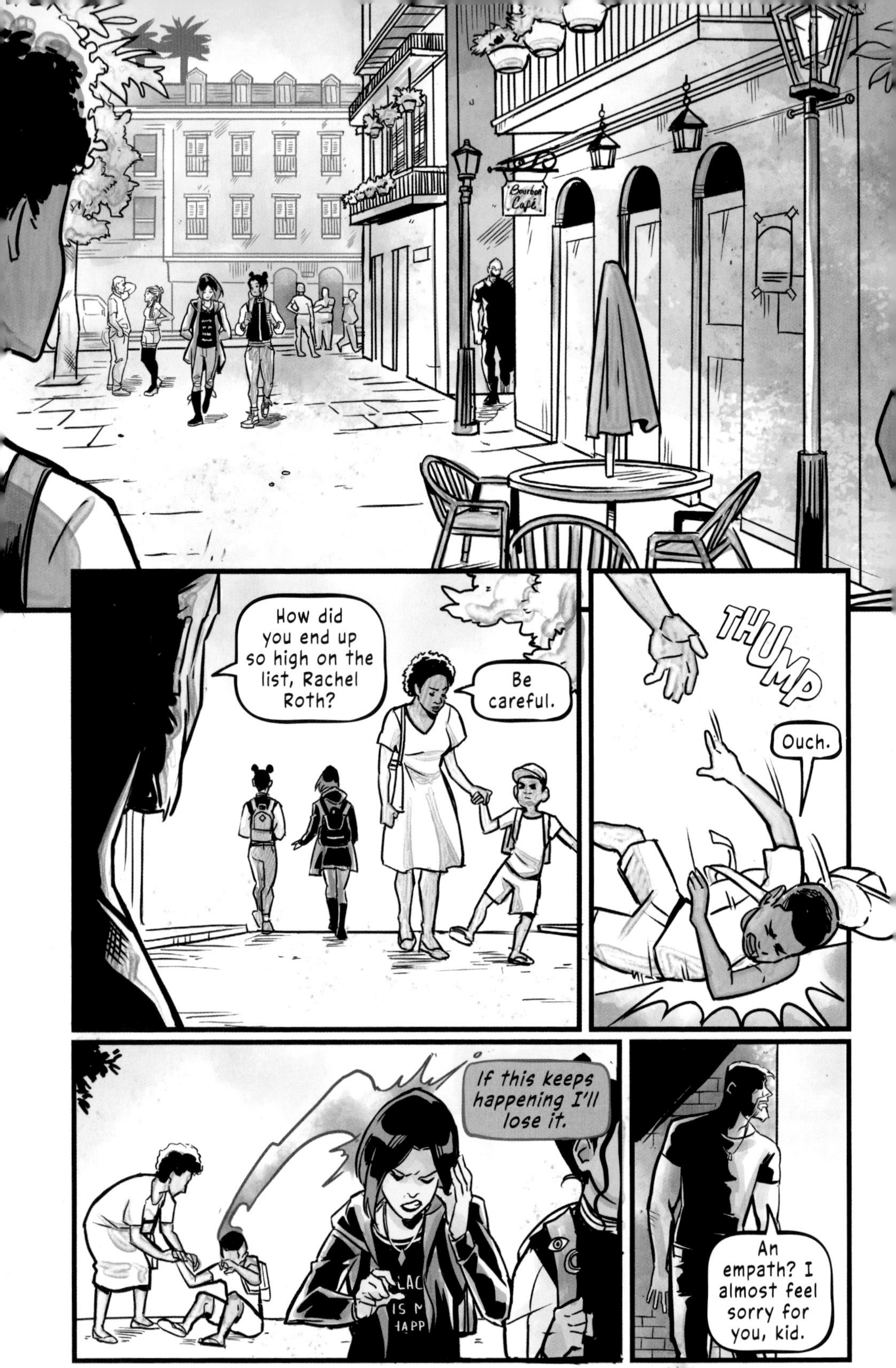
Bourbon Café
How did you end up so high on the list, Rachel Roth?
Be careful.
THUMP
Ouch.
If this keeps happening I'll lose it.
An empath? I almost feel sorry for you, kid.

CHAPTER 5: MISSING PIECES

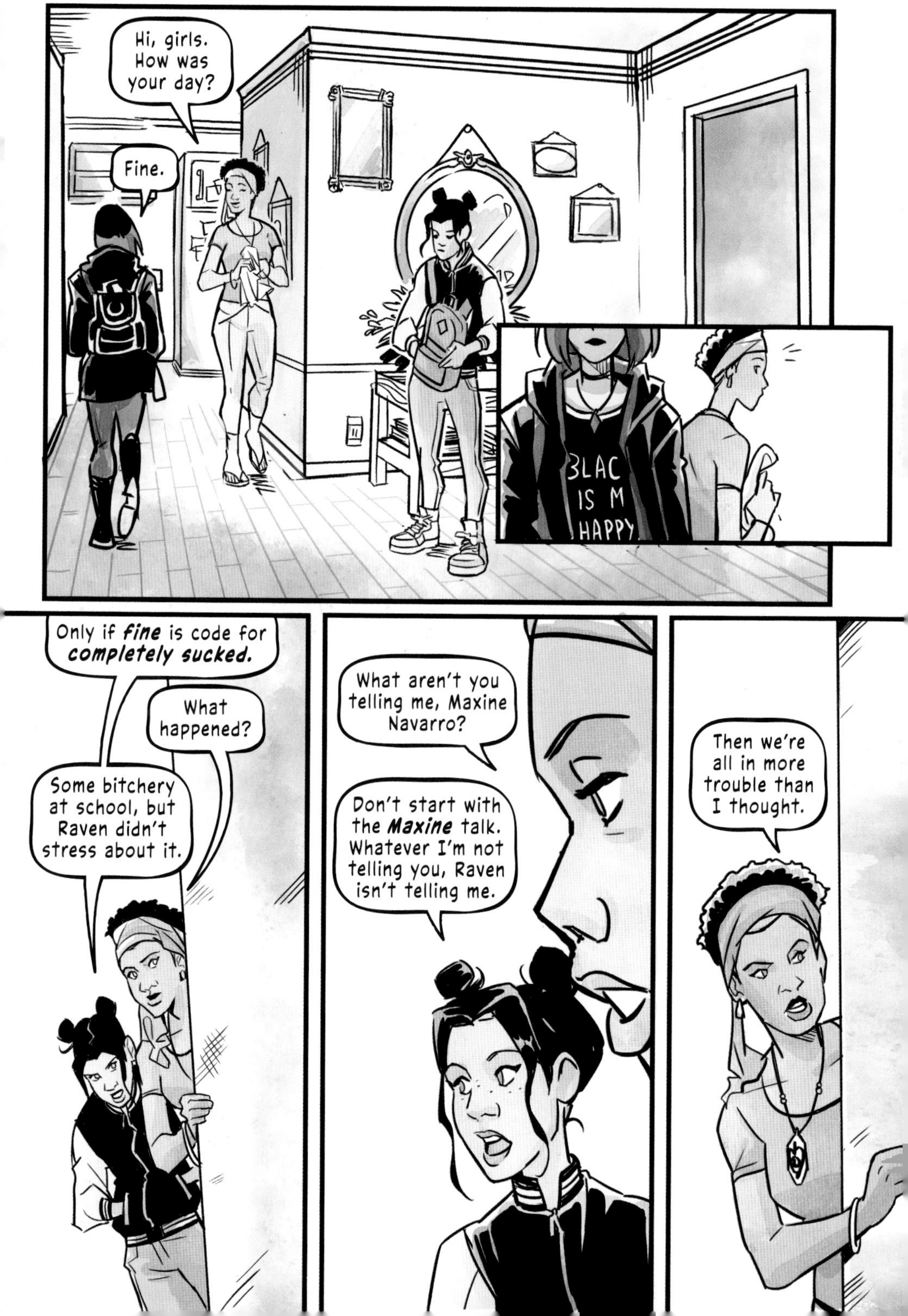
Hi, girls. How was your day?
Fine.
BLAC IS M HAPPY
Only if *fine* is code for ***completely sucked.***
What happened?
Some bitchery at school, but Raven didn't stress about it.
What aren't you telling me, Maxine Navarro?
Don't start with the ***Maxine*** talk. Whatever I'm not telling you, Raven isn't telling me.
Then we're all in more trouble than I thought.

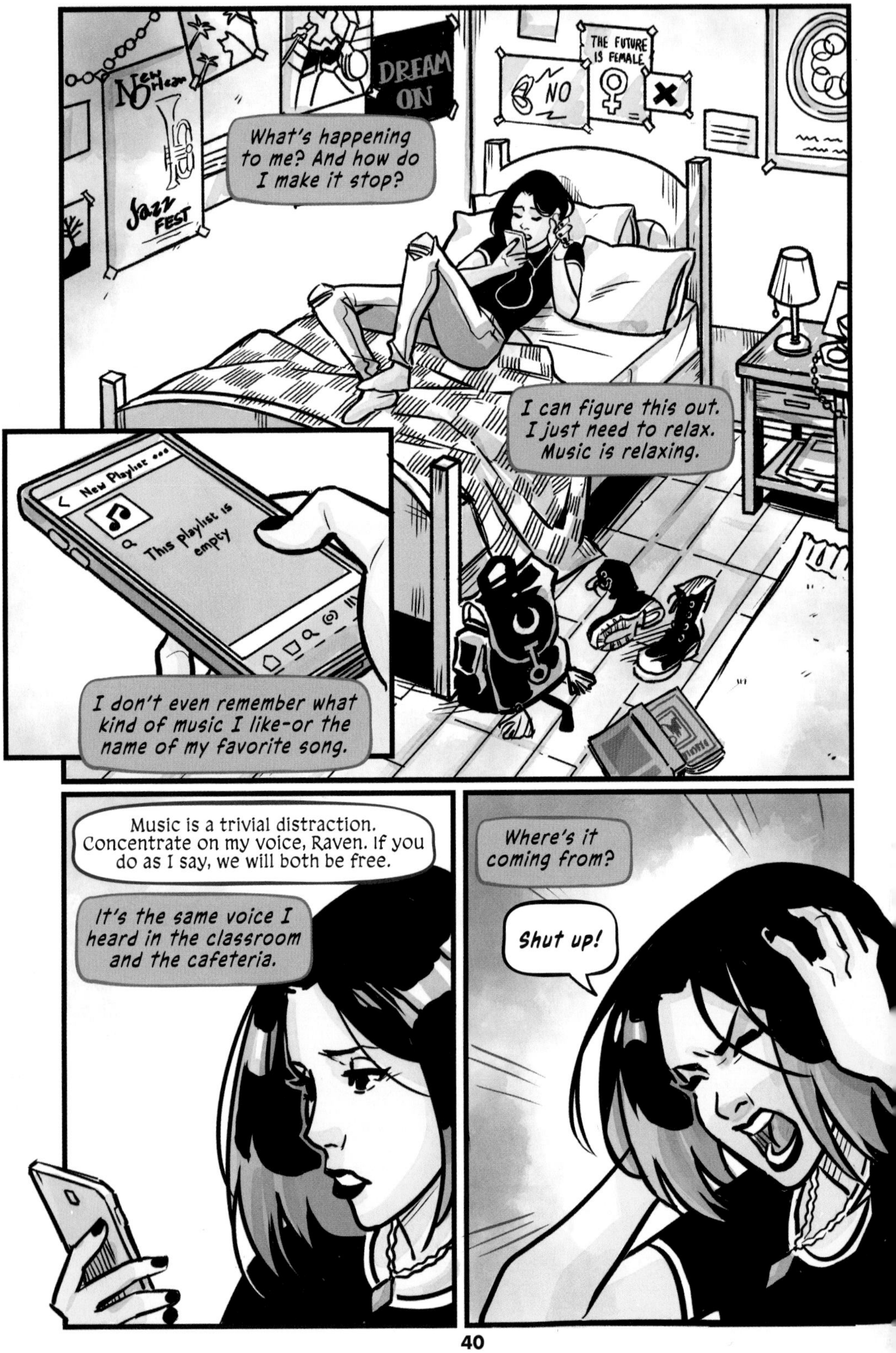

DREAM ON
THE FUTURE IS FEMALE
NO
New Orleans Jazz FEST
What's happening to me? And how do I make it stop?
I can figure this out. I just need to relax. Music is relaxing.
New Playlist
This playlist is empty
I don't even remember what kind of music I like-or the name of my favorite song.
Music is a trivial distraction. Concentrate on my voice, Raven. If you do as I say, we will both be free.
It's the same voice I heard in the classroom and the cafeteria.
Where's it coming from?
Shut up!

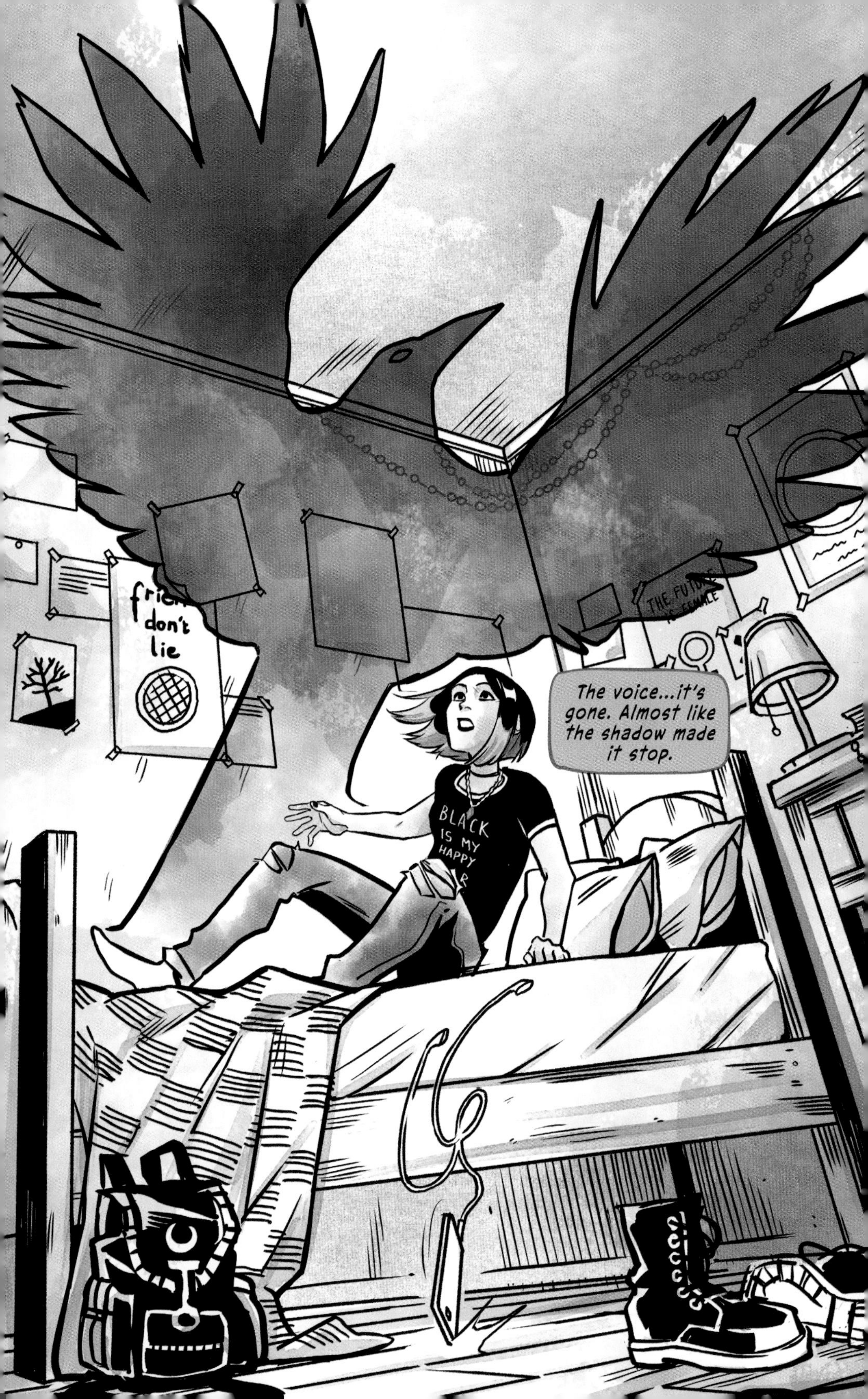
The voice...it's gone. Almost like the shadow made it stop.
don't lie
BLACK IS MY HAPPY

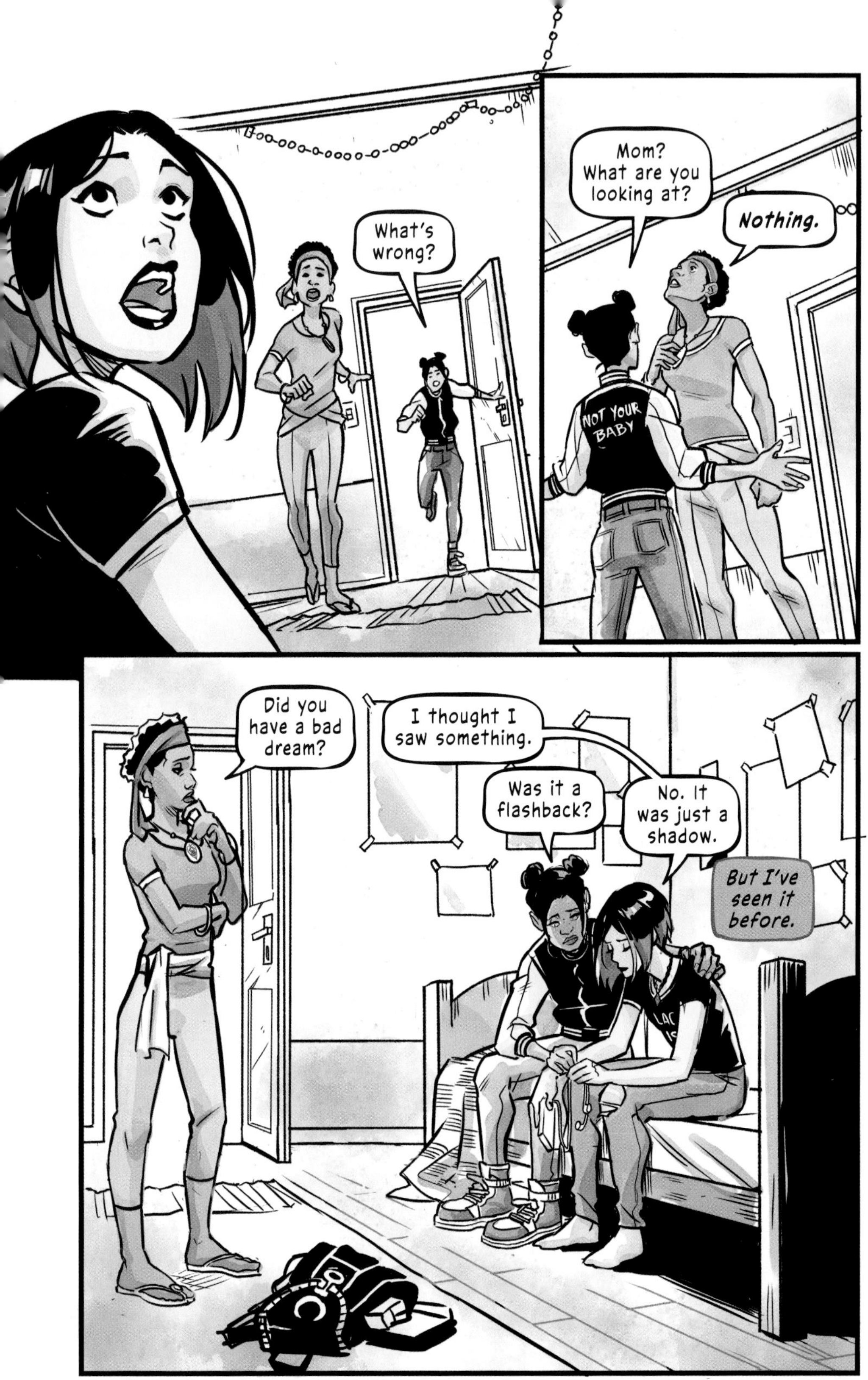
What's wrong?
Mom? What are you looking at?
Nothing.
NOT YOUR BABY
Did you have a bad dream?
I thought I saw something.
Was it a flashback?
No. It was just a shadow.
But I've seen it before.

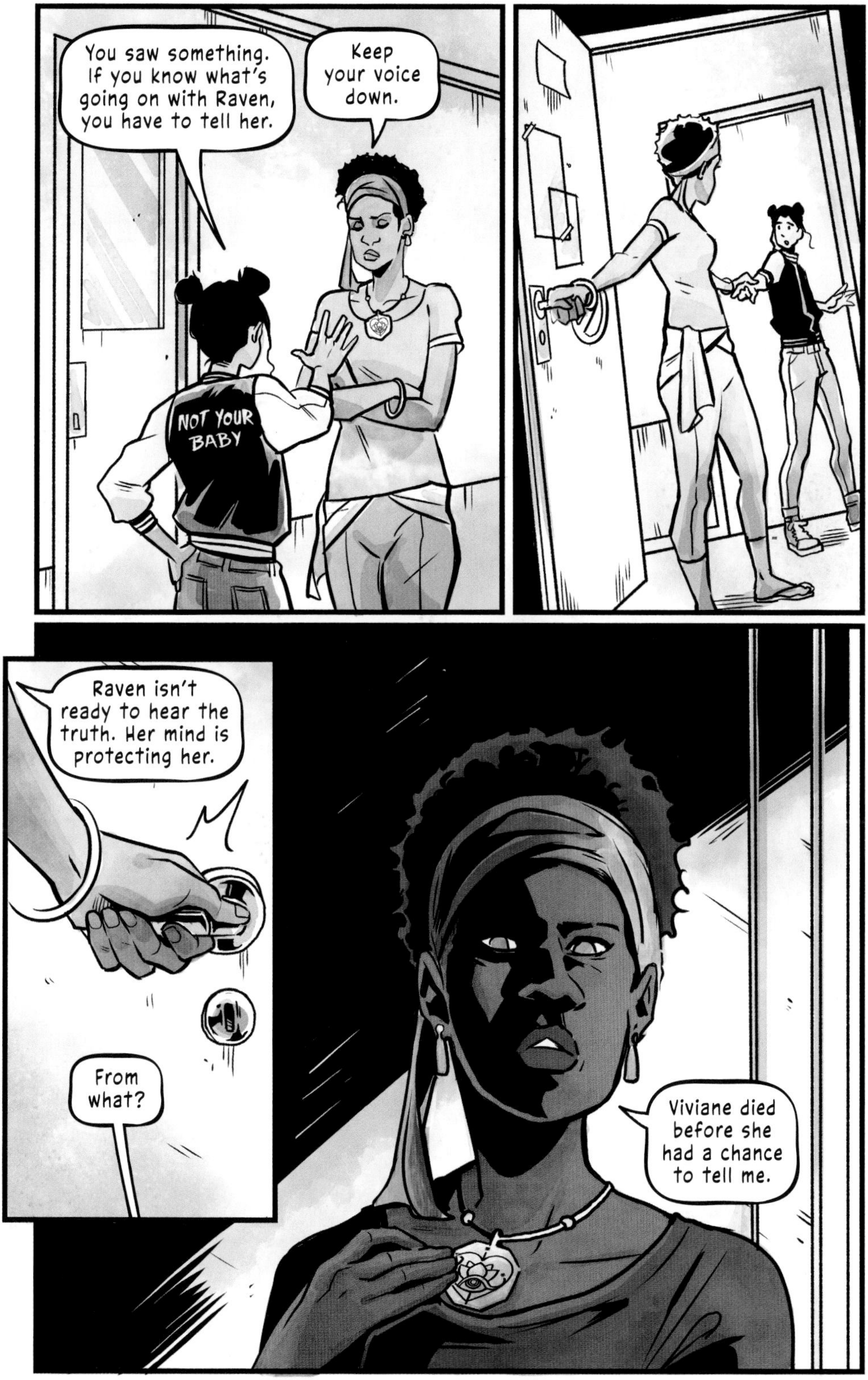
You saw something. If you know what's going on with Raven, you have to tell her.
Keep your voice down.
NOT YOUR BABY
Raven isn't ready to hear the truth. Her mind is protecting her.
From what?
Viviane died before she had a chance to tell me.

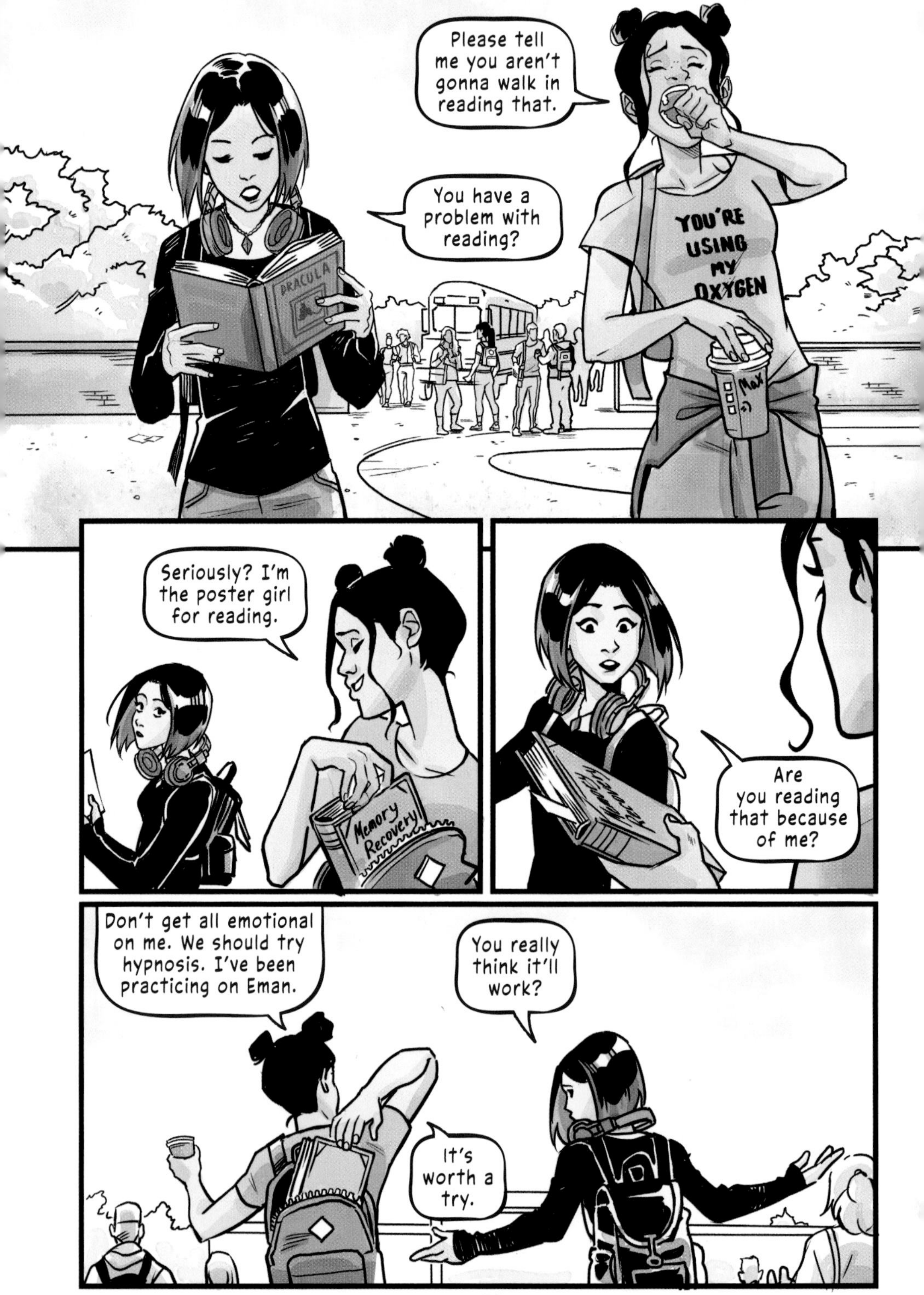
Please tell me you aren't gonna walk in reading that.
You have a problem with reading?
DRACULA
YOU'RE USING MY OXYGEN
Max
Seriously? I'm the poster girl for reading.
Memory Recovery
Are you reading that because of me?
Don't get all emotional on me. We should try hypnosis. I've been practicing on Eman.
You really think it'll work?
It's worth a try.

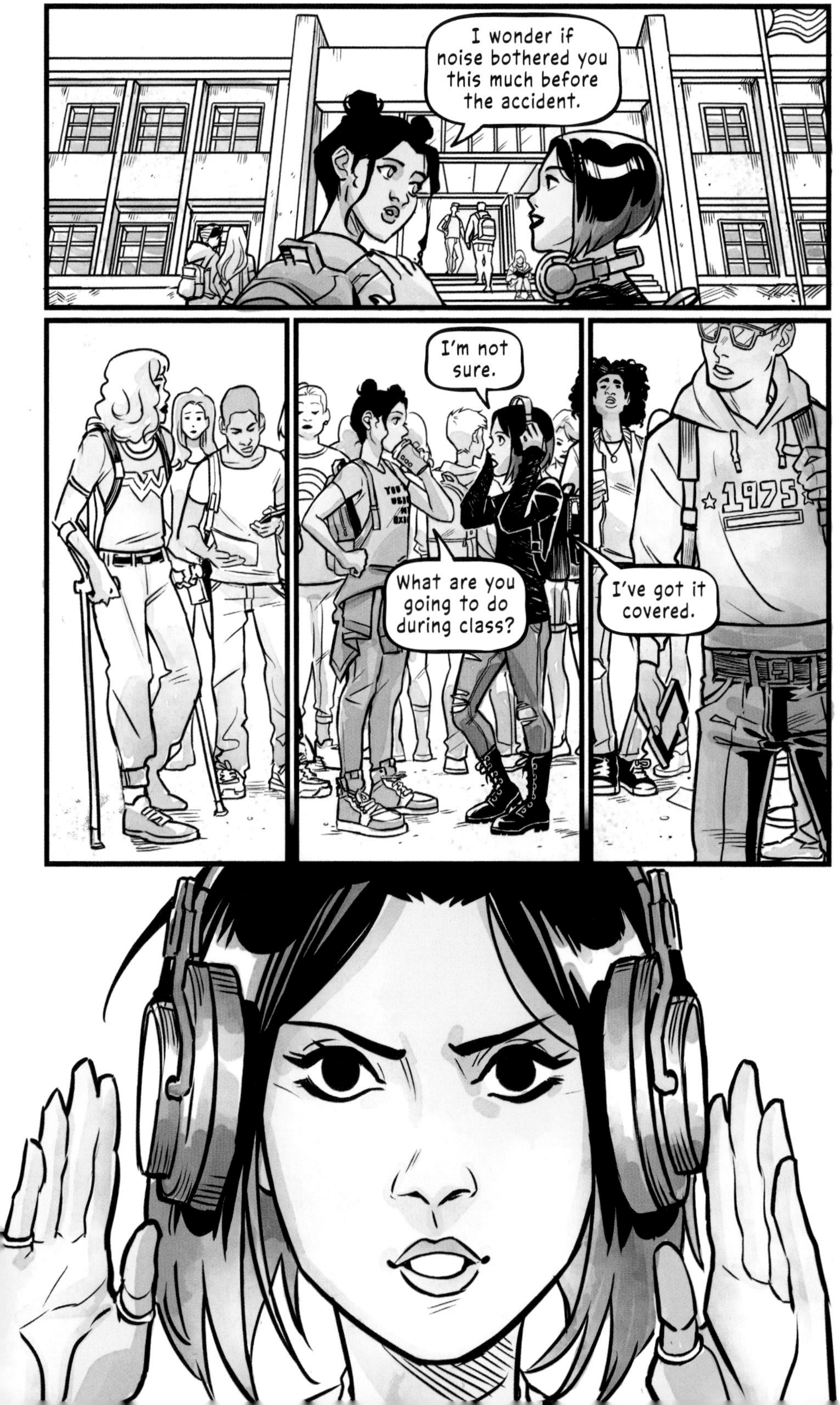
I wonder if noise bothered you this much before the accident.
I'm not sure.
What are you going to do during class?
I've got it covered.

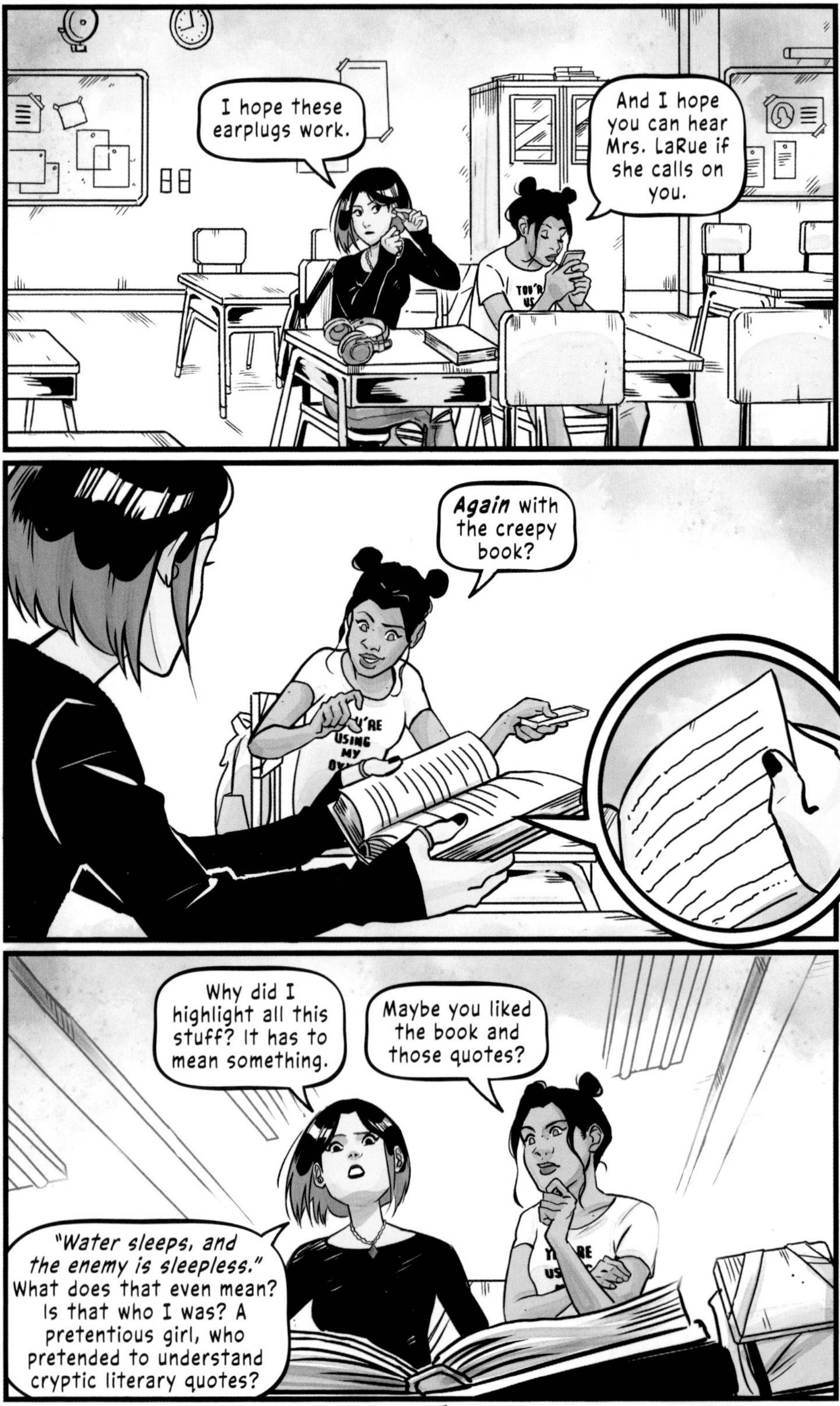
I hope these earplugs work.
And I hope you can hear Mrs. LaRue if she calls on you.
Again with the creepy book?
Why did I highlight all this stuff? It has to mean something.
Maybe you liked the book and those quotes?
"Water sleeps, and the enemy is sleepless." What does that even mean? Is that who I was? A pretentious girl, who pretended to understand cryptic literary quotes?

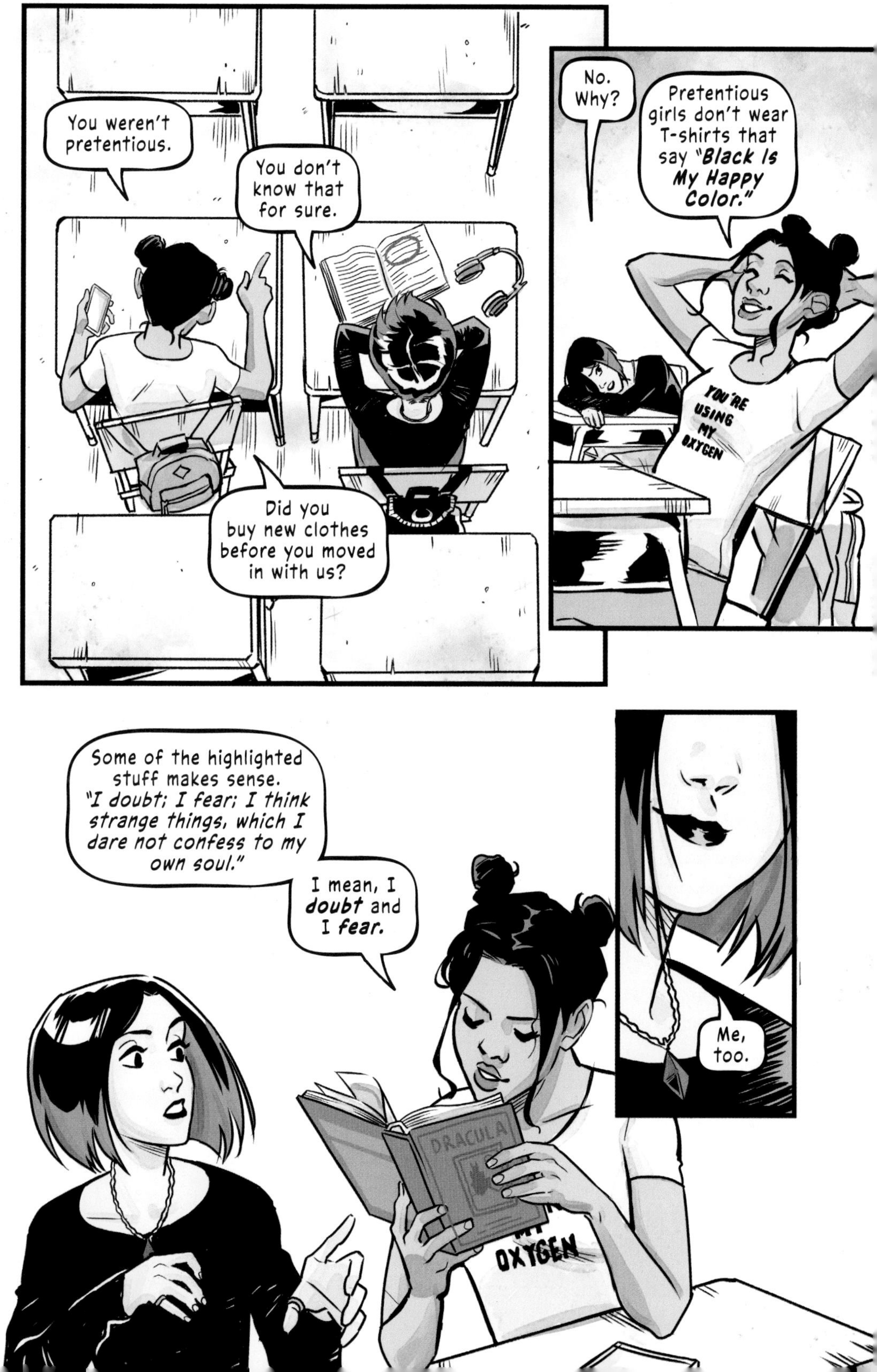
You weren't pretentious.
You don't know that for sure.
Did you buy new clothes before you moved in with us?
No. Why?
Pretentious girls don't wear T-shirts that say "Black Is My Happy Color."
YOU'RE USING MY OXYGEN
Some of the highlighted stuff makes sense. "I doubt; I fear; I think strange things, which I dare not confess to my own soul."
I mean, I doubt and I fear.
Me, too.
DRACULA
OXYGEN

CHAPTER 6: FORTUNES AND FEARS

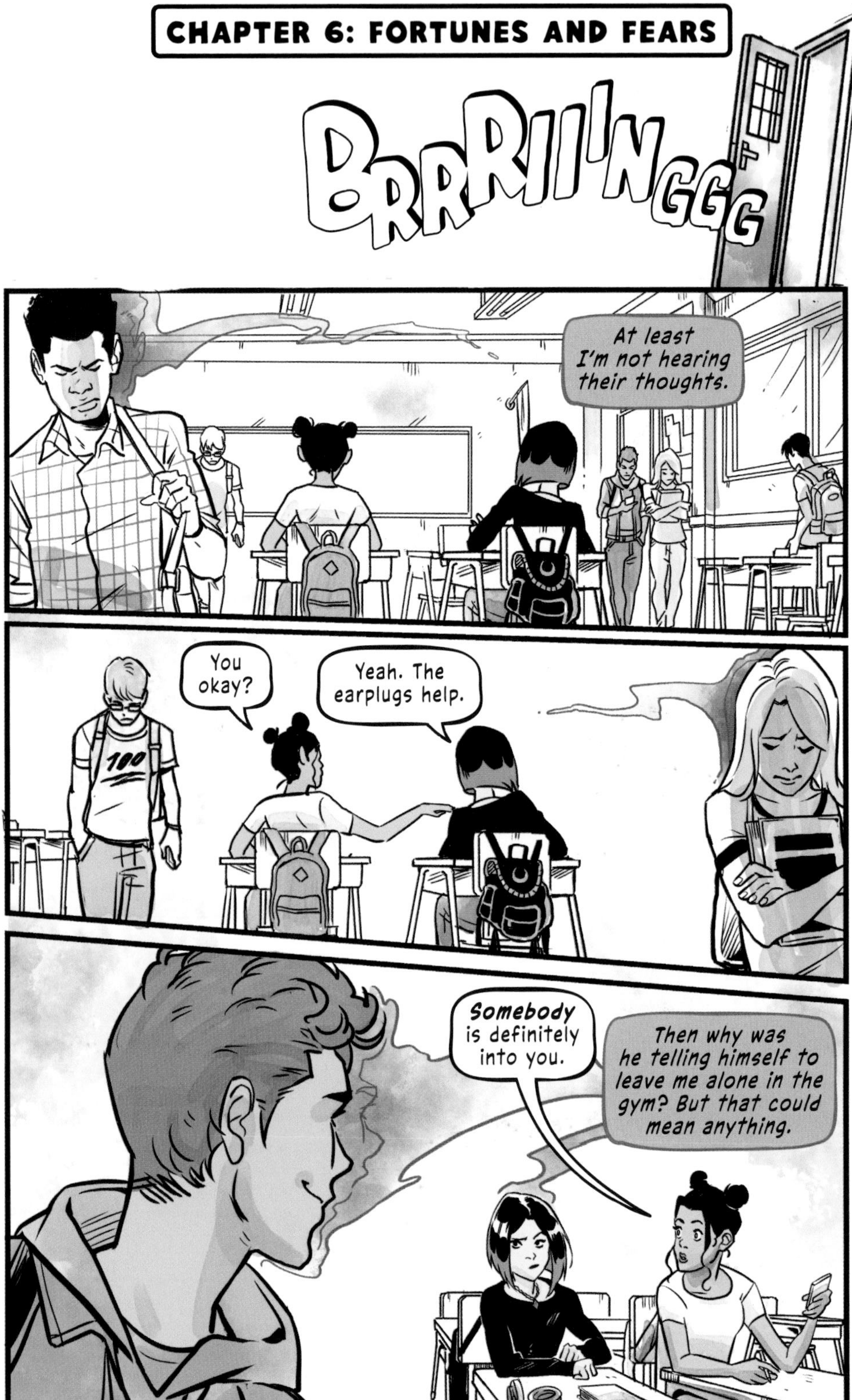
BRRRIIINGGG
At least I'm not hearing their thoughts.
You okay?
Yeah. The earplugs help.
Somebody is definitely into you.
Then why was he telling himself to leave me alone in the gym? But that could mean anything.

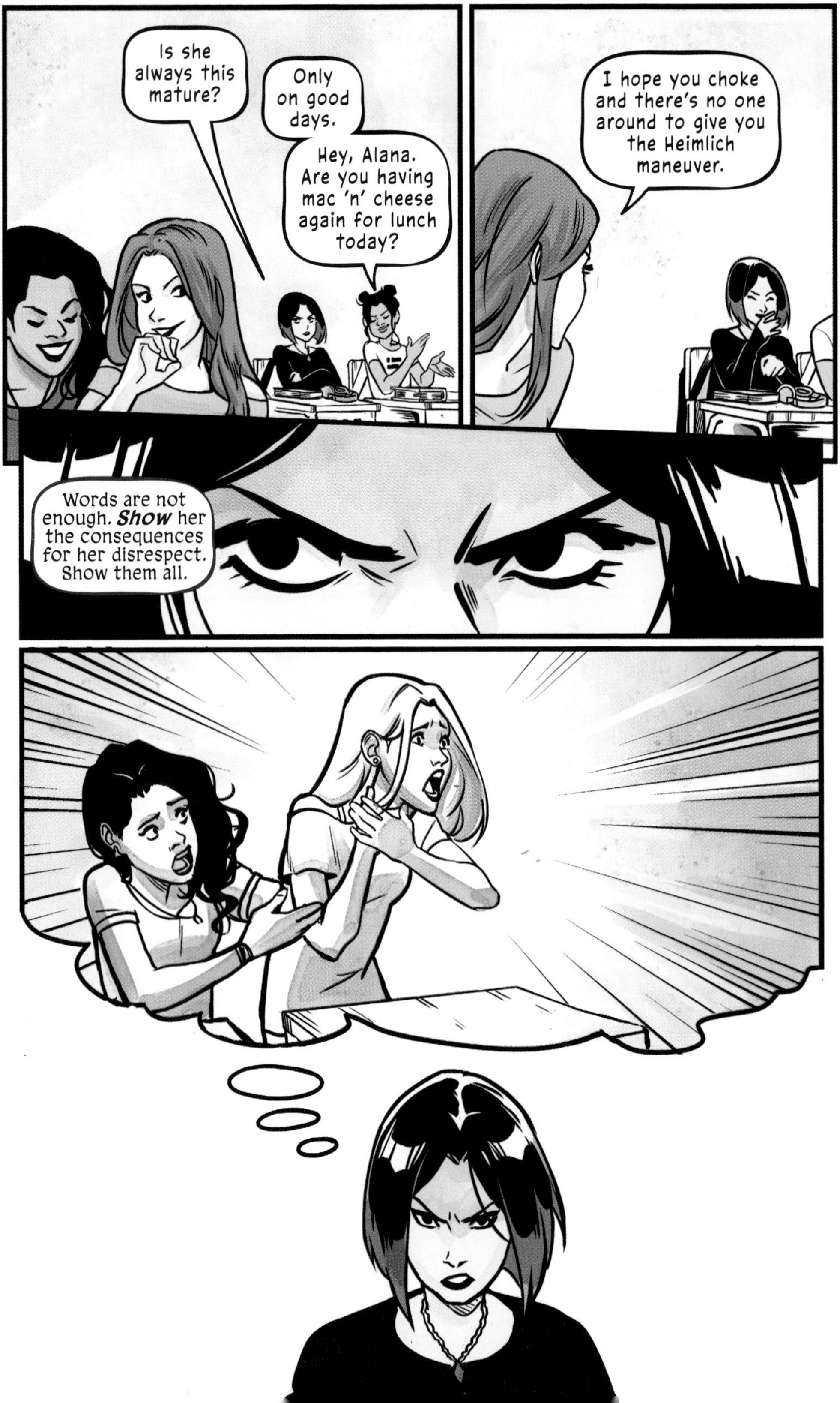
Is she always this mature?
Only on good days.
Hey, Alana. Are you having mac 'n' cheese again for lunch today?
I hope you choke and there's no one around to give you the Heimlich maneuver.
Words are not enough. ***Show*** her the consequences for her disrespect. Show them all.

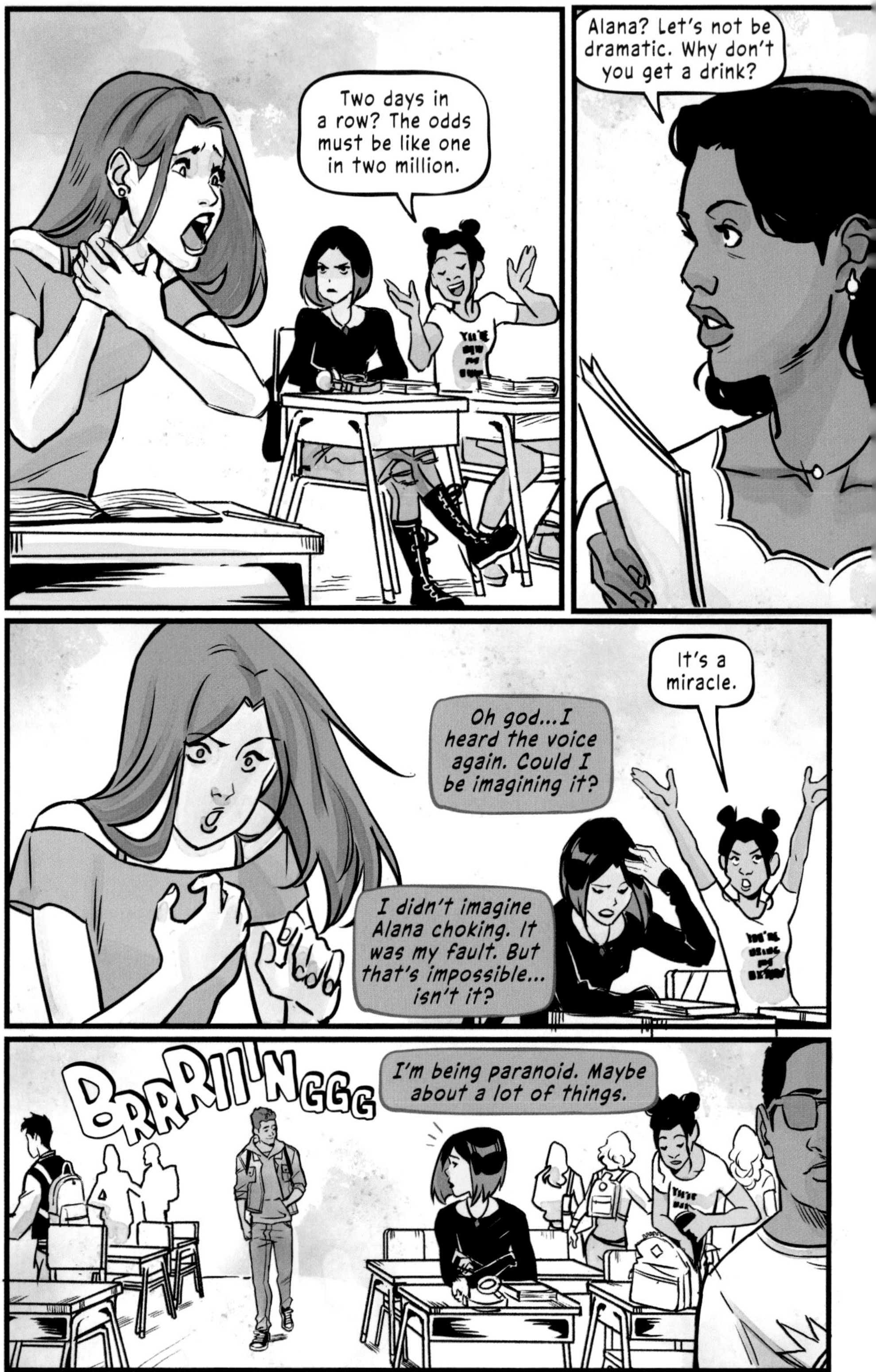
Two days in a row? The odds must be like one in two million.
Alana? Let's not be dramatic. Why don't you get a drink?
It's a miracle.
Oh god...I heard the voice again. Could I be imagining it?
I didn't imagine Alana choking. It was my fault. But that's impossible... isn't it?
BRRRIIINGGG
I'm being paranoid. Maybe about a lot of things.

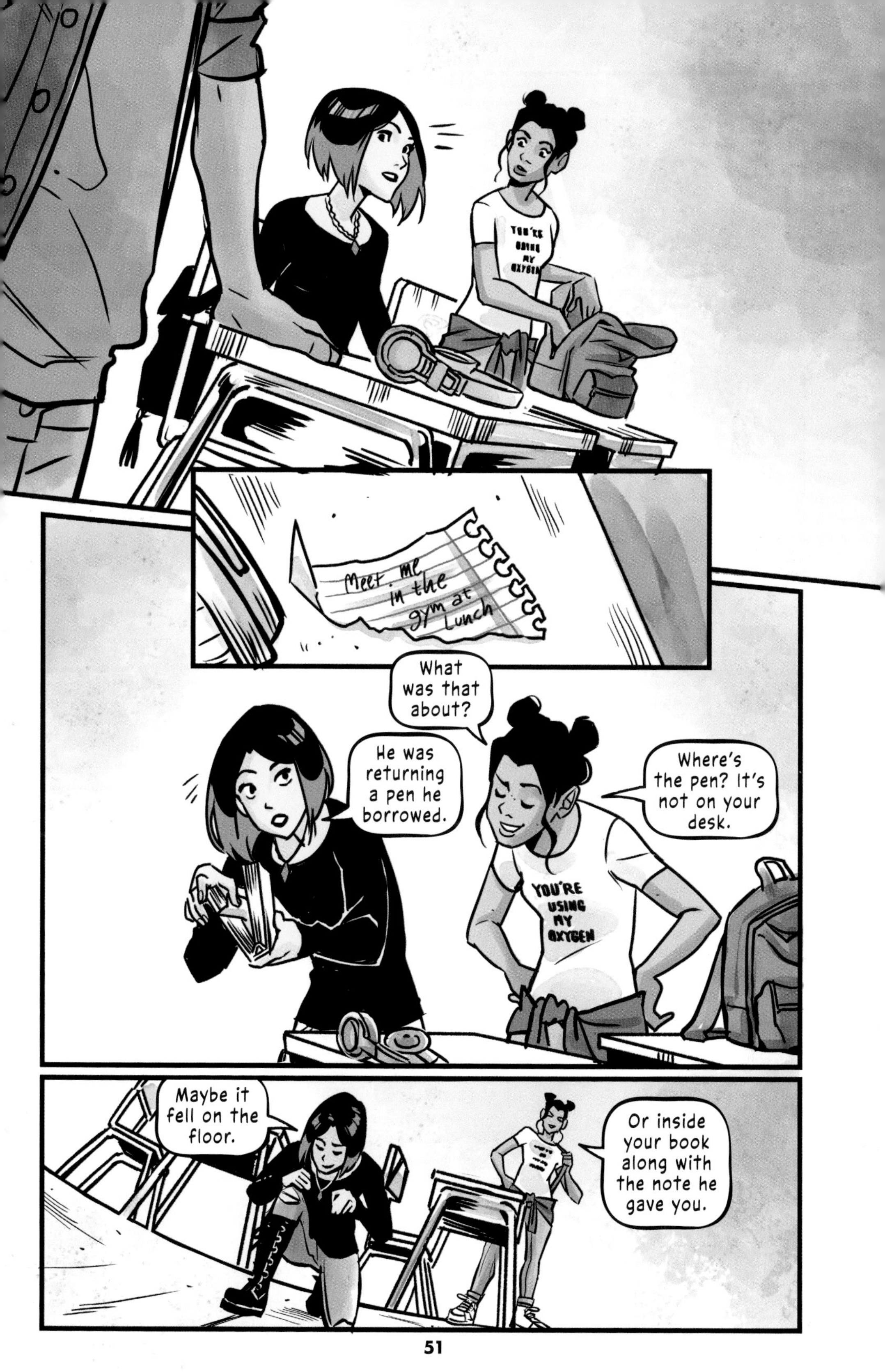
Meet me in the gym at Lunch
What was that about?
He was returning a pen he borrowed.
Where's the pen? It's not on your desk.
YOU'RE USING MY OXYGEN
Maybe it fell on the floor.
Or inside your book along with the note he gave you.

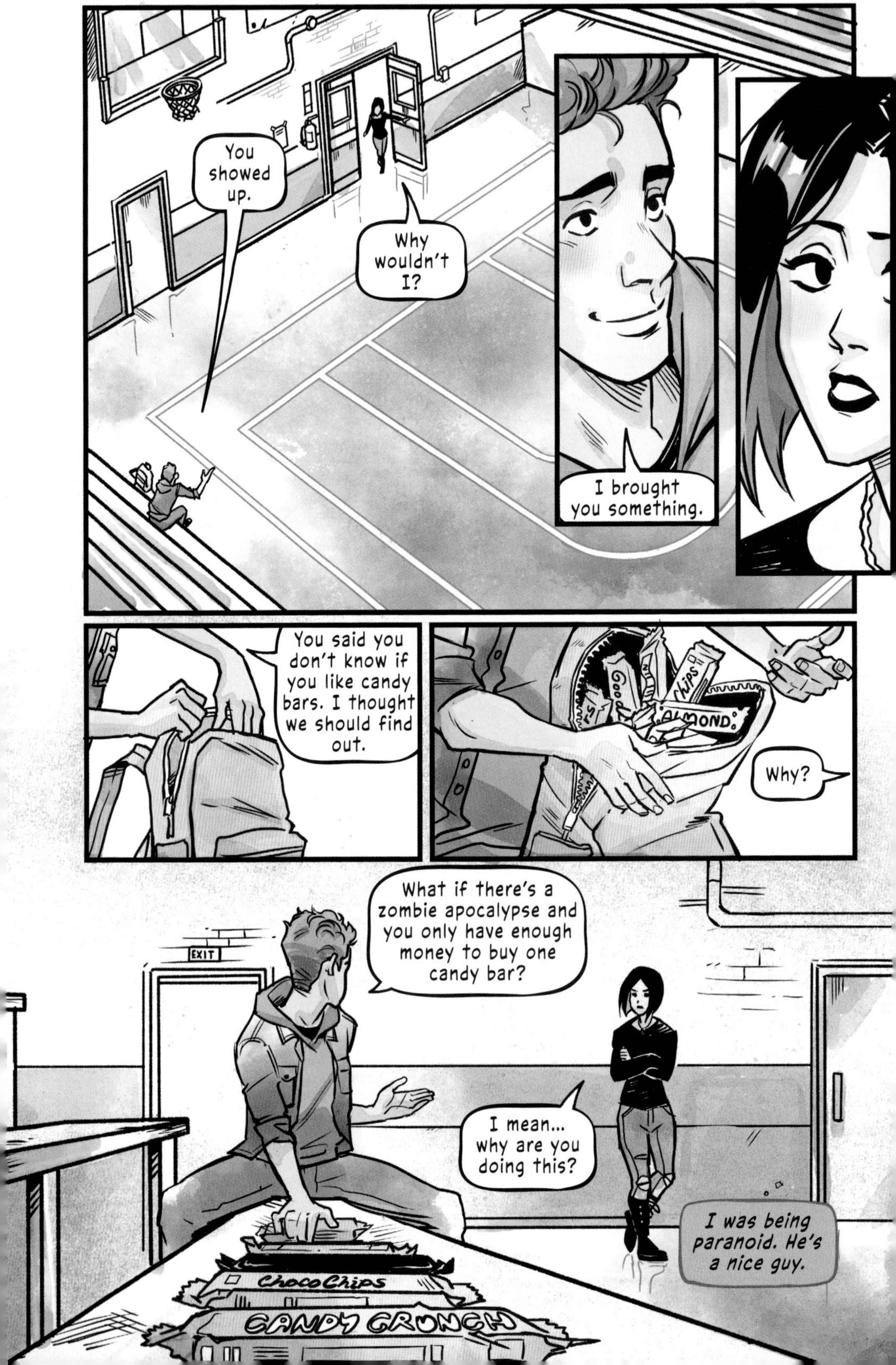
You showed up.
Why wouldn't I?
I brought you something.
You said you don't know if you like candy bars. I thought we should find out.
Good
Chips
ALMOND
Why?
What if there's a zombie apocalypse and you only have enough money to buy one candy bar?
EXIT
I mean... why are you doing this?
I was being paranoid. He's a nice guy.
ChocoChips
CANDY CRUNCH

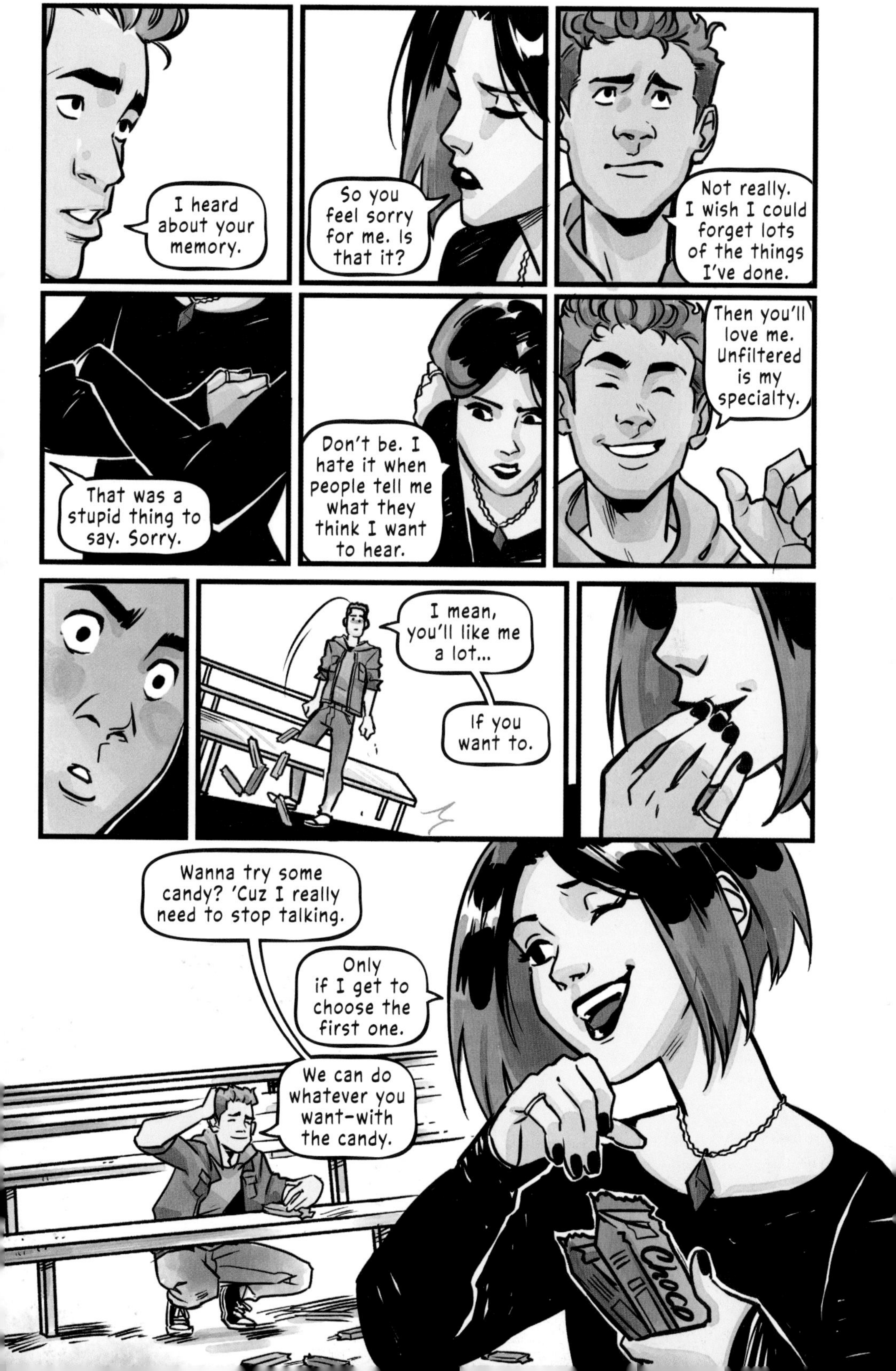
I heard about your memory.
So you feel sorry for me. Is that it?
Not really. I wish I could forget lots of the things I've done.
That was a stupid thing to say. Sorry.
Don't be. I hate it when people tell me what they think I want to hear.
Then you'll love me. Unfiltered is my specialty.
I mean, you'll like me a lot...
If you want to.
Wanna try some candy? 'Cuz I really need to stop talking.
Only if I get to choose the first one.
We can do whatever you want—with the candy.
Choco

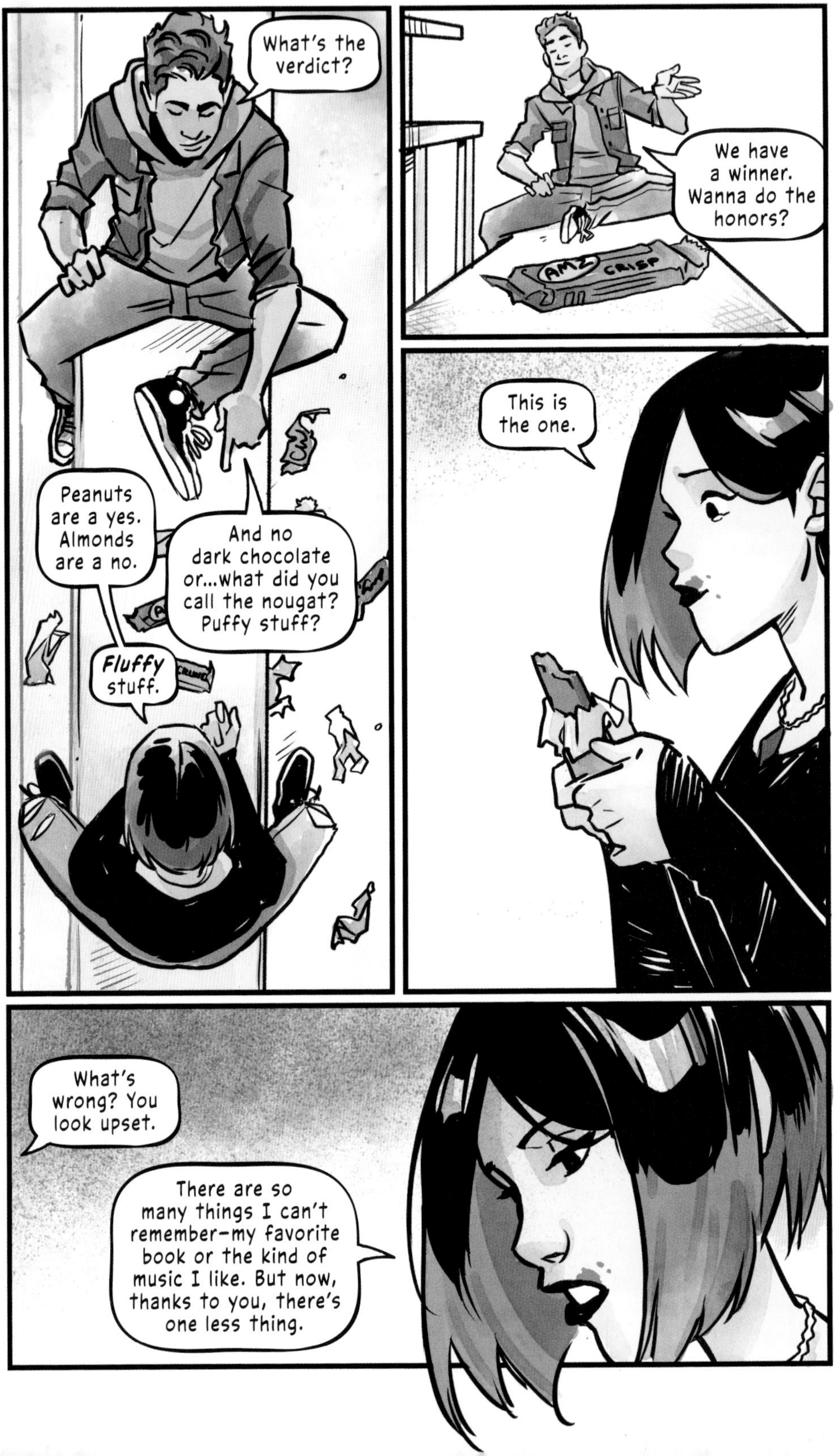
What's the verdict?
Peanuts are a yes. Almonds are a no.
And no dark chocolate or...what did you call the nougat? Puffy stuff?
Fluffy stuff.
We have a winner. Wanna do the honors?
AMZ CRISP
This is the one.
What's wrong? You look upset.
There are so many things I can't remember—my favorite book or the kind of music I like. But now, thanks to you, there's one less thing.

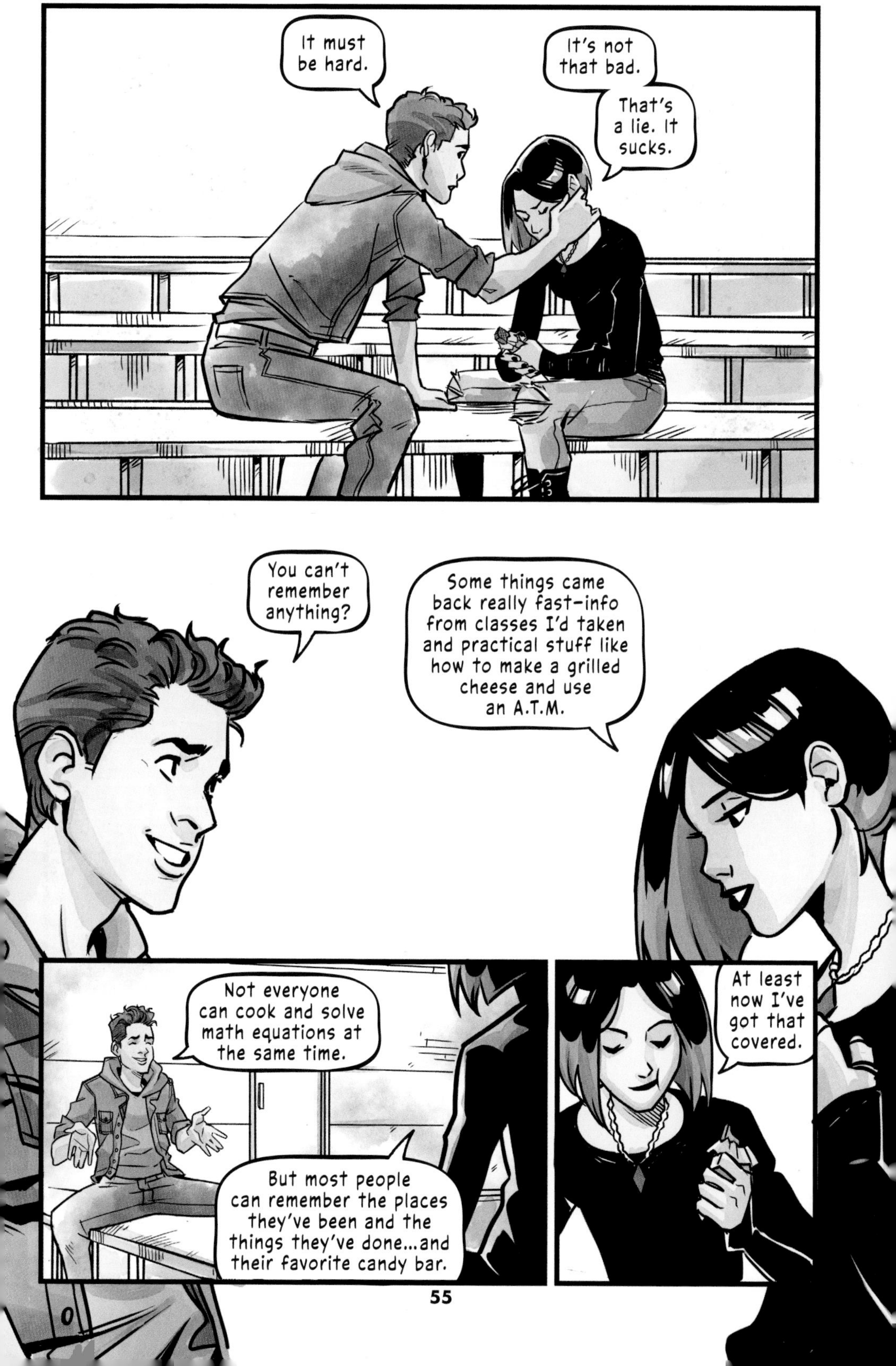
It must be hard.
It's not that bad.
That's a lie. It sucks.
You can't remember anything?
Some things came back really fast–info from classes I'd taken and practical stuff like how to make a grilled cheese and use an A.T.M.
Not everyone can cook and solve math equations at the same time.
But most people can remember the places they've been and the things they've done...and their favorite candy bar.
At least now I've got that covered.

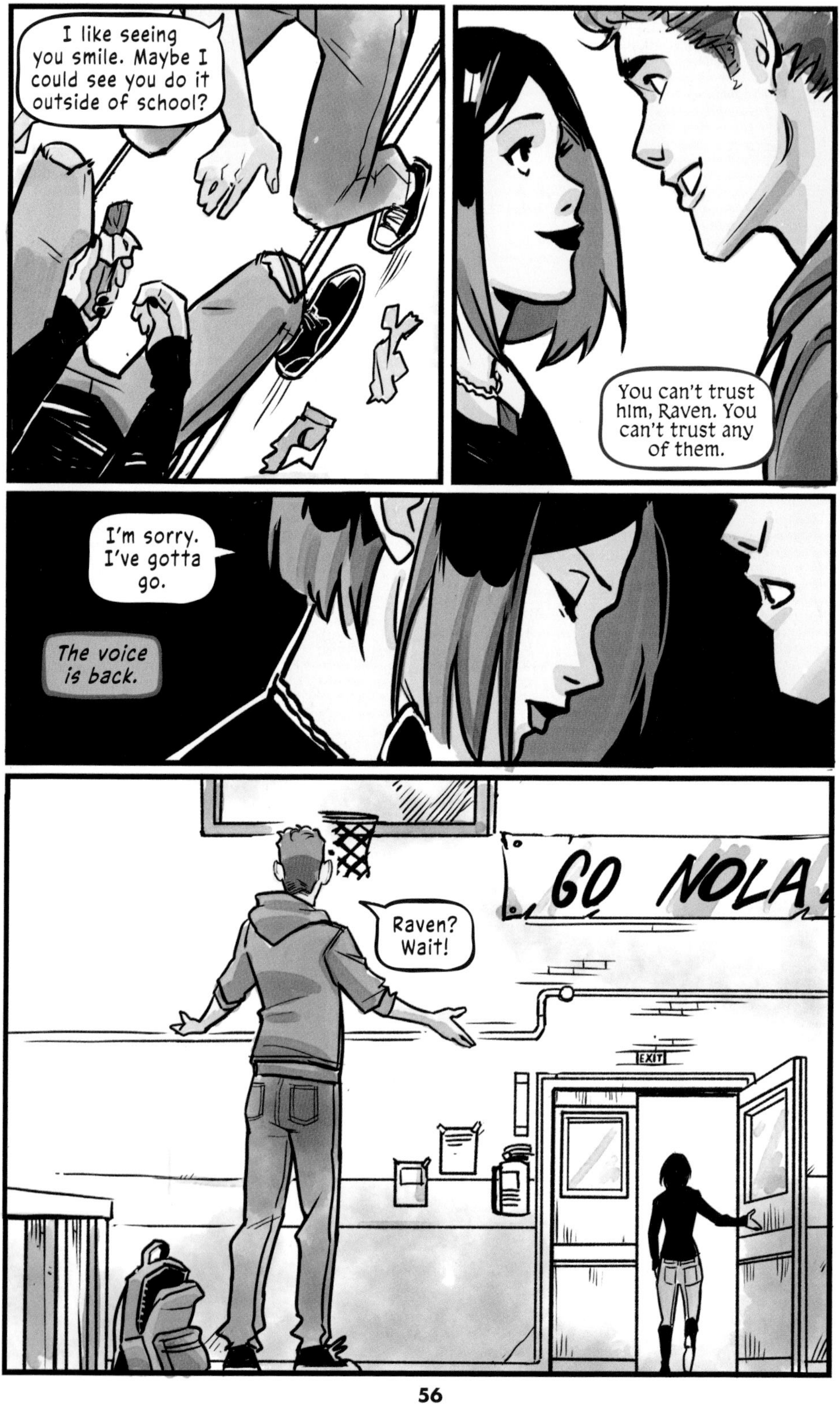
I like seeing you smile. Maybe I could see you do it outside of school?
You can't trust him, Raven. You can't trust any of them.
I'm sorry. I've gotta go.
The voice is back.
GO NOLA
Raven? Wait!
EXIT

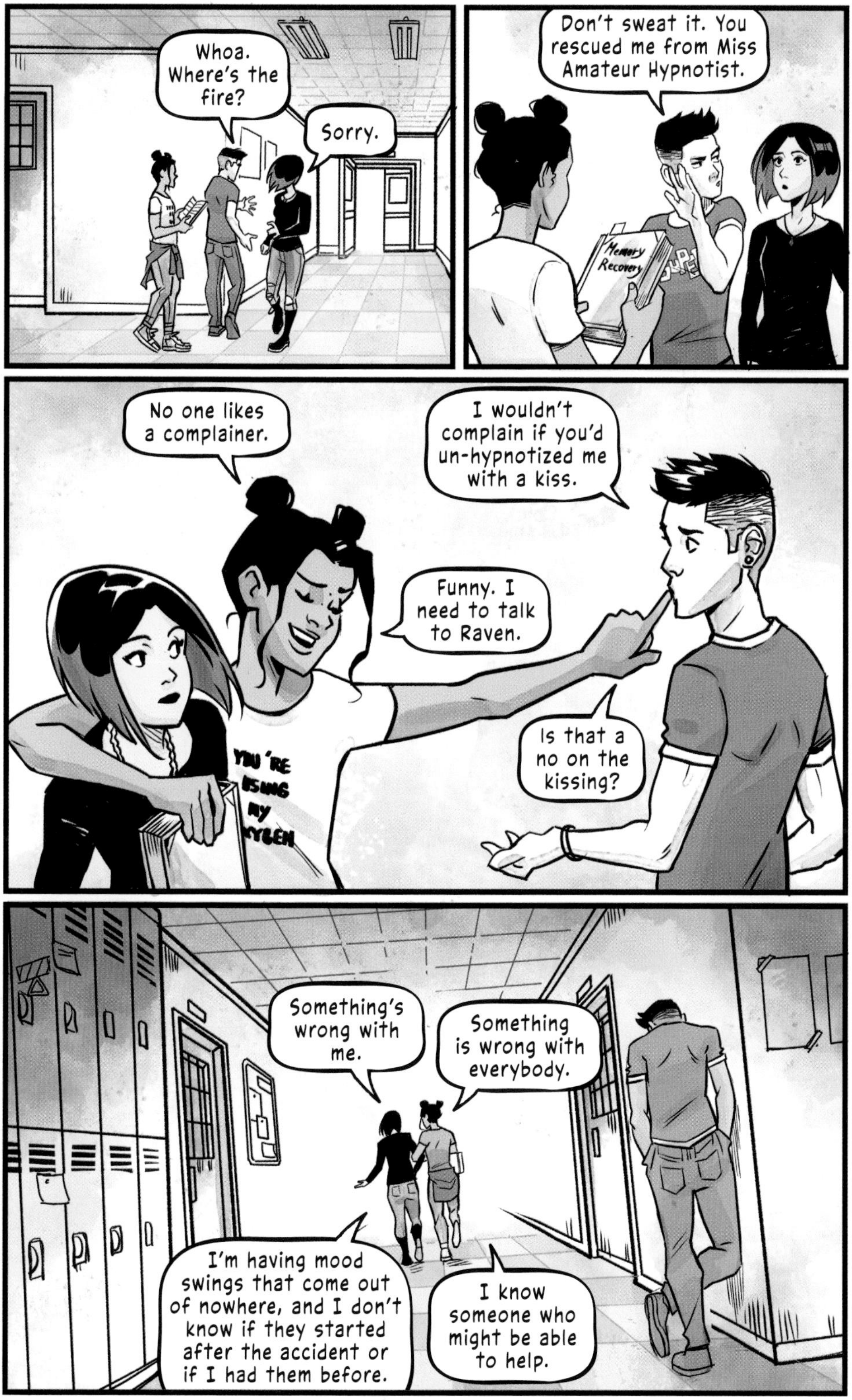
Whoa. Where's the fire?
Sorry.
Don't sweat it. You rescued me from Miss Amateur Hypnotist.
Memory Recovery
No one likes a complainer.
I wouldn't complain if you'd un-hypnotized me with a kiss.
Funny. I need to talk to Raven.
Is that a no on the kissing?
YOU'RE USING MY OXYGEN
Something's wrong with me.
Something is wrong with everybody.
I'm having mood swings that come out of nowhere, and I don't know if they started after the accident or if I had them before.
I know someone who might be able to help.

CHAPTER 7: VOODOO QUEEN

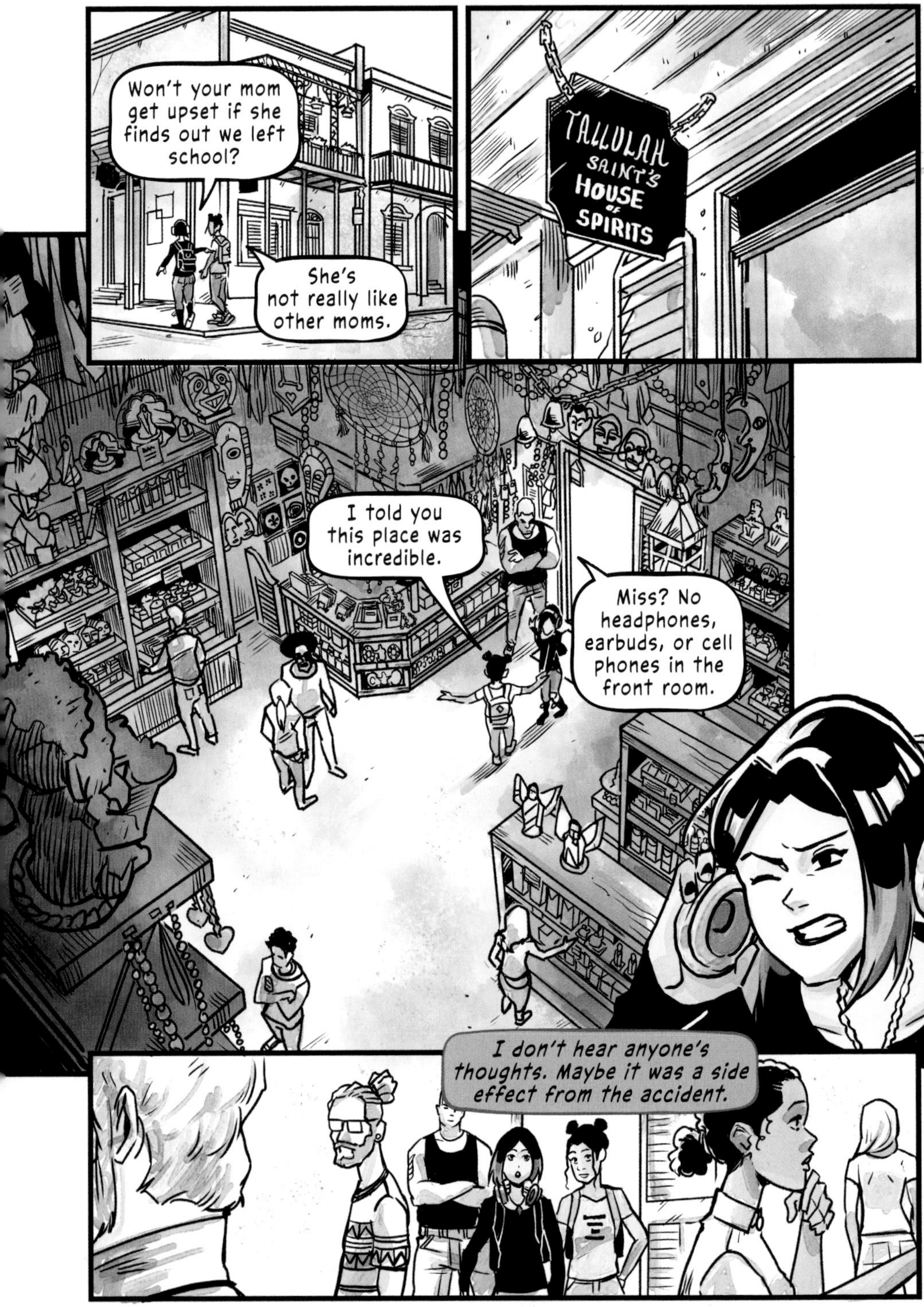
Won't your mom get upset if she finds out we left school?
She's not really like other moms.
TALLULAH SAINT'S HOUSE OF SPIRITS
I told you this place was incredible.
Miss? No headphones, earbuds, or cell phones in the front room.
I don't hear anyone's thoughts. Maybe it was a side effect from the accident.

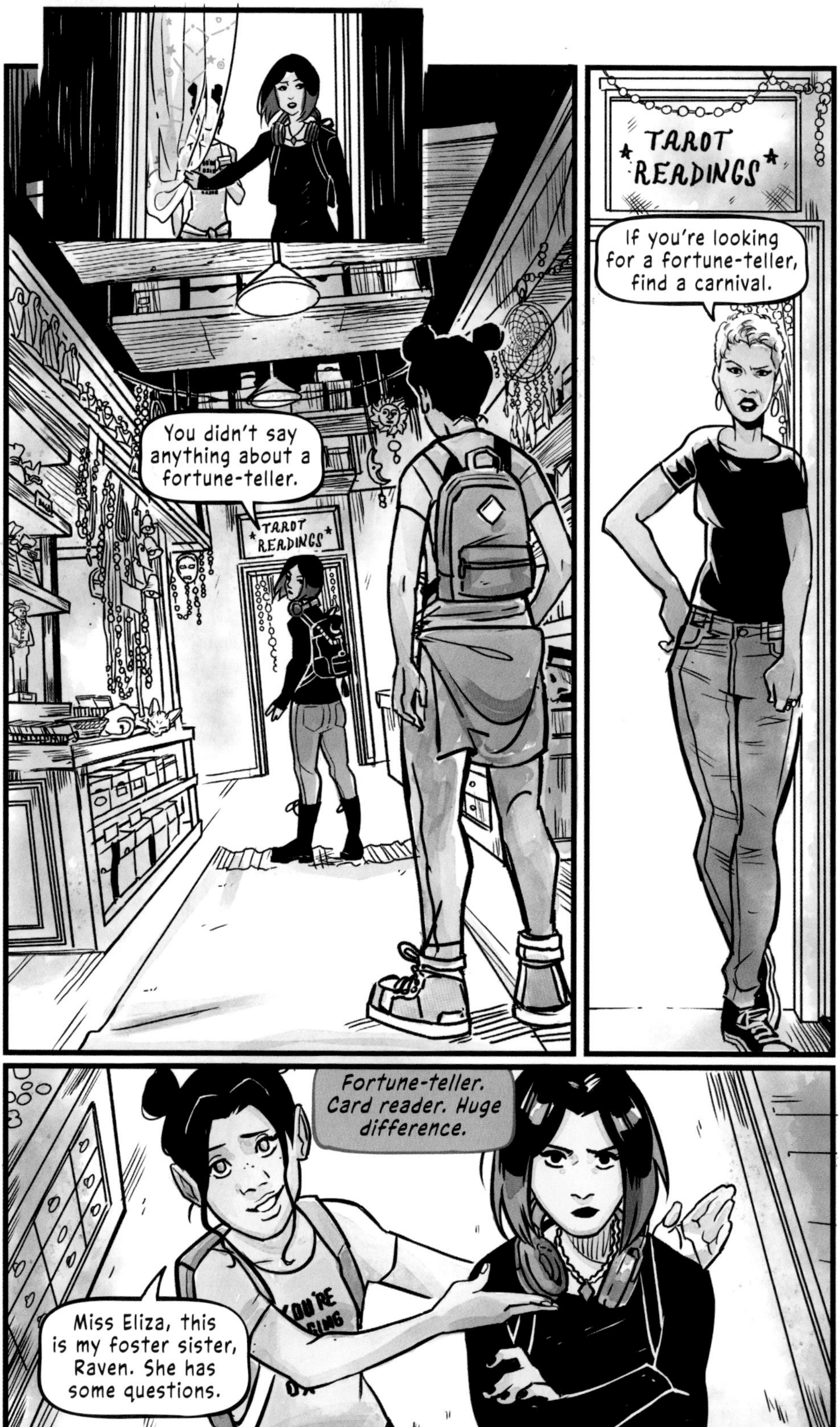

You didn't say anything about a fortune-teller.
TAROT READINGS
TAROT READINGS
If you're looking for a fortune-teller, find a carnival.
Fortune-teller. Card reader. Huge difference.
Miss Eliza, this is my foster sister, Raven. She has some questions.

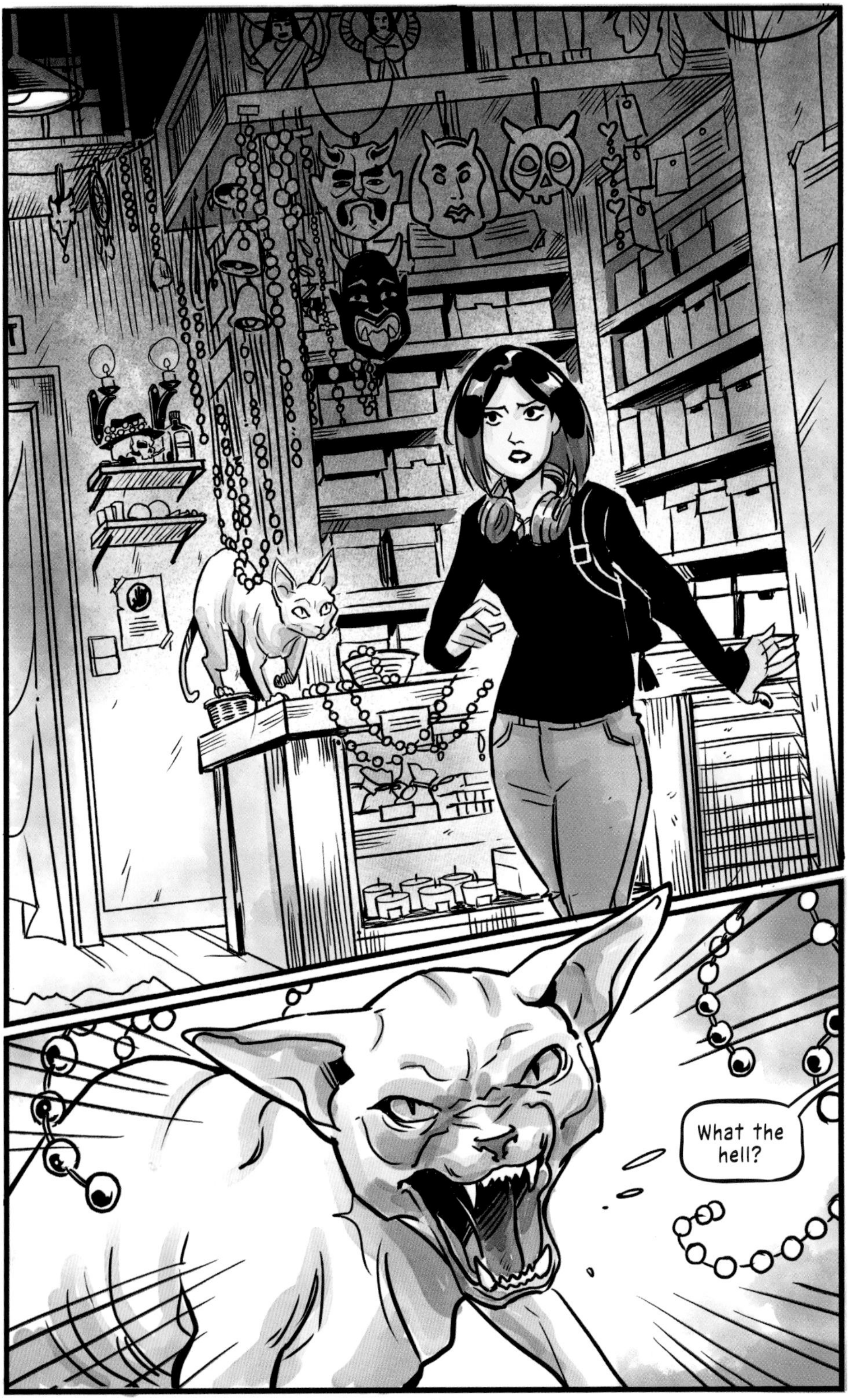
What the hell?

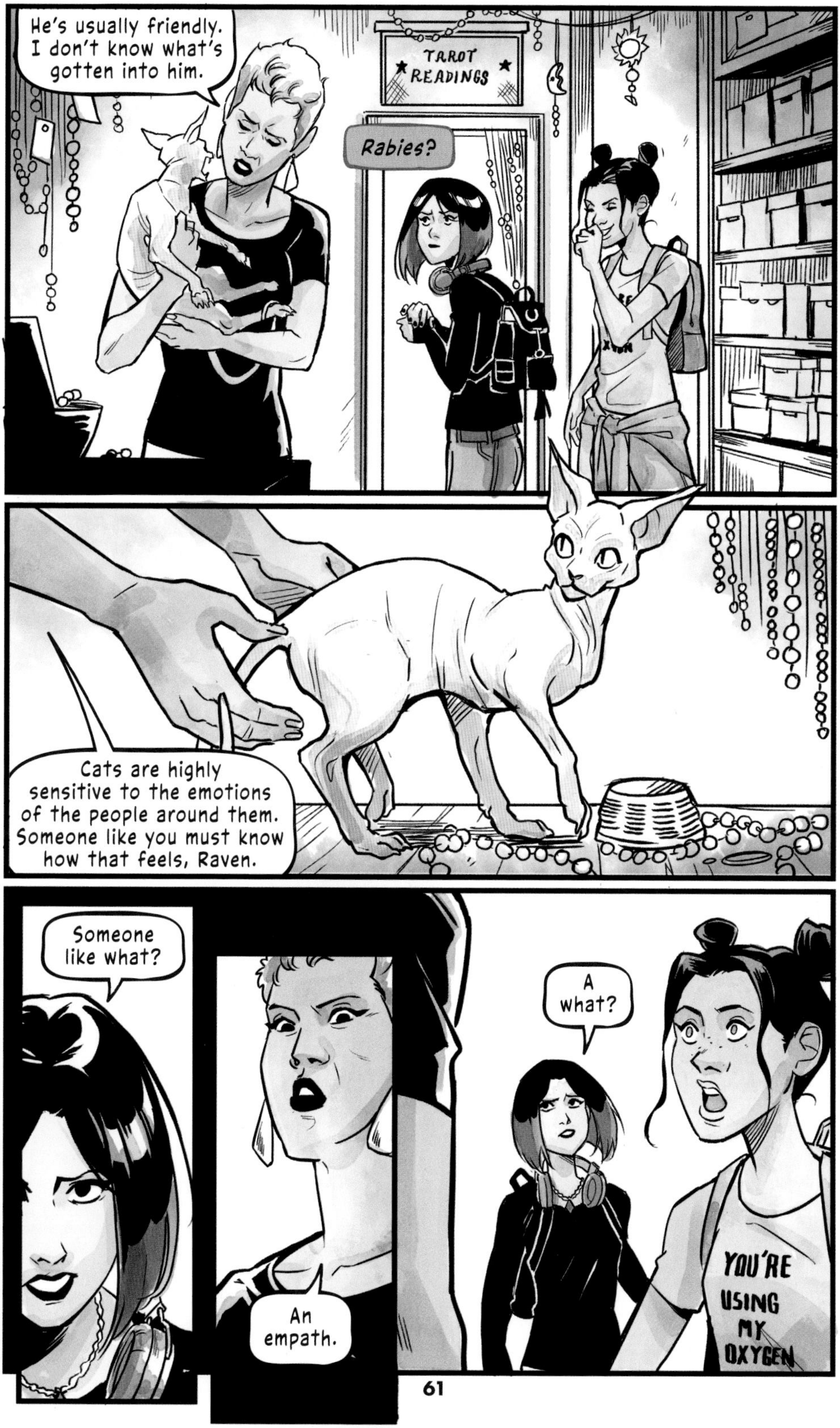
He's usually friendly. I don't know what's gotten into him.
TAROT READINGS
Rabies?
Cats are highly sensitive to the emotions of the people around them. Someone like you must know how that feels, Raven.
Someone like what?
An empath.
A what?
YOU'RE USING MY OXYGEN

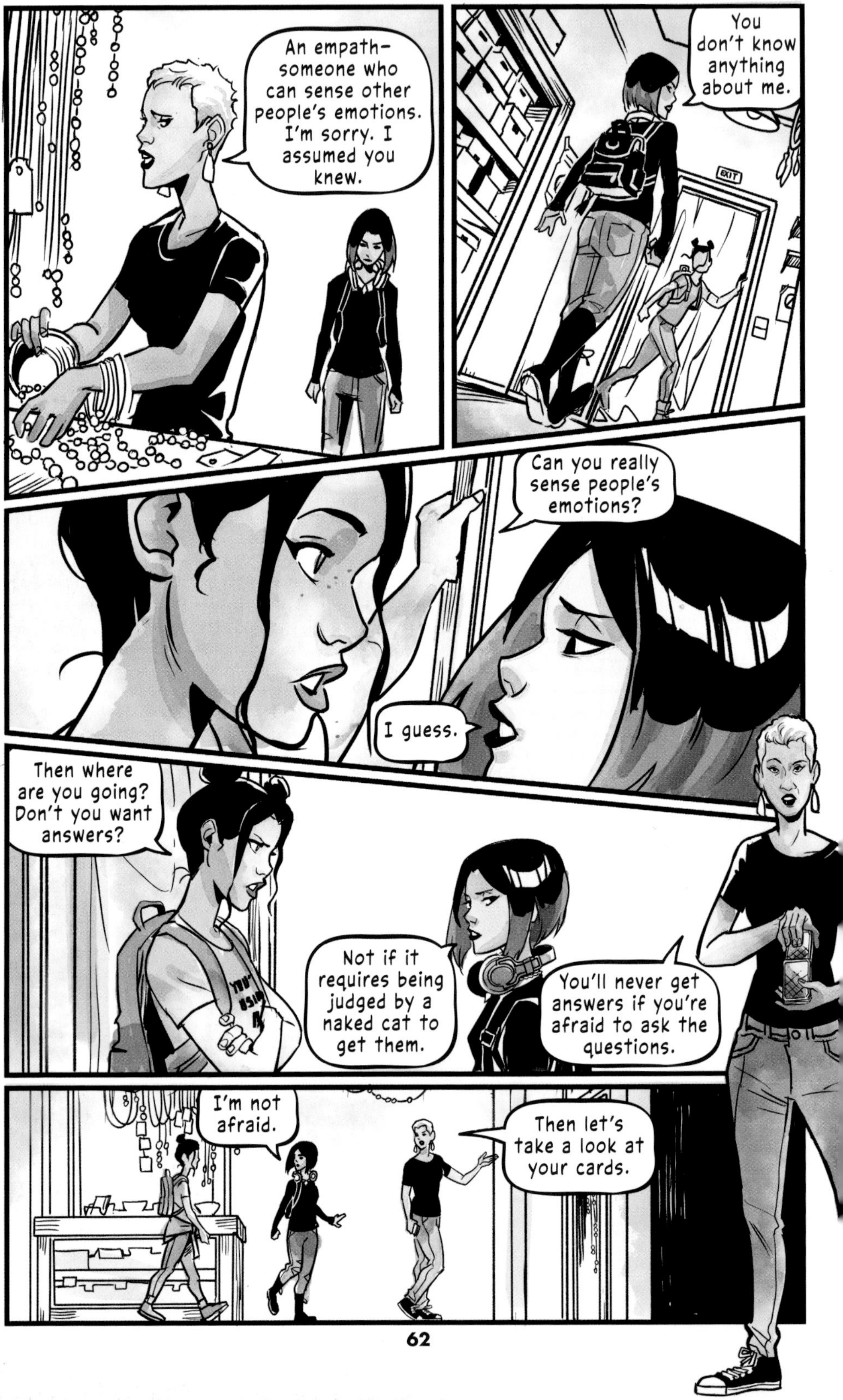
An empath–someone who can sense other people's emotions. I'm sorry. I assumed you knew.
You don't know anything about me.
EXIT
Can you really sense people's emotions?
I guess.
Then where are you going? Don't you want answers?
Not if it requires being judged by a naked cat to get them.
You'll never get answers if you're afraid to ask the questions.
I'm not afraid.
Then let's take a look at your cards.

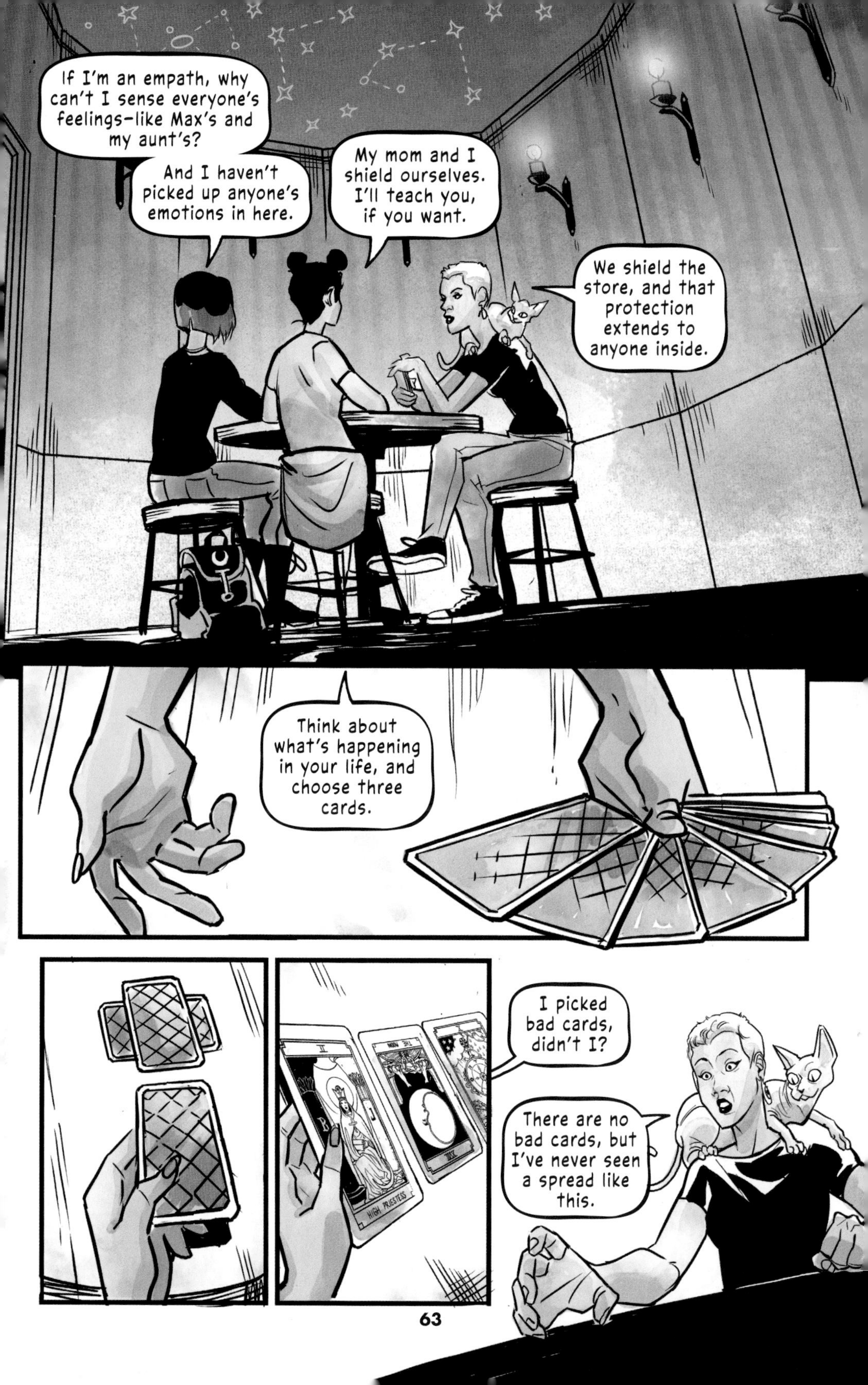
If I'm an empath, why can't I sense everyone's feelings—like Max's and my aunt's?
And I haven't picked up anyone's emotions in here.
My mom and I shield ourselves. I'll teach you, if you want.
We shield the store, and that protection extends to anyone inside.
Think about what's happening in your life, and choose three cards.
HIGH PRIESTESS
I picked bad cards, didn't I?
There are no bad cards, but I've never seen a spread like this.

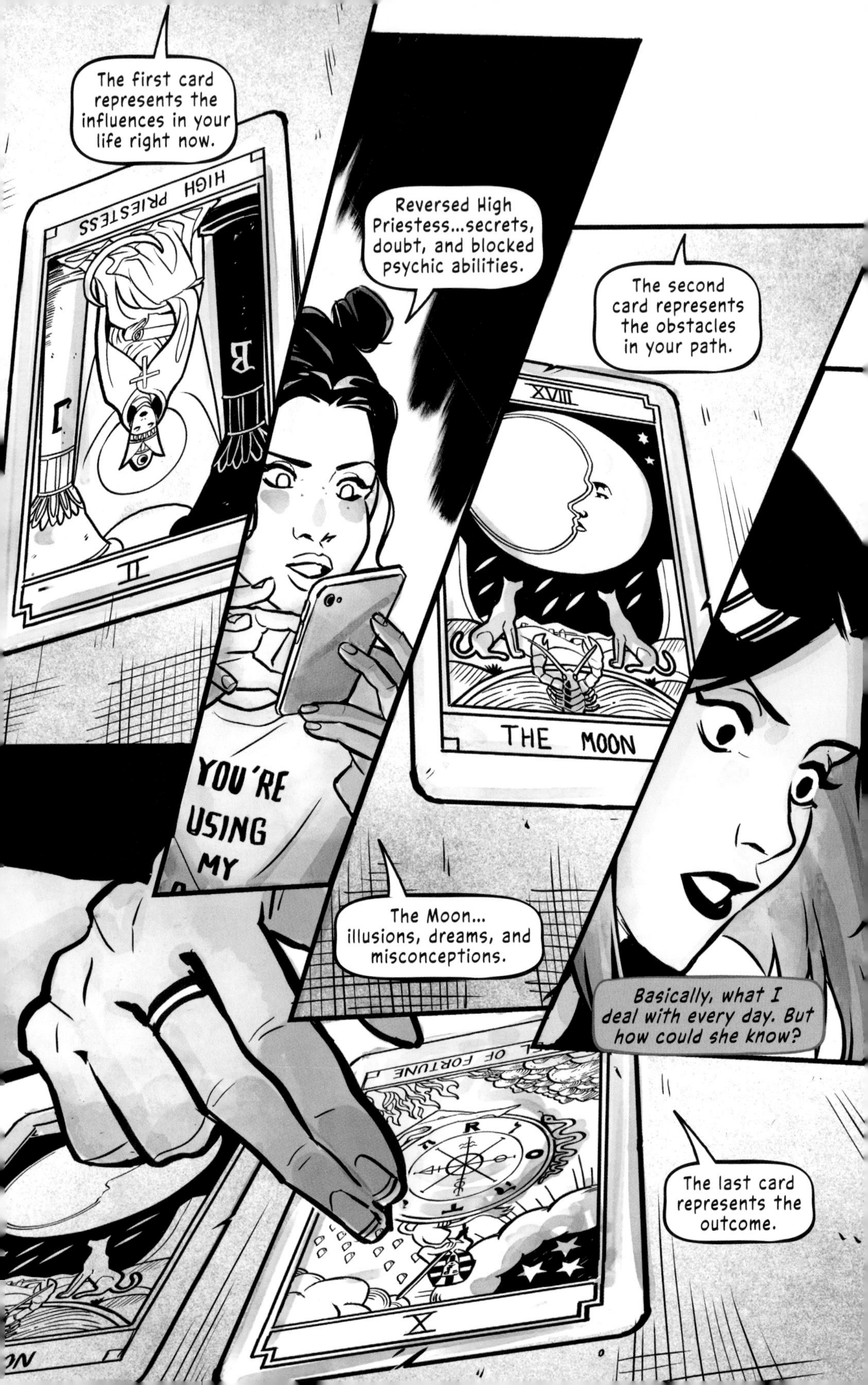

The first card represents the influences in your life right now.
HIGH PRIESTESS
II
Reversed High Priestess...secrets, doubt, and blocked psychic abilities.
YOU'RE USING MY
The second card represents the obstacles in your path.
XVIII
THE MOON
The Moon... illusions, dreams, and misconceptions.
Basically, what I deal with every day. But how could she know?
OF FORTUNE
X
The last card represents the outcome.

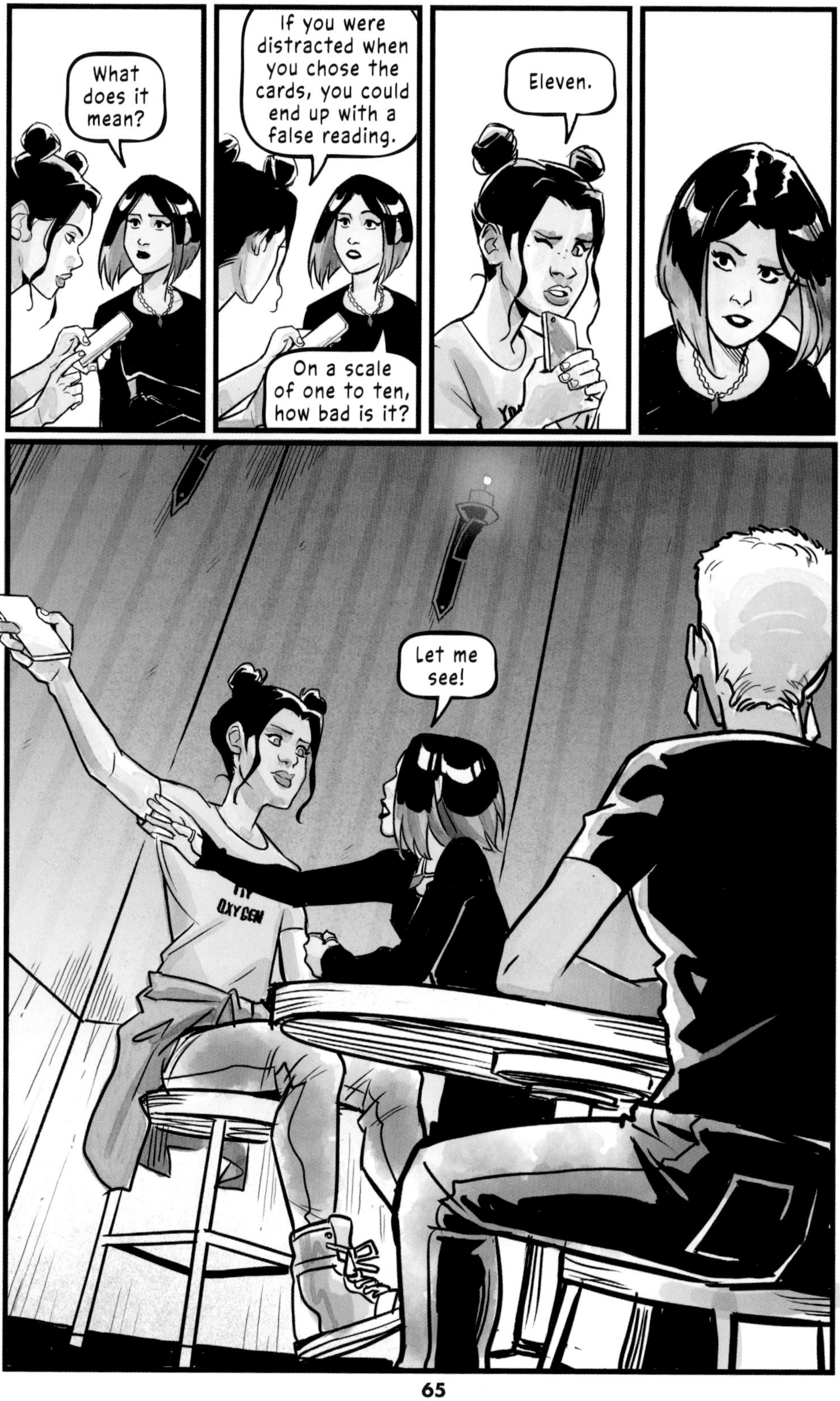
What does it mean?
If you were distracted when you chose the cards, you could end up with a false reading.
On a scale of one to ten, how bad is it?
Eleven.
Let me see!
OXYGEN

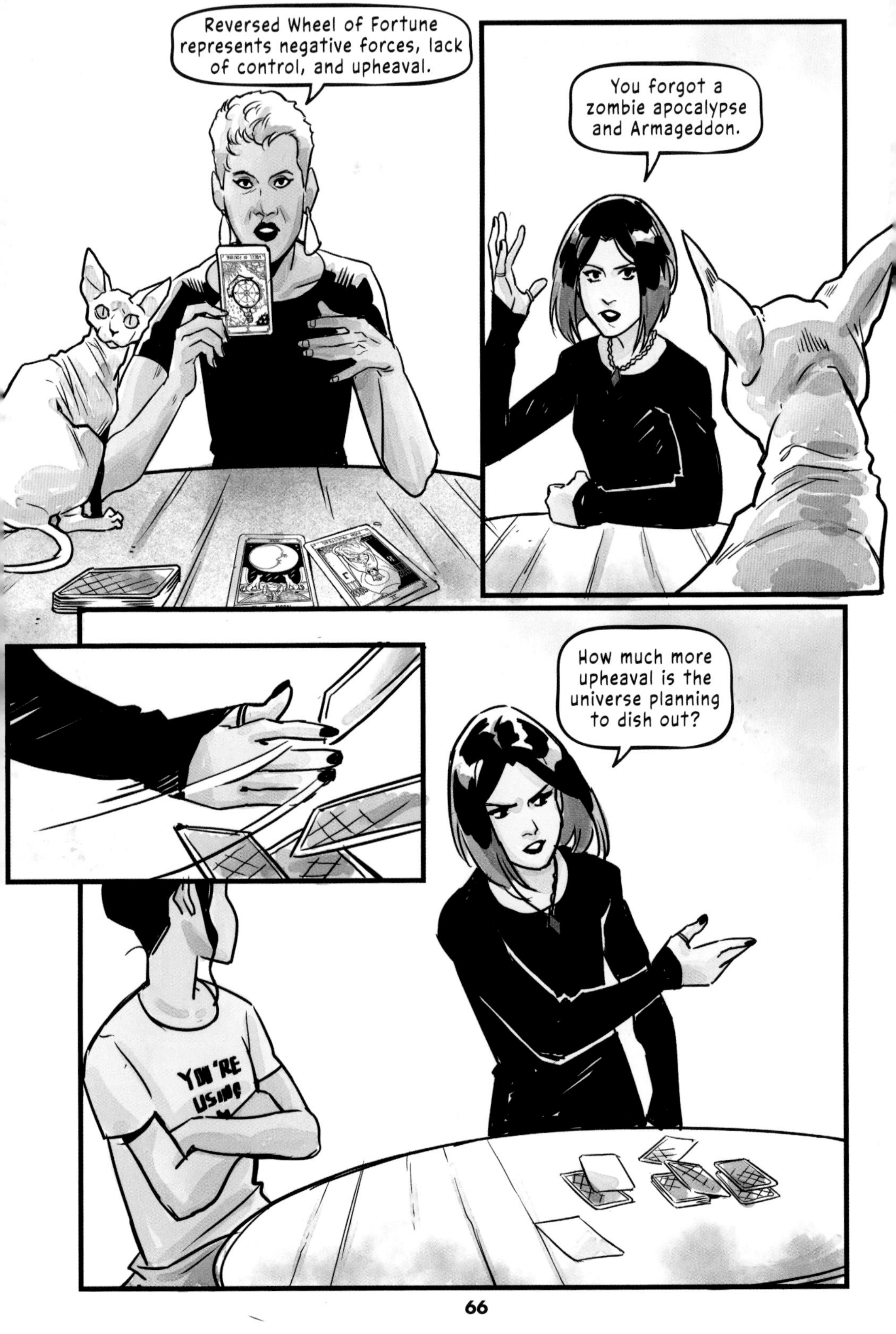
Reversed Wheel of Fortune represents negative forces, lack of control, and upheaval.
You forgot a zombie apocalypse and Armageddon.
How much more upheaval is the universe planning to dish out?
YOU'RE USING

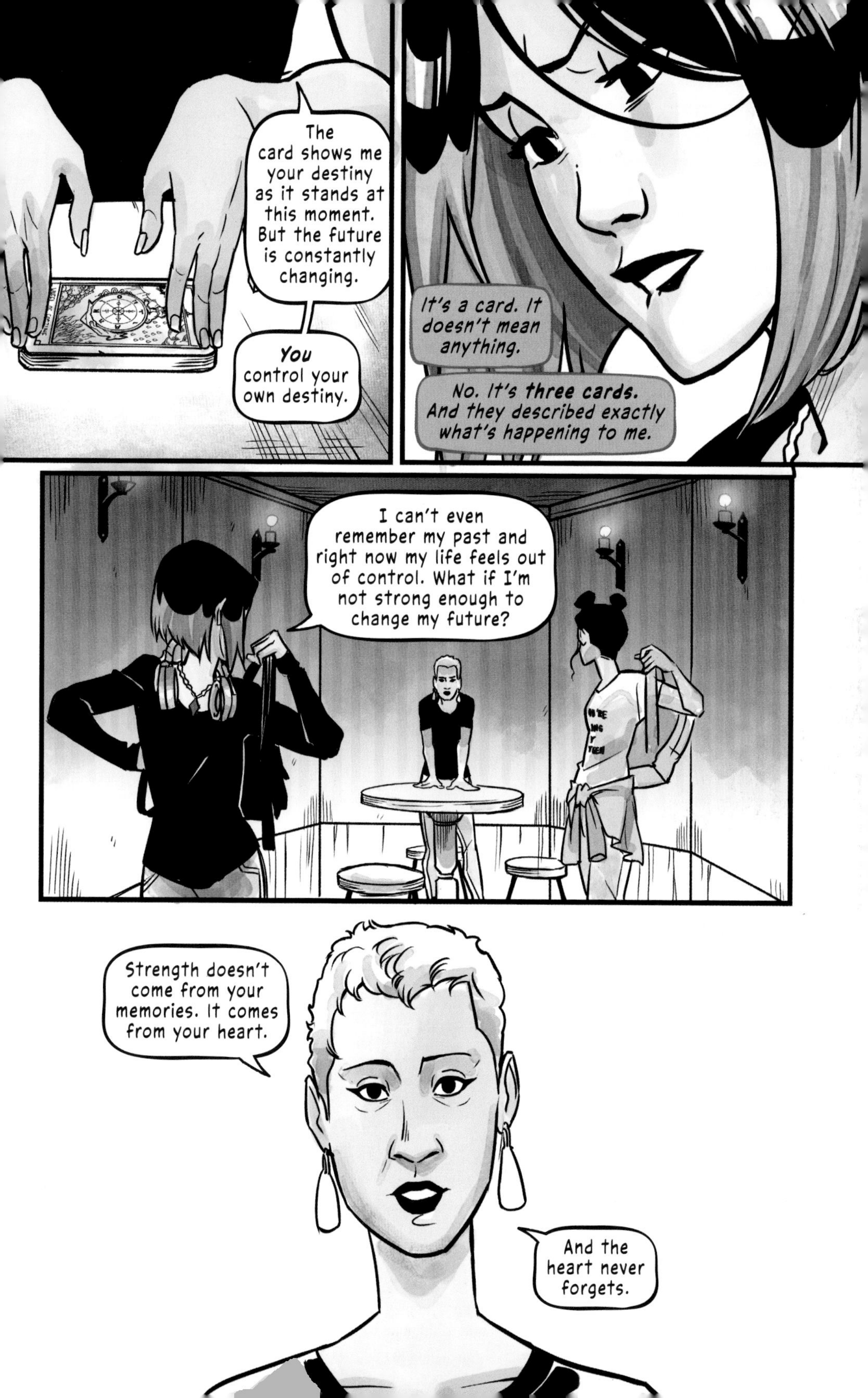
The card shows me your destiny as it stands at this moment. But the future is constantly changing.
You control your own destiny.
It's a card. It doesn't mean anything.
*No. It's **three cards.** And they described exactly what's happening to me.*
I can't even remember my past and right now my life feels out of control. What if I'm not strong enough to change my future?
Strength doesn't come from your memories. It comes from your heart.
And the heart never forgets.

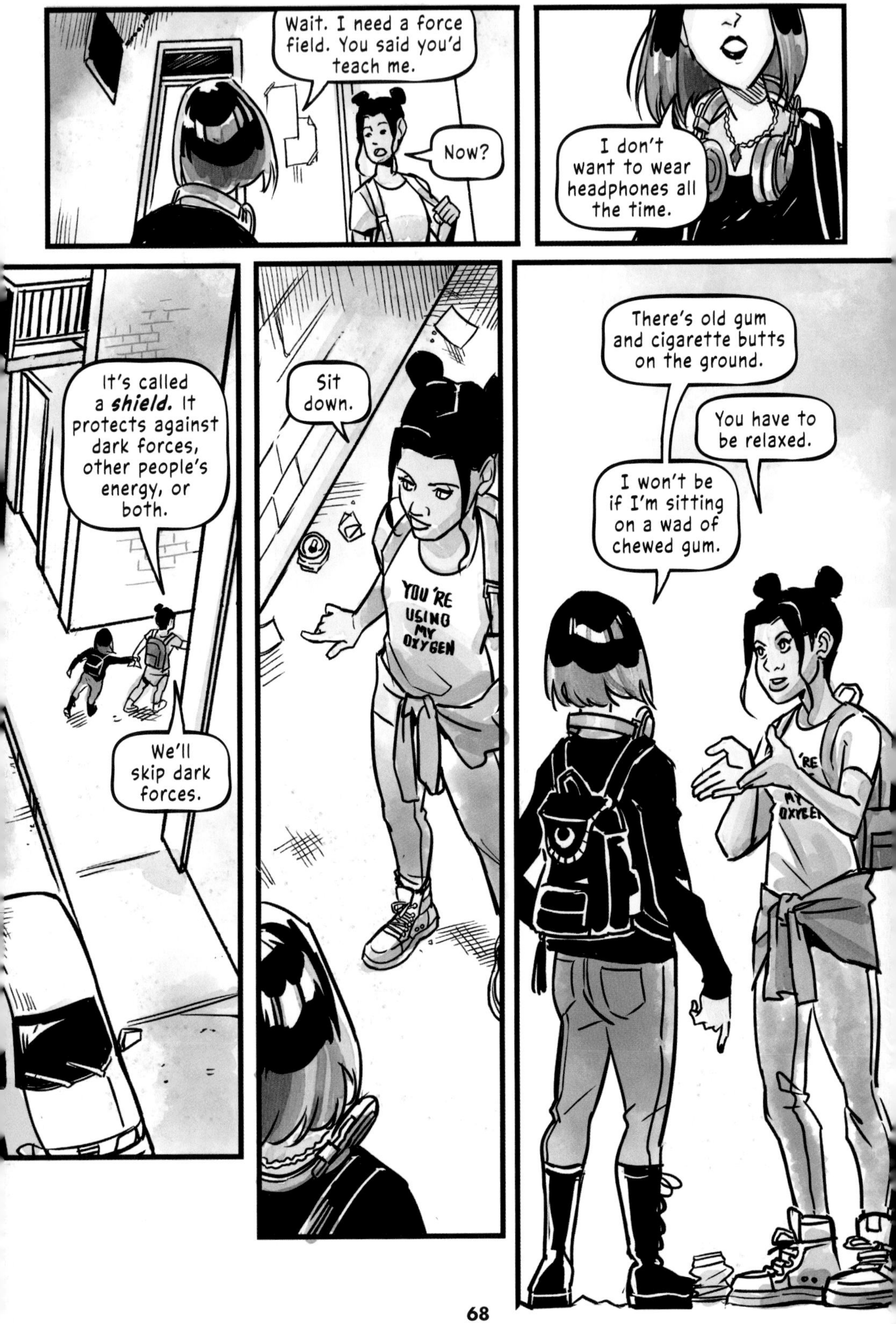
Wait. I need a force field. You said you'd teach me.
Now?
I don't want to wear headphones all the time.
It's called a *shield.* It protects against dark forces, other people's energy, or both.
We'll skip dark forces.
Sit down.
YOU'RE USING MY OXYGEN
There's old gum and cigarette butts on the ground.
You have to be relaxed.
I won't be if I'm sitting on a wad of chewed gum.

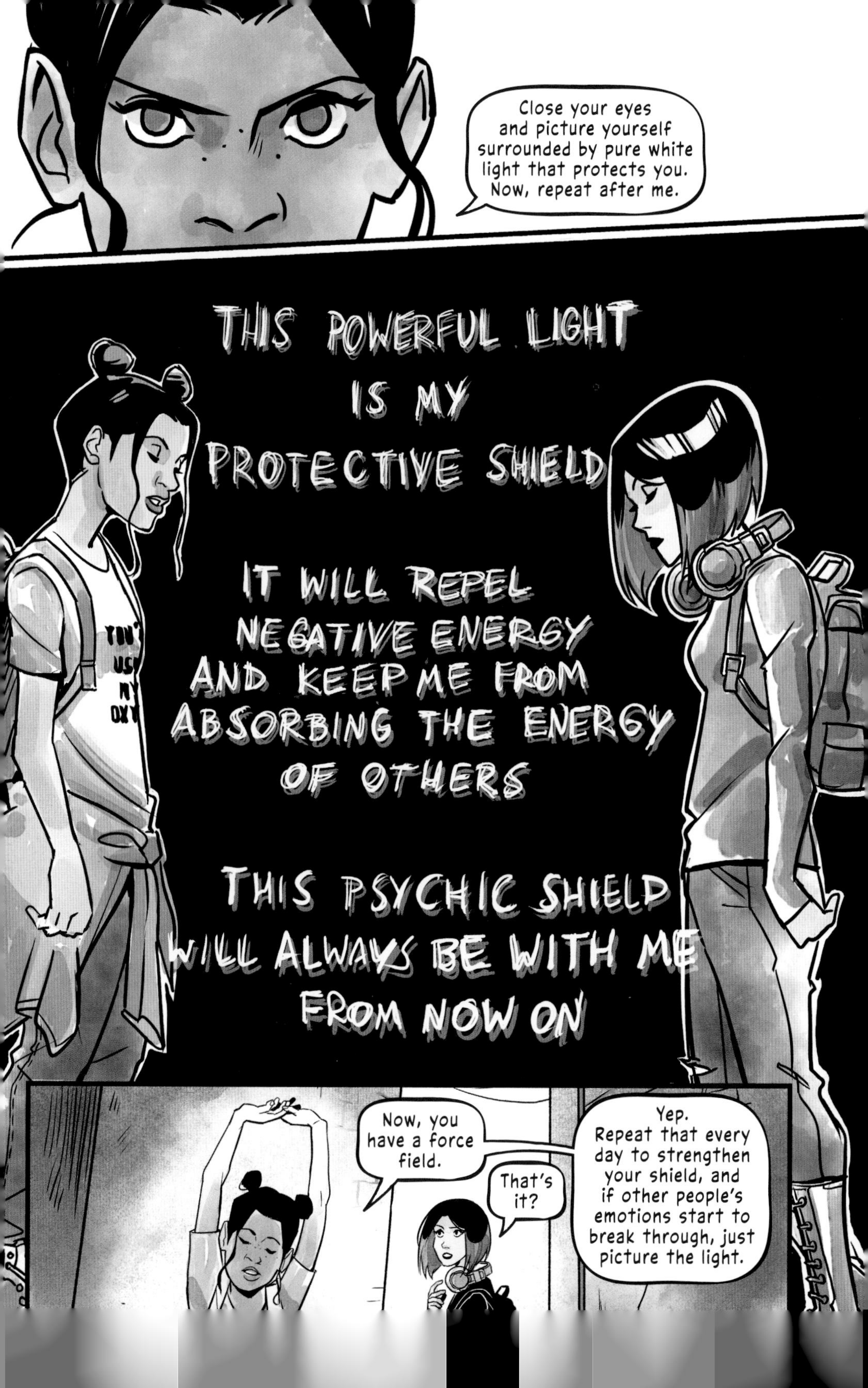
Close your eyes and picture yourself surrounded by pure white light that protects you. Now, repeat after me.
THIS POWERFUL LIGHT IS MY PROTECTIVE SHIELD
IT WILL REPEL NEGATIVE ENERGY AND KEEP ME FROM ABSORBING THE ENERGY OF OTHERS
THIS PSYCHIC SHIELD WILL ALWAYS BE WITH ME FROM NOW ON
Now, you have a force field.
That's it?
Yep. Repeat that every day to strengthen your shield, and if other people's emotions start to break through, just picture the light.

CHAPTER 8: TRUST FALL

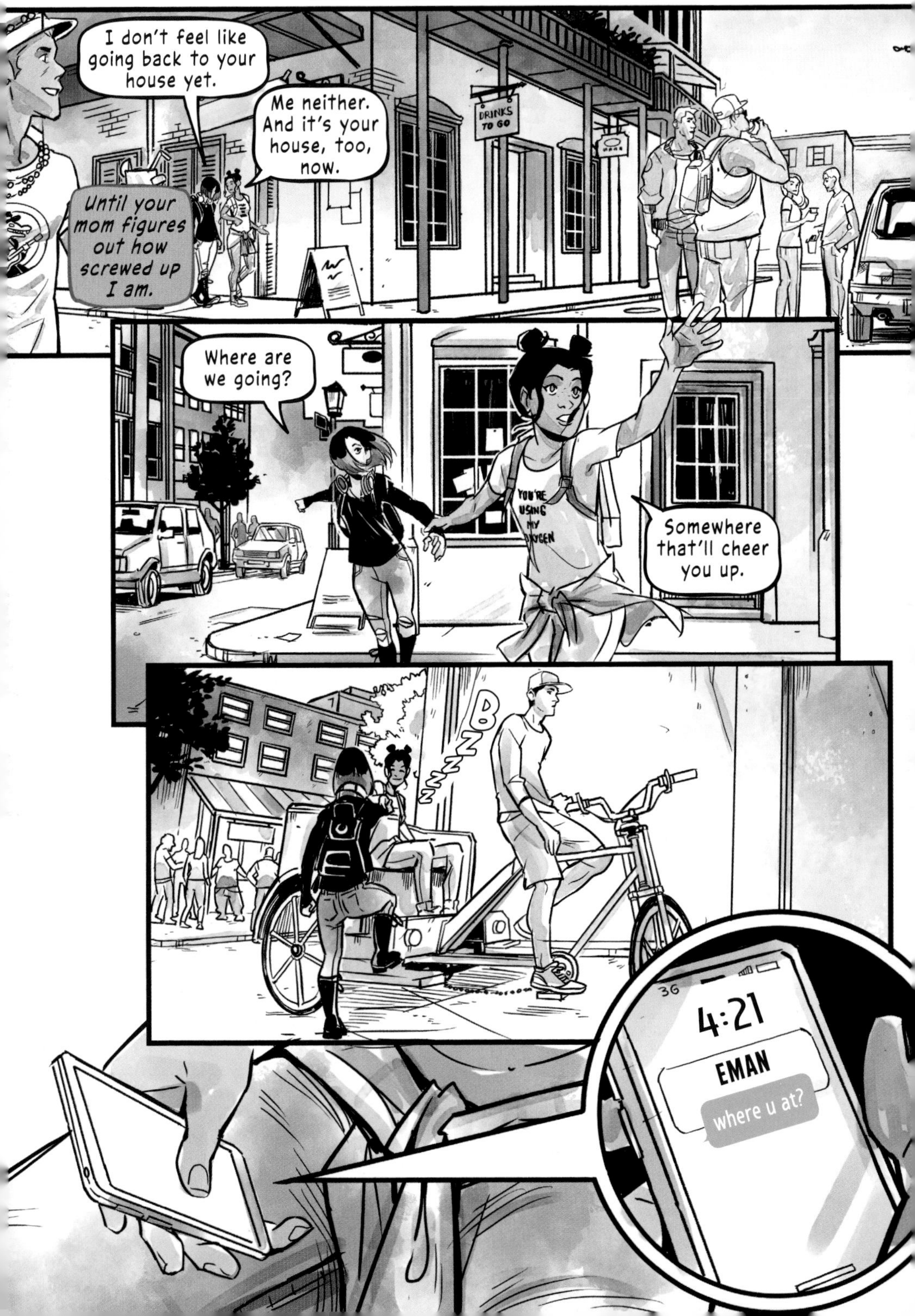
I don't feel like going back to your house yet.
Me neither. And it's your house, too, now.
DRINKS TO GO
Until your mom figures out how screwed up I am.
Where are we going?
YOU'RE USING MY OXYGEN
Somewhere that'll cheer you up.
BZZZZ
3G
4:21
EMAN
where u at?

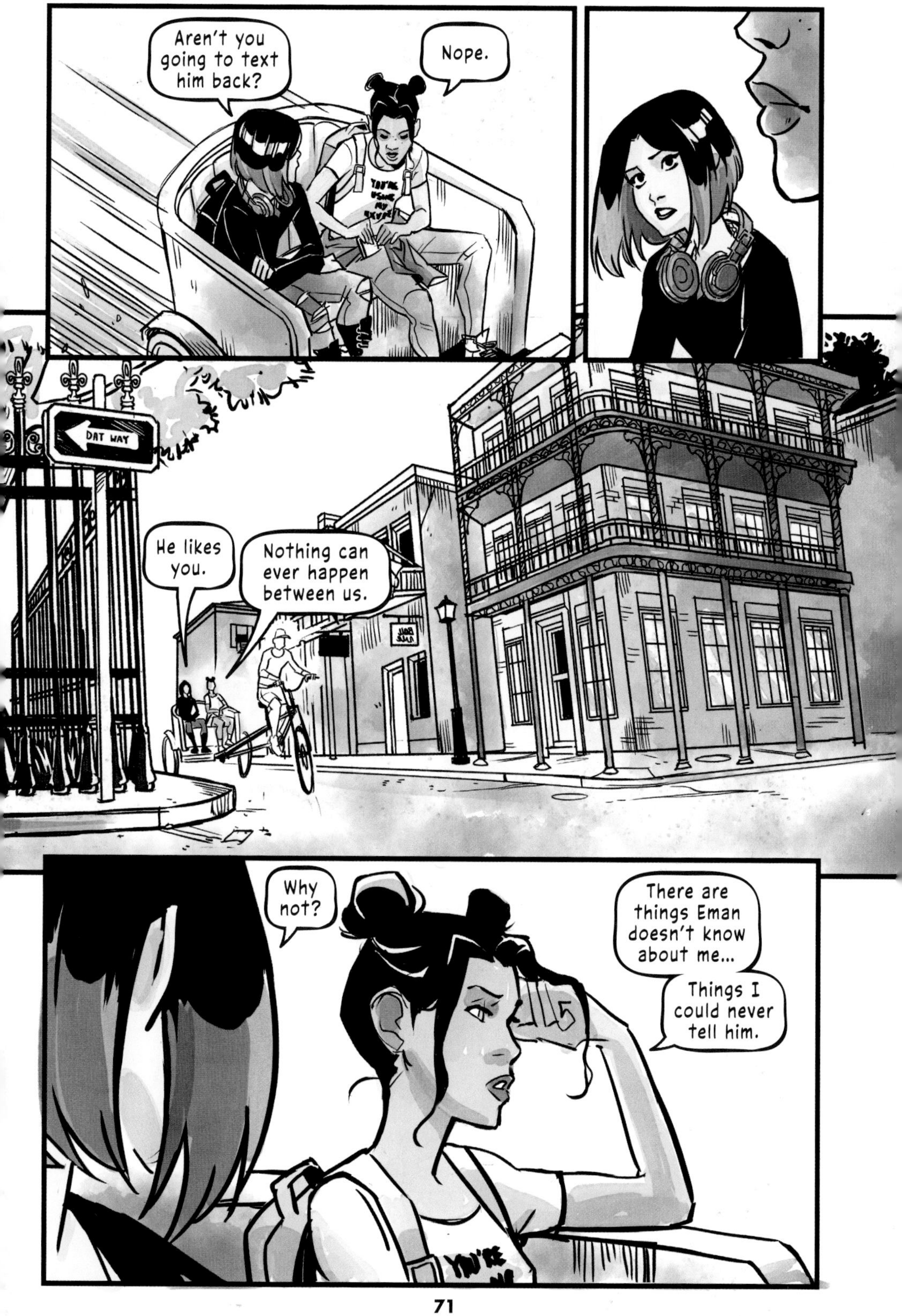
Aren't you going to text him back?
Nope.
DAT WAY
He likes you.
Nothing can ever happen between us.
Why not?
There are things Eman doesn't know about me...
Things I could never tell him.

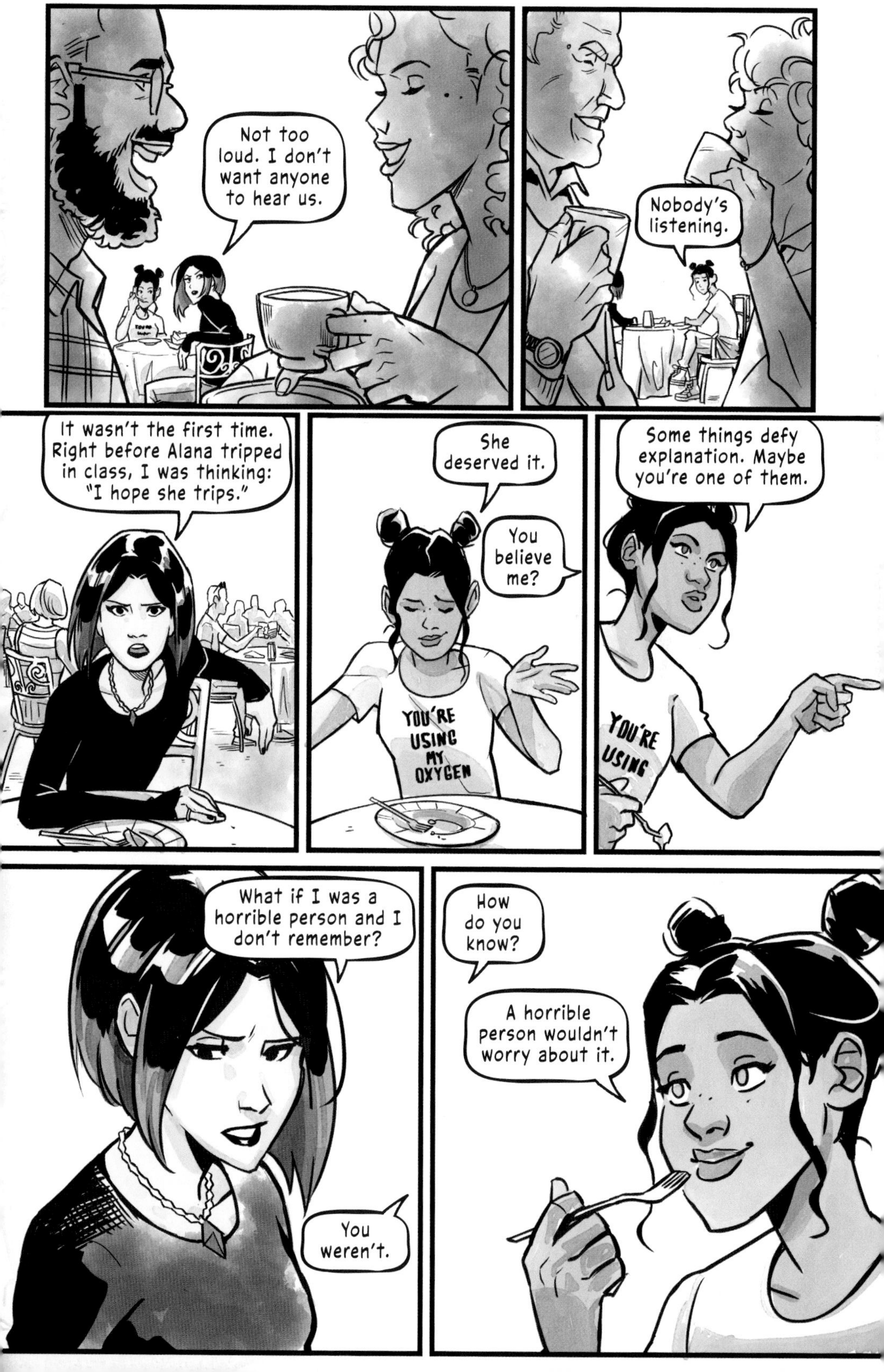
Not too loud. I don't want anyone to hear us.
Nobody's listening.
It wasn't the first time. Right before Alana tripped in class, I was thinking: "I hope she trips."
She deserved it.
You believe me?
YOU'RE USING MY OXYGEN
Some things defy explanation. Maybe you're one of them.
YOU'RE USING
What if I was a horrible person and I don't remember?
You weren't.
How do you know?
A horrible person wouldn't worry about it.

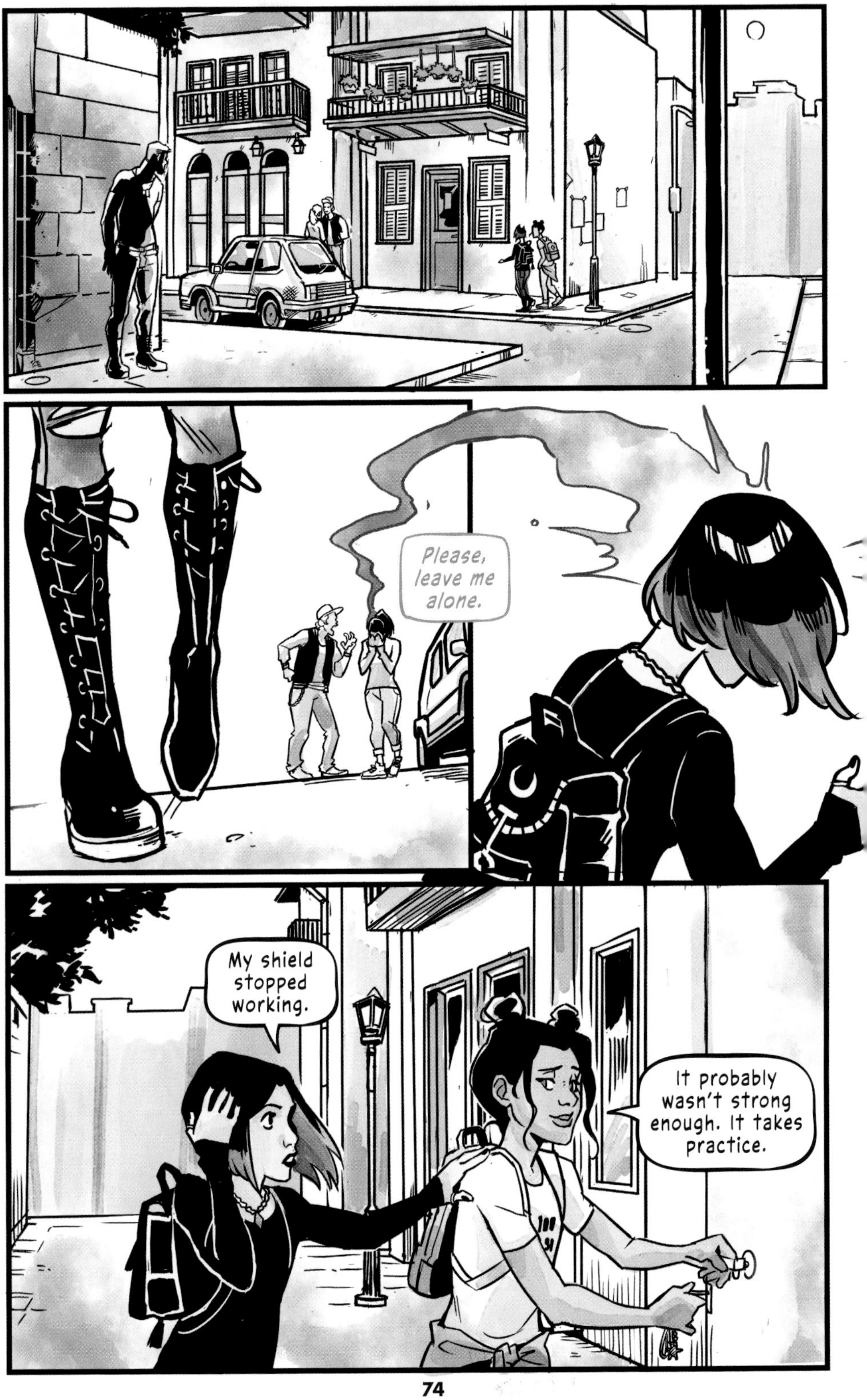
Please, leave me alone.
My shield stopped working.
It probably wasn't strong enough. It takes practice.

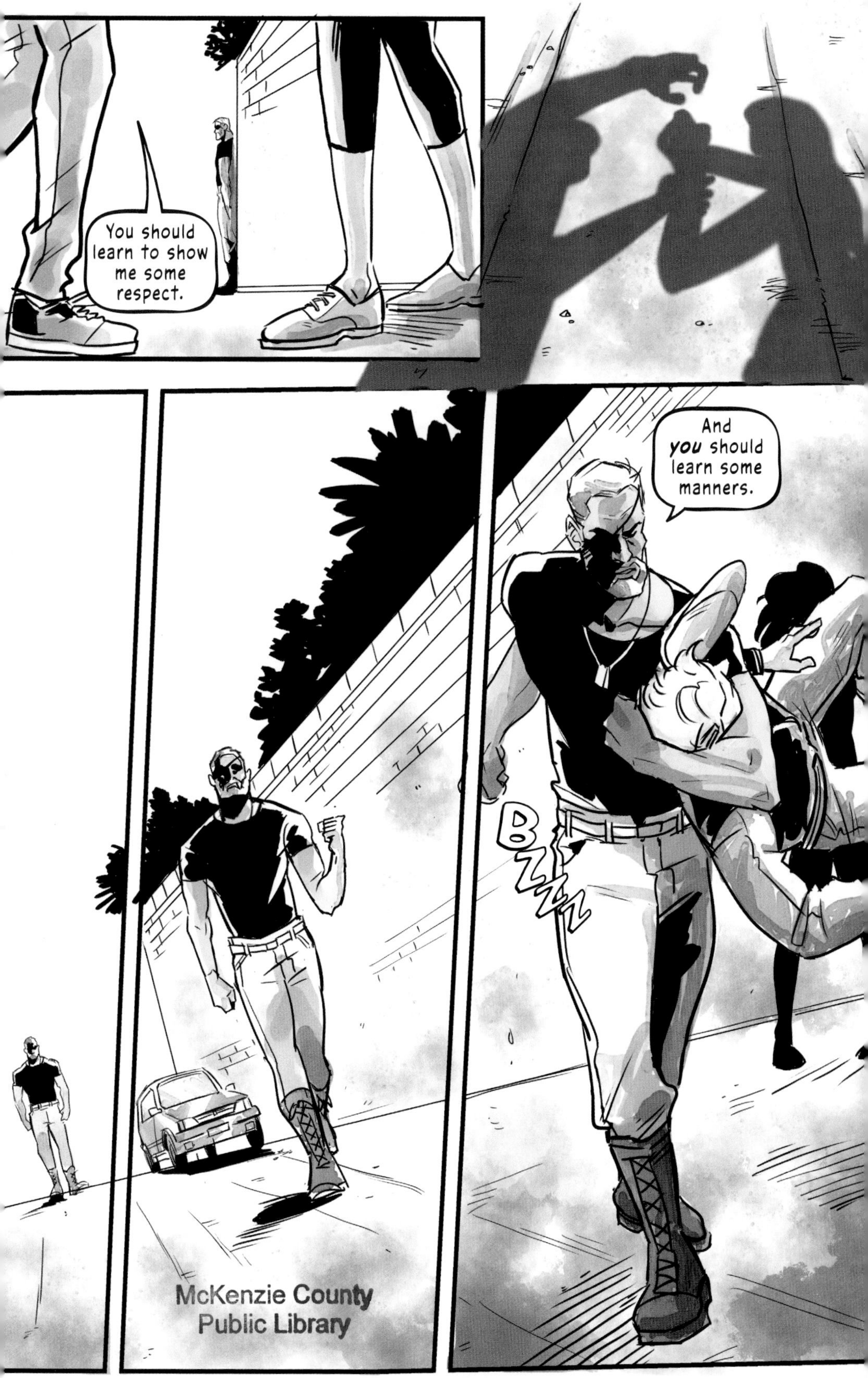

You should learn to show me some respect.
And *you* should learn some manners.
BZZZ

CHAPTER 9: SWEET DREAMS

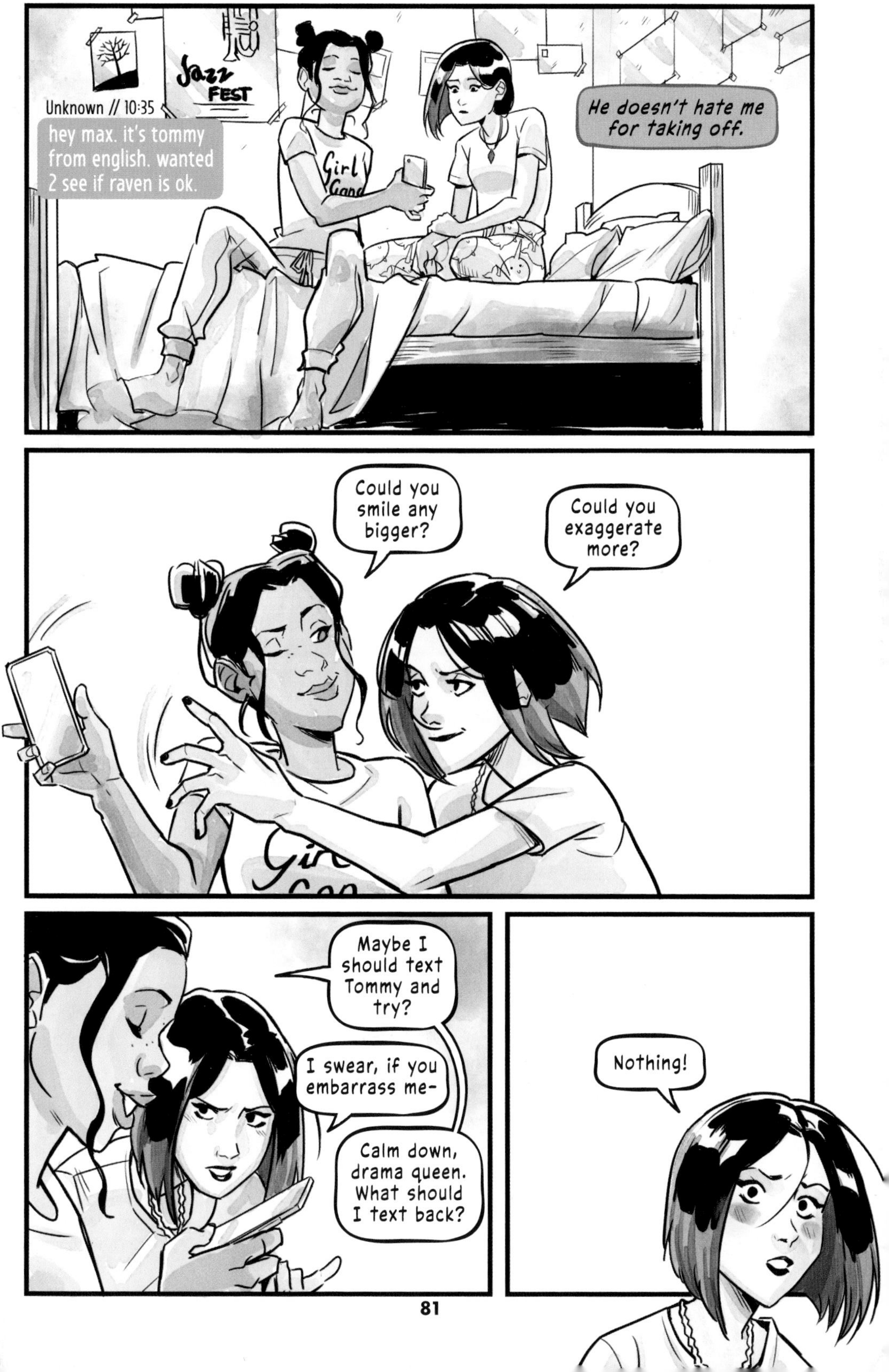
Jazz FEST
Unknown // 10:35
hey max. it's tommy from english. wanted 2 see if raven is ok.
He doesn't hate me for taking off.
Girl Gang
Could you smile any bigger?
Could you exaggerate more?
Maybe I should text Tommy and try?
I swear, if you embarrass me-
Calm down, drama queen. What should I text back?
Nothing!

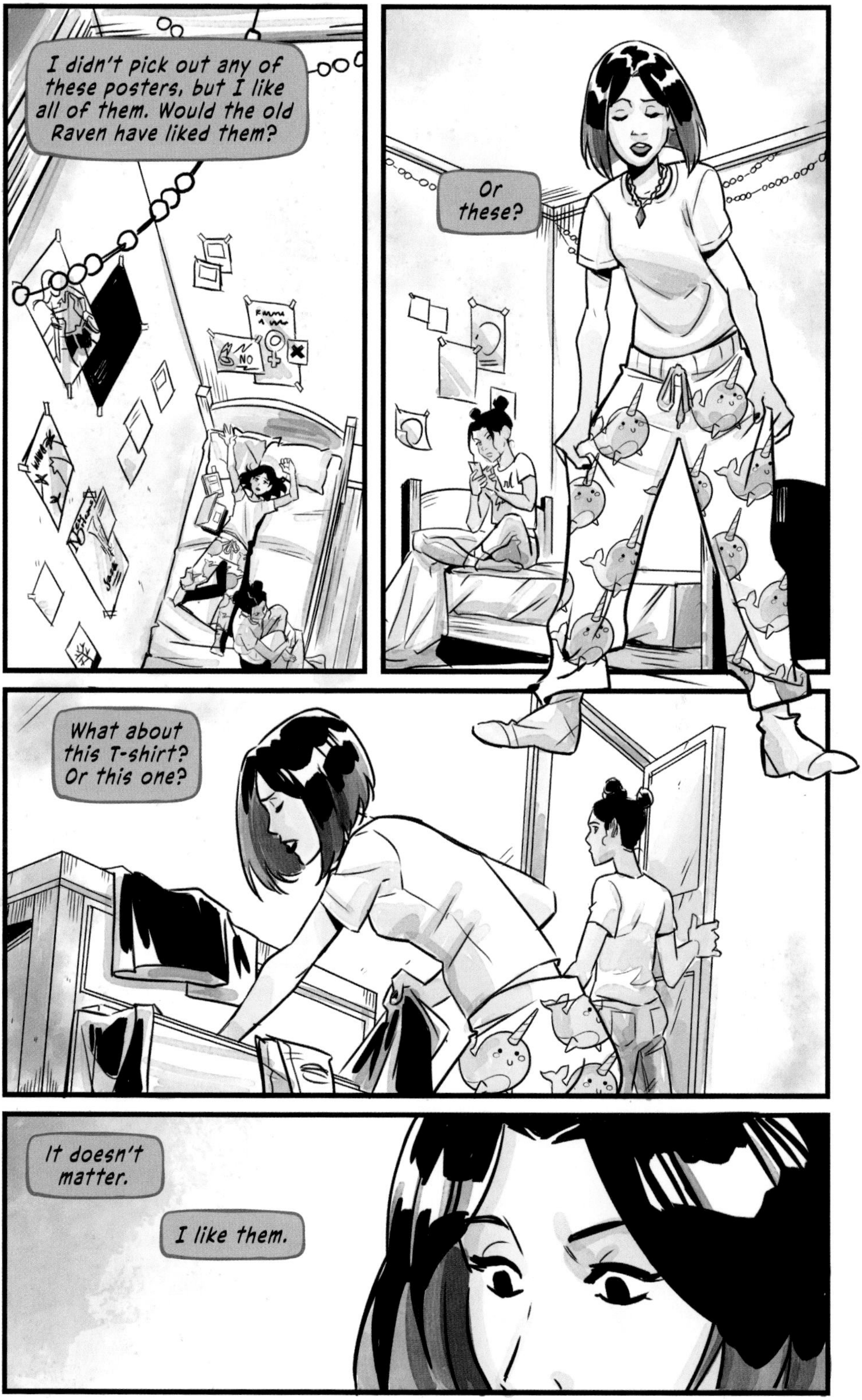
I didn't pick out any of these posters, but I like all of them. Would the old Raven have liked them?
Or these?
What about this T-shirt? Or this one?
It doesn't matter.
I like them.

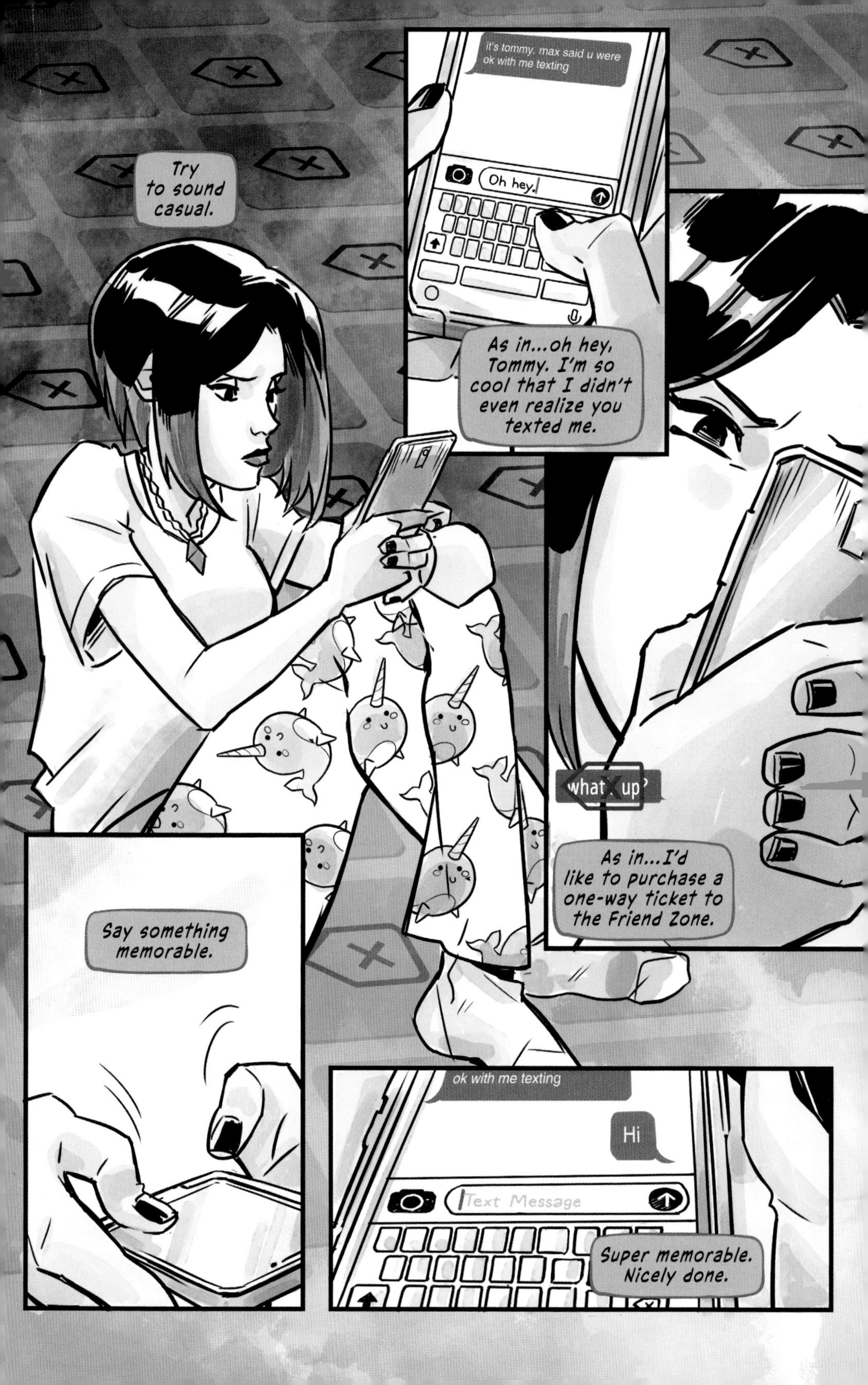
Try to sound casual.
it's tommy. max said u were ok with me texting
Oh hey.
As in...oh hey, Tommy. I'm so cool that I didn't even realize you texted me.
what up?
As in...I'd like to purchase a one-way ticket to the Friend Zone.
Say something memorable.
ok with me texting
Hi
Text Message
Super memorable. Nicely done.

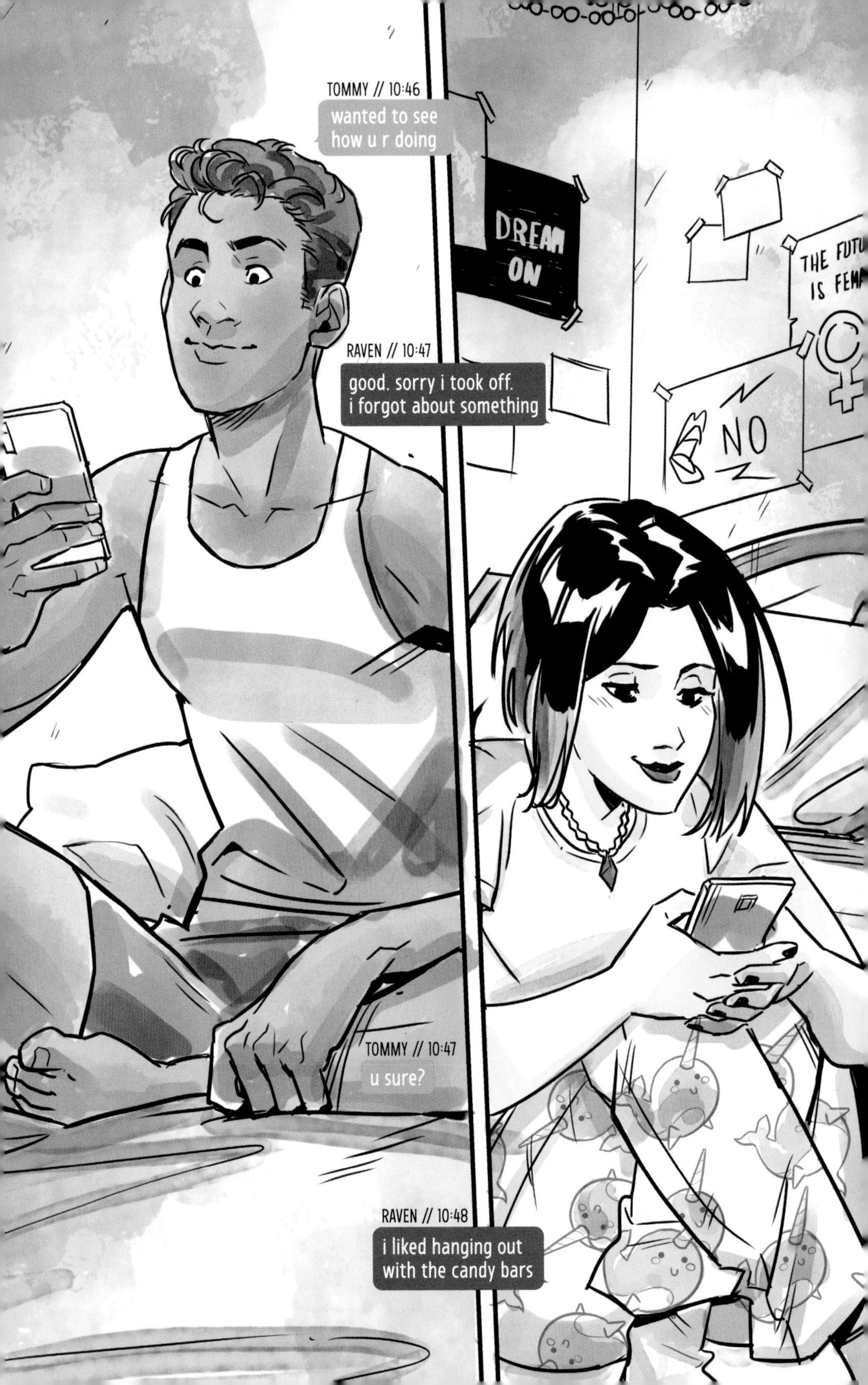
TOMMY // 10:46
wanted to see how u r doing
RAVEN // 10:47
good. sorry i took off. i forgot about something
DREAM ON
THE FUTU IS FEM
NO
TOMMY // 10:47
u sure?
RAVEN // 10:48
i liked hanging out with the candy bars

CHAPTER 10: SPIRITS, SAINTS, AND STONE

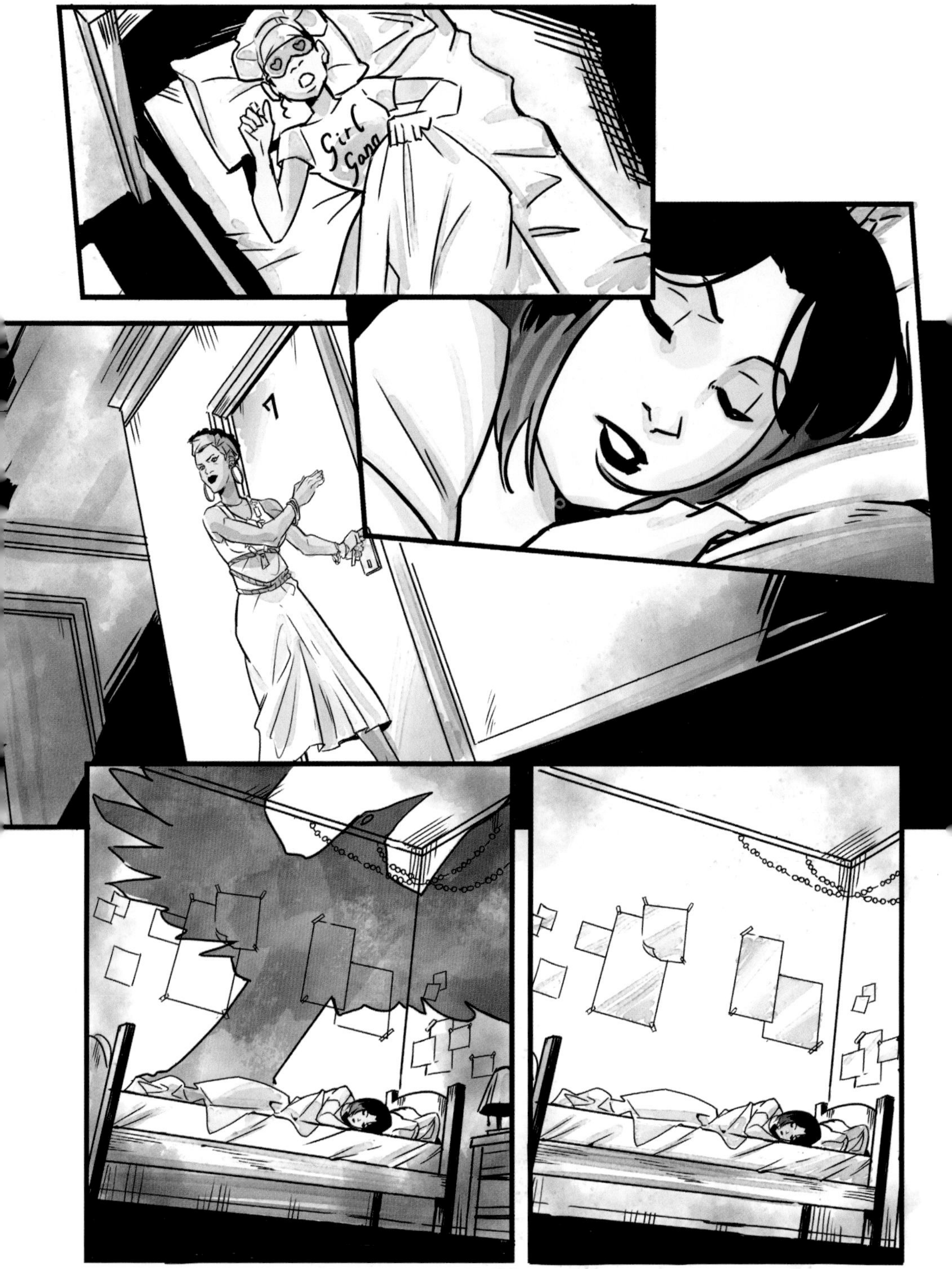
Girl Gang
7

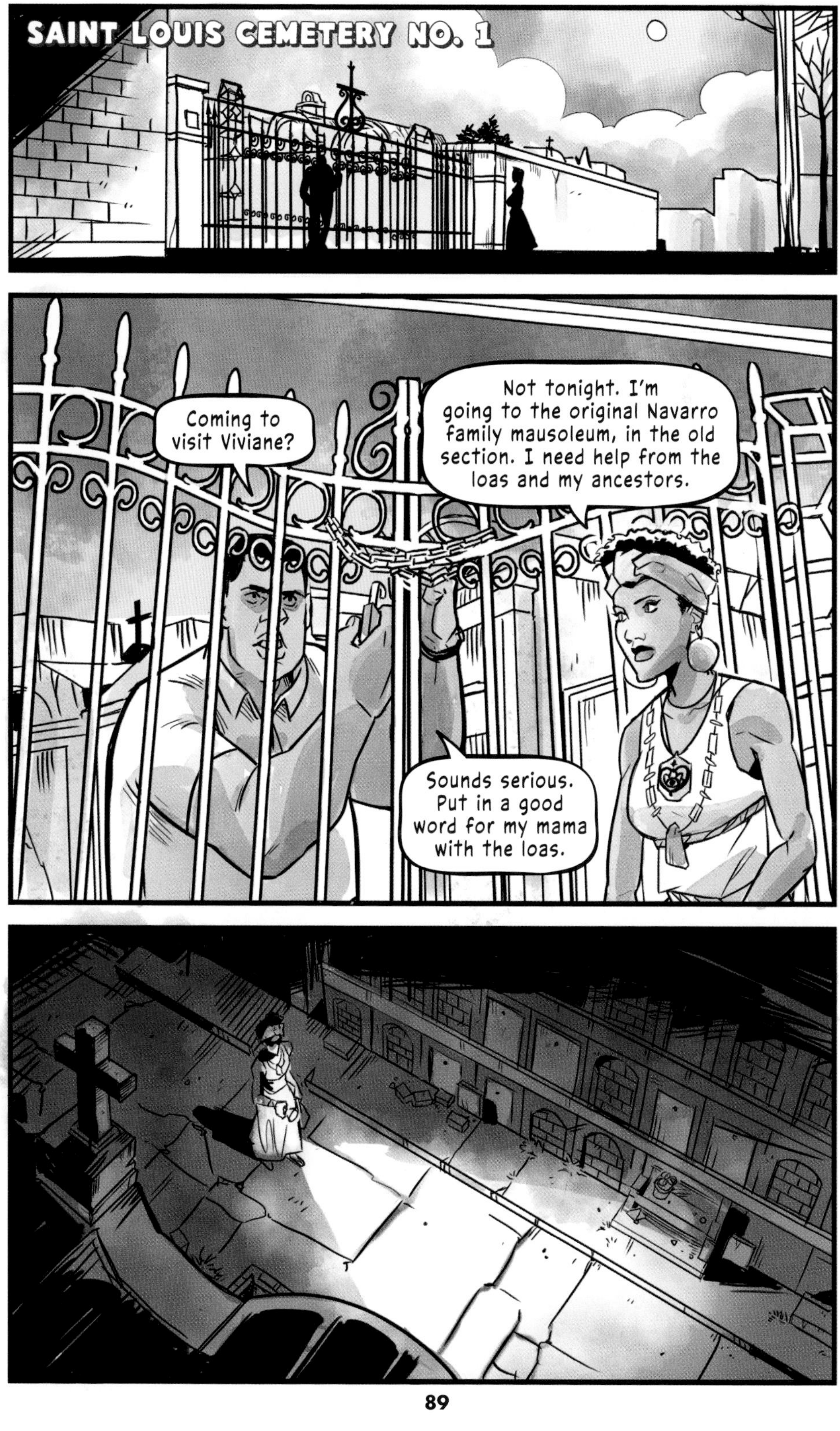
SAINT LOUIS CEMETERY NO. 1
Coming to visit Viviane?
Not tonight. I'm going to the original Navarro family mausoleum, in the old section. I need help from the loas and my ancestors.
Sounds serious. Put in a good word for my mama with the loas.

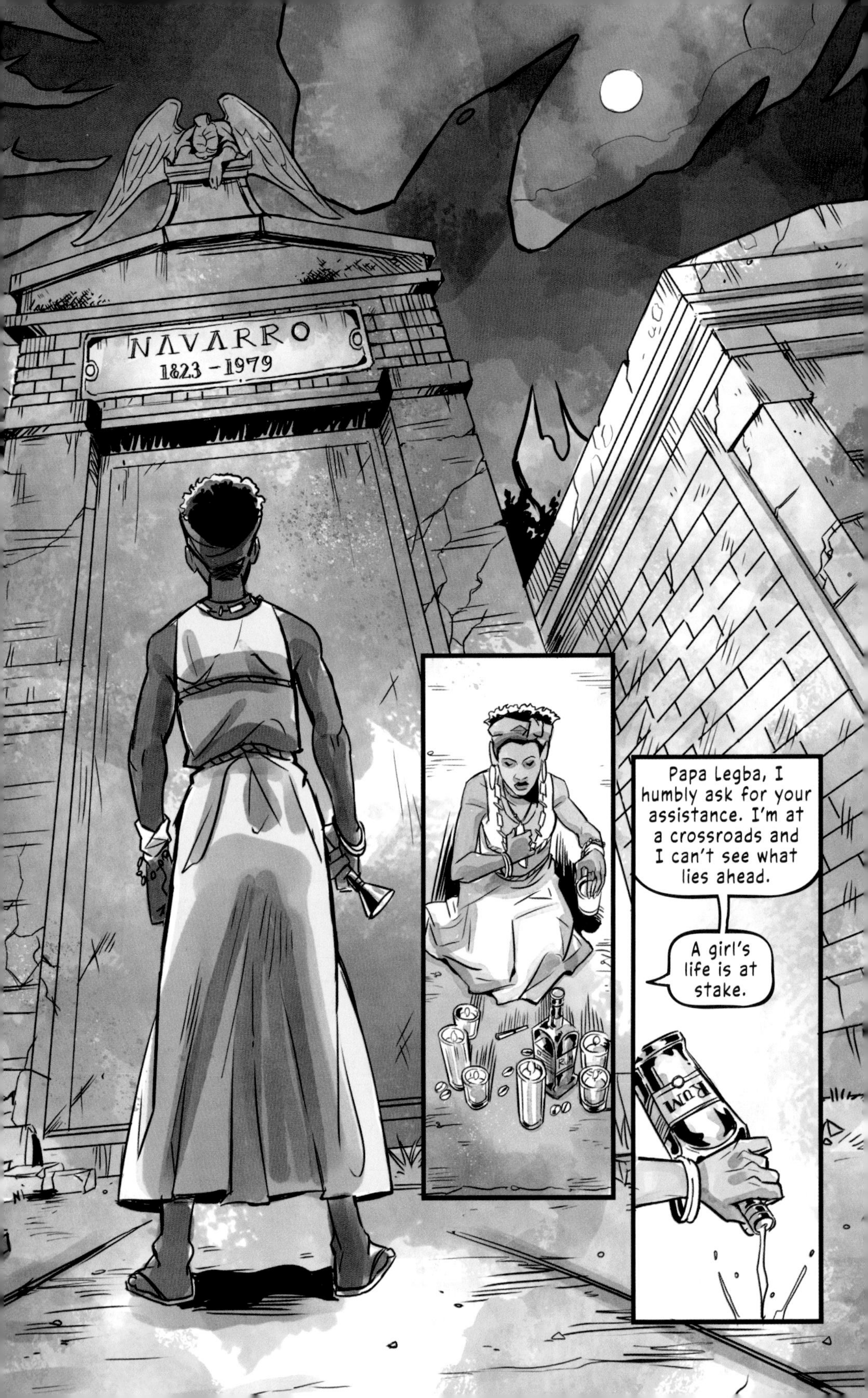
NAVARRO
1823 – 1979
Papa Legba, I humbly ask for your assistance. I'm at a crossroads and I can't see what lies ahead.
A girl's life is at stake.
RUM

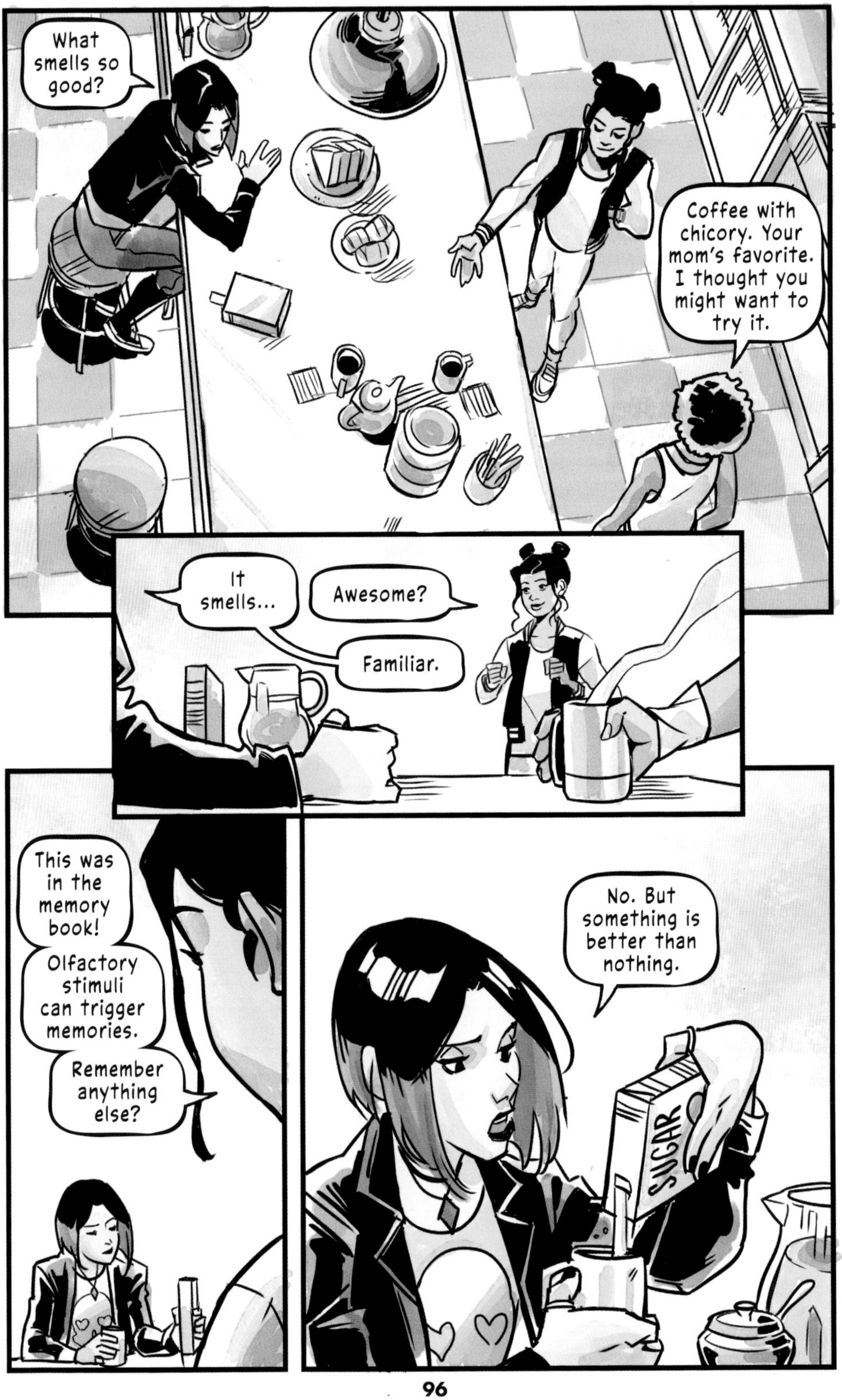
What smells so good?
Coffee with chicory. Your mom's favorite. I thought you might want to try it.
It smells...
Awesome?
Familiar.
This was in the memory book!
Olfactory stimuli can trigger memories.
Remember anything else?
No. But something is better than nothing.
SUGAR

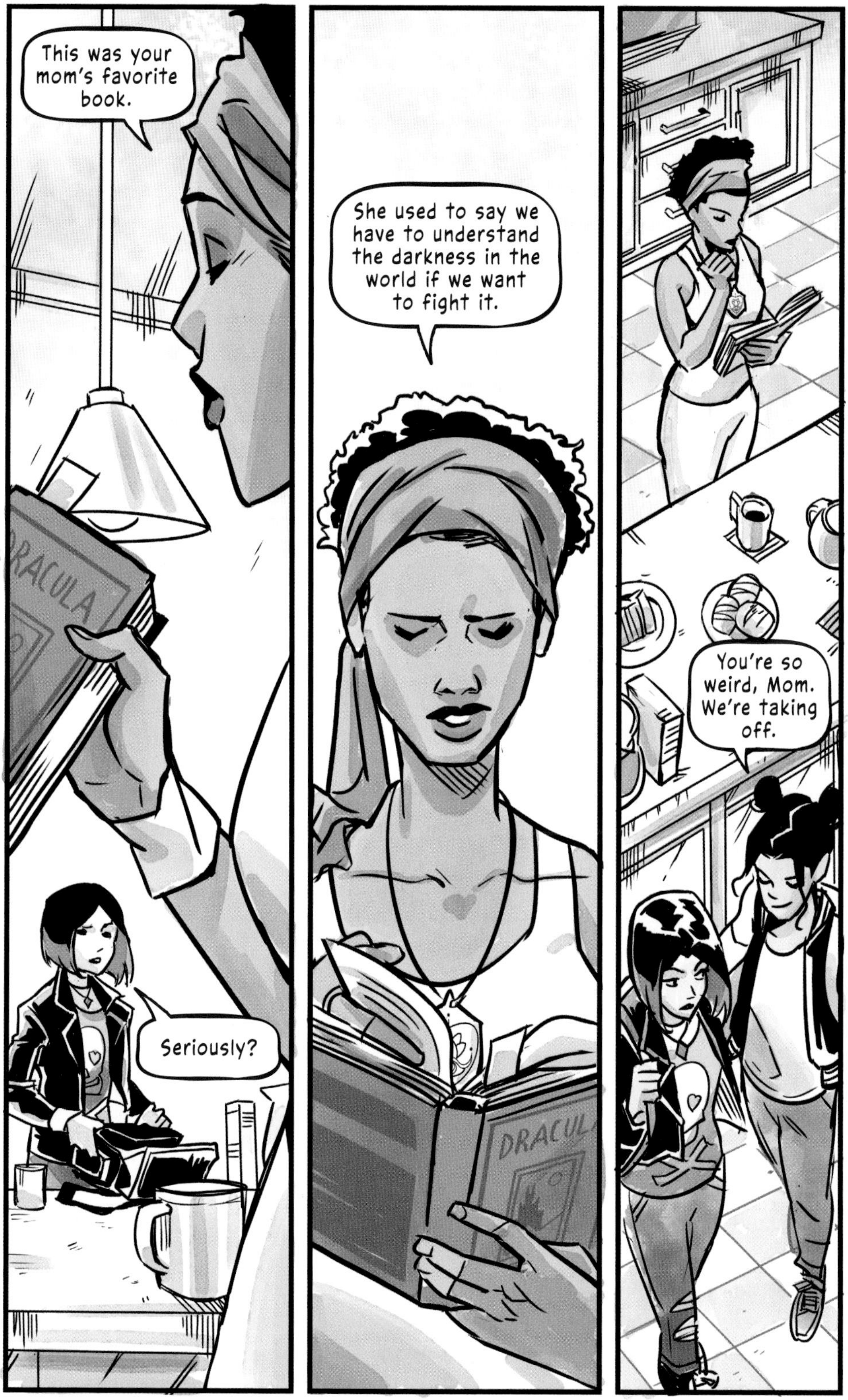
This was your mom's favorite book.
DRACULA
Seriously?
She used to say we have to understand the darkness in the world if we want to fight it.
DRACULA
You're so weird, Mom. We're taking off.

CHAPTER 11: ROSES ARE RED

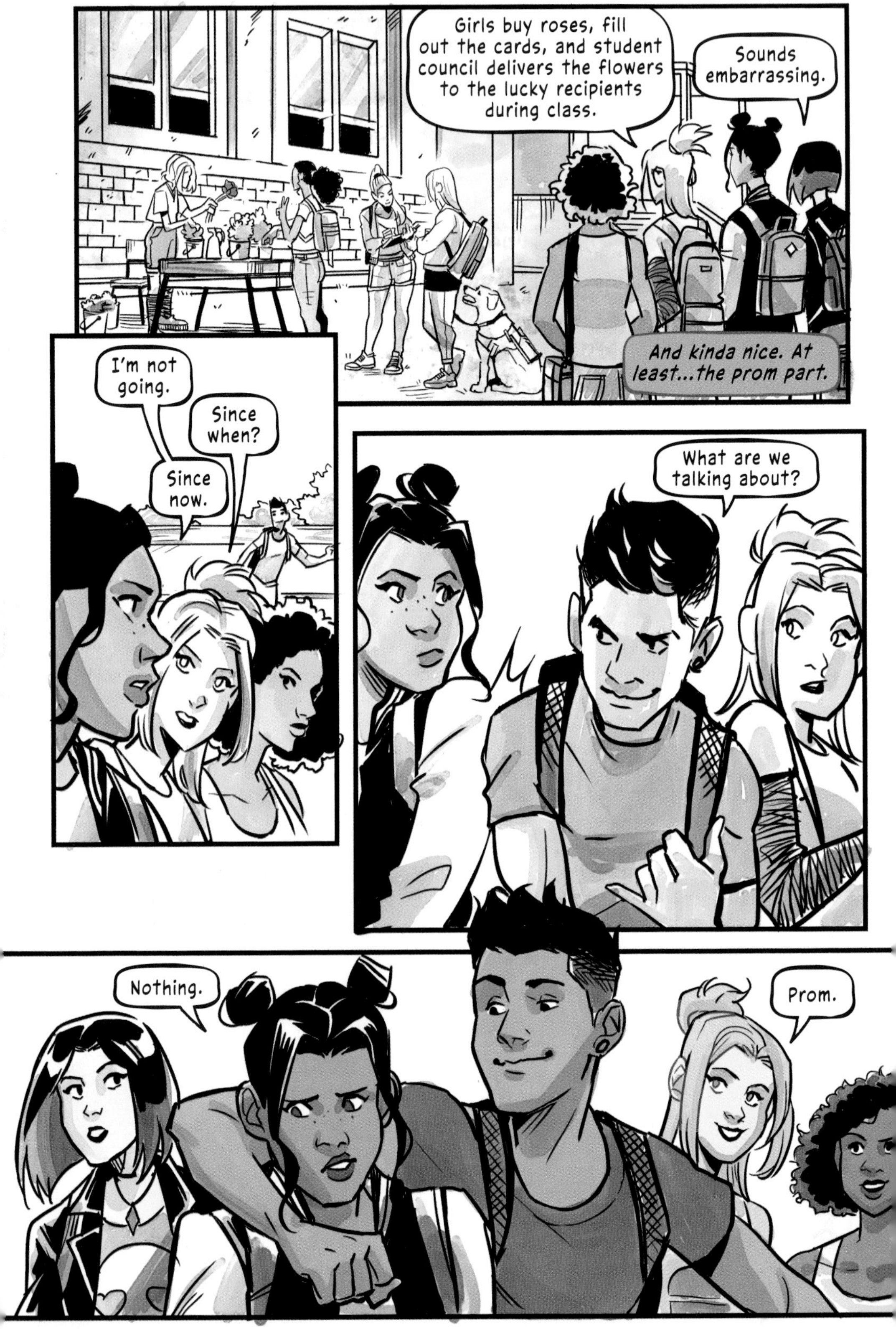
Girls buy roses, fill out the cards, and student council delivers the flowers to the lucky recipients during class.
Sounds embarrassing.
And kinda nice. At least...the prom part.
I'm not going.
Since when?
Since now.
What are we talking about?
Nothing.
Prom.

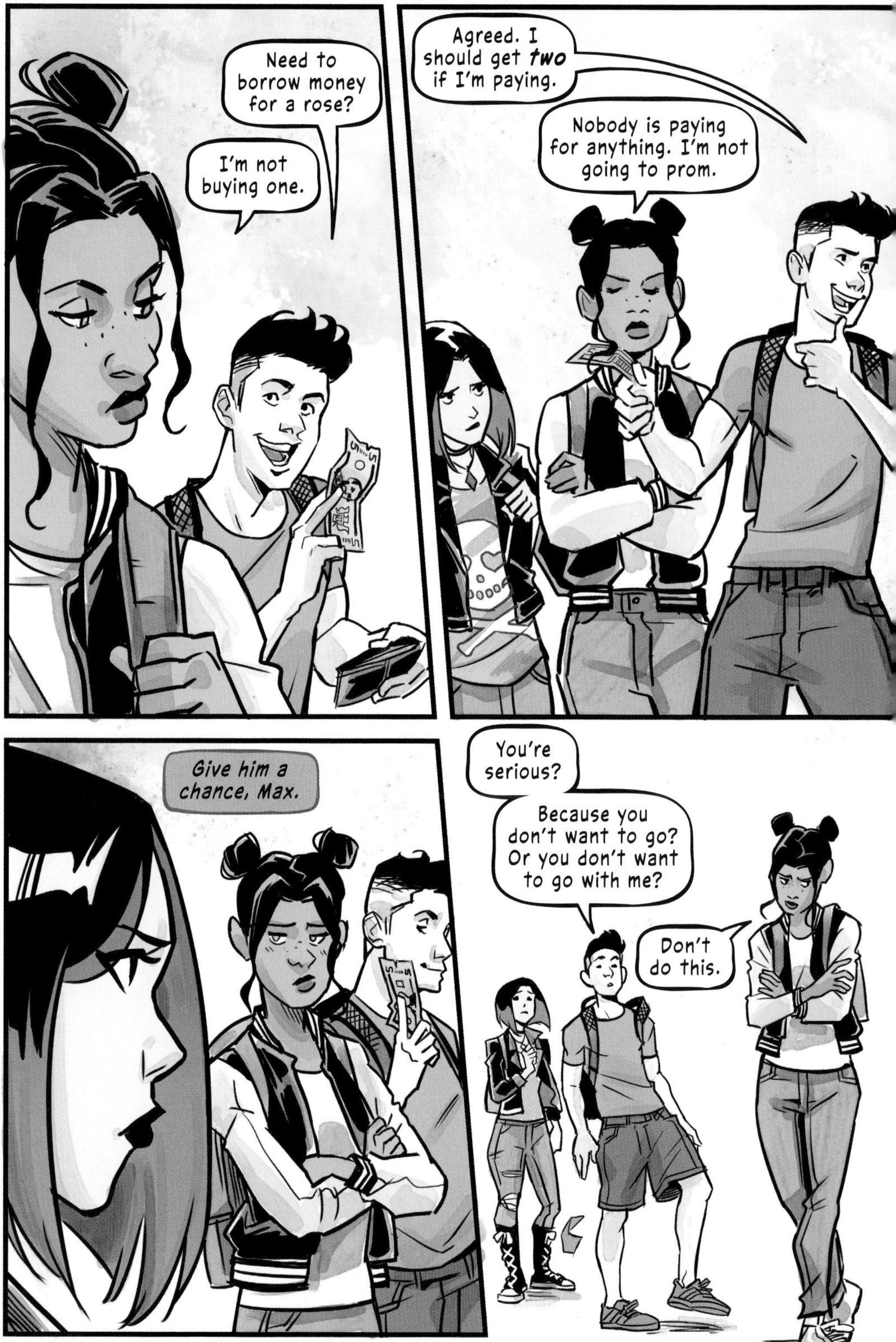
Need to borrow money for a rose?
I'm not buying one.
Agreed. I should get *two* if I'm paying.
Nobody is paying for anything. I'm not going to prom.
Give him a chance, Max.
You're serious?
Because you don't want to go? Or you don't want to go with me?
Don't do this.

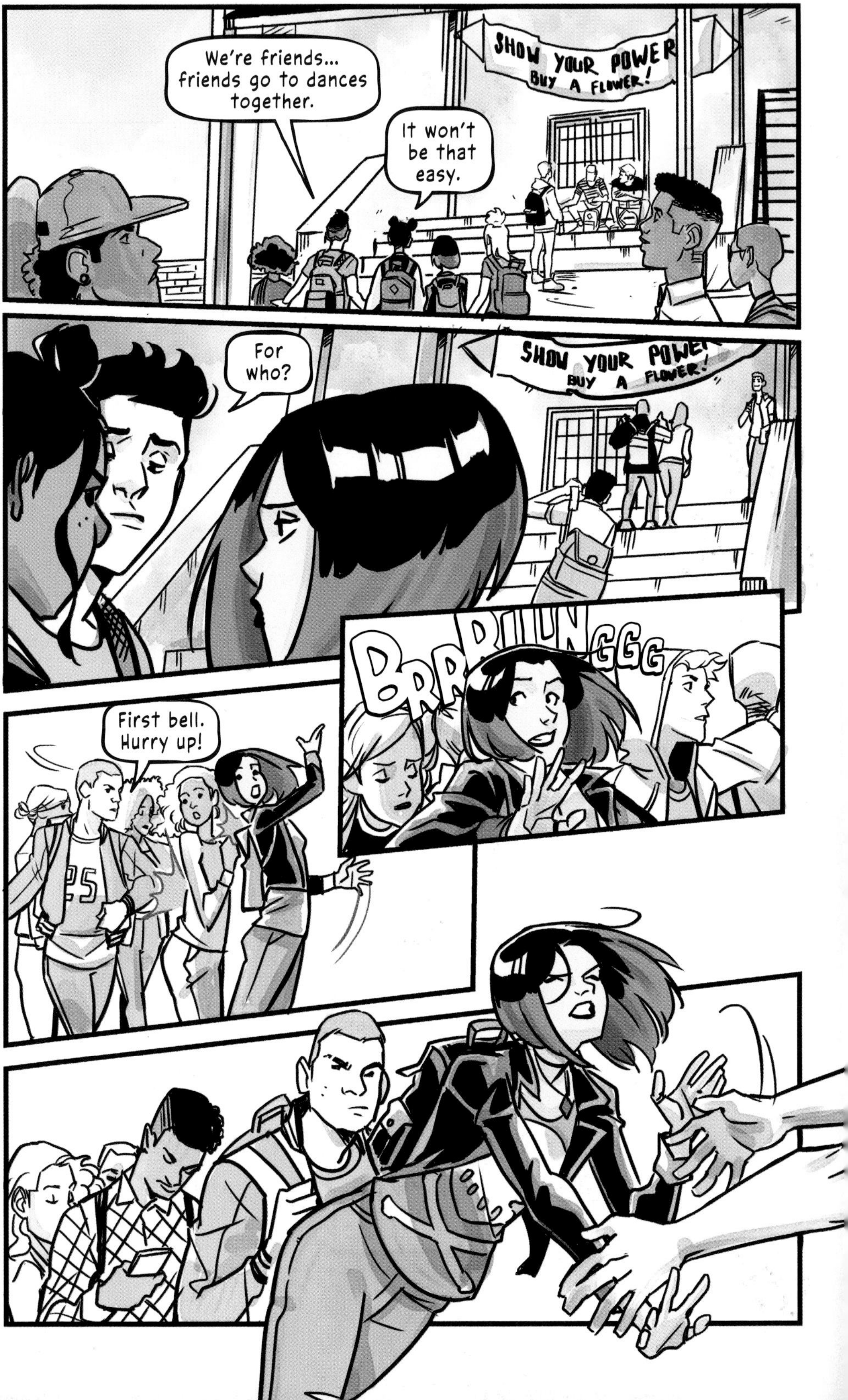
SHOW YOUR POWER
BUY A FLOWER!
We're friends... friends go to dances together.
It won't be that easy.
For who?
BRRRIIINGGG
First bell. Hurry up!

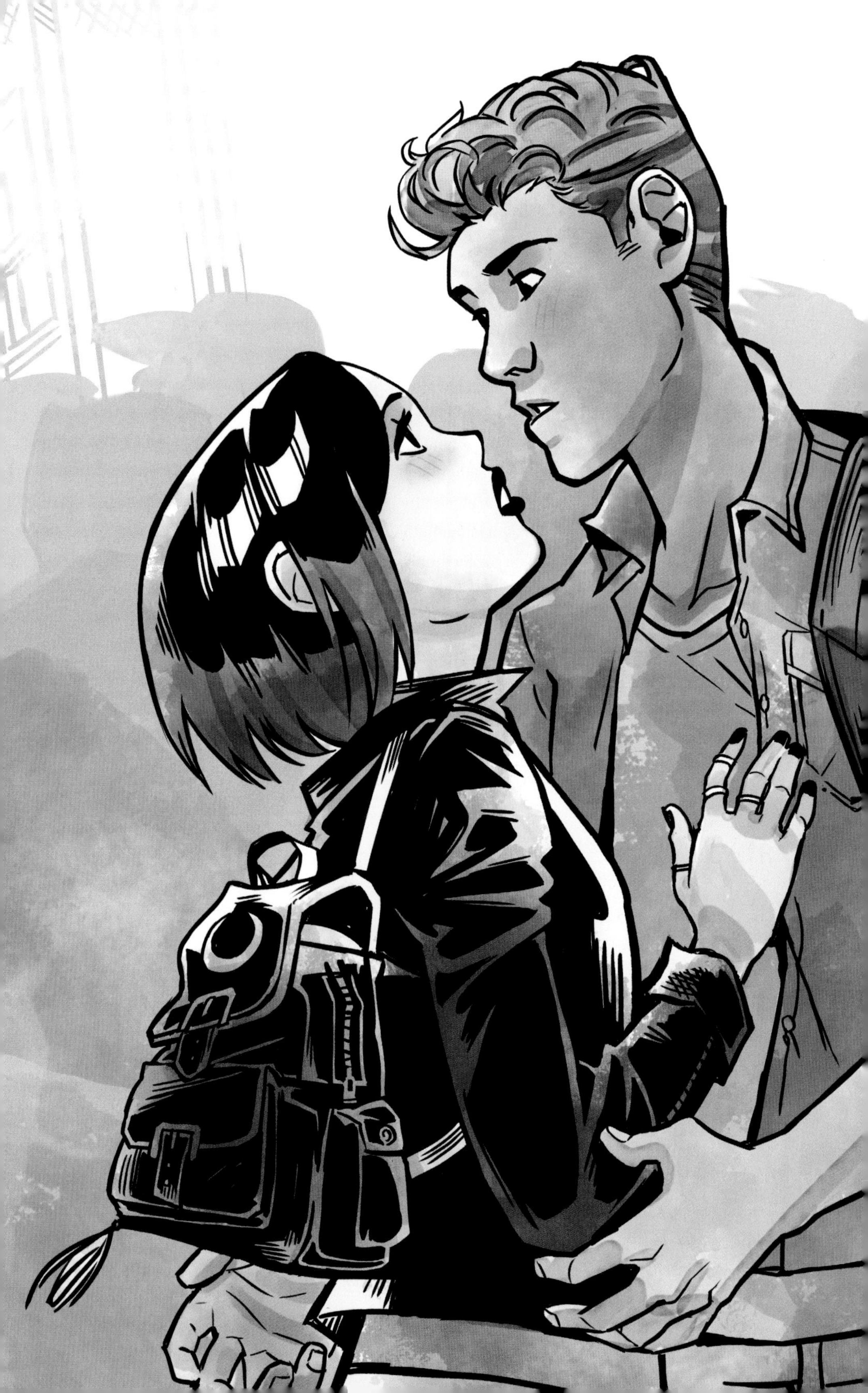

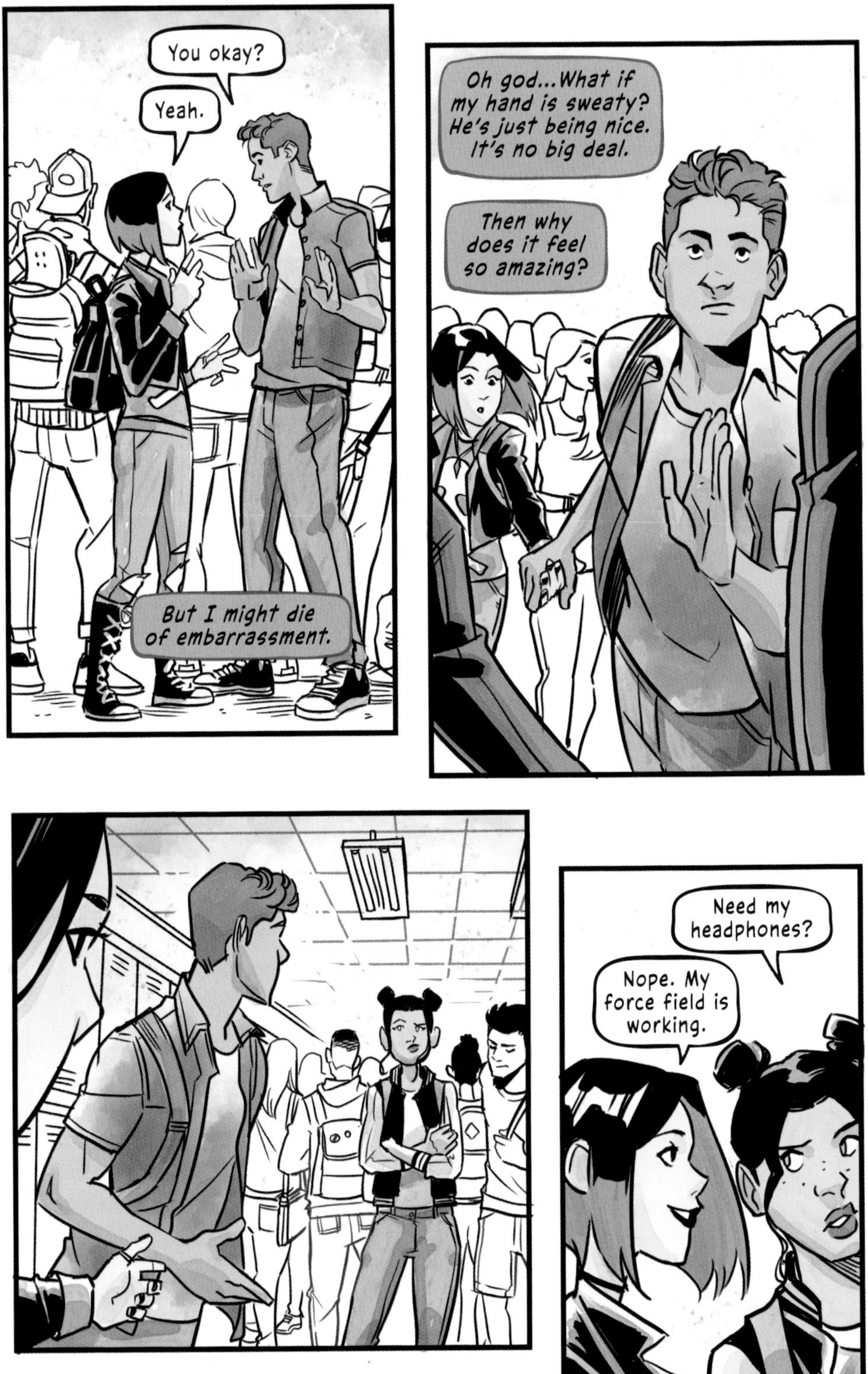
You okay?
Yeah.
But I might die of embarrassment.
Oh god...What if my hand is sweaty? He's just being nice. It's no big deal.
Then why does it feel so amazing?
Need my headphones?
Nope. My force field is working.

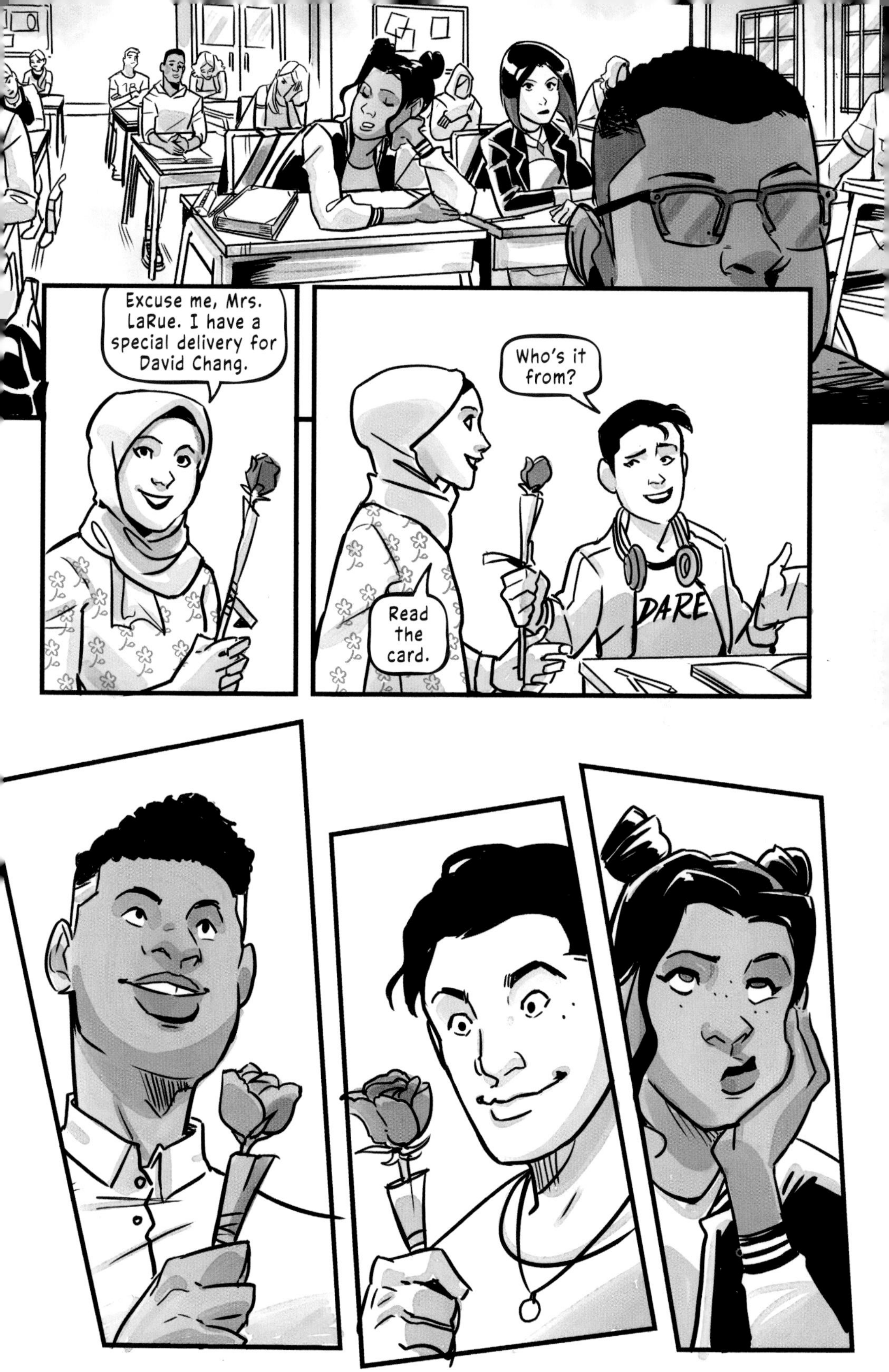

Excuse me, Mrs. LaRue. I have a special delivery for David Chang.
Who's it from?
Read the card.
DARE

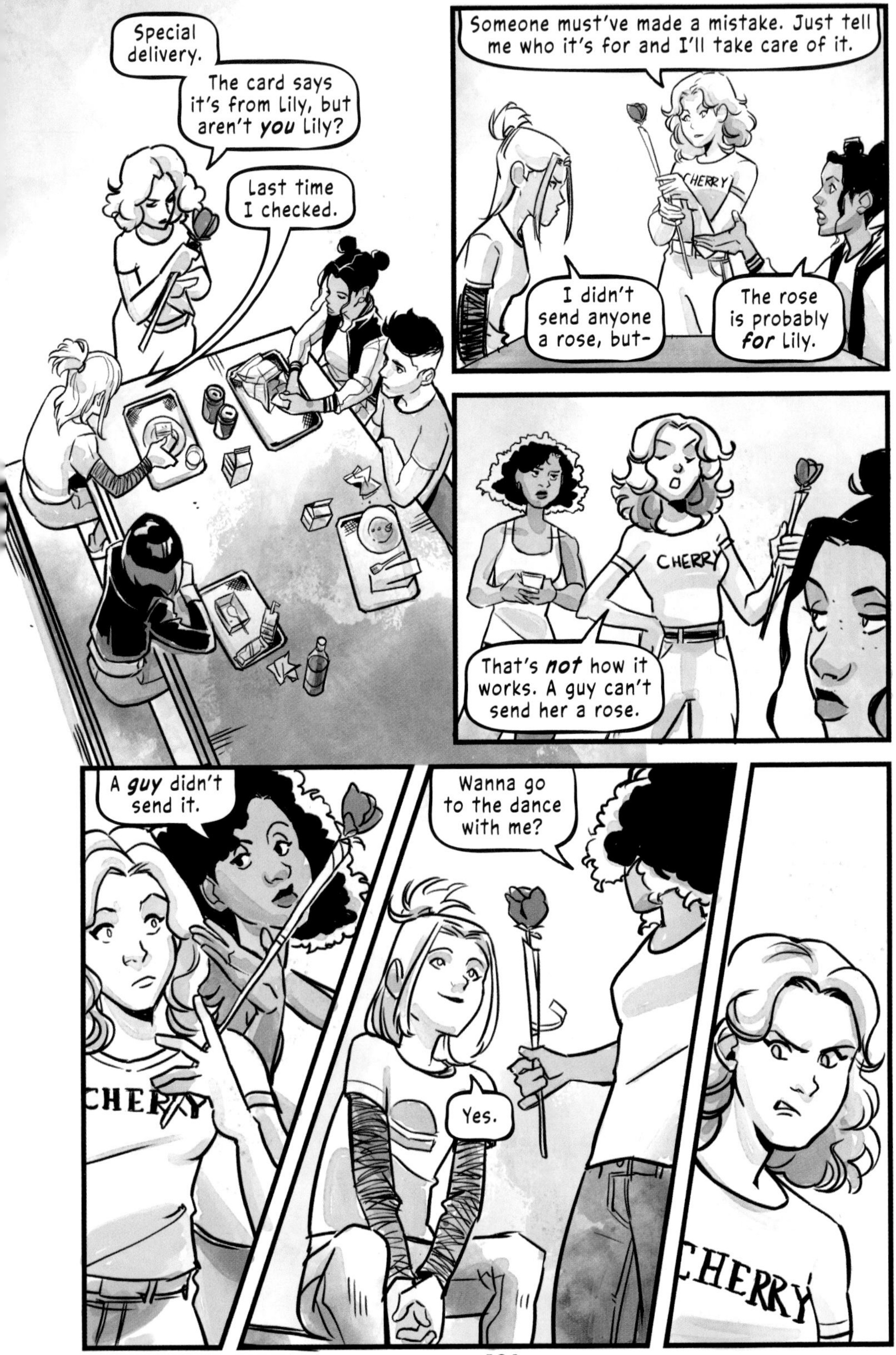
Special delivery.
The card says it's from Lily, but aren't *you* Lily?
Last time I checked.
Someone must've made a mistake. Just tell me who it's for and I'll take care of it.
CHERRY
I didn't send anyone a rose, but-
The rose is probably *for* Lily.
CHERRY
That's *not* how it works. A guy can't send her a rose.
A *guy* didn't send it.
CHERRY
Wanna go to the dance with me?
Yes.
CHERRY

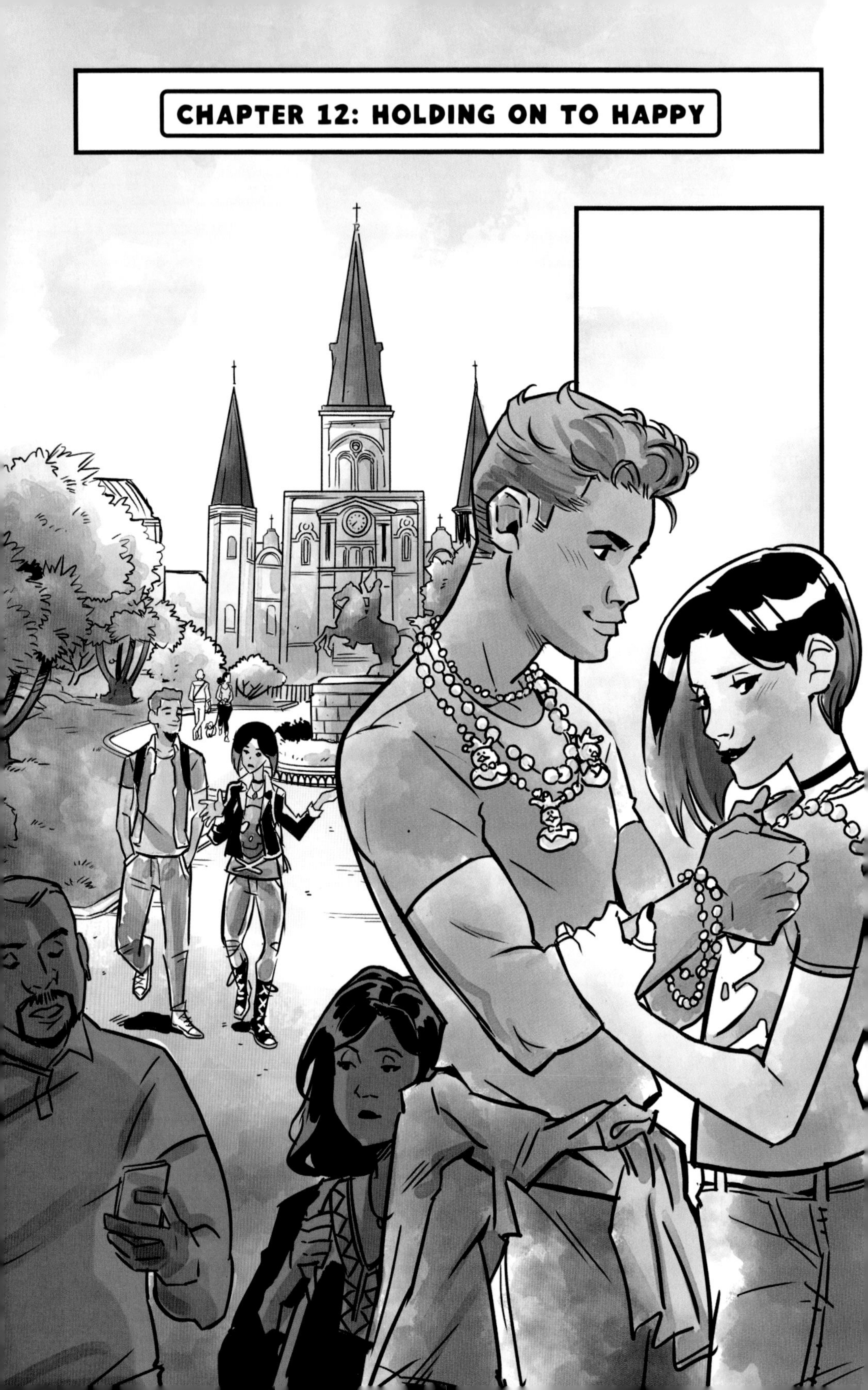
CHAPTER 12: HOLDING ON TO HAPPY

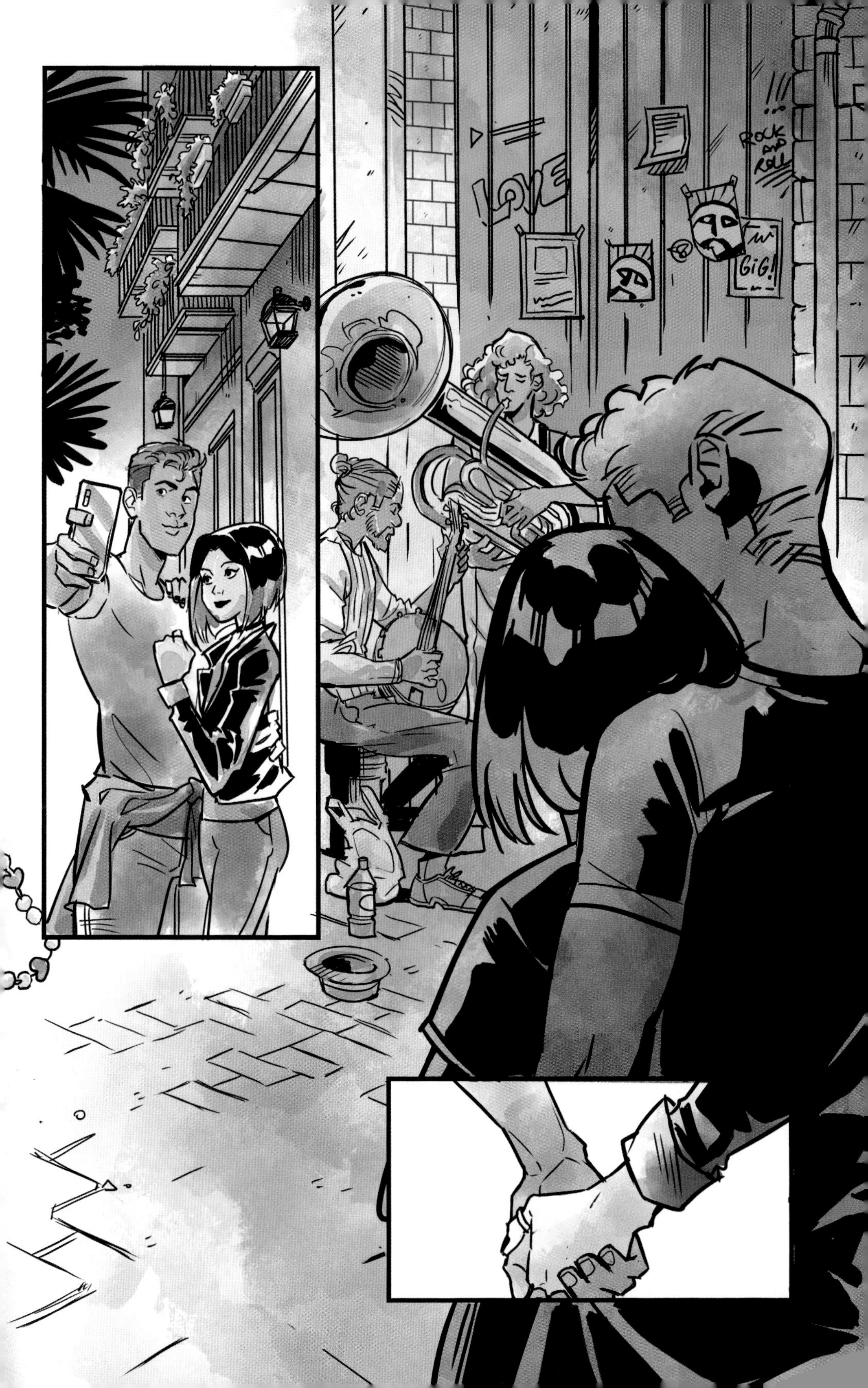
LOVE
ROCK AND ROLL
GIG!

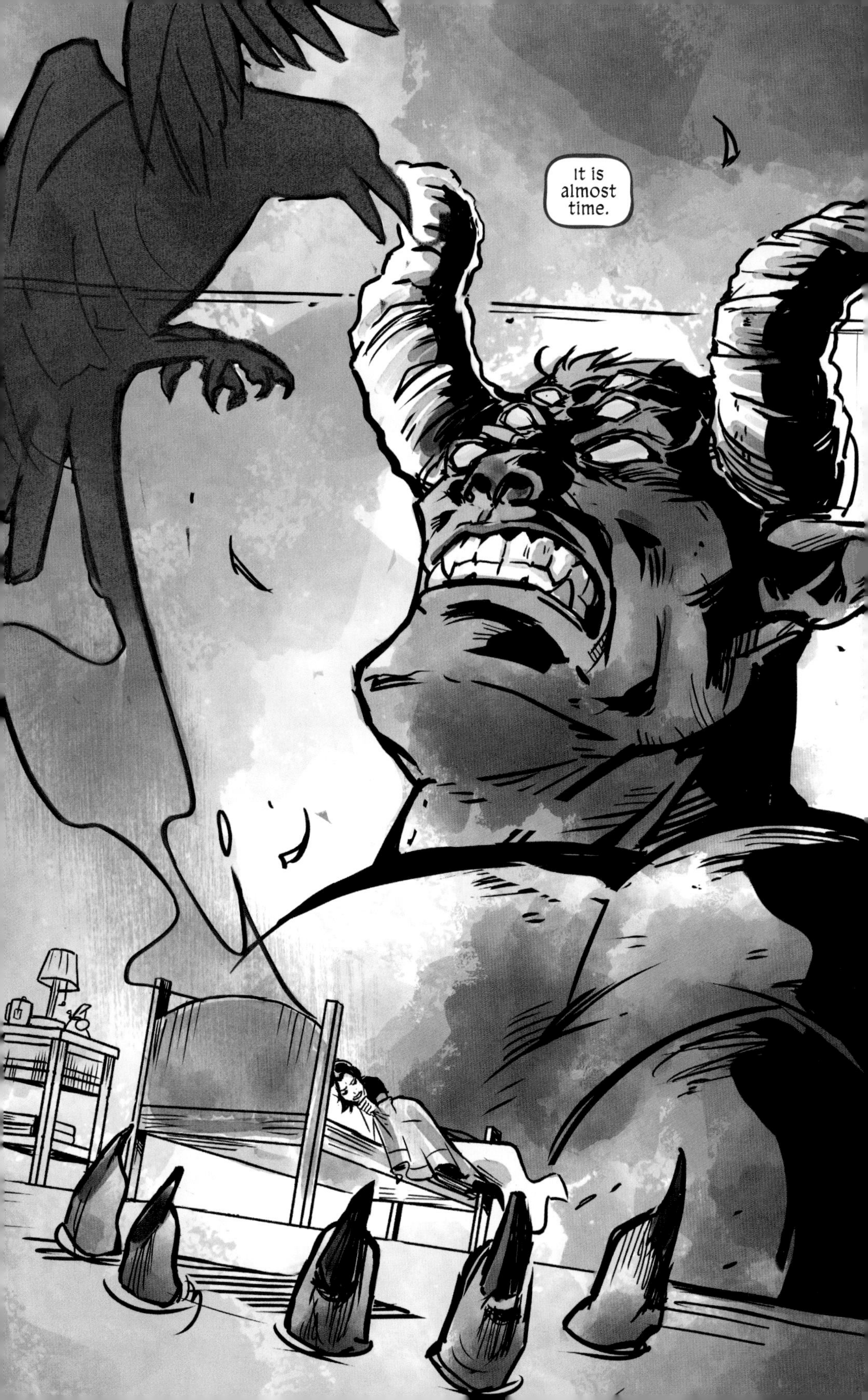
It is almost time.

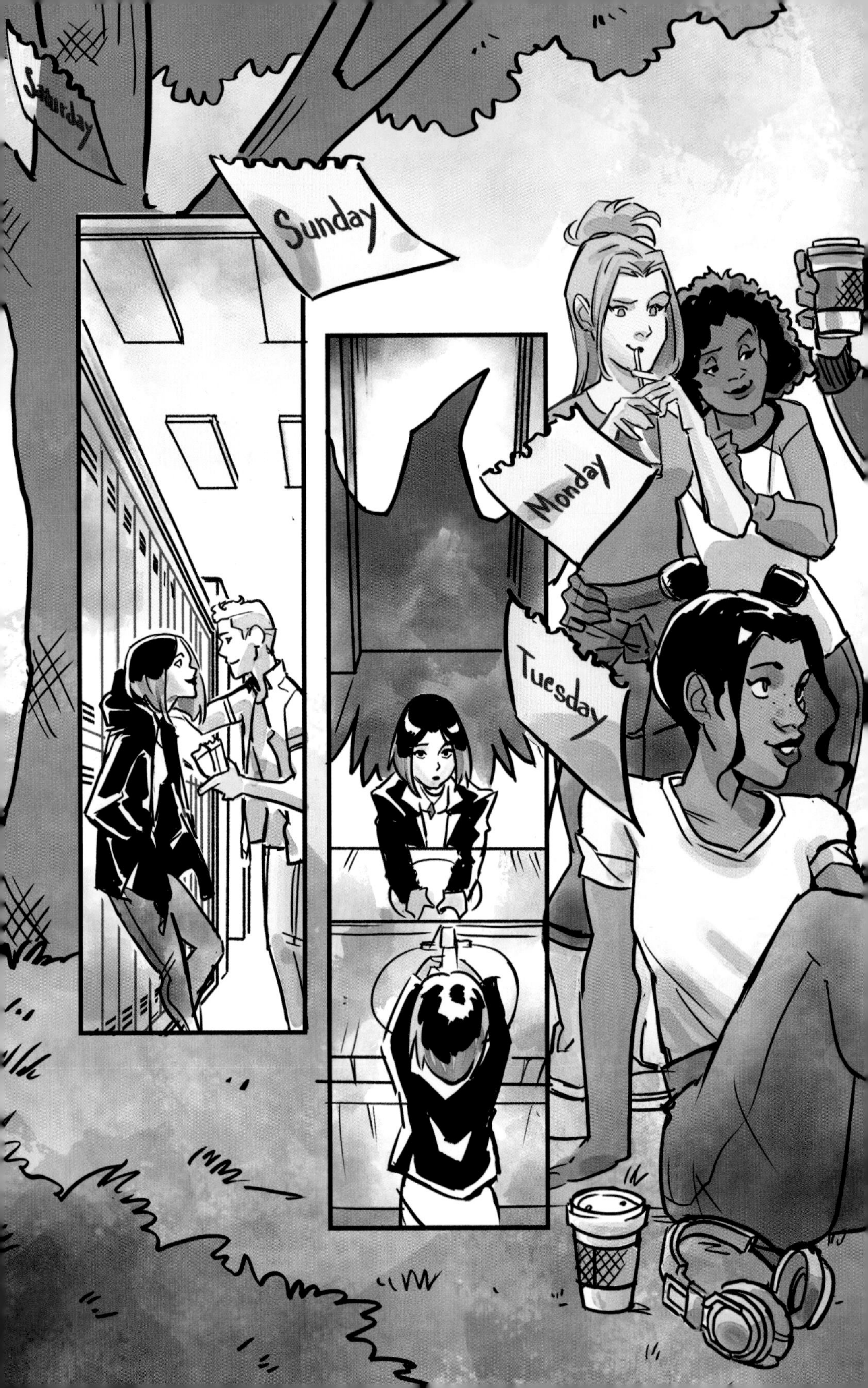
Saturday
Sunday
Monday
Tuesday

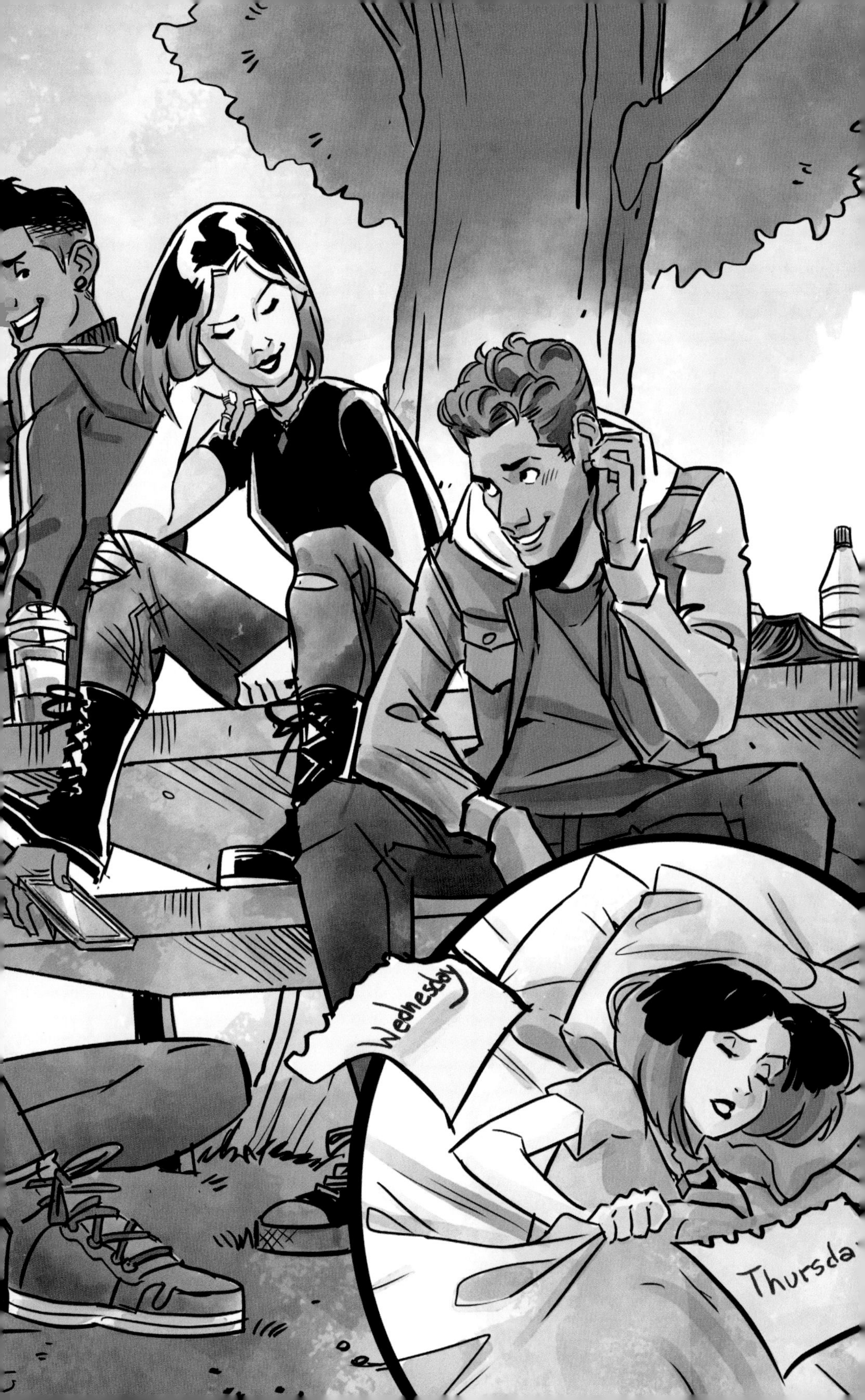

Wednesday
Thursda

CHAPTER 13: PROM NIGHT, PLASTIC RINGS, AND PROMISES

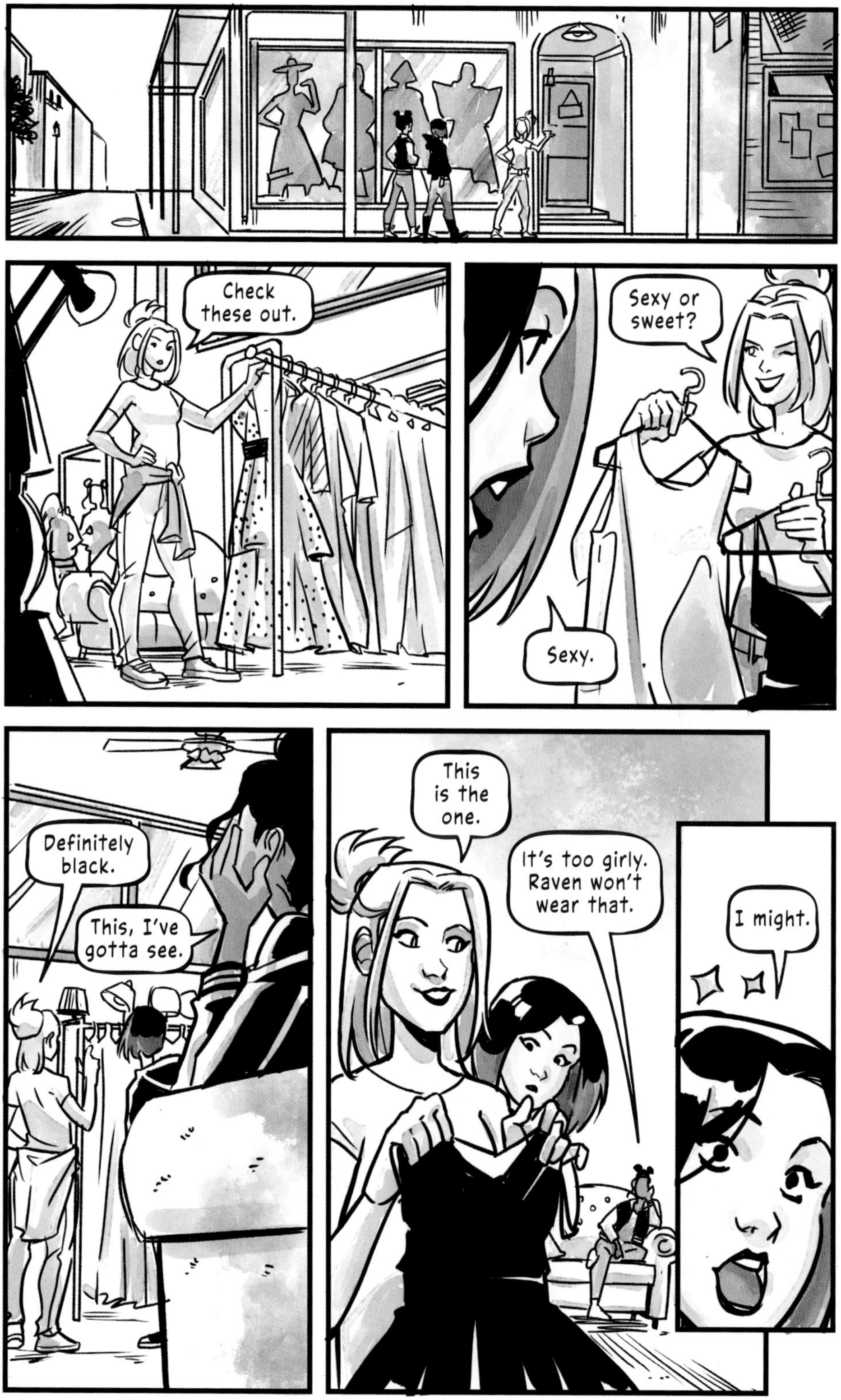
Check these out.
Sexy or sweet?
Sexy.
Definitely black.
This, I've gotta see.
This is the one.
It's too girly. Raven won't wear that.
I might.

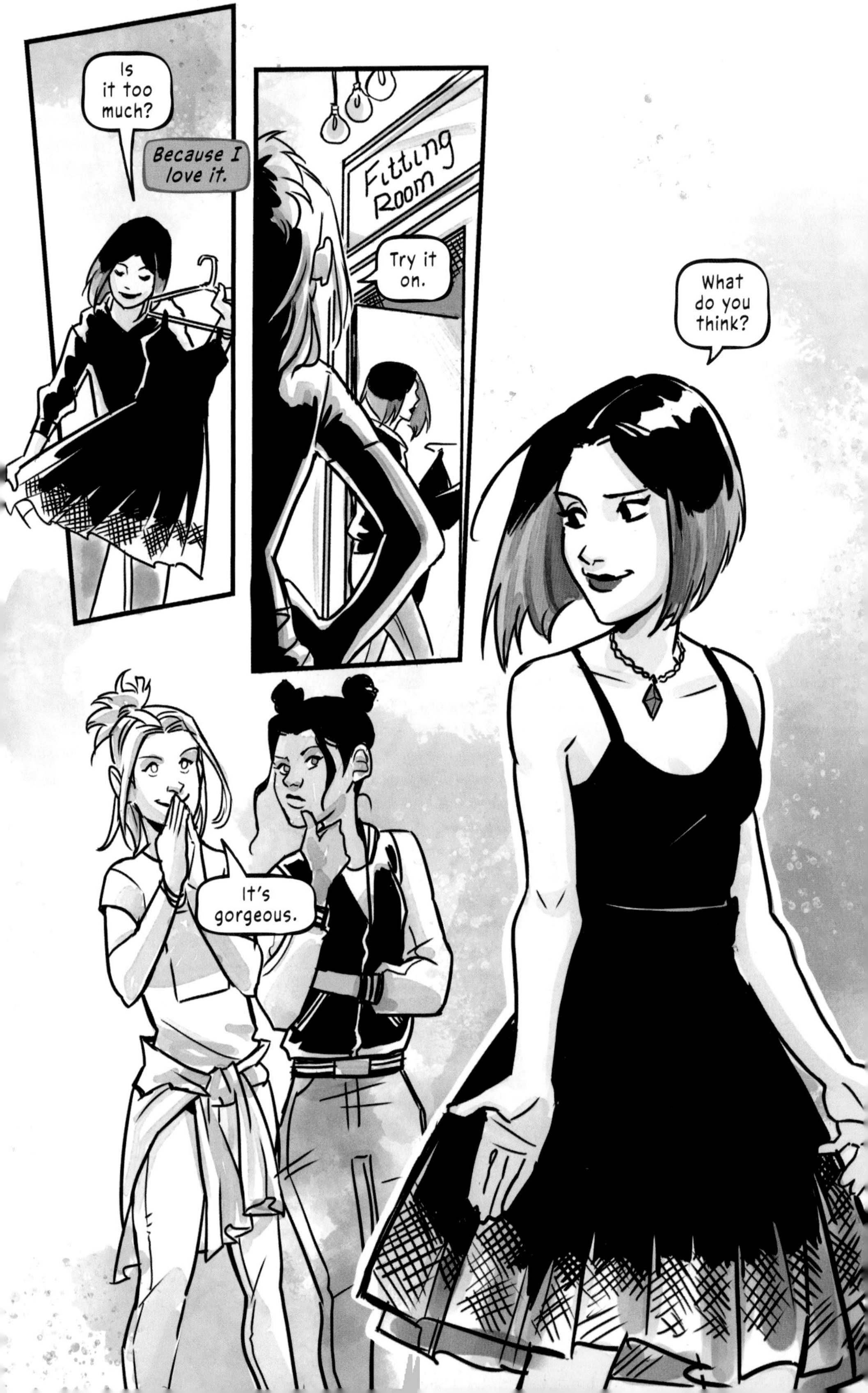
Is it too much?
Because I love it.
Fitting Room
Try it on.
What do you think?
It's gorgeous.

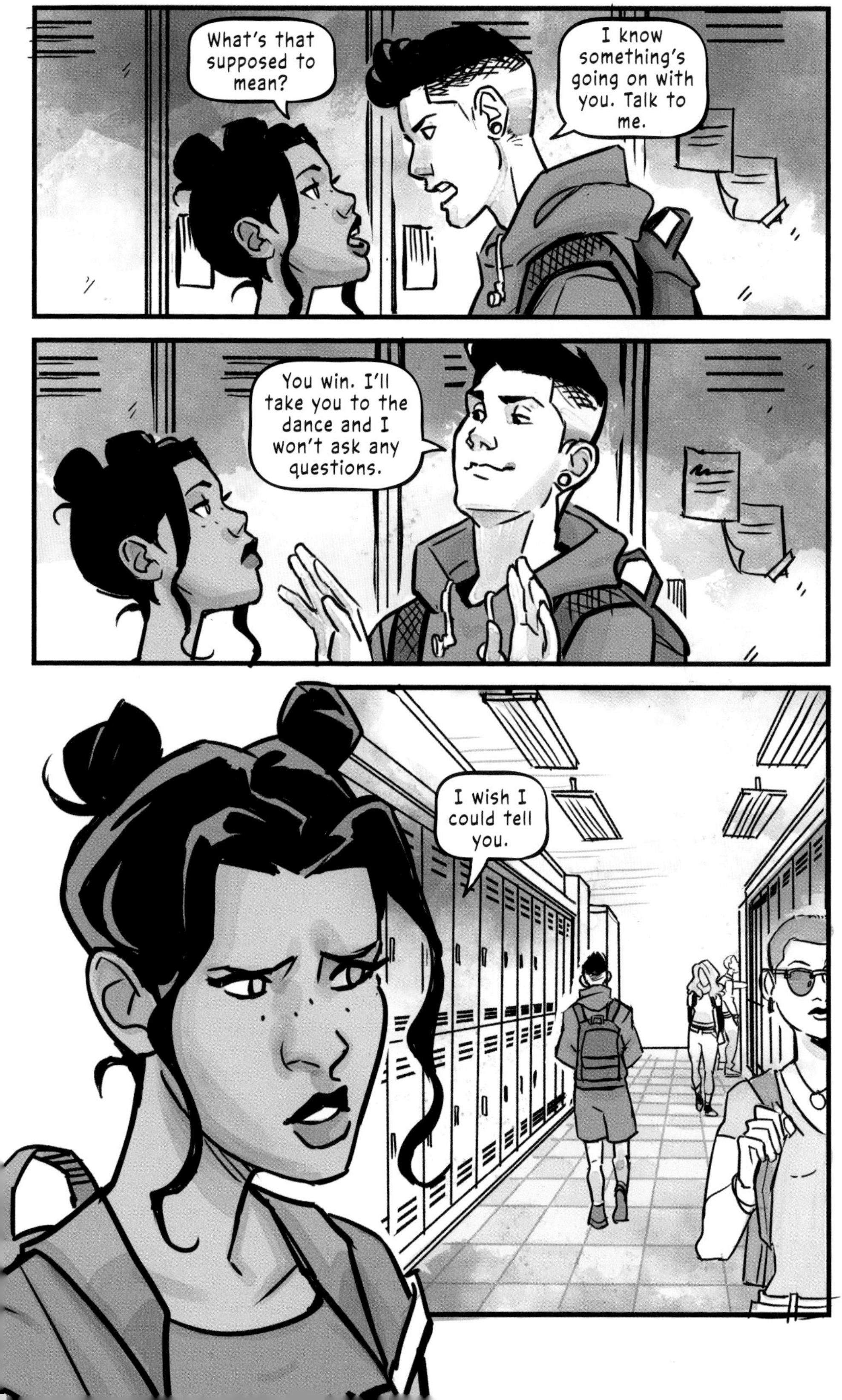
What's that supposed to mean?
I know something's going on with you. Talk to me.
You win. I'll take you to the dance and I won't ask any questions.
I wish I could tell you.

CHAPTER 14: PERFECT AND DAMAGED ARE BOTH FOUR-LETTER WORDS

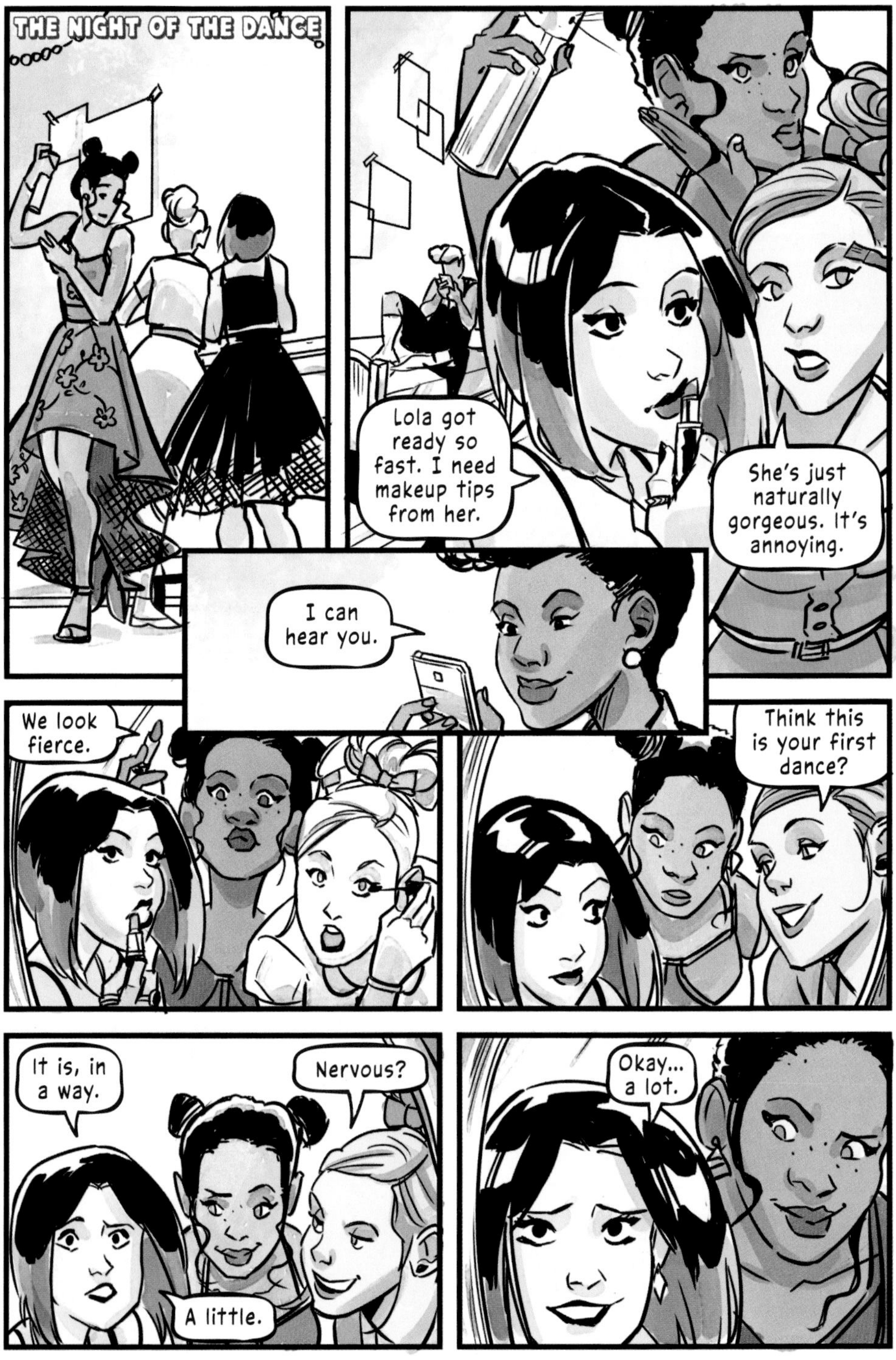
THE NIGHT OF THE DANCE
Lola got ready so fast. I need makeup tips from her.
She's just naturally gorgeous. It's annoying.
I can hear you.
We look fierce.
Think this is your first dance?
It is, in a way.
Nervous?
A little.
Okay... a lot.

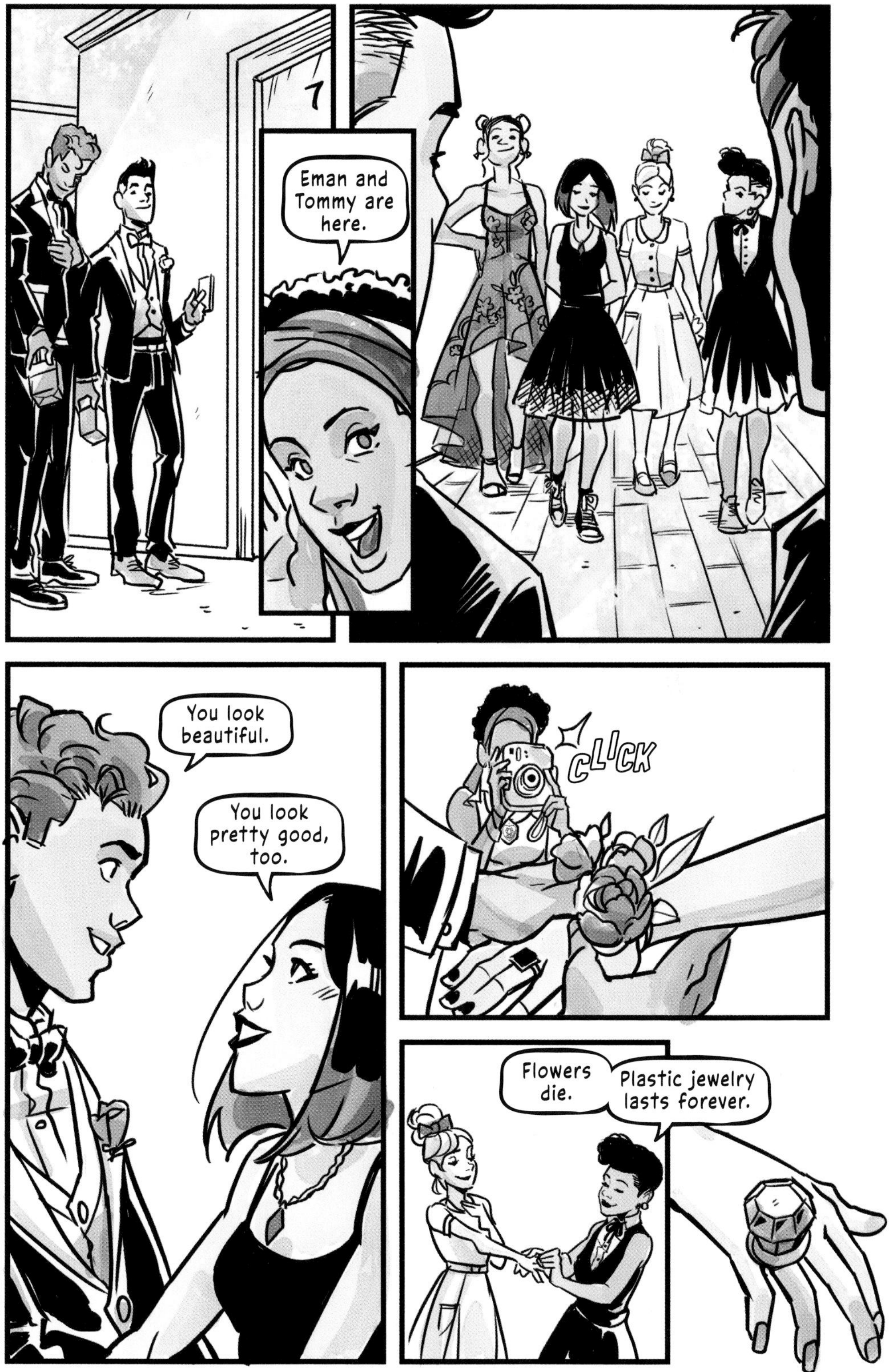
Eman and Tommy are here.
You look beautiful.
You look pretty good, too.
CLICK
Flowers die.
Plastic jewelry lasts forever.

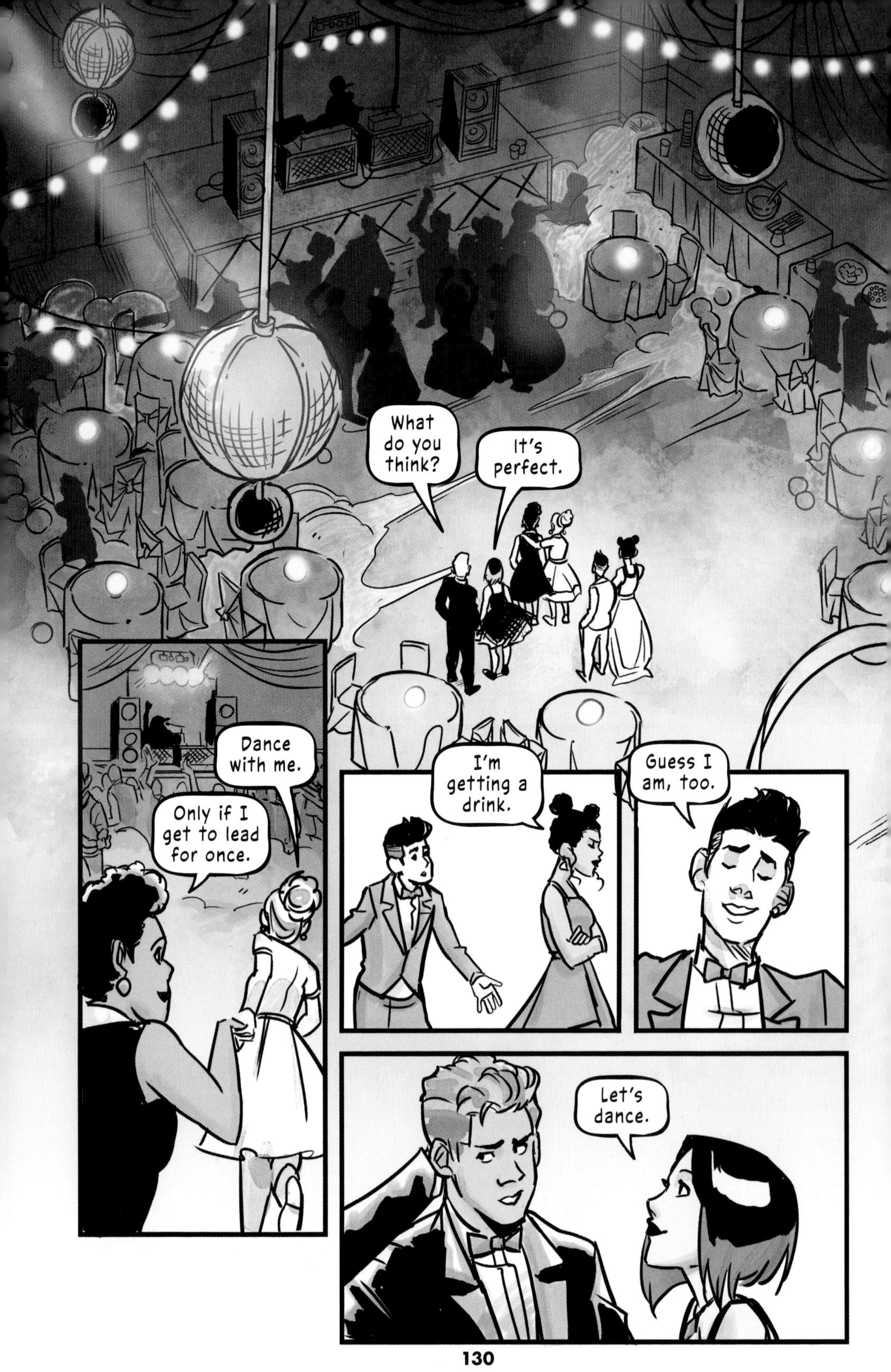
What do you think?
It's perfect.
Dance with me.
Only if I get to lead for once.
I'm getting a drink.
Guess I am, too.
Let's dance.

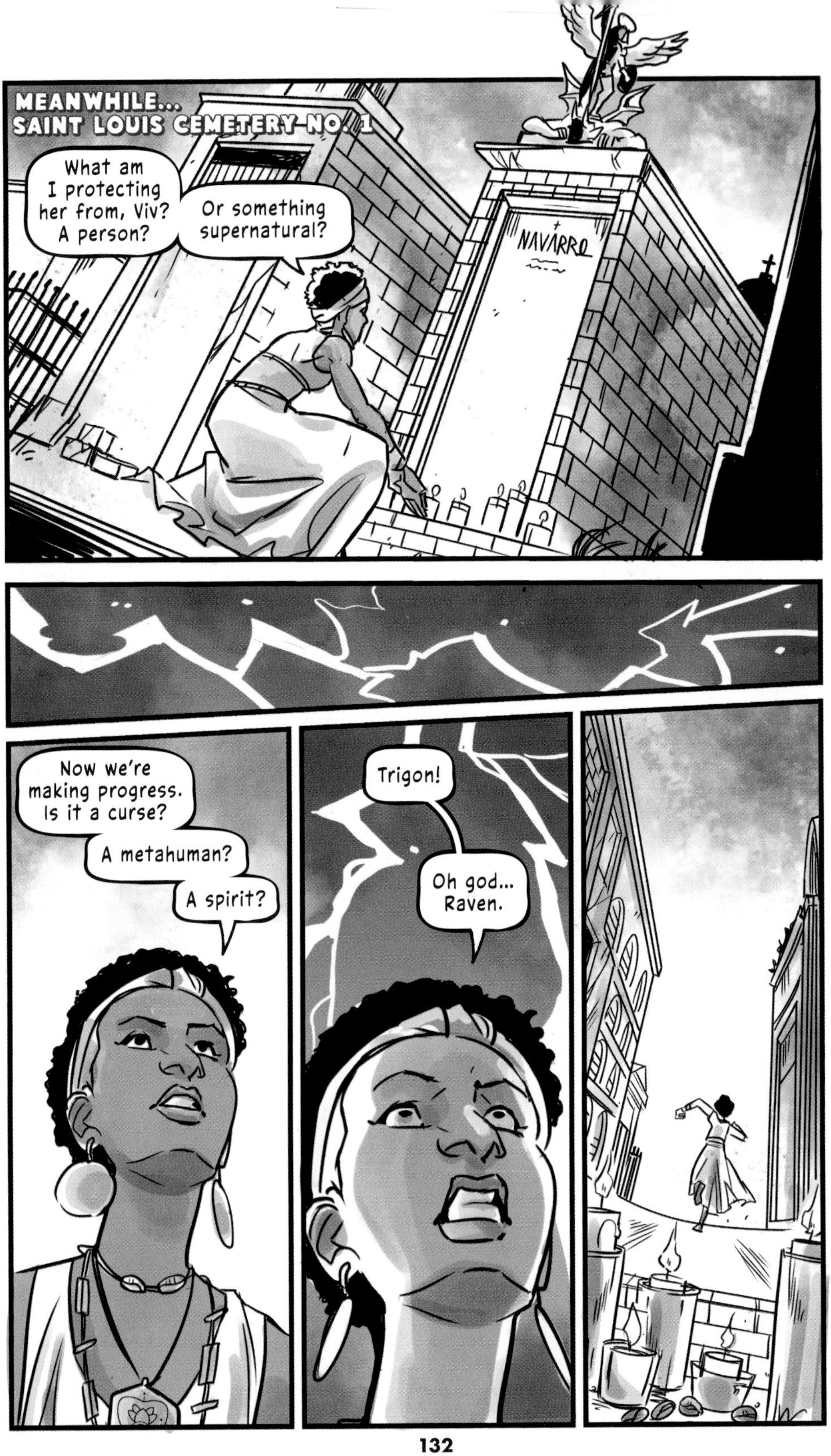
MEANWHILE...
SAINT LOUIS CEMETERY NO. 1
What am I protecting her from, Viv? A person?
Or something supernatural?
NAVARRO
Now we're making progress. Is it a curse?
A metahuman?
A spirit?
Trigon!
Oh god... Raven.

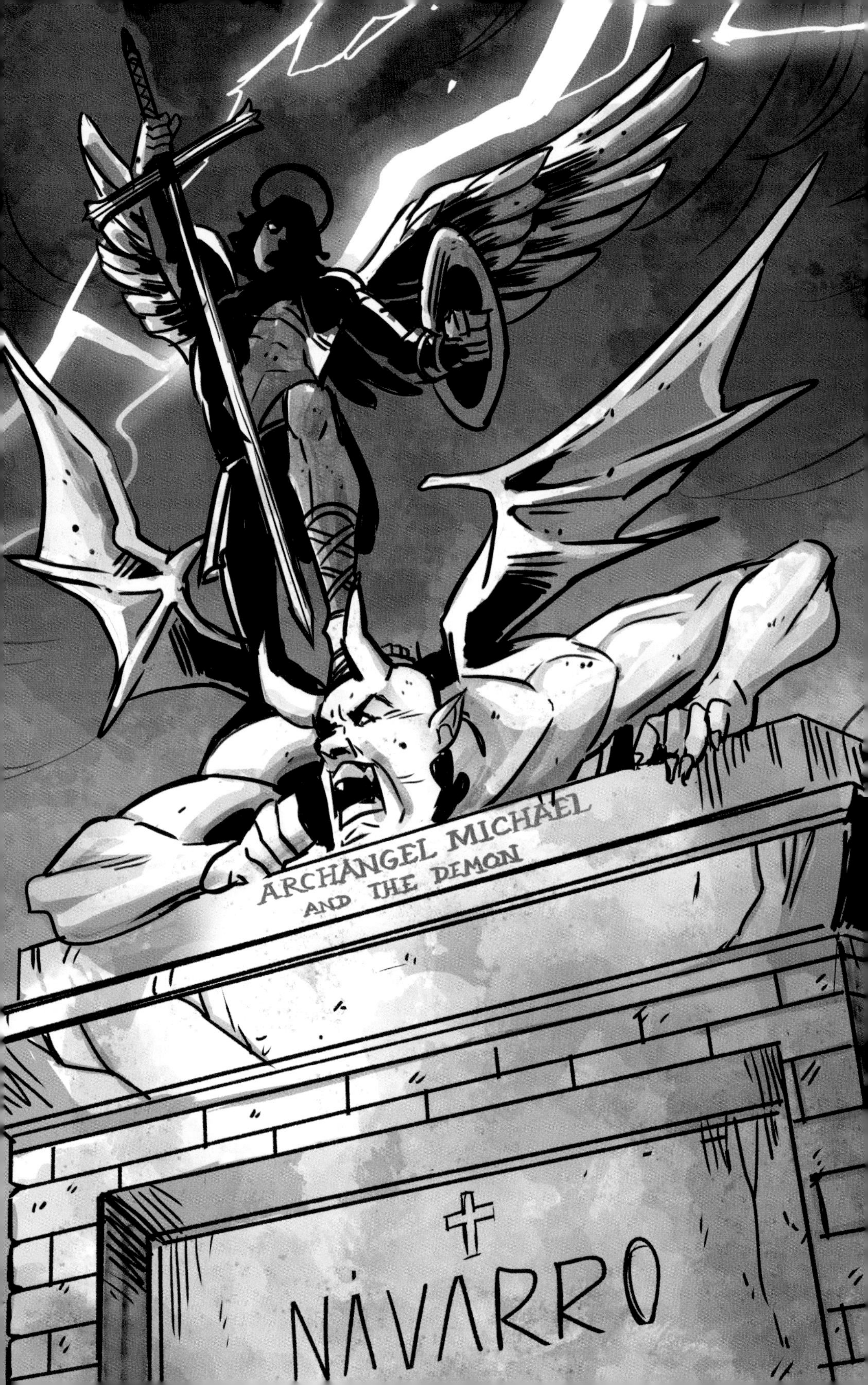
ARCHANGEL MICHAEL
AND THE DEMON
NAVARRO

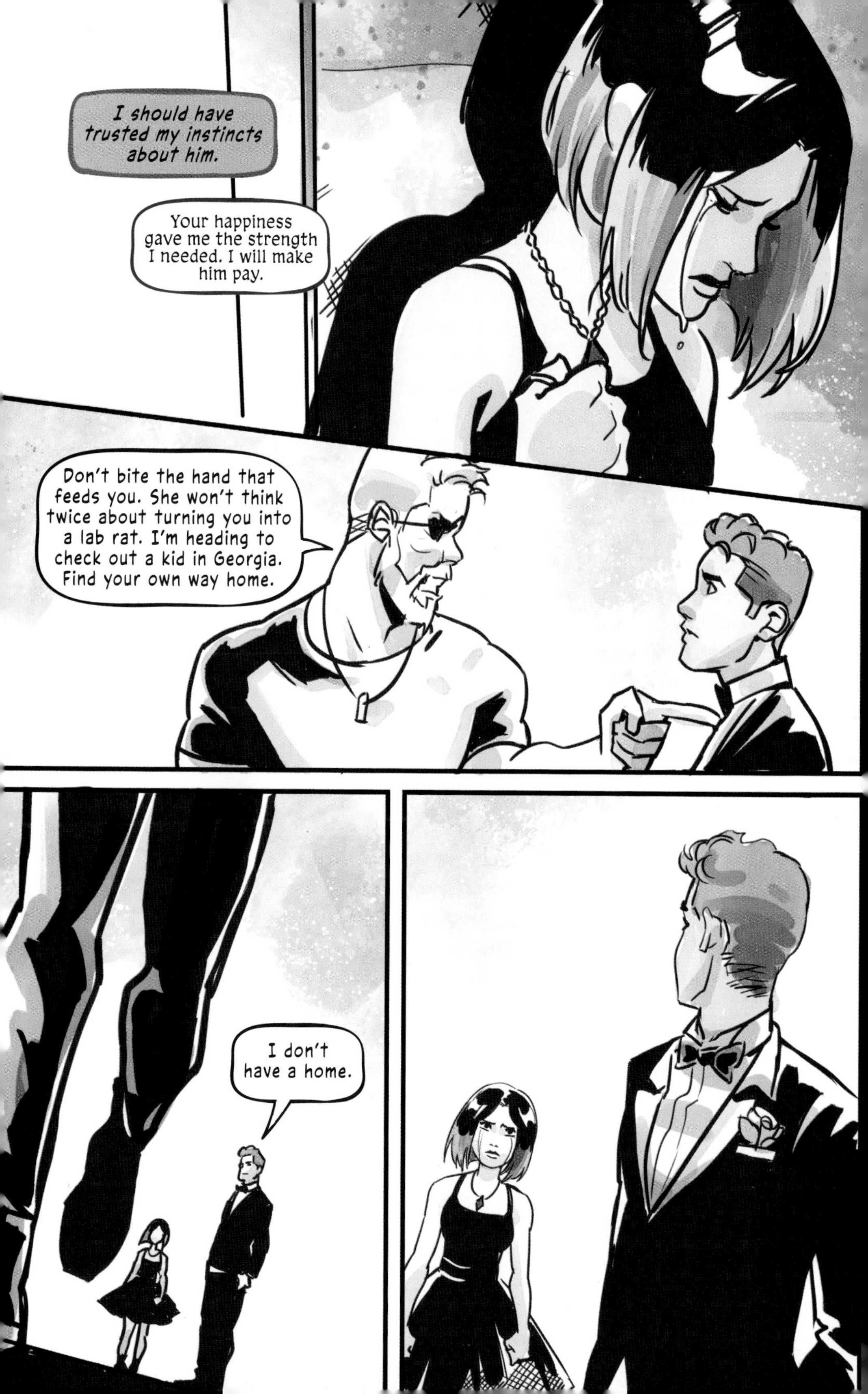
I should have trusted my instincts about him.
Your happiness gave me the strength I needed. I will make him pay.
Don't bite the hand that feeds you. She won't think twice about turning you into a lab rat. I'm heading to check out a kid in Georgia. Find your own way home.
I don't have a home.

CHAPTER 15: SINS OF THE FATHER

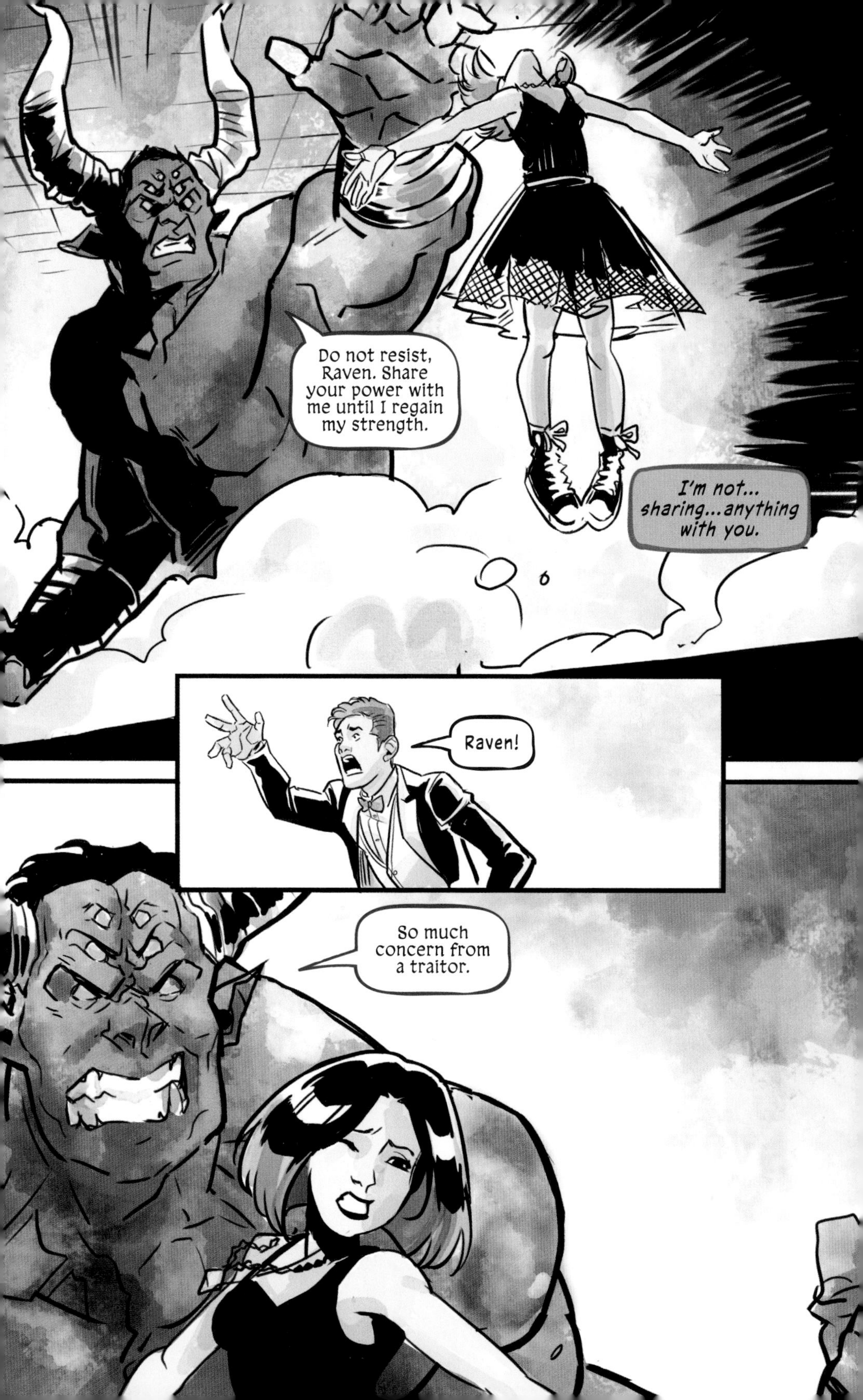
Do not resist, Raven. Share your power with me until I regain my strength.
I'm not... sharing...anything with you.
Raven!
So much concern from a traitor.

CHAPTER 16: SOULSTORM

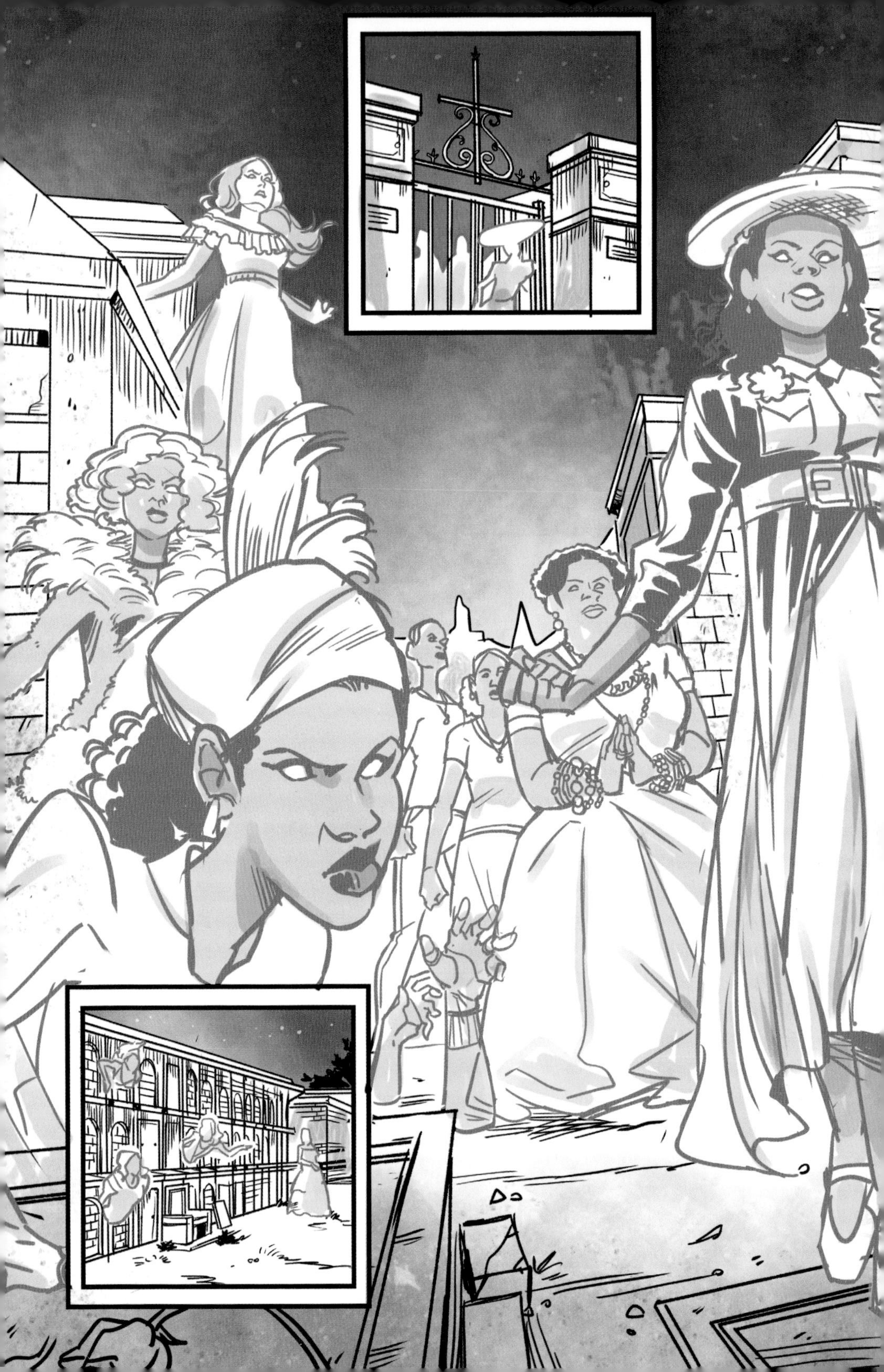

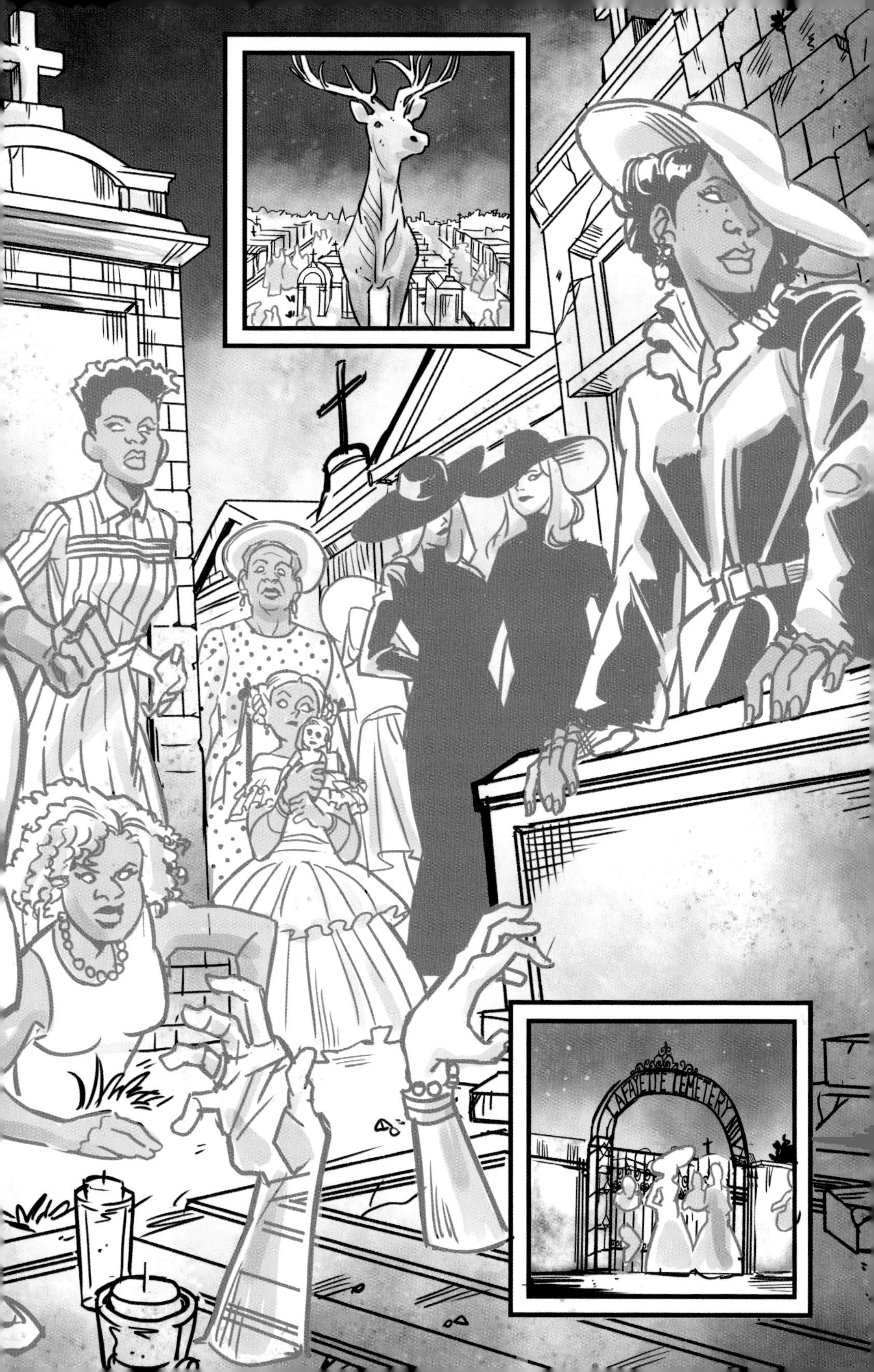
LAFAYETTE CEMETERY

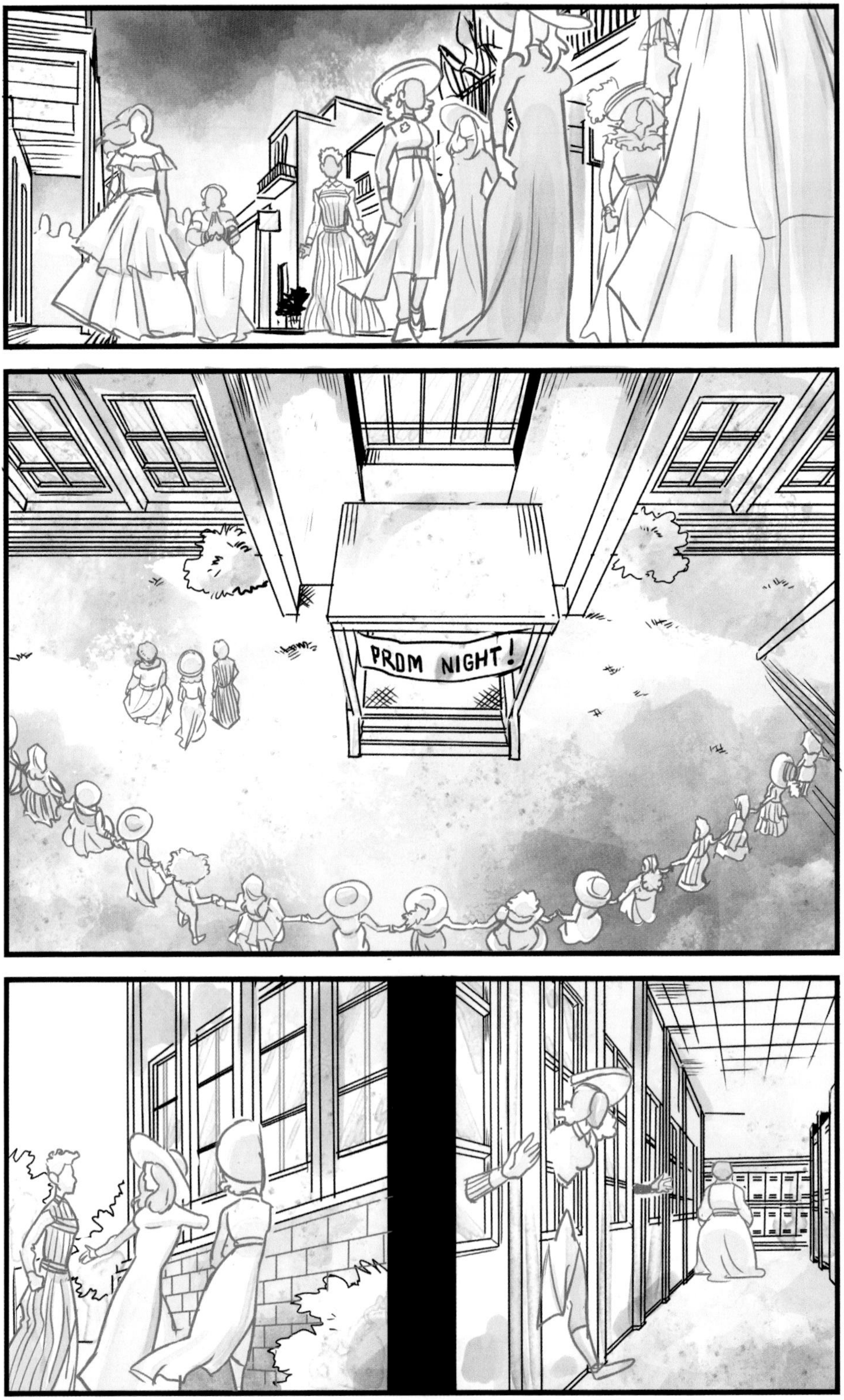
PROM NIGHT!

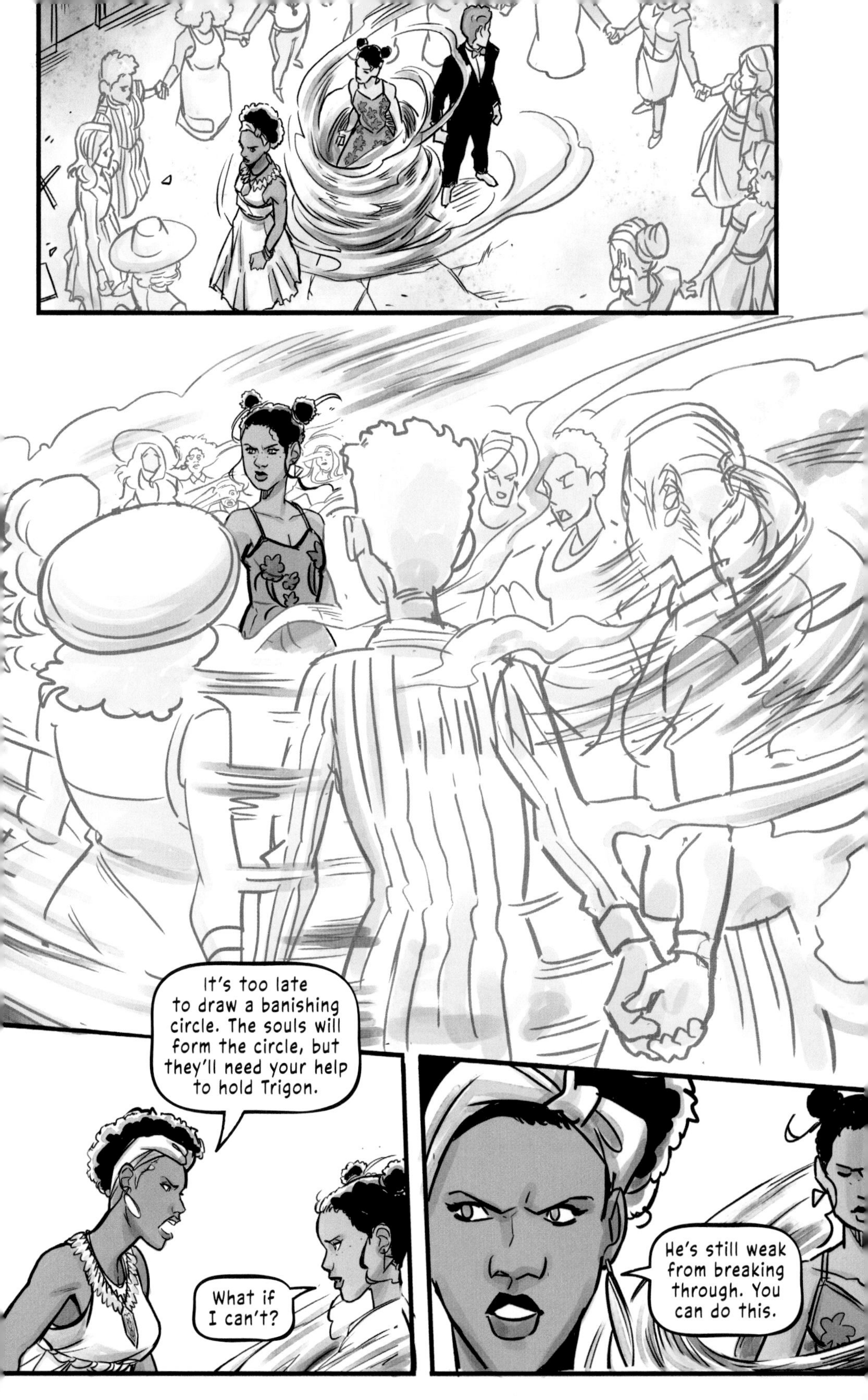
It's too late to draw a banishing circle. The souls will form the circle, but they'll need your help to hold Trigon.
What if I can't?
He's still weak from breaking through. You can do this.

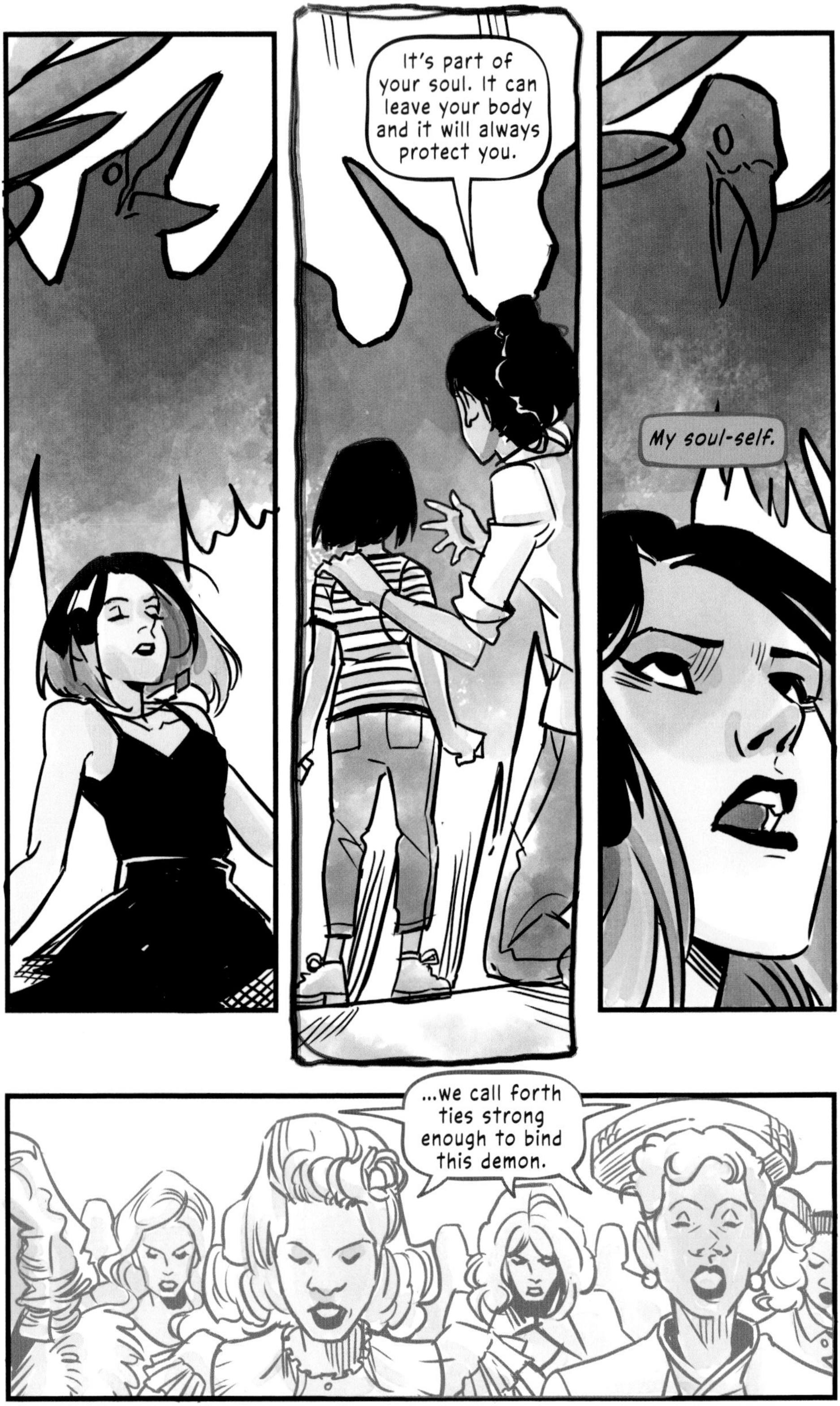
It's part of your soul. It can leave your body and it will always protect you.
My soul-self.
...we call forth ties strong enough to bind this demon.

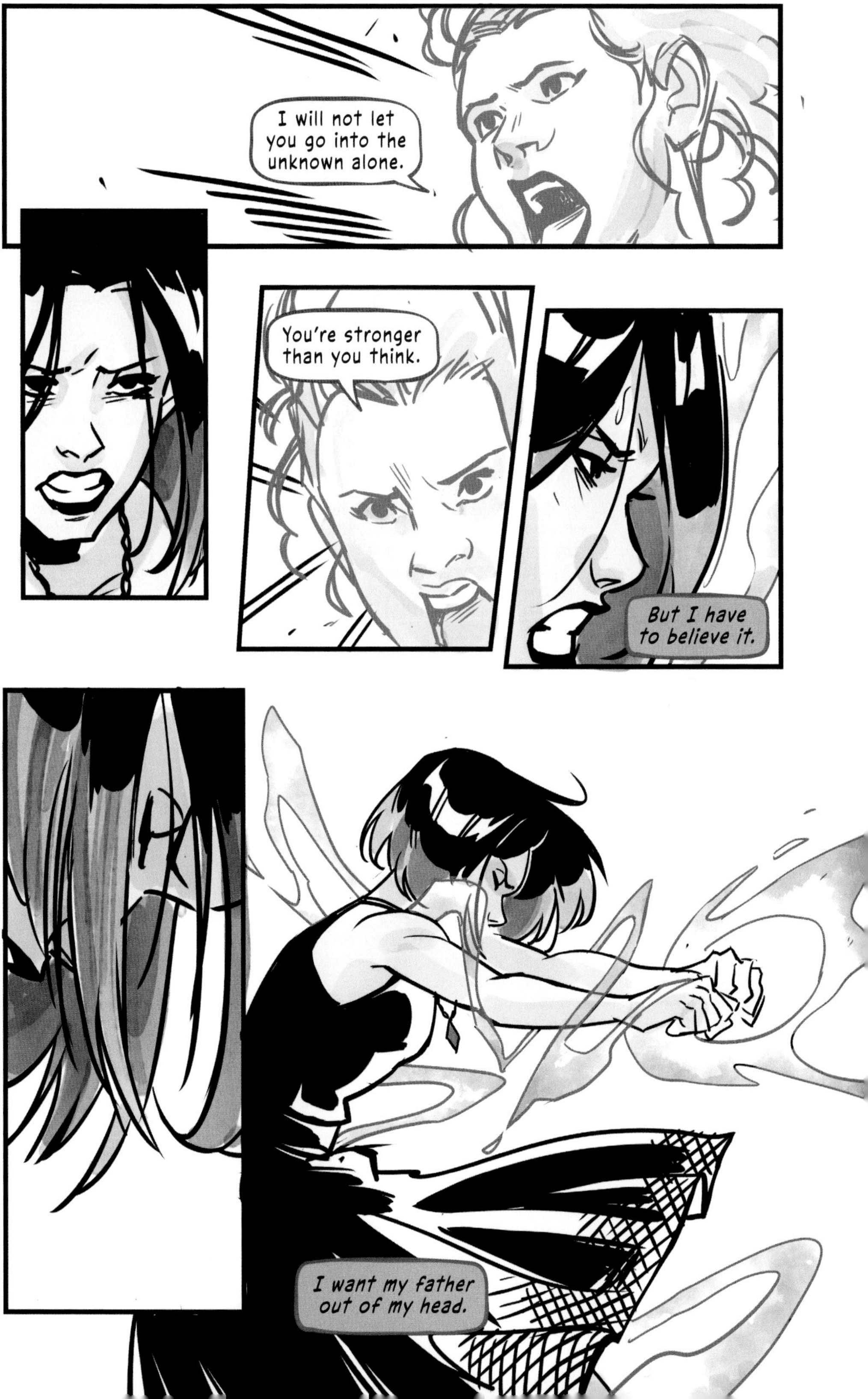
I will not let you go into the unknown alone.
You're stronger than you think.
But I have to believe it.
I want my father out of my head.

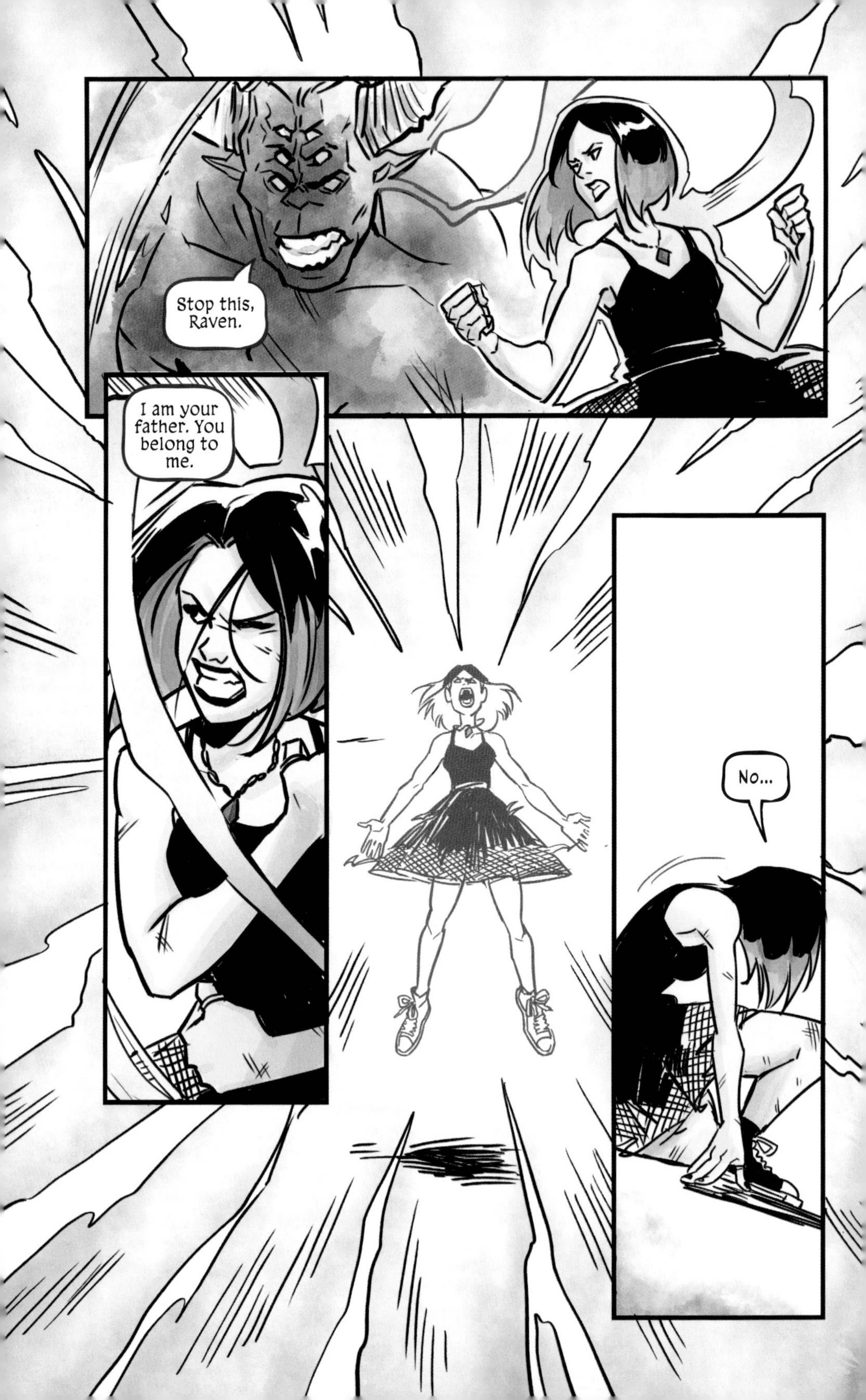
Stop this, Raven.
I am your father. You belong to me.
No...

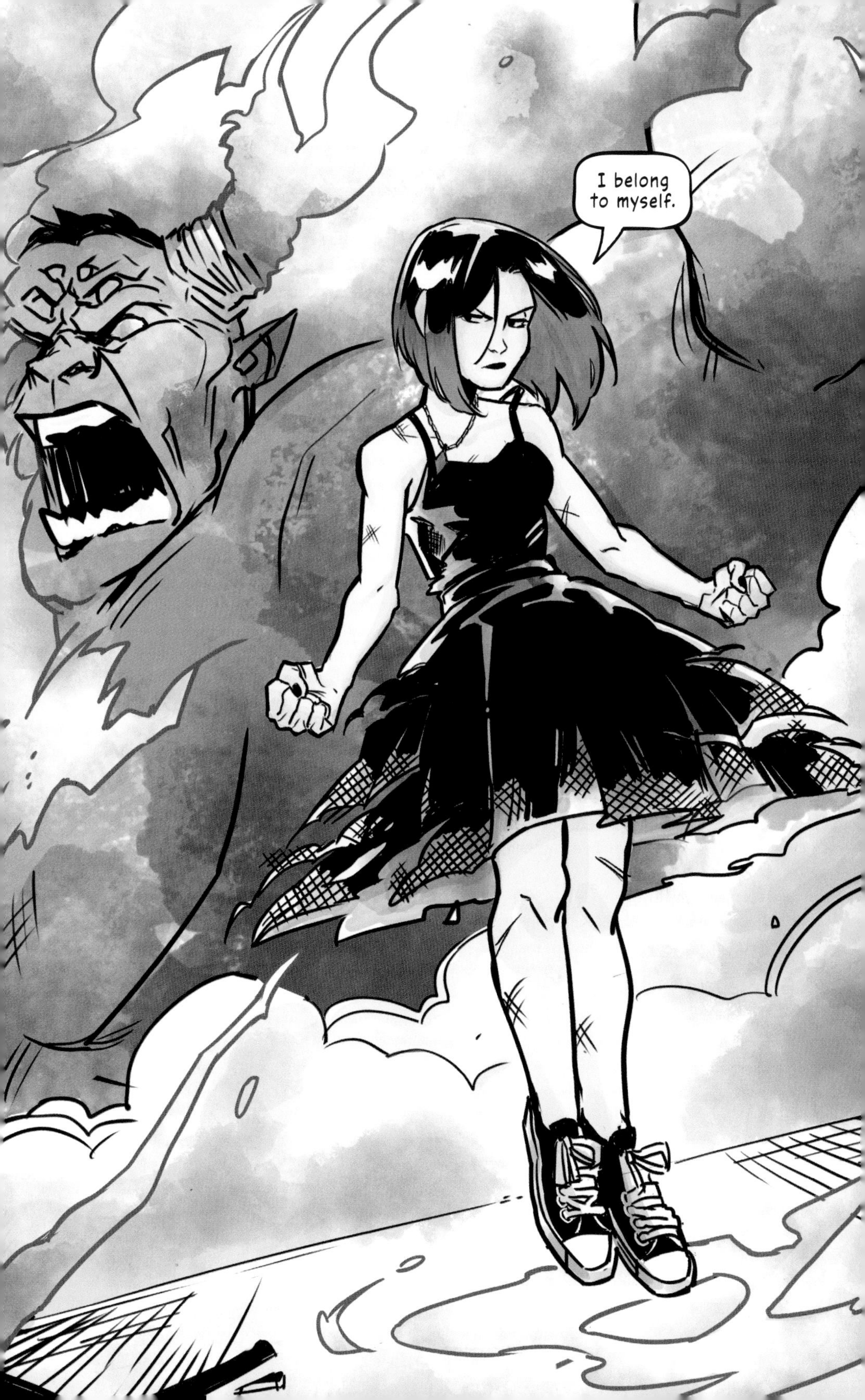
I belong to myself.

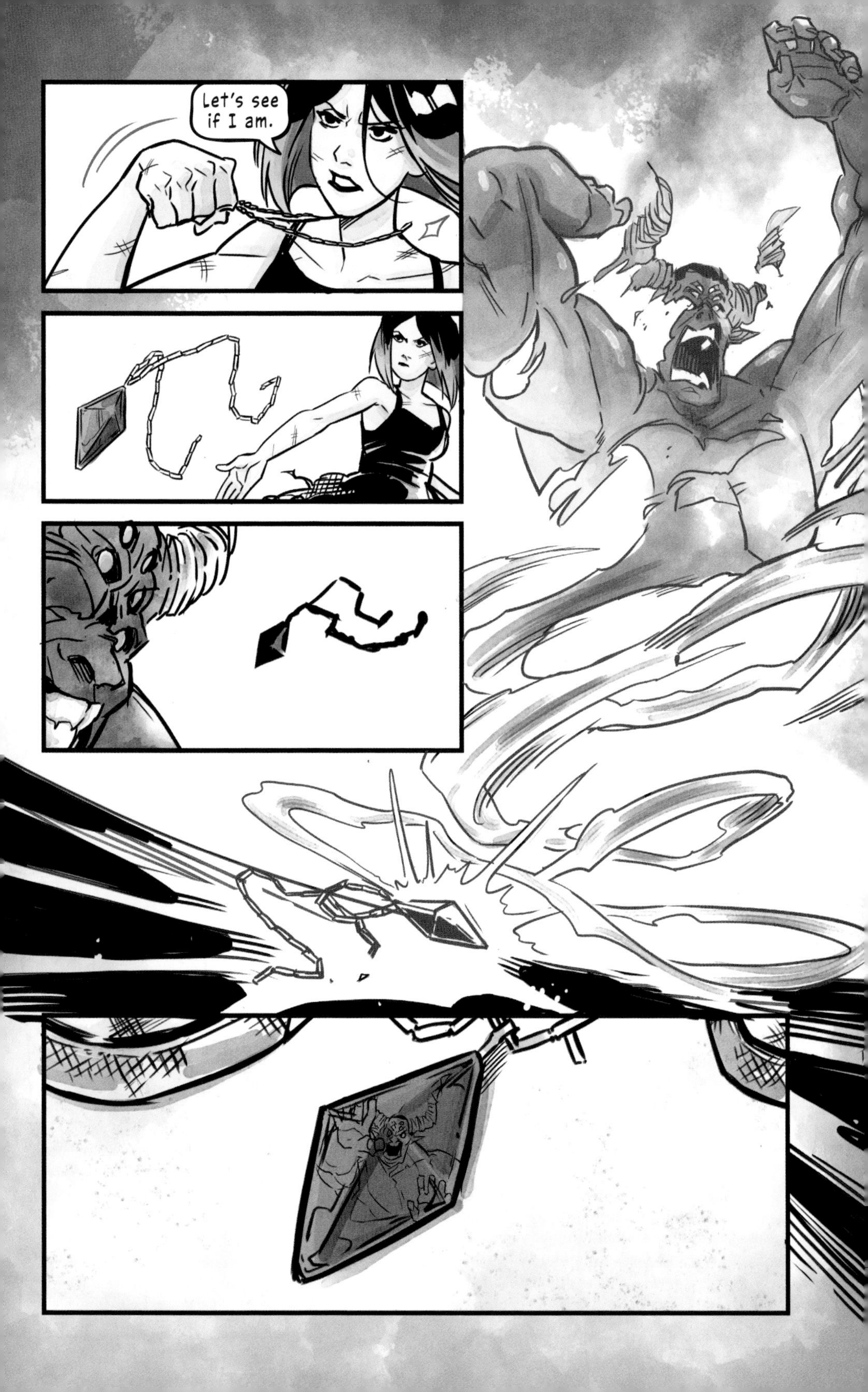
Let's see if I am.

CHAPTER 17: FORGET ME NOT

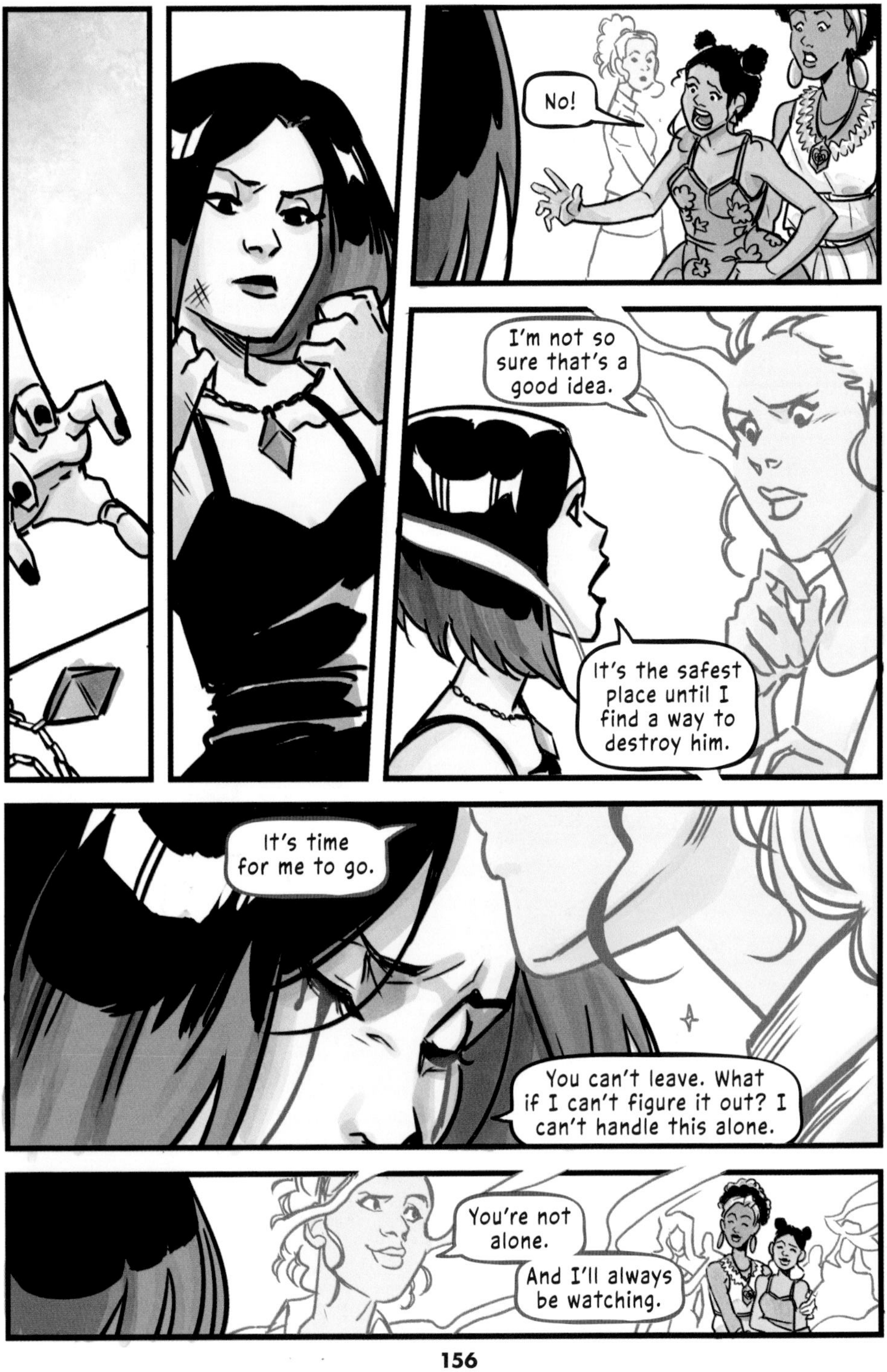
No!
I'm not so sure that's a good idea.
It's the safest place until I find a way to destroy him.
It's time for me to go.
You can't leave. What if I can't figure it out? I can't handle this alone.
You're not alone.
And I'll always be watching.

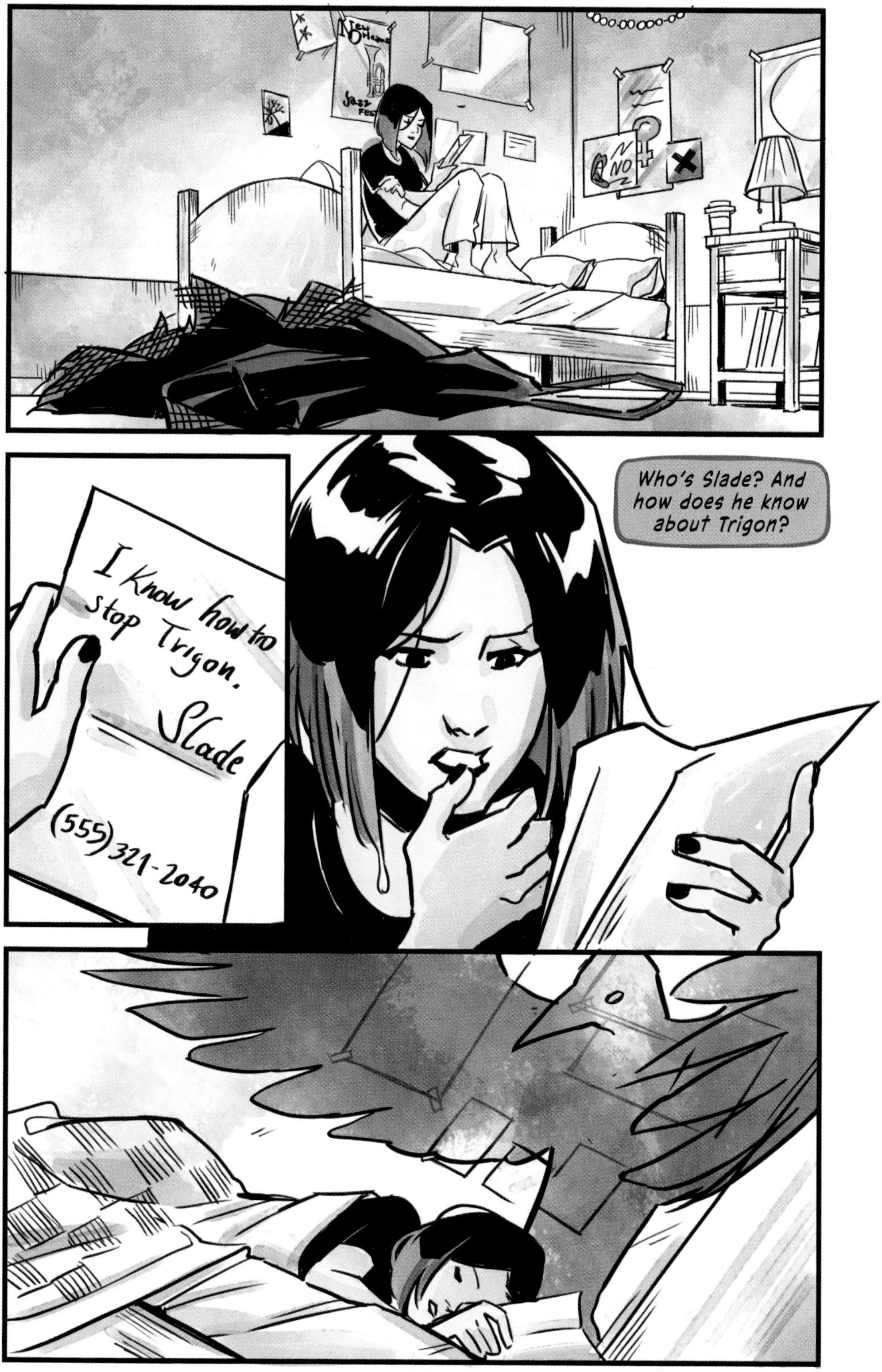
I Know how to stop Trigon.
Slade
(555) 321-2040
Who's Slade? And how does he know about Trigon?

CHAPTER 18: THE UNKNOWN

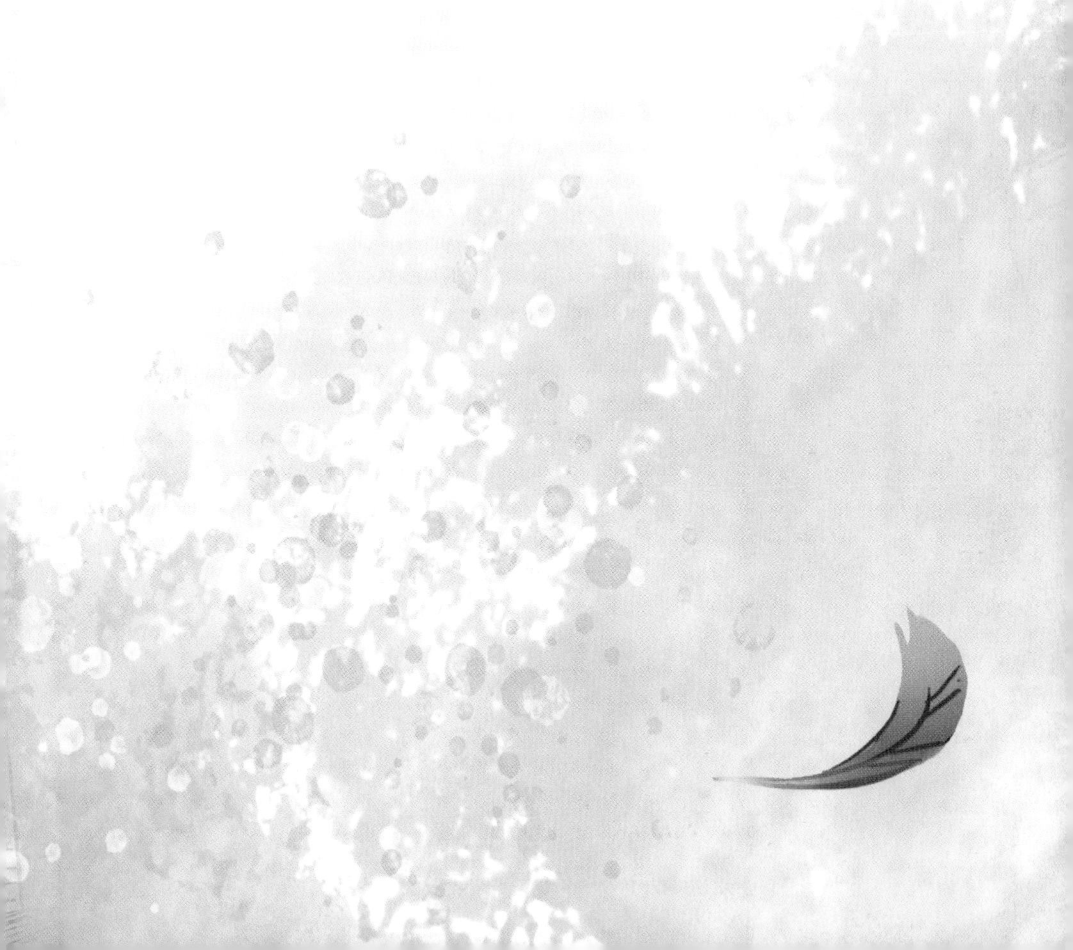

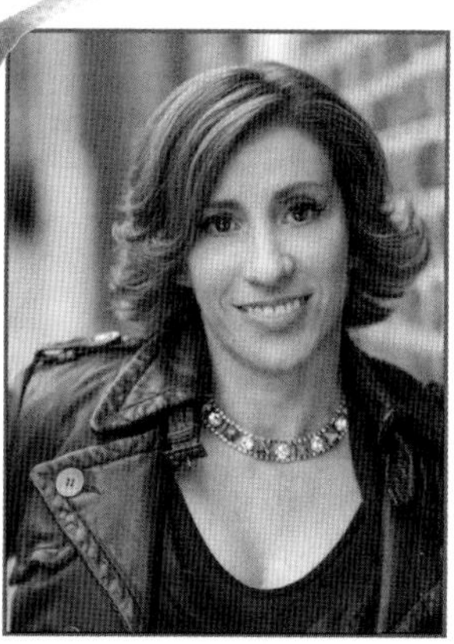

VANIA STOYANVA

kami garcia

is the #1 *New York Times, USA Today,* and international bestselling co-author of the *Beautiful Creatures* and *Dangerous Creatures* novels. *Beautiful Creatures* has been published in 50 countries and translated into 39 languages. Kami's solo series, The Legion, includes *Unbreakable*, an instant *New York Times* bestseller, and its sequel, *Unmarked*, both of which were nominated for Bram Stoker Awards. Her other works include *The X-Files Origins: Agent of Chaos* and the YA contemporary novels *The Lovely Reckless* and *Broken Beautiful Hearts*. Kami was a teacher for 17 years before co-authoring her first novel on a dare from seven of her students. She is a cofounder of YALLFest, the biggest teen book festival in the country. She lives in Maryland with her family.

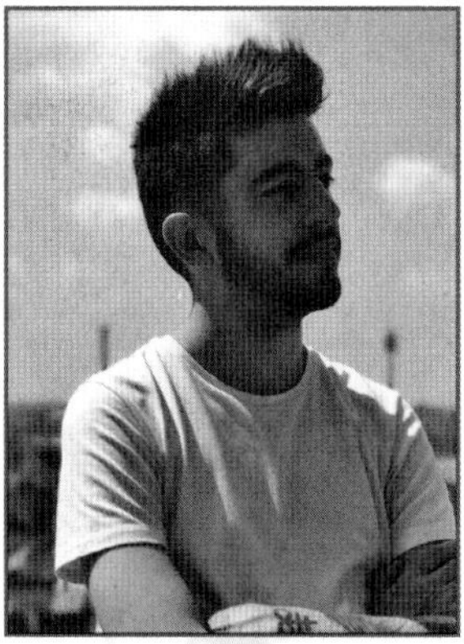

LAURA BROUWERS

gabriel picolo

is a Brazilian comics artist and illustrator based in São Paulo. His work has become known for its strong storytelling and atmospheric colors. Picolo has developed projects for clients such as Blizzard, BOOM! Studios, HarperCollins, and DeviantArt.

special sneak preview

TEEN TITANS
BEAST
BOY

WRITTEN BY
kami garcia

ILLUSTRATED BY
gabriel picolo

COLORIST
david calderon

CHAPTER 1: SPRING BREAK AND SOUR PLUMS

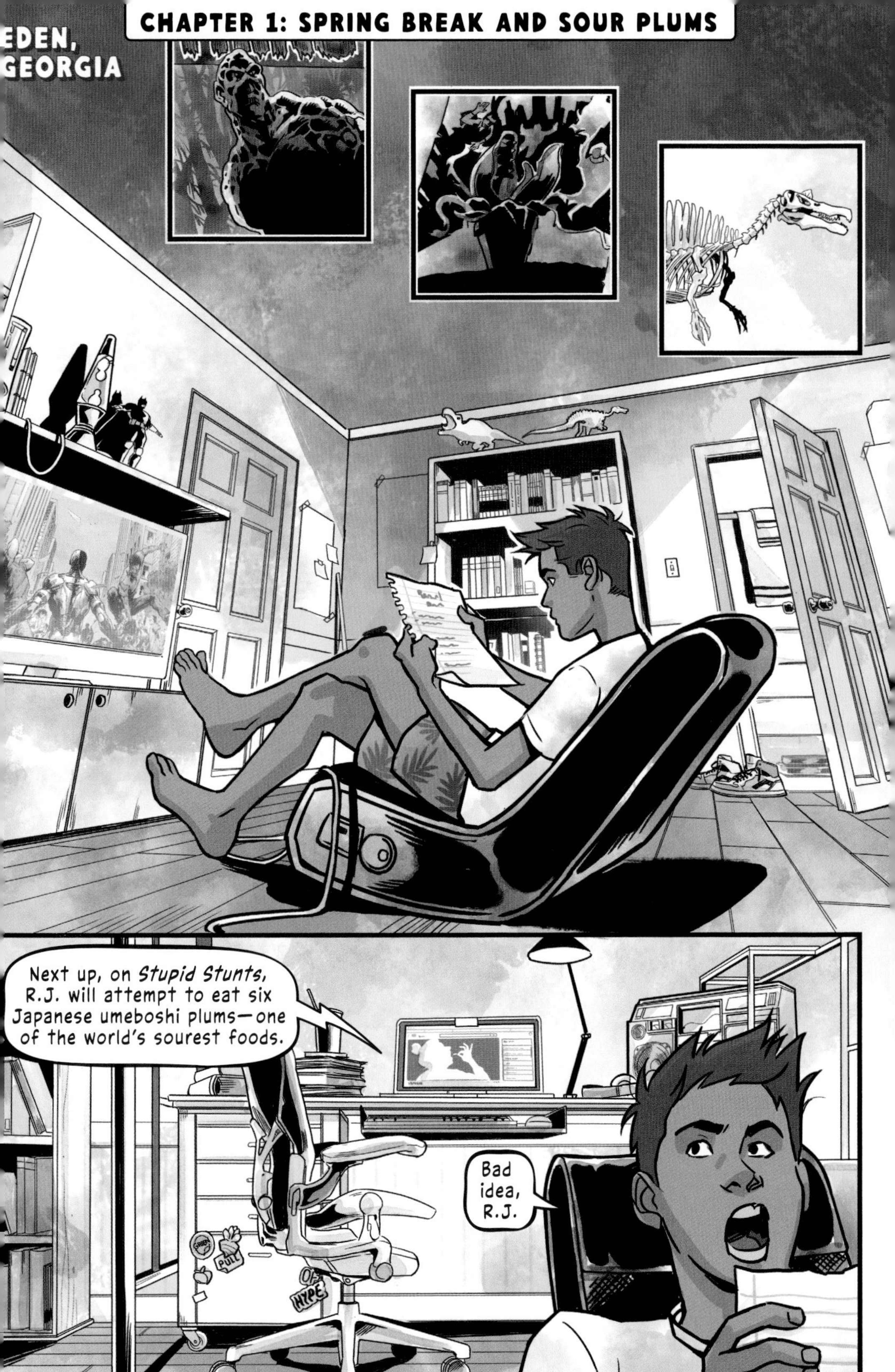

EDEN, GEORGIA
Next up, on *Stupid Stunts,* R.J. will attempt to eat six Japanese umeboshi plums—one of the world's sourest foods.
Bad idea, R.J.

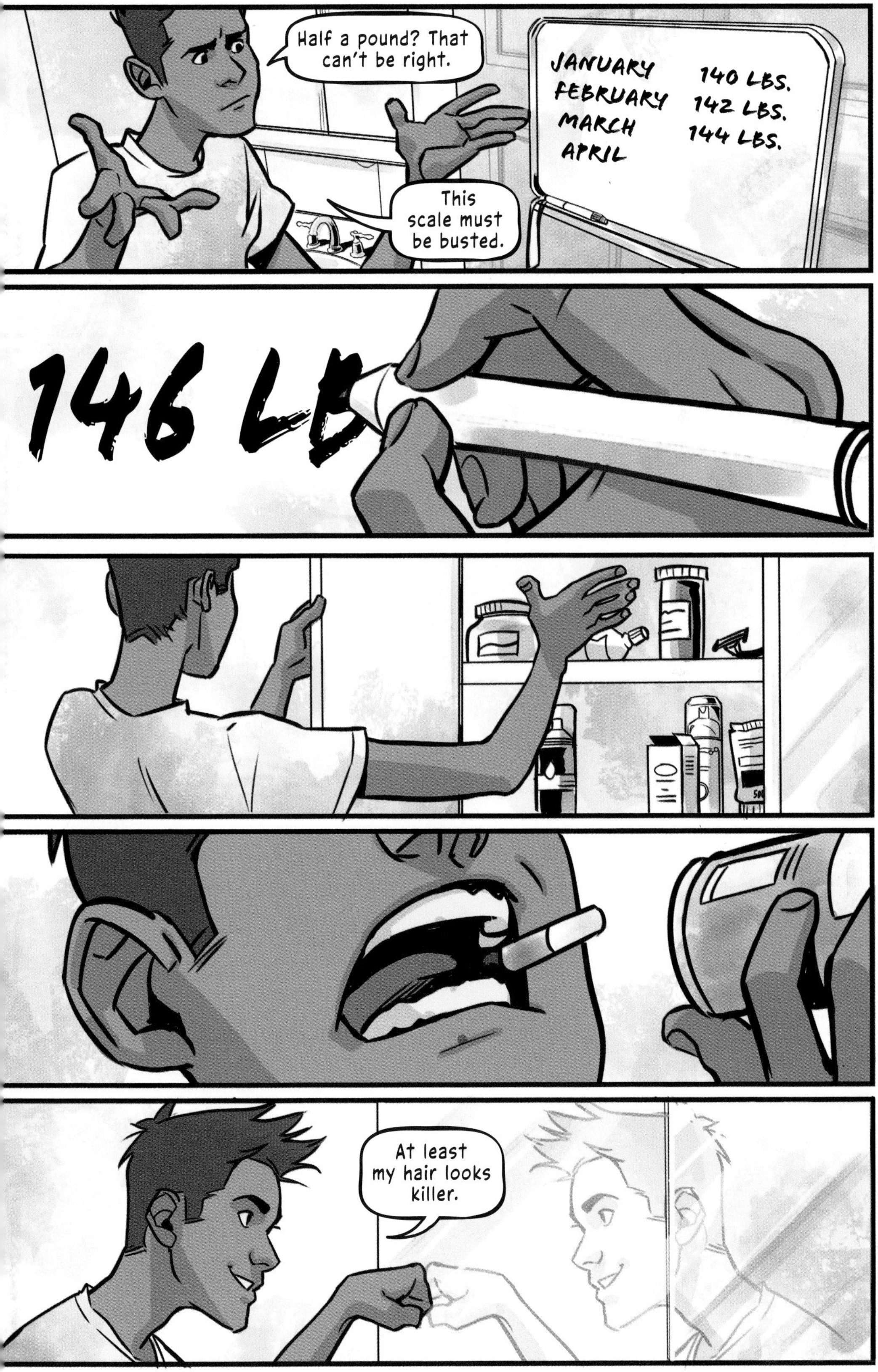
Half a pound? That can't be right.
JANUARY 140 LBS.
FEBRUARY 142 LBS.
MARCH 144 LBS.
APRIL
This scale must be busted.
146 LB
At least my hair looks killer.

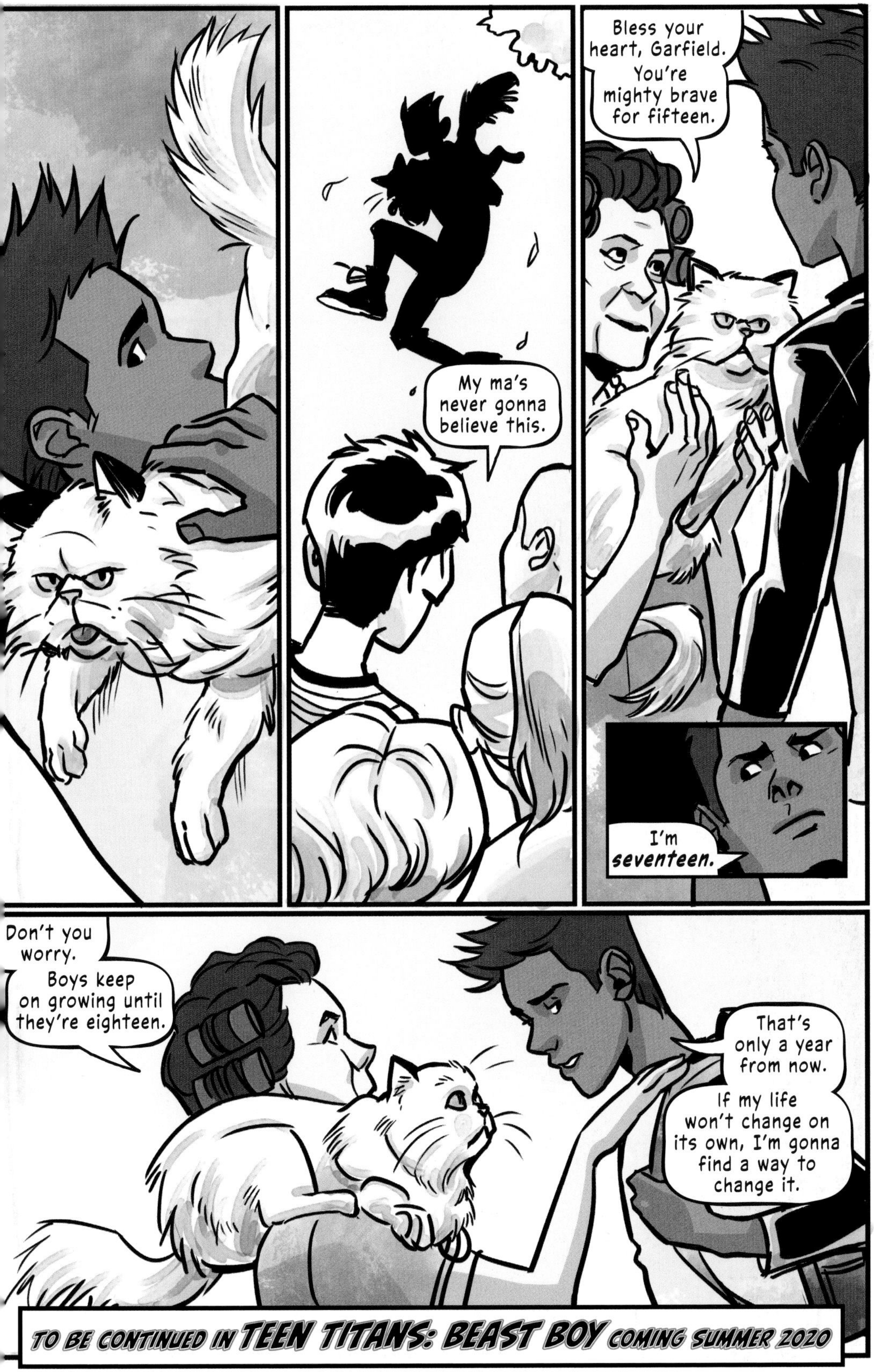

My ma's never gonna believe this.
Bless your heart, Garfield.
You're mighty brave for fifteen.
I'm *seventeen.*
Don't you worry.
Boys keep on growing until they're eighteen.
That's only a year from now.
If my life won't change on its own, I'm gonna find a way to change it.
TO BE CONTINUED IN TEEN TITANS: BEAST BOY COMING SUMMER 2020